SCANDALOUS SECRETS

Katharine knew far more about her bridegroom's secret life than he would have liked her to. She knew about St. Clair's high-born mistress, the irresistible, elegantly immoral Lady Sarah. She knew about St. Clair's voluptuous kept woman, the captivating Yvette. And she had learned more than she desired about his practiced skill at seduction and his legendary prowess as a lover.

But Katharine had a secret of her own. A secret that she prayed St. Clair would not discover. A secret that would put her at his mercy . . .

And mercy was what Katharine could not expect from a man whom she refused to admit to her bed even when she could not keep him out of her heart. . . .

THE REBEL BRIDE

More Regency Romance from SIGNET

THE
REBEL
BRIDE

by
Catherine Coulter

Ⓢ
A SIGNET BOOK
NEW AMERICAN LIBRARY
TIMES MIRROR

PUBLISHED BY
THE NEW AMERICAN LIBRARY
OF CANADA LIMITED

NAL BOOKS ARE ALSO AVAILABLE AT DISCOUNTS IN BULK
QUANTITY FOR INDUSTRIAL OR SALES-PROMOTIONAL USE.
FOR DETAILS, WRITE TO PREMIUM MARKETING DIVISION,
NEW AMERICAN LIBRARY, INC., 1301 AVENUE OF THE
AMERICAS, NEW YORK, NEW YORK 10019.

First Signet Printing, December, 1979

1 2 3 4 5 6 7 8 9

SIGNET TRADEMARK REG. U.S. PAT. OFF. AND FOREIGN COUNTRIES
REGISTERED TRADEMARK - MARCA REGISTRADA
HECHO EN WINNIPEG, CANADA

SIGNET, SIGNET CLASSICS, MENTOR, PLUME, MERIDIAN
and NAL BOOKS are published in Canada by The New American
Library of Canada, Limited, Scarborough, Ontario

PRINTED IN CANADA

COVER PRINTED IN U.S.A.

To

My sister, Diane

Thus in plain terms: your father hath consented
That you shall be my wife . . .
And, will you, nill you, I will marry you.
Now, Kate, I am a husband for your turn;
For, by this light, whereby I see thy beauty,
Thy beauty, that doth make me like thee well,
Thou must be married to no man but me . . .

—Shakespeare, *The Taming of the Shrew*

1

Julien St. Clair, Earl of March, flicked a careless finger over Yvette's plump belly, lay back on the large four-poster bed, and gazed beneath half-closed lids at the dancing patterns cast by the firelight on the opposite wall. He felt a sort of lazy satisfaction that, for the moment, relieved his boredom.

"I have pleased you, my lord?" She twined her fingers playfully in his fair curling hair, her own body languid from the pleasure he had given her.

"Of course, Yvette," he answered shortly, irritated that she disturbed the silence he wanted.

There was a flash of anger in her doe-brown eyes. She knew full well that she had pleased him but a short time before, and it galled her now to see him again remote and withdrawn. But from her long experience with noblemen, she realized that reproaches would gain her nothing. She let her face soften into a sensuous, inviting expression, and artfully lowered herself onto his chest, pressing her breasts against him. She slid her arms around his neck and gently tugged until he turned his face to hers. She smiled knowingly as he brought his arms lazily from behind his head downward through her chestnut hair, and began to explore her back and her buttocks, and to knead her full soft hips.

To Yvette's surprise, she soon felt a quiver run the length of her body and a low moan of pleasure escaped her lips.

In a graceful motion Julien rolled over on top of her. He met her trembling mouth and skillfully mingled his tongue with hers. His hands surged over her body, teasing, caressing, sweeping her with long, sensual strokes.

Julien watched her eyes widen and her lashes flutter involuntarily. Her mouth worked convulsively and she gave small cries of pleasure. A dull flush began to creep over her cheeks and her body trembled beneath him. She willed him urgently

1

to enter her, and he drew his body up as she guided him into her.

Though his body responded with rhythmic motion, Julien felt strangely detached from the woman writhing beneath him, unable to let himself feel the passionate intensity of her desire. Yet, he felt his breathing quicken as she reached her final tensing. He drove deep, heard her cries of passion, and let his body respond.

He allowed himself to be locked to her for one long moment before falling his length on top of her, his head beside her face on the pillow.

Yvette calmed and stilled her trembling limbs. She was certain this time that she had pleased him. Her own pleasure, she discounted. She waited for him to utter some slight words of endearment, but he lay quiet above her, his breath coming even.

Her body began to protest against his weight, but she did not move for fear of disturbing him.

"Yvette, what is the time?" he asked, his voice muffled by the pillow.

"It lacks but a few moments until ten, my lord," she said, a definite edge to her voice.

"Be damned!" he growled, rolling his body away from her. Yvette watched him rise from the bed and briefly stretch his tall muscular frame. As always, she was unable to look at him without admiring his body. For months she had called him her golden god. But now, she thought bitterly, he was a fickle god, leaving her with scarce a backward thought.

Her frustration grew as she racked her mind for a charmingly turned phrase to catch his attention. Finding herself unequal to the task, she sighed and raised herself up onto the pillow, pulling a cover over her body.

He drew on his white ruffled shirt and turned to look at her.

"I must leave, Yvette. I am promised to meet Blairstock at White's and am already late."

"When am I to see you again, my lord?" she asked with controlled sweetness, half-rising to go to him.

He halted her progress with an impatient wave of his hand, and replied with only casual interest: "That is difficult to say. I am meeting friends in the country for hunting and shall be absent from London for some time."

She sucked in her breath, now wary. He had not told her of his imminent departure from London.

He shrugged himself, not without some difficulty, into a coat of superfine blue cloth that was molded exquisitely to his broad shoulders, and strode over to her.

"I trust you will find sufficient to amuse you during my absence," he remarked indifferently. "I only ask that you not be too . . . indiscreet while you are still in my keeping." A faint sardonic look passed over his handsome face, rendering his gray eyes cold and hard.

"I . . . don't know what you mean," she stammered, her face draining of color.

"Oh, don't you, Yvette?" he inquired sternly. "In any case," he continued with careless emphasis, "we shall discuss the matter upon my return."

He picked up his cane and pulled his many-caped cloak around his shoulders and walked to the door. As he let himself out, he said over his shoulder, "Don't, I pray, underestimate the value of your favors. I assure you, Yvette, you are as fine a possession as any man could wish."

Julien closed the door quietly behind him and was gone. Yvette could hear his retreating footsteps as he took the stairs two at a time.

"Damn him!" she cried, wishing for something to hurl at the closed door. "All those fine lords! Arrogant crowing peacocks!"

As her ire cooled, a frown creased her white brow and she pursed her lips, now annoyed at herself for her own carelessness. She should have guessed that her capitulation to Lord Riverton would send his boasting, vain lordship to proclaim his triumph! It was a mistake she should not have made, a stupid, ill-timed blunder that had lost her, she was forced to admit, a very generous protector.

She pushed back the covers and rose slowly, her body aching from her exertions. She sat at her dressing table and began to brush out her tangled brown curls. She paused a moment to examine the undeniably alluring face and felt cheered. Lord Riverton was a rich man and appeared to enjoy her lisping English and her views of life in England, as well as the voluptuous attractions her body offered.

She sighed, momentarily cast down. She was fond of Julien, and he was after all an earl. She found herself gazing wistfully at her elegantly furnished room. She would miss this charming apartment and also, she reflected, a man skilled in the art of lovemaking. Julien could still surprise her by his ability to make her senses reel, to make her forget all her own wiles for giving him pleasure.

She rose from her dressing table, blew out the candles, and took herself back to bed. As pragmatic as she was passionate, she realized that it was just as well that Julien was leaving for the country; it gave her time to plan and assess Lord Riverton's intentions. It did not take her long to devise a plan which pleased her, and she fell asleep confident she could part the pinch-penny Lord Riverton from some of his precious guineas.

Julien hailed a hackney and directed the driver to make all haste to White's. He sat back against the rather worn cushions and stretched his long legs. The old wooden cab swayed precariously as the horse clip-clopped on the uneven cobblestones and Julien had to steady his position by holding the frayed leather strap. He felt now only slightly angered that he had shared Yvette with another man while she was under his protection. In all honesty, he knew that he had given her scant attention these last few months, his visits infrequent and for only one purpose. He had used her body to escape for brief periods of time from his growing restlessness. Yvette had been his choice recently over the lovely Lady Sarah, as he found it increasingly difficult to murmur the words of endearment and affection required of such a liaison. With Yvette he could behave exactly as he wished, for it was her duty to please him. He thought of her unsuccessful attempt at perfidy and felt faintly amused. He had no doubt that she would take care of herself; like a cat, she was, soft, purring, and quite able to land on her feet. He sighed and closed his eyes. He wished Yvette luck in her pursuit of Riverton.

When the cab drew to a halt in front of his club, he alighted quickly, paid the driver handsomely, and gave Yvette not another thought.

"Good evening, my lord." He was greeted at the door by one of White's renowned retainers, who after straightening from his low bow, deftly relieved Julien of his cane and cloak.

Julien nodded briefly. "Is Lord Blairstock here, Henry?"

"Yes, indeed, my lord. I believe his lordship is in the card room."

Julien made his way through the dark wood-paneled reading room, his steps muffled by the thick plush carpeting. Rich vellum-bound books lined the walls, and London papers lay in neat stacks on the heavy mahogany tables. He stopped a moment and thumbed through the *Gazette*, his eye caught by the latest bit of news of Napoleon's incarceration on Elba, an island that he now ruled as he had France.

"It is shocking, is it not, my lord, that the pompous Corsican held Europe so long in the palm of his hand?"

"Indeed it is," Julien replied, turning and proffering a slight bow to the arthritic Duke of Moreland.

The duke looked pensively down at the paper and continued in his slow, painstaking way: "It is quite beyond me how that upstart puppy achieved such power." He gave an eloquent shrug of his shoulders that brought a grimace of pain to his face. "But the French, you know, have always been an ... unsteady race."

Julien said gently, "Perhaps it is not so unfathomable a turn of events, your grace, when one considers the terrible plight of the French people even after the beginning of the revolution."

"I hope you are not becoming a republican, my boy. Something your late father would find most abhorrent," his grace chided.

"Being an Englishman, your grace, in a country where all men are treated with at least a modicum of justice, I do not think it 'republican' to comment with truth on the stupidity and blatant greed of the past French monarchs."

"Well said, my boy, well said." His grace beamed.

"If your grace will excuse me . . ." Julien said, taking the old duke's hand in his.

"Off with you, my lord. Do not forget to pay my compliments to your dear mother." The duke added more to himself than to Julien, "It is difficult to keep up with one's friends. . . ."

"My mother will be pleased, your grace." Julien smiled, not without affection, at the duke before turning and continuing his way to the card room.

He made his greetings to other acquaintances in his casual, easy manner as he progressed the length of the reading room. But he did not stop, reflecting with a grin that poor Percy would in all likelihood be in a great taking at having missed his dinner.

A footman opened a great paneled oak door to the card room and quickly closed it behind Julien, so as not to disturb the more sober club members in the reading room. The card room was ablaze with candles, in marked contrast to other, more sedate rooms in White's. It was a glittering company, loud and boisterous. Footmen seemed to be everywhere, scurrying from group to group bearing silver trays laden with quantities of drink.

Julien gazed around the room at the various tables until his eyes came to rest on Sir Percy sitting slouched with one elegantly clad leg swinging to and fro over the leg of a delicately wrought satin-covered chair.

He stood quietly for a moment behind Percy, noting with a shake of his head the small pile of guineas stacked in front of him. As Percy shoved most of the remainder toward the faro bank, Julien dropped a light hand on his shoulder.

"I see your luck is quite out tonight, Percy," Julien remarked, easing himself into a momentarily vacant chair next to his friend.

Sir Percy Blairstock turned a rather pale pair of blue eyes to Julien and remarked with a sniff: "Well, Julien, what other choice do I have but to game away my fortune? I suppose you were in the arms of one of your fair Cyprians and quite forgot our dinner engagement."

Julien smiled broadly, even white teeth flashing. "Quite accurate, old boy, but as you see, I did not forget. Your humble servant!"

"You conceited dog! You are no one's humble servant, March!" Sir Percy pushed back his chair and gathered up his remaining guineas.

"It appears that I have saved you from total ruin. Perhaps you owe me some words of thanks." Julien grinned and at the same time shook his head in refusal at a footman who offered him brandy.

"Ho, March! You do not play tonight?"

Julien turned away from the footman and Percy and calmly surveyed the dissipated face of Lord Devalnty, who appeared to be already deep in his cups. He had never liked the man, but he had been a friend of his father's, and therefore, in Julien's code, deserving at least of civility.

He gave a rather thin smile and responded easily: "As you see, sir, I am otherwise engaged with Blairstock here."

"And I for one am famished!" Sir Percy broke in. "Do come, Julien, let us try some of Pierre's delicious fish."

Julien shrugged his shoulders, rose, and bowed to Lord Devalnty. "You will forgive me, sir, I must see to the pressing needs of Blairstock before I am quite in his black books. Your servant, sir."

Lord Devalnty waved a thin, darkly veined hand and returned his attention to the faro bank.

"Reckless old fool! Never liked him above half," Sir Percy muttered darkly as he and Julien made their way from the card room.

"Tolerance, Percy, tolerance," Julien chided.

"But that wig, Julien . . . and he still paints his face. Did you see that ridiculous patch by his mouth?"

"A relic, Percy. Do not, I pray, be overly harsh in your judgment of Devalnty's oddities. Imagine how he must regard us with our elaborate cravats and artfully disheveled hair."

"My father used to tell me that wigs were full of lice," Percy pursued stubbornly.

Julien laughed but said only: "I fear if you dwell on that thought, Percy, you might well lose your appetite."

It was well after midnight when Julien and Percy left White's and walked in the dim moonlight toward Grosvenor Square to the St. Clair town house. Their comfortable silence was broken only by the clicking of their canes on the cobblestones until Julien said pensively: "You know, Percy, I grow quite tired of the fair Yvette. Can I depend upon Riverton to take her off my hands?"

Percy turned his head with some difficulty above his high starched shirt points, to gaze wonderingly at his friend. "She is a tidy morsel," he observed tentatively, trying to gauge Julien's mood. As Julien's countenance remained impassive and he offered no response, Percy remarked with some exasperation: "Good God, Julien, she has been in your keeping for but . . . what is it . . . five or six months?"

"Why, then, my dear fellow, don't you cut out Riverton, whom I understand is presently vying for her charms?" Julien asked, unperturbed.

"Quite above my touch, as you well know, March. Unlike you, I am cursed with a father who holds a tight rein on the purse strings!"

"Come, Percy, you know very well you could afford to maintain the fair Yvette if you were not so careless with your guineas at the gaming tables."

"That is quite easy for you to say, Julien," Percy commented with some bitterness. "In control of your own fortune and rich as Midas at eighteen . . . why, it makes my dinner churn at the thought!"

"As you will, Percy, but if you change your mind, you must move quickly, for I intend to dispense with her favors upon my return to London."

"Well, it is thoughtful of you to offer, March. But for the moment I and my pocketbook are quite content with less expensive bits o' muslin."

They fell into silence once again and Julien's thoughts were drawn back to the years he had spent learning to manage his vast estate after his father's early demise. And, of course, there had been his ever-complaining mother. It was with profound relief that he had installed her, according to her wishes, in a charming house in Brook Street to spend her days and evenings with an assortment of equally comfortably circumstanced dowagers.

"I say, Julien, when do you go to St. Clair?" Percy asked.

Julien pulled himself from his memories. "Tomorrow, I think. I will expect you and Hugh toward the end of the week."

"What sport do you offer besides shooting?" Percy asked slyly. Julien looked down at Percy's expectant face and said gently: "Fresh country air, Percy, nothing more."

"That is too bad of you, March!" Percy exclaimed.

"Of course, we shall enjoy François's excellent cooking to maintain our spirits in the evenings." Julien poked the head of his cane into Percy's expanding stomach.

Percy did not seem to take this amiss and was much mollified.

"That is at least a concession. Do you mind if I give François a recipe for stewed mutton? My man is quite unable to get it just right."

Julien laughed, picturing such a confrontation between Percy and his emotional, artistic chef. "You certainly may try, but be prepared for the most comprehensive of Gallic oaths!"

He reflected on François's past tirades and added: "Perhaps you had best not, Percy, for I have known the good François to brandish his butcher knife with the most foul intentions!"

Percy's eyes widened and he recalled his sire's expostulations on the instability of the French. He decided it best to forget any improvements on his mutton and changed the subject abruptly. "I trust we will play at cards. I expect to lose a fortune to you, you know."

"I keep telling you, Percy, be more careful with your discards. You stake too much on the chances of winning a big hand. It's your head you must use, not that elusive entity you call intuition!"

Percy ignored this advice, for he had heard it before, and said smugly: "Well, I know that Hugh will put you in your place, for a better card player I have yet to find! Then we will see how well you practice your own advice."

"We shall see." Julien grinned, his calm unruffled. "Although you know I shall do my best to see your fondest hopes thwarted."

Percy refused to be drawn, his thoughts turning again to the epicurean delights he would enjoy at St. Clair.

2

Julien's journey to St. Clair occupied the better part of two days. As he tooled his curricle at a smart pace on his way north, with only his tiger, Bladen, for company, he felt again an unsettling restlessness that even the promise of excellent shooting and the thought of comfortable evenings spent with his friends did not abate. A faint crease on his forehead was the only visible sign that anything disturbed the Earl of March. Had Bladen seen his master's face, he would have probably thought him displeased with a new hunter or perhaps with a wager lost at cards. But he did not have an opportunity for such speculation, for Julien kept his gaze fixed on the road ahead, over the heads of his beautiful matched bays.

As Bladen handled the payment of tolls at the various stages, brooking no nonsense from the toll takers, Julien was left to his thoughts, undisturbed.

He had not been to St. Clair for some months, and his visit now was prompted not by the cares of the estate but by motives he himself could not define to his satisfaction. He thought to break free of the admittedly comfortable restraints that were binding him to a round of activities that held little pleasure for him, for there was a growing emptiness that nagged at him whenever he slowed his frantic pace.

Perhaps, he reflected, as he flicked the thong of his whip over the head of his leader, he would be able to speak to Hugh. Unlike Percy, Sir Hugh Drakemore was an older, settled man who seemed to know his way. In their long years of friendship, Julien had never known Hugh to react with anything but an amiable equanimity to the vagaries of his fellowman. But then, what would he say to Hugh? Certainly he could not complain that he was tired of his wealth and title, for he most assuredly was not. No, it was something else, something that was elusive, just out of his reach.

He had found himself looking searchingly at Percy the night before, noting the small yet obvious signs of dissipation about his eyes, the once-athletic body that was now running to fat. Percy had quizzed him often about being a fixture at Gentleman Jackson's boxing salon, a pursuit, however, that kept Julien's body hard and muscular. Percy seemed to devote his energies, indeed his life, to gaming, women, and drink. Now it occurred to him that he was being a hypocrite criticizing his friends. How was he different from the pleasure-seeking ton, flittering brightly in the evenings, hurling themselves into the gaiety? Surely his head ached just as abominably as his friends' the mornings after consuming quantities of brandy.

Beyond making this silent observation, Julien found that this train of thought was inordinately frustrating and inconclusive. Perhaps, he thought, this visit to St. Clair was just what he needed. But his lips twisted ironically at this wishful conclusion. He was still seeing St. Clair as the place of happiness and innocent adventure of his boyhood, with dragons to slay and fair maidens to rescue.

He urged his horses to a faster pace. Fine-blood cattle, they jumped forward, a well-trained extension of his arm. They forced him to concentrate on his driving, for the road was narrow, even dangerously so.

The slightly built Bladen hung on tightly, shaking his head. His master always drove to an inch, but he had never seen him increase his horses' pace on such a winding, narrow road. He thought fleetingly that his master was driving as if demons were after him. He paused, alarmed by this thought, and swung his head around quickly to search the road behind them. Seeing nothing but clouds of dust raised by the curricle, he shrugged his shoulders and wondered whether demons were not invisible. He turned his attention on the road ahead, thankful now more than ever that his master was an excellent whip.

Late the following afternoon they passed through the village of Dapplemoor, which lay but a few miles to the west of St. Clair. The village seemed practically empty save for a few ducks that swam lazily in a small pond at the center of the green.

"Everybody be home having their dinner, milord," Bladen observed, having surveyed the quiet village.

"Do not despair, Bladen," Julien tossed over his shoulder. "We shall be at St. Clair in but a short time."

"Aye," Bladen agreed, reflecting with some pleasure on the meal that would be ready for him. He tightened his grip once again as his master passed out of the village and spurred his horses forward.

Julien felt a quickening within as they entered St. Clair park. Giant oak trees lined the drive, forming a lush green ceiling of leaves. Only slight beams of sunlight penetrated through the dense covering. He mused that these giant oaks would remain as they were, long after the St. Clairs were dead and forgotten.

The oaks came to an end when they burst onto the graveled drive that wound around in circular fashion in front of the mansion. Julien drew his horses to a halt in front of the great stone steps.

The last rays of sunlight cast their gold hue on the thick stone walls that rose up two stories, extending at the four corners to form round Gothic towers. Julien was seized by a feeling of agelessness, of being drawn back into time, away from the modern society of London. As he gazed at his home, he could not but respect his hard-willed ancestors who had ensured his birthright. St. Clair had been gutted on two occasions, the last being over one hundred and fifty years ago during the interminable battles between Charles I's royalist troops and Cromwell's Roundheads, but the earls of March had simply scrubbed down the smoke-blackened stone walls and rebuilt the interior. Julien knew as a simple fact that if war again ravaged England he would do just as his ancestors had done. St. Clair must never be allowed to fall into ruin.

No sooner had Julien alighted from his curricle than the great doors were thrown open and Mannering, the St. Clair butler for over thirty years, made his way down the ancient stone steps to greet his master. Julien's eyes lit up at the sight of his old retainer. He knew full well that the smooth running of St. Clair was due in great part to the faithful competence of Mannering.

Mrs. Cradshaw, St. Clair's housekeeper, followed closely on the heels of Mannering, her plump, simple face alight with pleasure.

"Welcome home, my lord," Mannering boomed in his rich, deep voice, bowing low.

"It is certainly good to be home, Mannering. I trust all goes well with Mrs. Mannering?"

"As well as can be expected, my lord, considering the years are making us all a bit rickety."

Mannering beamed at the young earl, pleased that his lordship was never too high in the instep to be concerned about those in his employ.

"Master Julien!" Mrs. Cradshaw bustled forward and swept Julien a deep curtsy.

Julien encircled the small, plump woman in his arms, a wide smile on his face.

"Your prodigal has returned, Emma. Is it too much to hope that there will be some blueberry muffins beside my plate this evening?" He gave her a gentle hug and released her.

"Fancy that, Edward," Mrs. Cradshaw exclaimed, turning to Mannering. "Master Julien never forgets his blueberry muffins."

"Indeed not. Moreover, François will not be arriving until well after dinner tonight. Far too late to turn up his artistic nose at my tastes!"

"What can you expect from Frenchies? Why, I had it on the best information that the Frenchies don't even know what blueberries are!"

"Why, Mrs. Cradshaw, I have it from my best sources that the French think blueberries fit for only pigs and Englishmen!" Julien responded, a pronounced twinkle in his eyes.

"Oh, Master Julien, you're bamming me!" she pronounced, tapping him reproachfully on the arm.

"Now, Emma," Mannering interposed, "his lordship looks worn to the bone."

He turned to Julien and continued formally: "Your rooms

are all ready, my lord, and since I do not see your valet"—he paused slightly to leave no doubt that he found Timmens an unnecessary encumbrance—"I myself will attend your lordship tonight."

Julien was amused by the rivalry between his two households, but managed to maintain a serious expression. Poor Mannering! If he only knew that Timmens considered himself quite put upon to be dragged into the wilds of the North, into the company of persons he considered to be outlandishly uncivilized. Julien gave a brief moment's thought to the dusty state of his normally gleaming Hessians. He could almost hear Timmens' high reedy voice reproaching him.

Julien nodded his agreement to Mannering and made his way through the great front doors, past several footmen and two giggling maids who had peeped their heads around a corner to peer at him.

"I always feel that I should be removing my armor rather than a meager cloak and hat," Julien remarked as Mannering divested him of these accoutrements.

"Indeed, my lord," Mannering agreed, pride ringing in his voice.

Like many great houses of its age, St. Clair opened its oaken doors directly into an awesome hall, whose walls were covered with ancient tapestries and brightly lit flambeaux. Suits of highly polished armor stood upright around the great room. Julien had always the impression that at a moment's notice they would spring forward into action to defend St. Clair, and as a boy he had joined them in many an imaginary battle. A wistful smile played over his lips and it was with a conscious effort that he turned his attention to Mrs. Cradshaw.

"I find myself quite famished. Could I have my dinner—with, of course, the blueberry muffins—in about an hour?"

"Certainly, my lord." She gave him a sideways glance as if to remind him that he was no longer among that rackety pack of good-for-nothing servants in London, who could not be trusted to take proper care of his lordship.

Julien strode to the main staircase, a dark oak affair that dominated a goodly portion of the hall. He touched the ornately carved railing, aware that it glowed shiny and bright under the careful ministrations of Mrs. Cradshaw. He slowed his step halfway up the stairs, turning his gaze for a moment to the portraits of past earls and their wives on the wall beside him. They had been a prolific line, he thought, mentally adding to this number of portraits the scores of others that hung in the gallery. The portraits reminded him that the St. Clairs had inherited father to son in an unbroken stream of earls until the present, an unusual occurrence in itself. Julien could readily imagine his father hurling abuse at his head for all eternity should he not marry and produce the necessary male child. It had all seemed rather absurd to trouble himself with such thoughts, for he was young and quite healthy, certainly more so than his nominal heir at present, a distant sickly cousin who would become the eighth earl should Julien depart this world without a son. On his next birthday Julien would be twenty-eight, a reasonable enough age to take a wife and beget a future Earl of March.

He was certain that this decision would please his Aunt Mary, sister to his mother, who had been voluble on the subject of his marriage from the moment he had passed his twenty-fifth birthday. He could always count on her, after all formal amenities were done, to look at him with narrowed eyes and inquire after his plans to modernize the nursery wing at St. Clair. Over the past three years he had crossed the portal of her rather dark and airless house in London knowing that in the drawing room he would face a nervous debutante, elegantly clad, awaiting his inspection.

Julien looked up, surprised that he had reached his room. A footman appeared and quickly flung open the massive door. Like the hall below, the master bedchamber was awesome in size and filled with heavy furniture that dated from Tudor times. It had crossed his mind to wonder how the impeccably clean Mrs. Cradshaw managed to move the ponderous pieces in order to sweep beneath them. But it was the huge canopy bed that Julien most appreciated. The Tudor earl who was responsibile for its construction must have been a giant of a man, for the bed was nearly seven feet long and almost as wide. Julien could not be displeased at this, for he himself was well over six feet and suffered unending discomfort at inns and at his friends' houses.

While Mannering directed footmen in the preparation of the bath, Julien walked over to a brightly burning fire and eased himself into a large leather chair. He negligently loosened his cravat and with a sigh of comfort stretched his long legs out before him.

What more could a man wish for? he asked himself lazily. Somehow the thought of a wife's domestic chatter intruding on the majestic silence of this ancient chamber was unimaginable to him. In any case, he thought with a grimace, its sole purpose would be to grate on his nerves.

Having done justice to Cook's innumerable dishes, Julien rose, sated, and walked from the formal, rather somber dining room to the sixth earl's library. Julien never felt quite at his ease in this room, for it was uniquely his father's. All Tudor influence was swept away, replaced by pale blue satin hangings and light, delicately carved French pieces from the last century. Lush, light-blue-patterned Aubusson carpets covered the cold stone floor, and even the massive carved fireplace had been removed and replaced by a light-colored Italian marble. He could still picture his mother, a descendent of a long, proud heritage of drafty castles in the North, casting scathing comments at her husband's folly. Since his father's death some ten years ago, this room and indeed all of St. Clair was Julien's alone, to do with as he pleased. But he had vowed long ago that the library would remain just as it was, the only tangible expression of his father's taste at St. Clair.

There was an overlarge winged chair that stood near the fireplace, quite out of place with the other exquisitely wrought pieces. It was his father's chair and Julien always found himself grateful that his sire had relaxed his taste in this one instance to the demands of comfort.

It was in this chair that Julien sat himself, stretching his Hessians to the glowing fire.

Mannering approached him, gave a slight cough to gain his attention, and turned inquiring eyes to the untouched plate of Mrs. Cradshaw's blueberry muffins that he had carried with him from the dining room.

Julien said ruefully: "Good God. Mannering, am I quite undone? I fear I shall find myself in Mrs. Cradshaw's black books."

Mannering ventured tentatively: "Mrs. Cradshaw will understand, my lord."

Julien waved his hand to the small table at his side. "No, Mannering, I do not wish to brook her displeasure my first evening home. I promise you, I shall do them justice before the evening is out."

Mannering set the plate of muffins at his side and made his way to the sideboard to fetch a decanter of claret. A smile flitted over Julien's face as he recalled Mannering's herculean struggle to assist him into his form-fitting coat. He had shown unbounded relief when Julien divested himself of his own boots, a task that would most certainly have shaken Mannering's dignified image of himself. Perhaps, he thought, Mannering would not now think his valet, Timmens, a bad sort after all.

"Will that be all you require, my lord?"

Julien, aware of his old retainer's fatigue, said quickly: "Yes, Mannering. Do retire now, I will snuff all the candles when I go up."

Mannering turned and strode in his stately manner from the library, softly closing the double doors behind him.

Julien leaned forward and poured himself a glass of claret. He took a sip and sat back, savoring the quality. He began absently to twirl the stem between long, slender fingers, his thoughts turning to Percy and Hugh, whom he expected to arrive the next evening. He discovered now that he regretted having invited them to join him here. Aside from the fishing and shooting, the time he would spend in their company promised to be no different from his activities in London.

Julien frowned; he decided after a long drink of claret that he was simply becoming hermitic.

A ghost of a smile played over his lips as he pictured Percy's boredom at being incarcerated in the country. He found himself concluding, without much regret, that in all likelihood Percy and perhaps even Hugh would depart St. Clair after but a few days.

The claret curled about warmly in his stomach and he began to grow drowsy. Unenthusiastically he eyed the muffins, and found himself unable to take even a nibble. He would take them to his room and down several the next morning before breakfast.

He fell asleep not long thereafter, comfortably stretched his full length on the large Tudor bed, his head clear of the effects of too much drink. It was a pleasant condition, one he had seldom experienced in the past several months.

3

Julien awoke later than he had intended the following morning and upon opening his eyes found himself looking up into his valet's perturbed face.

"Good God, Timmens, what a face to be greeted with after a pleasant night's sleep!"

"Good morning, my lord," Timmens said stiffly. He gave an audible sniff of displeasure and helped Julien to rise from his bed.

"Come, man, surely things are not so bad as all that. I assure you that even though my Hessians and coat have suffered in your absence you will not find them quite beyond repair."

"I have already endeavored, my lord, to restore your Hessians, though it was," he added in the voice of one sorely tried, "an experience that I would not care to again repeat."

Julien paused a moment, now fully awake and aware that the sensibilities of his stiff-lipped valet were ruffled to the extreme. "Of course I have missed your fine service, Timmens," Julien said, his voice cajoling.

Timmens, somewhat mollified by this admission, allowed himself to unbend and competently assisted his master to dress.

Finally dressed, Julien was at the point of escaping to his breakfast when he chanced to see the plate of muffins beside his bed, still untouched. An expedient solution occurred to him and he eyed the still-muttering Timmens. Deciding that Timmens could use a trimming for his martinet ways, he turned to his valet and said suavely: "Timmens, you see the muffins here by my bed. As a reward for your excellent service this morning, I require you to enjoy at least two of them before allowing the maids to enter the room."

Timmens darted his rheumy eyes to the muffins, bemused by this ambiguous token of praise. He realized that his master was awaiting his answer and said blankly: "Yes, my lord. Thank you, my lord."

Not more than an hour later, in fine good humor, Julien mounted his Arabian mare, Astarte, and rode out of the park at a comfortable canter to inspect his lands.

Bright sunlight poured down through the crisp morning air, as if bending all of its brilliance on St. Clair. With a great sense of well-being, Julien turned Astarte onto an open field and gave her her head. His body moved smoothly with hers, swaying in rhythm to her firm stride. The chirping of birds and the gentle rustle of leaves and foliage was a welcome change from the ever-present noise of the London streets.

Julien quite lost track of time, and some minutes later, realizing that Astarte was breathing heavily with exertion, he reined in, straightened in the saddle, and looked about him. A short distance ahead lay a large wood, forming a near-circle around him. He saw with vague interest that he was no longer on St. Clair land.

"Come, Astarte, let us see what lies ahead."

Julien made out a small path just to his left that led into the woods and click-clicked Astarte forward. The floor of the woods was green with spongy moss that deadened the sound of Astarte's hooves.

All too soon the trees began to thin and Julien could make out a small clearing but a few yards ahead. Suddenly he knew he was not alone. He was not certain how he knew, except that his ears had grown used to the sounds of the forest.

He allowed Astarte to move slowly forward toward the clearing. His vision no longer blocked by the trees, he stiffened at the strange sight that met his eyes.

There, in the small clearing not twenty yards away from him, stood two men, pistols raised properly in front of their faces, standing back to back.

Good Lord, he thought, appalled, they are going to duel!

There were no seconds, no one but the two duelists, who now began to pace away from each other, one man's voice calling out the paces in a loud, clear voice: "One, two, three . . ."

Julien gently dug his heels in Astarte's side and she obediently moved forward, making no sound until they reached the edge of the clearing.

Fascinated, Julien stared fixedly at the two men.

"Eight, nine, ten!"

The men turned in quick smooth motions and faced each other. One of the men pulled up his pistol in a quick, jerky movement, stiffened his arm, and fired.

The gun's report rang through the silence of the woods. The bullet missed its mark, for the other man remained standing, and now, in what seemed an endlessly cruel delay, slowly raised his pistol and aimed it toward his opponent's heart.

Julien found himself frozen into inaction, his hands clenching the reins. The man stood proud and stiff, waiting, without a sound.

With a nasty laugh the man fired. To Julien's horror, his opponent grabbed his chest, gave a loud moan of pain, staggered forward, and finally fell heavily to the ground.

The spell broken, Julien dug his heels, and Astarte leaped forward. He pulled up short not ten yards from where the man lay, and jumped from his horse. With unbelieving eyes he saw the man who had committed this needless murder stand leaning against a tree, holding his sides in laughter.

Ignoring him, Julien strode quickly to the prone figure and knelt down beside him. The man was pitifully small and slight of build. Julien gathered the lifeless figure into his arms, and suddenly overwhelmed with fury, yelled at his murderer, who now stood in shocked silence, as if aware of the enormity of what he had done: "You damned fool! What in God's name have you done, man?"

The man raised his hand in a helpless gesture, but seemed unable to come forward and speak.

To Julien's shock, the slight figure in his arms began to struggle violently, and he gazed down for the first time into the face of the fallen man. A startled pair of the greenest eyes he had ever beheld looked up at him in confusion.

The green eyes did not waver from his face, but did blink in rapid succession. Well-formed lips parted in an "O" of surprise, and dimples peeped through on white cheeks.

"Why, sir, I think you have much mistaken the matter!"

"But you're a . . . girl!" Julien gasped.

"That, sir, is a statement I cannot argue with," she said with the greatest composure, the dimples becoming more pronounced.

Finding himself for the moment speechless, Julien instinctively dropped his arms from about her shoulders. With the utmost unconcern she pulled herself away and came up to her knees, her hands resting lightly on her thighs.

"Harry," she called, laughter lurking in her low musical voice, "I do believe that we have given the gentleman a shock! Stop standing there like a gaping ninny and come here!"

Julien, finding that his addled senses were returning to normal, looked up to see a young man come toward them, a sheepish grin on his cherubic face. He rose slowly to his feet and turned to look down at the girl, a pronounced scowl on his face. Julien was beginning to feel very much the fool, a condition of which he was not at all fond. His eyes narrowed dangerously on the girl's face and he demanded coldly: "Are you in the habit, my girl, of playacting at such deadly games?"

The dimples quivered and his indignation grew. She turned to him and said in a composed voice: "When you have recovered from your ruffled sensibilities, dear sir, you will realize that it was not we who interrupted you. This is Brandon land, and how my brother and I wish to spend our time is certainly no concern of yours!"

"Now, Kate, I pray you, the gentleman was but worried," the young man hastily interposed, planting himself in front of the girl.

Turning to Julien, he said apologetically: "I do beg your pardon, sir. Kate, here, must needs know all the masculine sports."

He indicated with no little embarrassment the now-indignant girl, who jumped angrily to her feet and turned on her brother.

"Really, Harry, there is no reason for you to apologize! The gentleman"—she cast a martial eye briefly on Julien— "was trespassing!"

"I do beg your pardon, ma'am," Julien retorted, his voice heavy with sarcasm.

Harry cast a quelling glance at his sister and quickly extended his hand to Julien. "Harry Brandon, sir. And this is my sister, Katharine."

Julien stiffened, but after one look at the young man's pleading eyes, unbent and extended his own hand.

"St. Clair. I believe my lands lie not far distant from yours."

"So you're the Earl of March!" Kate declared, eyeing him up and down with unabashed curiosity.

Julien raised haughty brows and replied frostily: "Why, yes, I do have that honor."

The snub was unmistakable, but to Julien's chagrin, the girl merely continued to regard him with frank inquisitiveness, her head cocked pertly to one side.

"Yes, I suppose it could be regarded as an honor . . . to some," she remarked blandly.

A glint came to his eyes. So she wanted to cross verbal swords with him, did she! He said swiftly, "Particularly so to . . . ladies of breeding!"

He subjected her to a thorough appraisal and rested his gray eyes coldly on her tight-fitting breeches. He expected her to blush to the roots of her hair and to stammer incoherently, for he had many times achieved this result with but the mildest of set-downs.

His well-ordered world received a slight shock when the girl replied to this cheerfully, all the while brushing leaves from her breeches: "I suppose it is difficult to evince breeding when one is engaged in a duel." She raised her wide eyes to Julien's face and added brazenly: "But you must admit, dear sir, that breeches are much more the thing when one must fall down and play dead! And it was my turn this time to get fatally wounded! Harry insisted."

Before Julien could recover sufficiently to make a suitable rejoinder, she added, seeming to ponder the problem: "Perhaps it is a sad trial to gentlemen of your breeding and . . . age, to accept such trifles with equanimity."

For the first time in his life, Julien Edward Mowbray St. Clair, Earl of March, found himself without a word to say.

"Kate, really!" Harry expostulated, giving his sister a light buffet on the shoulder.

He turned to Julien in an agony of embarrassment. "Sir, please forgive her tongue. She doesn't mean what she says! She's only funning," he finished lamely, casting a dark sideways glance at his recalcitrant sister.

"Harry, how dare you side against me with this . . . this person!" She stomped a booted foot, the green eyes flashing daggers at her brother.

Julien looked back and forth between the pair and felt a muscle twitch at the corner of his mouth. Although he found the manners of this hoydenish girl deplorable, the situation was ridiculous to the extreme, and he could not help breaking into a grin.

"Miss Brandon," he said gravely, gazing into Kate's upturned face, "please accept my profound apologies. You look most charming in breeches!"

She shot him a look of pure mischief and replied demurely: "But, sir, I could not look more charming in breeches than you do!"

Julien would have infinitely preferred to take his hand to her breeched backside, but realizing in all truth that this pleasure must be denied him, threw in his hand and gave up the battle. He managed to quell his feelings of wounded consequence, threw back his head, and gave way to a shout of laughter.

"Where, Miss Brandon, have you and your brother been hiding yourselves? I count it my misfortune not to have met the pair of you before!"

Harry replied quickly to forestall any further impertinence from Kate: "It is not so strange, my lord. You are not often here."

Julien felt a quite odd sensation, equally vague and undefined as the nagging thoughts that had pursued him to St. Clair. He turned slowly to Harry and said thoughtfully: "No, Harry, I believe you are right. My visits have been infrequent and of singularly short duration up until now."

"Do you plan to stay long this time, my lord?" Harry pursued, thankful for an unexceptionable topic of conversation. He felt very nearly green with anxiety at the thought of having offended their noble neighbor.

Julien was silent for a moment. He found himself looking at Katharine and felt again the odd sensation, that spread now like a surge deep within him. She had removed her tight-fitting hat, and clouds of thick, rich auburn hair fell about her shoulders and waved gently down her back nearly to her waist. She was oblivious of him and did not look up, occupied with winding the thick masses of hair into long plaits and tucking them under her hat.

Julien tore his gaze away from her and answered Harry shortly: "It is a possibility, Harry . . . a possibility."

"Oh, Lord, Mannering! I had clean forgot Sir Percy and Sir Hugh are to arrive for dinner." Julien cast a rueful look at his butler, all the while peeling off his riding gloves.

"It is nothing to concern yourself with, my lord," Mannering allowed, smoothing invisible creases from the gloves Julien handed him. "It is merely, my lord, that Mrs. Cradshaw is hesitant to accord their lordships chambers without your approval."

Julien felt a tug of impatience. "Very well, Mannering, have Mrs. Cradshaw allot their lordships the Green Room and the Countess's Chamber."

Mannering nodded his agreement and gave a discreet but quite audible cough, clearly indicating to his master that this was not his only concern. Julien was well aware of his butler's roundabout ways of securing his attention, and thus fixed his eyes on Mannering. "Out with it, Mannering. I promise you I shall not fly into a great rage."

Mannering gave another cough and gazed at a point just beyond Julien's left ear. "It is the Frenchman, my lord," he said with finality. He brought his focus back to his master, as if to ask instructions, his point clearly made.

"The Frenchman? You refer, I presume, to François, my chef," Julien hazarded.

"Of course, my lord," Mannering affirmed, surprised at his lordship's failure to instantly grasp so obvious a fact.

A sense of foreboding descended over Julien and he asked gravely: "You may tell me the truth, Mannering. Has a scullery maid fled St. Clair in terror of her life?"

Aghast at such a suggestion, Mannering drew himself up and said with dignity: "It is not *our* staff, my lord. As I said, it is the Frenchman. He swears that he cannot be expected to be . . . an artist . . . in such a backward, barbaric kitchen. That, I think, my lord, is the gist of what he said, his English being so bad." He did not add that in his opinion it would be not at all a bad thing were the raving chef to fling out of the kitchen and remove his voluble presence elsewhere, preferably far from St. Clair.

Julien knew, of course, even from the restrained account Mannering had given, that François was in quite a taking. If Percy and Hugh were not to sit down to an empty dinner table, he must soothe his chef's outraged sensibilities. Damn, he should never have ordered Francois to accompany him here! He'd done it primarily for Percy, who always proclaimed a violent dislike for sturdy English fare. Julien recalled that he would not be overly displeased if Percy and Hugh found St. Clair quite a bore and departed posthaste for London. Perhaps, his thinking continued serenely, it would not be such a catastrophic occurrence were François to leave in a huff.

Having reached this happy conclusion, Julien favored

Mannering with an indifferent shrug of his shoulders and said with the greatest unconcern: "Mannering, please inform François that if he finds his accommodations here not to his liking, he will be paid his quarterly wages and driven to Dapplemoor to catch the mail coach back to London. And, if you please," Julien continued, "have a footman fetch Stokeworthy and ask Cook to send me a light luncheon. I will be in the library."

Mannering's jaw dropped. In that instant, his respect for his master soared to heights heretofore unknown. "Fancy," he repeated in awed tones later to Mrs. Cradshaw, "his lordship was as calm as you please and ready to let the Frenchman go without a blink of an eyelash!"

As Julien partook of cold chicken and crusty bread, he was informed by Mannering, who was unable to contain the news, that upon hearing of his master's sentiments, François had abruptly ceased his French ravings and in a burst of enthusiasm declared that his lordship and his guests would have the finest, most exquisite dinner his culinary skills could achieve.

Julien recieved this news with mixed feelings. He shrugged, deciding that at the very least, he would suffer no more tantrums from the fellow.

His luncheon finished, Julien made his way to the Estate Room, for generations the account room of the earls of March. As he awaited his agent's arrival, he let his mind wander back to his curious encounter that morning with the Brandons. "What an impertinent chit," he said half-aloud, but without displeasure. Though he had openly derided the girl's clothing, he could not help dwelling briefly upon her slender figure, emphasized by the tight breeches. And the long, thick russet tresses. He was mildly surprised that he had not until now made her acquaintance, nor that of her brother, Harry. But then, since he was at least eight years Harry's senior, it was no wonder that their paths had not crossed in his youth. They would have been but children when he departed for Eton. Brandon . . . Brandon. Of a certainty, now that he thought about it, the name was known to him. He wondered with a questioning frown why his father had never talked of the family, nor, for that matter, met with them socially.

He was forced to end this line of thinking when there came a knock on the door.

"Enter," he called.

Stokeworthy, the St. Clair agent, appeared in the open

doorway, his long thin face, rather like a horse's, Julien had always thought, wearing an apologetic look.

Julien rose. "Ah, do come in, Stokeworthy. It is certainly good of you to come on such short notice. I do hope it did not inconvenience you."

He took the older man's bony hand into his and gave it an enthusiastic shake.

"I wish to apologize, my lord, for my tardiness, but you see, Mrs. Stokeworthy's niece has come down with a chill and the house is at sixes and sevens." Stokeworthy fastened his watery eyes on his master's face, hoping to see no displeasure. Unknown to Julien, he would have preferred to spend much more time than he did here in the Estate Room at St. Clair, and had welcomed his summons here, albeit on short notice, with profound anticipation. He found invariably after his visits with the earl that Mrs. Stokeworthy quite fell over his words. The folk of Dapplemoor would pay his household unexpected visits, listening with avid attention to any tidbits of gossip he chose to relate about the Earl of March.

Julien was concerned by Stokeworthy's news.

"Given your niece's illness, perhaps you would rather return home. We could meet again in several days, when you have no other worries on your mind."

"Oh, no, my lord," Stokeworthy exclaimed, sorry that he had ever mentioned the chilled niece. "I assure you, my lord," he continued firmly, "that a man's presence is never the thing in the sickroom!"

"If you are certain . . ." Julien temporized.

"Very sure, my lord," Stokeworthy affirmed. He ceremoniously pulled a sheaf of papers from his time-worn case to emphasize his point.

Julien and Stokeworthy spent the next several hours poring over accounts and calculating the sums his tenants' crops would likely fetch at market. It had been a good year at St. Clair; not too much rain and not too much snow. The county had fared well and the St. Clair coffers would prosper, as would the pocketbooks of his tenants.

Julien trusted Stokeworthy implicitly, as his father had before him. He was pleased, even more so than usual after Stokeworthy's glowing account of St. Clair's prosperity, that his father had brought this man into his employ. Many people had been surprised at his father's choice, Julien had learned not many years past. It seemed that the garrulous Mrs. Stokeworthy bore a striking resemblance to Julien's grandfather, and if the rumors were true, Mrs. Stokeworthy was but one of his grandfather's by-blows.

It occurred to Julien that his father, a man of unwavering moral standards, must have found it unnerving to be in contact almost daily with the several men and women who so closely resembled him. Julien had asked his father once about his grandfather's vagaries, but had received such a stern, uncompromising set-down that he quite vowed to take his inquiries elsewhere. Although Julien had never known his grandfather, he had believed all the stories since he first looked closely at the portrait of his grandfather that hung in a darker corner of the gallery. He could almost picture his bewigged grandsire with his full sensual lips, the lewd twinkle in his gray eyes, swooping down astride a great black charger on unsuspecting village maidens.

Julien was unaware to this day that the locals had embroidered upon the facts and his grandfather's exploits had become romantic legend in Dapplemoor to pass the time in the long winter months. Nor would it have overpleased him to discover that the folk hereabouts compared him more often with his righteous, moral father than his dashing, amorous grandfather.

Fortunately not privy to these facts, Julien continued to pride himself on his courteous, scrupulously polite treatment of the local folk.

After sharing a glass of sherry with Stokeworthy, he saw the good man off, consulted his watch, and deemed it time to change into evening apparel.

A few minutes after Julien descended the staircase, the exquisite folds of his neckcloth perfectly placed, Mannering informed him of the imminent arrival of Sir Percy and Sir Hugh.

"It appears, my lord," Mannering announced, "that their lordships have journeyed together." He motioned a footman to open the great oak doors to admit them.

"Lord, Julien, what an outlandish place!" Percy exclaimed the minute he entered.

Mannering relieved him of his cloak and hat and stood stiffly aside, in offended silence, as Percy stepped forward to shake Julien's hand.

Hugh appeared but a moment later, a calm smile of pleasure on his intelligent face. He bade a polite good evening to Mannering, who unbent a trifle, and removed his cloak and hat.

"Feel as if I've stepped back into the pages of my history books," Percy continued irrepressibly, letting his gaze travel about the hall.

"I know just what you mean, Percy," Julien agreed good-humoredly.

He turned to greet Sir Hugh Drakemore, who remarked in his well-bred voice: "A beautiful estate, Julien. As you know, my great-aunt Regina lives not twenty miles to the west, and I count this like a visit home."

Julien beamed with unspoken pride. "It is a pleasure to have you here, Hugh." Taking Percy into the conversation, he continued: "I trust this madcap here did not overturn you on your way here."

"Dash it, Julien," Percy interrupted, his honor impinged, "you know full well I would do nothing of the kind! Why, Hugh himself said he had never had a more comfortable trip!" Percy bent his gaze pointedly at Hugh.

Never one to let down his friends, Hugh said with unruffled composure: "Quite true. I was particularly comfortable when Percy took the reins."

Julien raised an incredulous eyebrow, and Percy, unwilling to have this subject pursued to greater depth, abruptly announced: "Dash it all, Julien. Getting late, you know, and I am quite famished!"

Hugh regarded Percy with a frown of disapprobation but forbore to comment on his outrageous demand. Julien interposed quickly, knowing the vociferous appetite of his friend.

"Quite right, Percy. Why do not you and Hugh repair to your rooms and change." He added somewhat apologetically: "You see, Percy, I cannot have guests to dinner in their traveling clothes. It would do a great disservice to my consequence."

"Humph!" Percy grunted. "You are a dog, Julien. You wish us to change simply because you do not wish to feel foolish alone in your evening clothes."

Julien laughed his agreement at this pronouncement. "You have found me out, Percy. But you must bear with me."

Hugh stood quietly waiting for Percy to join him. "We shall not be long, Julien, unless"—he cast a quizzing glance at Percy—"our exquisite here must needs dandify himself."

Julien could not resist a rueful grin, thinking of the half-dozen neckcloths he had ruined before achieving his own elegant appearance. He turned to Mannering. "Sir Hugh and Sir Percy will now go to their rooms. If you will please have a footman escort them."

"Very well, my lord." Mannering bowed in his most formal manner, as if to impress upon Sir Percy that St. Clair was indeed an earl's establishment.

"Mannering tells me that the lake is abundant with trout, Hugh," Julien commented as he walked with his friend across the east side of the lawn toward St. Clair lake.

Hugh inhaled the fresh morning air and hiked his fishing gear more securely over his shoulder. " 'Tis a pity Percy would not rouse himself, for the country air is quite invigorating." He turned his dark eyes to Julien, a smile breaking his usually composed features.

Julien laughed. "What! Percy up and about before noon? Why, it is unheard of, Hugh. And you know that Percy can't stand to see the 'beasts' wriggling around on the string when you haul them in!"

Hugh inclined his head in agreement and paused a moment to look about him. "I own you must be proud of your hands and home, Julien."

"Yes," Julien answered slowly. "I suppose I am proud." Like Hugh, he turned momentarily to gaze back through the trees to the sun-bathed east tower which commanded a magnificent view of St. Clair lake and the vast meadows and hills beyond. He turned back to Hugh and added: "When I am here, I scarce ever miss the racket of London. Particularly this time."

"Why this time in particular?" Hugh asked.

Julien pulled the branches of a bush from their path before he turned to Hugh, a silent smile on his face that did not reach his gray eyes. It was strange, he thought, but he did not at all have the inclination to speak frankly to Hugh. As a matter of fact, he realized with a start, the vague, unsettling feelings had quite vanished. He felt content and would have preferred to be striding to the lake by himself, enjoying the quiet and peaceful surroundings. But Hugh was here, and he must be a gracious host.

"Do forgive me, Hugh. I must be woolgathering this morning. What did you ask?"

Hugh cocked an eyebrow and gazed intently at his friend.

Never one to pry, he cooled his curiosity and said: "It was nothing, Julien. You say the trout are abundant?"

"So Mannering has informed me." At that moment they broke through a small circle of trees and the unruffled blue water of St. Clair lake greeted them.

"A magnificent prospect, is it not, Hugh?"

"Yes, indeed," Hugh affirmed warmly.

As Julien gazed about him, he chanced to see something move to his left, close to the water's edge. "Who the devil can that be?" he muttered aloud, his eyes darkening.

"Perhaps Mannering has informed others of the abundant trout," Hugh said with gentle humor.

"The devil!" Julien ejaculated. "This is certainly private land and I intend to find out just who thinks he has the right to fish in my lake!" Julien turned swiftly and strode in the direction of the trespasser. He called over his shoulder: "Stay here, Hugh. I shall be back shortly."

Julien walked rapidly and quietly, the dewy, thick grass cushioning any sound his boots might have made. He drew up short in surprise, for the intruder was but a lad. The boy was sitting cross-legged, a rude, homemade fishing pole held firmly in his hands. He was gazing intently at the water, completely absorbed.

Concentrating on my trout! Julien thought angrily.

There was something faintly familiar about the lad but Julien could not quite put his finger on it. He strode up behind the boy and said in his most peremptory voice: "And just who, my lad, gave you permission to fish in my lake?"

The boy jumped in surprise and the fishing pole fell from his hands into the water. As he tried frantically to retrieve it, he cried out angrily: "How dare you give me such a fright! Now look what you've done! How absolutely odious . . ." The words died abruptly as the boy whirled on his heels to face his accuser.

Julien found himself gazing into the face of Kate Brandon, dressed again today in her boy's breeches, her hair tucked under an old leather hat.

"You . . ." she breathed, quite as surprised as he.

Julien was the first to recover his wits. "I wish you good morning, Mistress Kate." He bowed low in front of her. "I trust you find the fishing good here . . . on St. Clair land."

Kate scrambled to her feet. At his thrust, she had the grace to blush, but added quickly in her defense: "Your agent,

Stokeworthy, gave me permission to fish here. You know," she confided easily now, "it is quite the best spot in the area."

"St. Clair is honored by your accolades, Miss Brandon," Julien said stiffly. Oddly, he found himself somewhat put out by her confidence. Had she no maidenly shyness? He chanced to see her fishing basket and inquired in a surly tone: "And just how many of my trout are now at this very moment snug in your basket?"

Kate chose to ignore this and declared sharply: "It appears to me, sir, that you are . . . quite tight! After all, what can a few fish mean to the great Earl of March!"

"No more tight than your breeches, madam!" he retorted, doing his utmost to best her.

He should have guessed that such a stricture would in no way discomfit her. Indeed, she replied in a confiding tone: "Quite right of you to notice. You see, I have had to wear this pair for the past two years, Harry's breeches being now too large for me. They are, I assure you, a bit confining."

She turned toward the water, shaded her eyes with her hand for a moment, and then brought her gaze back to Julien's face.

"It is a pity you gave me such a start. You see," she explained, seeing the blank look on Julien's face, "it took me quite two weeks to whittle that pole so that it was just right. Harry thinks himself far too grown-up and would not help me. Now it is gone! I hope you are satisfied, sir!" She glared at him with her enormous green eyes.

There could be nothing else outrageous that she could say. Julien shook his head and said gravely: "Miss Brandon, you will, of course, allow me to make reparations. In fact, my friend over there"—he turned and waved to Hugh to come to them—"has equipped himself with several fishing poles. It is likely he can be convinced to part with one of them."

"Why, that is quite handsome of you," Kate announced with approval. The dimples peeped out irrepressibly.

"What an unaccountable girl you are, Miss Brandon! You must be quite a trial to your family!"

He had meant only a simple jest, but at his words her face fell ludicrously and the green eyes darkened. She looked away from him and he saw her lips draw into a tight line of unhappiness.

Unsure of what had upset her, he stretched his hand out in an unconscious gesture. "Miss Brandon, I did not mean to . . ."

he began. He was unable to finish, which was probably just as well, for he had no idea of what he would have said. Hugh approached and stood beside him, gazing in some surprise at the breeched boy.

With an effort, Julien turned to Hugh and said: "Hugh, I would like you to meet Miss Katharine Brandon. Her family lives somewhat west of Dapplemoor."

"Lady Katharine Brandon," she corrected. Kate stretched out her hand to Hugh, who for want of something better, extended his own hand and clasped her slender fingers.

The green eyes twinkled. Julien was relieved to see that whatever had made her unhappy was for the moment forgotten.

She gave a winsome smile to Hugh and said simply: "Do forgive me, sir. I fear that curtsying in breeches is quite beyond my abilities."

Hugh blinked rapidly several times. Calling on the great aplomb and polish that he had acquired over the years, he managed to reply with equanimity: "Do not disturb yourself, Lady Katharine. I quite understand. Though I have, myself, never endeavored to curtsy in breeches, I do think it would be an awkward and unpleasing sight."

Julien had observed this exchange with only half his attention. The other half was focused on her initial revelation. "Lady" Katharine Brandon. Her father, then, was no local squire as he had first imagined. Or perhaps her mother was of very high rank. Why had he not then been introduced to this noble family who lived in such proximity to St. Clair? He wondered briefly if the Brandons were impoverished. If this were the case, they might prefer to live in relative seclusion, being unable to entertain the local gentry.

Julien turned his full attention back to Hugh and Katharine, who had reached a comfortable pause in their exchange of amenities.

"Unfortunately, I startled Lady Katharine and she dropped her fishing pole in the lake. And, Hugh, I have handsomely offered her one of yours!"

Hugh, a gentleman to the tips of his well-manicured nails, quickly answered: "It would be my pleasure, Lady Katharine. Please make your selection. I have but three poles with me, but I have been assured by Julien that they are of the finest quality."

Kate glanced at Julien with a gleam of amusement before

bending over the three poles laid out by Hugh. Upon careful inspection, she rose, quite enthusiastic over her choice.

"How very fine it is . . . and such balance!" she cried. "Now I shall be able to pull in every trout that takes a nibble!"

Julien gave a bark of laughter, his shoulders shaking. "Be my guest, Lady Katharine, be my guest! Consider the meager contents of my lake at your disposal."

She joined wholeheartedly in his laughter. "How very *noble* of you, my lord!" she exclaimed.

Even before Mannering handed him the daily post from London on a silver salver, Julien's nostrils quivered at the unmistakable scent of Lady Sarah's exotic perfume. It usually amused him that he could smell the Lady Sarah's heavy musk scent at a soiree before actually seeing her. But today he found himself a bit put out; even the letter from his mother, who found perfume an irritant to her nerves, was tinged with the cloying scent.

Julien tossed the letters on an elegant French writing table and halted Mannering as he turned to go. "Mannering, do stay a moment."

"Yes, my lord?"

"I find myself abominably ignorant about some of our local gentry. The Brandons, to be exact." He paused a moment, alert for any signs of change in his butler's impassive countenance. Seeing none, he continued: "The name is, of course, familiar to me, and I have but recently met for the first time the Brandon offspring. Quite a charming pair, incidentally. What can you tell me of the family?"

Mannering's eyes lit up for a brief instant and his thin lips curved into a smile. "Ah, yes, the Lady Katharine. A most delightful young lady, if you will pardon my saying so, my lord. And of course Master Harry, too."

Julien was intrigued by his normally staid butler's praise of any person not directly connected with the St. Clair family or household.

"But who are they?" he persisted.

Mannering, who prided himself on his intimate knowledge of every noble family within two days' ride of St. Clair, cleared his throat ceremoniously.

"Sir Oliver Brandon, the Lady Katharine's father, is a baronet who is considered quite an outsider here, having arrived in only the last thirty years. His family lives, I believe, in the Lake District, near Widemere. The Lady Sabrina, his lordship's late wife, was the only daughter of the McCelland laird, a most powerful lord whose father fought for Prince Charlie in forty-five. Unfortunately, my lord, I am unable to recount how the Lady Sabrina met Sir Oliver," Mannering admitted, disappointed that he had been unable to ascertain these facts.

"In any case, my lord," he continued, "I have been given to understand that the McCelland laird forbade the marriage, and the Lady Sabrina and Sir Oliver . . . eloped." Mannering's nostrils flared in condescension at the very mention of such an action. "Sir Oliver also was cast out by his family, his father, as I understand, being none too fond of Scots."

"You mean, Mannering, that the McCelland laird considered the Brandons beneath his touch?"

"Quite, my lord. As you know, their union produced the Lady Katharine and Master Harry. The Lady Sabrina died some six years ago, from an inflammation of the lung, most say."

"Most say, Mannering?"

"Well, if you will forgive my saying so, my lord, it is my opinion that the Lady Sabrina died of . . . unhappiness." Realizing that this statement sounded woefully sentimental, Mannering hastened to add: "Sir Oliver is not a very kind man, my lord, and the Lady Sabrina's years with him were not contented ones."

Mannering's story of the Lady Sabrina brought to Julien's mind Kate's unhappy look when he had mentioned her family. But he merely nodded and asked Mannering with calculated sharpness: "Then why have I not met the Brandons? If they have been here thirty years, well, I have been here nearly twenty-eight years myself!"

A sense of foreboding descended over Mannering as his master fixed him with a hard stare, reminding him forcibly of the late earl. The earl had drawn him out about the Brandons, and he had already said far too much to avoid answering his question. He had been silent for so many years, in keeping with the late earl's wishes, that he found himself quite at a loss as how best to proceed.

He gave his characteristic cough and began with painstaking slowness:

"As your lordship knows, the two Brandon children were

too young for your notice when you lived at St. Clair. Master Harry was barely out of short coats when you departed for Eton." Mannering paused, hoping for a reprieve, but the earl began tapping his fingertips in obvious impatience.

"Yes, yes, I know all that, Mannering. Get to the point, man!"

"Yes, my lord. You see, my lord, your late, esteemed father did not deal well with the Brandons. It seems that your lordship's grandfather was regarded by the Brandons as being of ... questionable reputation where females were concerned."

Julien laughed. "A rake and licentious womanizer is what you mean, is it not, Mannering?"

Mannering fixed Julien with an offended stare, the like of which Julien had not seen since he was a boy.

"One hesitates to speak ill of the dead, my lord, particularly when the person is one's late master, and an earl."

"I stand corrected, Mannering," Julien said gravely. He had to remember that he was not in London, where such appellations of persons living or deceased were mundane occurrences.

"Please continue, Mannering. You say my father and mother had a ... falling-out over Grandfather's questionable reputation?"

"If I may venture to say so, my lord," Mannering continued, now warming to his subject. "Sir Oliver Brandon is a staunch Methodist and overly rigid in his moral views. It seems that the Lady Sabrina's personal maid was found to be ... in the family way. The girl swore it was your grandfather, the earl. Sir Oliver, so I was informed, beat the girl soundly, cast her out, and never again spoke to your grandfather. As you know, my lord, your own father was a very proud man, as is of course proper. Although his late lordship did not always agree with your grandfather's conduct, he thought it disgraceful that a *mere* baronet should dare to condemn an Earl of March, much less cut the acquaintance!"

"The light dawns, Mannering." Julien could picture with not much difficulty how his father and mother would react to such an impertinence. It took him but a moment to shrug off his irritation at not being told all this as he realized that Mannering would in all likelihood be able to tell him more about Katharine.

"As you know, Mannering, the Lady Katharine is a somewhat ... unusual young lady. The two times I have met her, she was dressed in breeches, quite like a boy. As a matter of fact, she is forthright in her manners and speech, very unlike the daughter of a rigid Methodist."

"Perhaps I have acted . . . precipitately, my lord. During the past several years, your lordship being rarely here, Mrs. Cradshaw and I have become well acquainted with the young lady and have let her spend much time here. Mrs. Cradshaw and I have a liking for Lady Katharine. As you can imagine, my lord," Mannering hurried on, "a young lady of her high spirits is sadly out of place in Sir Oliver's household, particularly after the death of Lady Sabrina, her mother. She is certainly not an *encroaching* young lady, my lord. It is just that she . . . needs friends."

"You say she is not an 'encroaching' young lady, Mannering?" Julien inquired gravely.

"Quite true, my lord."

To Mannering's relief, his master gave a little chuckle and placed his hand on his shoulder. "You have acted quite right in this matter. I only regret that my presence here prevents the Lady Katharine from fully enjoying herself on St. Clair land."

Julien dropped his hand and turned his view toward the large French windows that gave a brilliant view of the front lawn. He said under his breath, "As you say, she is in need of friends."

"I beg your pardon, my lord?" Mannering asked, thinking his master's low-spoken words meant for him.

"It is nothing, Mannering. I thank you for the information."

Left alone, Julien again gazed out into the peaceful summer scene. So Kate had made friends with his staff. Quite a feat, he thought, considering Mannering's strict adherence to propriety. A lady in breeches! He realized that he was smiling, not a lazy, mocking smile as was his habit, but a tender smile.

"I must be becoming a half-wit," he muttered half-aloud. "Taken with an impertinent, outrageous . . ."

Julien turned and walked slowly back to the center of the room. He wondered if Kate had been in his father's library. He could picture her pouring tea dressed in a gown of . . . perhaps green velvet, her beautiful thick auburn hair piled high on her head. Unaccountably, he found this picture of domesticity not at all alarming and he was loath to let it slip from his mind. He shook his head, bemused. He very much wanted to see Kate again.

The next several days passed pleasantly enough for Julien, though he and Hugh did not see Kate Brandon again on their outings. For the most part, he and Hugh rode, hunted, and fished together. Percy seemed quite content at this arrangement, planning the evening's menus with François each morning, perusing the London papers, and napping in the afternoons.

Had Hugh told Julien that he was not particularly good company, Julien would have been surprised. Long accustomed to Julien's quickness of wit and good-humored cynicism, Hugh found it quite odd that he seemed distracted, his responses vague and not at all to the point. He regarded his friend covertly on several occasions and speculated on the cause of Julien's preoccupation. Finding no likely answers, he concluded that as Julien seemed not to wish to speak of what was bothering him, his as well as Percy's presence at St. Clair was not at all what Julien needed.

And so it was Hugh, and not Percy, who announced at dinner one evening that he really must return to London. He bent a stern eye on Percy and began to enumerate various reasons why Percy, also, should accompany him.

"After all, my dear fellow," he addressed Percy, "we have enjoyed Julien's hospitality for quite long enough. And you, Percy, have a horse running at Newmarket next week. Since I have wagered on your horse to win, I feel it only right of you to return with me and see to his training," he added. He absolved himself of this harmless lie, for his motives were, after all, of the purest.

Percy, who had a bite of creamed artichoke hearts in his mouth at that moment, paused his chewing and said shrewdly: "Don't take me for a flat, Hugh! You know very well that Julien wishes us miles from here." He turned his light blue eyes on his host and added with a shrug: "Although I cannot imagine why."

"Hold, both of you," Julien quickly interposed. "I assure you that nothing could be further from the truth. As for Percy's horse, Hugh, why, the nag hasn't a chance of winning! There is no reason why either of you should think of leaving so soon."

Julien would have said more, but he became suddenly

aware that Percy was merely regarding him with a stare of disbelief. As for Hugh, he became suddenly preoccupied with the dissection of a leg of broiled chicken.

"Must be a woman," Percy announced, unwittingly hitting the mark.

Julien felt a dull red flush creep over his face. He gave a wry grin, realizing that Percy was exceedingly acute.

Percy took another bite of the creamed artichokes and pondered the problem. Upon swallowing, he remarked cordially: "Can't imagine where you met a woman in such an outlandish place!" Oblivious of Julien's heightened color and a puzzled look from Hugh, he concluded imperturbably: "Do hope that Riverton has taken the fair Yvette off your hands, old boy. Ah, and the poor Lady Sarah . . ."

"Really, Percy!" Hugh exclaimed, sensing Julien's discomfort. "You go too far. How Julien wishes to conduct himself on his own lands is certainly none of your concern."

Unruffled by this stricture, Percy once more bent his gaze on Julien's face and said a trifle glumly: "Must be serious, Hugh. Never seen him make such a cake of himself over his mistresses. Good Lord, he's been miles away from us for the past three days! Didn't even blink an eyelash when he lost twenty pounds to you in cards last night." Percy knew he had concluded with a fact of irrefutable consequence.

Julien found himself at a loss for words, a condition he was becoming rapidly used to. Lord, had he been so obvious? He quickly picked up his glass of claret and downed it in one gulp. He met Hugh's eyes over the rim of his glass and saw the light of comprehension spread over his face. Only Hugh had met Katharine.

At that moment Hugh seriously doubted the powers of his own intellect. He felt somehow that his ability to comprehend his fellow humans had grossly betrayed him. Good God . . . a woman! Kate Brandon! He could not believe he had been so blind. He consoled himself with the fact that in his long acquaintance with Julien he had never observed him treat any of the endless bevy of charming debutantes with anything but polite indifference. Why, it was not long ago that he had confided to Hugh that he found the chatter of young females quite beyond his limits of endurance. He had always taken his pleasure with older women, who were experienced in the games of flirtation and love, and were, above all, married. Or with his mistresses. Hugh blinked; how could such a change be wrought by a mere girl in the country? All he could actually remember of her person was that she was a pretty, laughing girl with enormous green eyes. But she was wearing breeches . . . and that wretched old hat pulled down over her ears! He gazed up at Julien, a tiny frown furrowing his brow. His friend had always been fastidious in all things, and in particular, in his choice of women.

Percy was quite satisfied with himself, as his devastating pronouncement had reduced the assembled company to silence. Having had the last word, he returned his attention to his dinner. What Julien chose to do with his women was no concern of his. He merely hoped that he had not become ensnared with some ill-bred, conniving wench. But then, he thought, Julien was such a proud, arrogant man; he would never besmirsch his noble lineage.

Julien pushed his plate aside and eyed his friends with wry good humor. He wondered if they thought him mad. He found to his own surprise, however, that it had never occurred to him to deny Percy's comments. If he tried now, he would only appear the more ridiculous. He broke the short silence and remarked in a level voice: "Have I been such poor company, Hugh? Come, Percy, you cannot say that you wish to leave François's cooking."

Percy lost all patience and exclaimed, waving his fork at Julien: "Dammit, Julien! Like Hugh, I have no desire to remain and watch you mooning after some girl. Why," he sputtered, "it's positively unnerving! Maybe it's something in the country air," he concluded with a laugh. "I, for one, certainly do not wish to catch it!"

"Percy—" Hugh began.

"Now, don't you prose at me, Hugh," Percy interrupted. "Why, it was you who suggested leaving." He sat back in his chair and regarded Julien with an owlish stare.

Hugh reddened, and a sharp set-down was on his tongue when Julien threw up his hands, his sense of humor over this odd situation engaged. "Leave him be, Hugh. It is quite the first time he is able to crow, albeit he resembles more a stuffed peacock than a lean scavenger!"

The tension was broken and both Hugh and Percy were grinning at him good-naturedly.

"I wondered when you'd get your wits back, Julien. Damned glad that you haven't quite lost all your senses!" Percy remarked mischievously.

"I strive, Percy, I strive." Julien looked down at his glass and swished the claret from side to side. The deep red reminded him of Kate's luxurious auburn hair. She's bewitched me, he thought, his pulse quickening. He thought of her green eyes and the dancing dimples. Lord, he was completely besotted! Strangely enough, he found that he was not at all distressed by his condition. It struck him forcibly that he wanted Kate—not simply a summer idyll to end with the coming of fall: he wanted her by his side.

He raised his face to his friends and said matter-of-factly: "Perhaps it is better if you return to London. I would find it unnerving to go a-wooing with the two of you smirking behind my back." Ignoring the startled looks, he concluded with quiet determination: "I intend to return to London with my bride."

Percy's eyes grew round with wonder and disbelief. Hugh chewed meditatively on his lower lip before saying slowly: "I suppose it is the Lady Katharine Brandon . . ."

Percy interposed, "Ah, at least I can set my mind at rest . . . no ill-bred country wench for the great Earl of March!"

Annoyed, Julien snapped, "Of course not, Percy. She is a lovely . . . high-spirited young lady!"

Percy ignored Julien's outburst. He regretted momentarily his lack of exertion during their visit; he would have liked to have at least seen her. He turned to Hugh. "You have met her, I gather?"

Hugh felt exceedingly uncomfortable. If he told Percy about his only meeting with this unconventional young lady, about her breeches and her odd manners, it would be all over the clubs upon Julien's return to London. And since Julien seemed bent upon making the young lady his bride, he knew that such a story would make her entry into the ton a not-altogether-pleasant experience.

At last he answered Percy, his voice calm. "Yes, Percy, I have met her. I have yet to see her equal. An altogether unforgettable young lady."

He was aware that Julien was regarding him with an amused grin.

"Hmm," was all that Percy said to this glowing, albeit ambiguous description. He stroked his chin and sighed deeply. Julien being leg-shackled was in itself an appalling thought, for their gay evenings, bachelors all, would come to an end. But perhaps, he thought, the new countess would be fond of entertaining, and that would mean many delicious dinners prepared by François. Percy's blue eyes brightened at this prospect, and in sudden good humor he rose and thrust his glass forward.

"Come, Hugh," he commanded cheerfully, "let us congratulate Julien. A toast to the new Countess of March!"

Hugh was quick to follow Percy's lead and the two men turned to Julien, clicked their glasses together, and drank deeply.

Julien rose slowly. The last week and a half compressed itself into but a moment. A toast to the Countess of March. . . . He silently bid farewell to a life that now seemed inordinately boring, downed his own glass, and in a burst of excitement demanded another toast.

Two vintage bottles of St. Clair claret were consumed before the three men finally separated and departed shakily, each to his own room.

It was quite late the following morning when all three friends finally emerged from their rooms, their eyes blurry and their heads heavy.

Under the efficient command of Mannering, mountains of luggage were assembled in the hall and strapped onto Percy's great carriage.

"An altogether . . . unforgettable week, Julien," Hugh remarked lightly as he shook his friend's hand.

"Lord, Hugh, you are never to the point!" Percy exclaimed. "A deuced unsettling experience, if you ask me."

"Rest assured, Percy, that the next week will be far more unsettling for me," Julien replied, a confident grin belying his words.

Percy leaned out of the carriage window and mocked: "Wish you luck, old boy. If you need help, Hugh and I will be more than willing to serve as your faithful emissaries!" Without waiting for a reply, Percy shouted to the driver and the carriage lurched into motion.

A ghost of a smile flitted over Julien's face as he stood watching the carriage rumble down the graveled drive and disappear into the park. He had no doubt that the most difficult part of entering into the married state would be surviving the jokes of his friends. He retraced his steps and made his way to the library. As he passed by several portraits of past earls of March, he chanced to look up. Their painted eyes seemed to regard him with approval, their faces no longer accusatory. If he had been wearing a hat, he would most certainly have proffered them an elegant bow. As it was, he merely grinned and let his thoughts turn most willingly to Katharine. Katharine St. Clair, Countess of March.

His footstep was light as he entered the library and eased himself comfortably into the large chair beside the fireplace. He pursed his lips and formed a sloped roof with his long slender fingers, tapping them thoughtfully together as he contemplated his strategy.

It was but a short time later that he uncoiled gracefully from his chair, tugged the bell cord, and ordered Astarte to be saddled.

4

"I do wish you did not have to leave so soon, Harry. You know how wretched it is here without you." Kate Brandon spoke dolefully and her shoulders dropped pitiably.

"Now, Kate, it will not be long, only until Christmas," Harry said bluffly. He clumsily patted his sister on the arm to comfort her.

"Aye," Kate said, reverting to her Scottish mother's tongue, "but 'tis still over four months, Harry."

Harry searched his mind for sage words, reassuring words, for he was, after all, her elder brother. He could think of nothing except the warning that he had given her many times before: "I beg of you, Kate, take care that Sir Oliver does not find out about your escapades during the day. You know as well as I what he would do."

It gave Harry a start to see her woebegone expression vanish and a curiously cold and hard look take its place. "Do you take me for a simpleton, Harry? Of course I know what he would do. He would beat me within an inch of my life.

We both know it is quite a habit with him," she added with deadly contempt.

Harry was appalled that she could speak with such hardness. The picture of Kate as a child rose in his mind—her laughter, her openness, Kate tugging on his coattails begging to be included in his games.

"Lord, Kate, why does he hate you so?"

His voice shook with impotent fury. He had argued with his father on several occasions, in an attempt to draw Sir Oliver's anger onto himself. He felt a miserable coward, for he seldom succeeded.

"When Mother was alive, he was not so . . . cruel," he said, to himself more than to Kate.

Kate cut him short, her voice grim. "No, Harry. He became so toward me before mother died. Of that I am certain."

Harry grasped her shoulders and in a sudden protective gesture pulled her against him. She was alarmingly stiff. He thought back to his mother's funeral and felt a stab of pain. He had been at Eton that year and had been home rarely, savoring his freedom and his image of being quite grown-up. It was after the funeral that he had sensed a change in his father.

Kate relaxed against him but did not speak. It had been many years since Harry had held her, and he became aware that he was holding not just his little sister, but a woman. Maybe that is the reason, he thought, Sir Oliver finds it painful to be with Kate, for she so closely resembles our mother.

Kate drew back from the circle of Harry's arms and looked out over the poorly kept lawn. She despised herself for her weakness. If she lost her pride, she would have nothing else.

"It's that damned religion of his," Harry muttered from between clenched teeth. "I wish I could burn all those ridiculous musty books of his!"

To his surprise, Kate turned back to him and gave a mirthless laugh. "Do not curse his religion, Harry, for I in truth find it my salvation. You know, he is scarce aware of my existence, at least during the day. Even Filber dare not disturb him in his theological studies."

Harry's lips tightened in disdain as the stern lecture he had received from Sir Oliver but an hour earlier came back to his mind.

"Damnation, the only thing he can think about is his infernal wages of sin," he muttered.

Kate's eyes brightened for a moment in tender amusement. "What, dear brother, you do not intend to become a Methodist?"

Kate was rewarded, for Harry gave her a twisted grin, the frown fading from his forehead.

"Hold a moment, Marcham," Harry called, seeing his valet emerge from the stable with their horses.

At that moment Kate felt immeasurably older than Harry. She looked at his blond curls brushed and pomaded into what he had stiffly informed her was the latest style. His breeches and waistcoat were of severe, somber color, but she knew that before he arrived at Oxford he would change into the florid yellow patterned waistcoat he had shown her one evening when Sir Oliver had retired.

"My dear, poor Marcham is sadly weighted down. Are you certain that you intend to be gone only four months?" Her voice was playful, and she tugged gently on his sleeve.

Harry replied to Kate's sally with a rather perfunctory smile. Despite his best intentions, he was impatient to be gone, and in truth, he did not know what to say to her, nor what he could do about her future. He knew that Sir Oliver was encouraging the suit of that provinicial oaf Squire Bleddoes. It was altogether ridiculous, for Kate was far too wellborn for such a marriage, and besides, she had told him she would have nothing to do with that "prosy bore." This he had understood, but when she had blithely informed him that remaining her own mistress did not seem at all a bad thing, he was shaken. Kate knew very well that his fondest wish was to join a crack cavalry regiment; she must also realize, he thought despairingly, that it would be impossible for her to accompany him. Lord, what a mull! Perhaps when he returned for the holiday at Christmas, he and Kate would think of something.

Harry drew on his gloves and leaned over to kiss Kate lightly on the cheek. It occurred to him that there might be danger from another quarter.

"Kate," he said earnestly, his blue eyes narrowing, "do not forget the Earl of March. You cannot be sure that he will not tell Father of our escapade. Most probably he's high in the instep and proud as a peacock . . . can't tell what he might do."

Kate looked at him and smiled, a woman's smile. She replied in a calm voice, as if reassuring a child: "I will be careful, Harry. Do not worry yourself about it. I think that . . . his lordship would never stoop to such paltry and petty behavior."

Harry was a bit put out by her calm assumptions about the Earl of March. It was at times like this that Harry wished Kate were more docile, more accepting of her older brother's advice and counsel. He had the nagging doubt, grown stronger in the past several years, that he was no match for her quick tongue, that it was she who had the stronger will.

Harry shook himself free of this not-altogether-pleasing image of himself. After all, it was rather stupid of him to regard his sister—a mere girl—as a possible superior to him. Was he not to be Sir Harry Brandon of Brandon Hall someday? And if Kate had not yet married upon the demise of Sir Oliver, it would be he, Sir Harry, who would arrange her life and give her direction.

Seeing the rather benign smile on her brother's boyish face, Kate thought that she had succeeded in keeping their leave-taking as unemotional as possible. She remarked lightly: "I think the horses grow impatient, my dear. You may rest assured that I shall avoid Sir Oliver assiduously, as well as that alarmingly persistent suitor of mine."

Harry was immeasurably relieved. Kate was acting her usual self again. He quieted his conscience with the thought that before too many more months passed, he would find a solution to her problem.

Kate added in a quizzing voice: "Do read at least one book this time."

"Well, don't you kill anyone with your dueling pistol!" he retorted after a moment of concentrated thinking.

There was a sudden sound behind them, and Kate whirled about. It was only Filber, the Brandon butler, come to wave good-bye to Harry. She breathed a sigh of relief, knowing that Sir Oliver would openly condemn brother and sister spending too much time together. It was strange, she thought fleetingly; it was as if their father thought her a bad influence on Harry.

"You did say good-bye to Father?" she asked nervously, still expecting to see his tall, gaunt frame appear at any minute in the open doorway.

"Yes," he replied shortly. He did not wish to think again of his sire's preachings. But he too looked over his shoulder.

"Good-bye, Master Harry," Filber called, thinking that Harry had turned to receive his words.

"I will see you at Christmas, Filber," Harry returned warmly. Somehow, Filber fitted his picture of the proper father much more than did Sir Oliver.

"Well, old girl, do keep out of trouble," Harry said heartily. Kate did not answer, afraid that her words would betray the light, unconcerned face she presented to her brother.

Harry swung himself on his horse and signaled Marcham to do the same. He kissed his fingers in good-bye to Kate and whipped his horse about.

He turned and waved once again before disappearing from sight. Kate raised her own hand in silent reply.

She had certainly succeeded in cheering him, and she supposed now that she should feel quite noble. After all, it was not his fault that he was a male and therefore free to go and do as he pleased. But it seemed a cruel twist of fate, she thought. She felt rather sorry for herself.

She stood unmoving, striving to control such uncharitable thoughts. A gentle breeze ruffled her hair. Unaccountably, she found that her thoughts turned to the Earl of March and the amicable morning she had spent fishing with him and Sir Hugh Drakemore at St. Clair lake. Her depression eased and in an unconscious gesture her hands tugged at her outmoded gown. His lordship had shown himself to be witty and entertaining; his descripitons of the sights and activities of London stirred her imagination. She had jokingly told Sir Hugh that the earl might as well be telling her of the Taj Mahal, for London, to her, was just as remote.

The corners of her mouth lifted. She remembered his laughter when she spoke whatever was on her mind. He was a delightful companion, willing to cross verbal swords with her. Perhaps she had found a friend. But for how long? The Earl of March never stayed at St. Clair for any extended period of time. As a matter of fact, even now he might have already returned with his friends to London.

She turned slowly and walked back into the hall. Her spirits plummeted. She wondered if she would ever see him again.

Kate was not left long to ponder this question, for that very afternoon, as she sat disconsolately at her piano doing

great injustice to a Mozart sonata, Sir Oliver unceremoniously interrupted her, his voice filled with cold suspicion: "I
am informed, daughter, that the Earl of March is calling."
He pursed his thin lips together and his rather close-set eyes
drew closer together. "He calls ostensibly to visit with me. A
fact that I have difficulty crediting. Would you be so kind as
to tell me where you have made his lordship's acquaintance?
And be quick about it. Men of his rank do not like to be
kept waiting. Tell me the truth, girl, for I do not like to play
the ignorant fool!"

Though Kate trembled inwardly, she was long used to her
father's peremptory attacks, and her expression never
changed. Her mind worked furiously. She could certainly not
tell him the truth, for his retribution would be swift and unpleasant. She calculated rapidly that there was at least a slim
chance to come through this unscathed, and if her attempt
failed, the result would be the same in any case.

She looked at her father, who was openly glaring at her,
and quite undaunted, she replied calmly: "Last week Harry
and I were riding through the village. His lordship, as it happened, was visiting his agent, Mr. Stokeworthy. It would have
been unforgivably rude of us not to introduce ourselves, under the circumstances. His lordship mentioned that he might
call, as he had never made your acquaintance, Father," she
added mendaciously.

As her eyes did not waver and her improvised story sounded plausible to Sir Oliver, he merely grunted and said sharply: "Well, then, girl, you might as well come along with me
and perform the proper introductions. I only hope that the
present earl is not the dissolute arrogant sinner that his
grandfather was. Probably top-lofty like his father," he added
under his breath.

He strode out of the room and Kate rose and followed
him, her mouth suddenly gone quite dry. She did not have
time to ponder the earl's intentions for visiting Brandon Hall.
Had she dared, she would have rushed to her room and
changed from her well-worn yellow muslin gown with its girlish sash tied under her breasts. She ran her tongue nervously
over her lips and in an unconscious gesture tugged at the
gown to make it longer.

At the door of the drawing room her father had the good
manners to allow her to enter the room first.

The earl stood by the fireplace, elegantly dressed in riding clothes, looking quite at his ease.

Kate forced her leaden feet to move forward. She extended her hand and greeted the earl with tolerable calm.

"It is good to see your lordship again."

Julien clasped her slender fingers in his hand. Before he could make a suitable response, Kate continued quickly: "I have been telling my father how Harry and I met you at Mr. Stokeworthy's house. I told him," she hurried on, "that you expressed a wish to pay us a visit. It is delightful that you have come."

Julien gave only an infinitesimal start at her story. She raised large, beseeching eyes to his face, and he saw the fear in them. He gave her hand a slight squeeze before releasing her, and turned to greet Sir Oliver.

He extended his hand and said with exquisite good manners: "A great pleasure, sir, to finally meet you. I count it provident that I met Master Harry and Lady Katharine so conveniently in the village, for I have long wanted to reestablish good relationships with the Brandons."

Kate gazed with something akin to awe at her father, who had received the earl's suave and fluent speech with an almost obsequious deference. His hard eyes softened and he clasped the earl's outstretched hand with the greatest alacrity.

"Indeed, my lord," he uttered in a mellifluous voice. "I am greatly honored that you have deigned to call." He gave a slight cough that reminded Julien forcibly of Mannering, and added in an apologetic voice: "I presume your lordship is aware of the rift between our two families. An unfortunate affair, and if your lordship is willing, best now forgotten."

Julien executed the most elegant of bows and replied smoothly: "I count myself grateful that you wish it to be so, sir."

Kate cast a furtive glance at the earl. She had the strangest feeling that what had just transpired between her father and the earl had not, indeed, could not, have really happened. Why, her father's very attitude was one of a condemned criminal being pardoned by royal command!

Suddenly she felt quite gauche and provincial. She became acutely aware of her old dress and the scuffed sandals that were all too visible beneath her hemline.

Sir Oliver turned to his daughter, who was standing literally openmouthed. Damn the girl, she looks like a gaping idiot! he thought angrily. He ground his teeth but managed to moderate his voice: "Katharine, will you please see that Filber brings in the sherry? His lordship is undoubtedly needful of refreshment."

Kate nodded and hurried to the door. In all likelihood, she thought, Filber had already heard his instructions through the closed door and was probably now fetching the sherry and glasses.

"Yes, Lady Kate, right away," Filber said, before Kate had time to speak.

"Very acute of you, Filber," she remarked wryly as the butler hurried to the dining room.

Kate walked quickly to a mirror and regarded her messed hair with vexation. She was trying to smooth down errant curls when it occurred to her to wonder if the earl were here merely to mock her and her father. She felt a wave of humiliation at her father's behavior and at the thought that the earl had seemed to find nothing amiss with such deferential treatment. She paced the floor waiting for Filber to bring the sherry.

Sir Oliver rubbed his hands together and asked the earl to be seated. Kate was only partially right in her assessment of his attitude. Certainly he was impressed at his lordship's courteous condescension to visit Brandon Hall, but more than that, he was aware that the earl was as yet unwed. It did not take him long to see the earl as a possible answer the number of bills that lay piled on his desk.

Julien would not have been at all surprised had he known what Sir Oliver was thinking. In fact, he found himself watchful of Kate's father, hoping that he had made a favorable impression and that the natural desire of a parent to see his progeny well placed in the world, and, he thought cynically, to line his own pockets, would work to his advantage. He had not been deceived by Sir Oliver's deferential treatment of the Earl of March. Having read the fear in Kate's eyes, he realized that to his family Sir Oliver was an altogether different man.

As it happened, neither of the men's thoughts were at all perceptible on their faces or in their painfully polite and mundane conversation. Bonaparte was always a safe topic and Julien in his most respectful manner elicited Sir Oliver's opinion.

"It has now been nearly three months that Napoleon has

been on Elba," he began. His choice of topics seemed at first an excellent one, for Sir Oliver immediately sat forward in his chair, his eyes blazing.

"Would, for the safety of all men's souls, that the Allies had not allowed the monster to live! For years I trembled for fear that an invasion of those degenerate French Catholics would throw our land back into the hands of the papists!"

Julien blinked, but Sir Oliver was too moved to notice. He exploded in sudden religious furor: "I would have sought them out and destroyed them and all their loathsome, filthy idols!"

"Quite right," Julien said calmly. "A Catholic England would be intolerable." He wondered if Sir Oliver were not a bit mad.

Sir Oliver gave a start. Perhaps he had been a bit too dogmatic in stating his view. He said in a more moderate voice: "We must pray that the Allies are able to keep Bonaparte on Elba."

"As I understand," Julien added gravely, "the French people have welcomed back the Bourbons with open arms. Louis seems quite firmly planted on the throne."

Julien was greatly relieved to see Kate return, followed by the butler bearing a silver tray. He rose quickly until Kate seated herself on a small sofa facing him.

While Filber served the sherry, Julien was freed for a few moments to regard his future wife. He was not at all disappointed by Kate's appearance. He had wondered how she would look not dressed in her boy's clothes, and although the gown she wore was rather outmoded, he was delighted at her slender beauty. The rich auburn hair was long down her back and secured with a simple ribbon. He wondered how she would react to her new station; as his countess, she would have anything that she wished.

He frowned as he saw her hands twisting nervously at the folds of her gown. She would not meet his eyes, and alternately gazed from her lap to her father. There was no vestige of his spirited, self-assured Kate. He felt hesitant to address even the most innocuous of comments to her for fear that her answers would draw down the wrath of her father after he left. He contented himself with simply enjoying her presence until he would have the opportunity to speak with her alone.

"It is a pity, my lord," Sir Oliver said jovially, "you have just missed my son, Harry. He left but this morning to return to Oxford."

Aware of the obvious pride in Sir Oliver's voice, Julien was quick to respond. "Yes, a fine young man. He wishes perhaps to be a scholar?" Julien asked politely.

Kate choked on her sherry and Sir Oliver cast her a blighting look. He remarked with some reluctance: "No, it would be, of course, my wish, but Harry is intent on being in a cavalry regiment. You know boys, my lord, they wish for adventure."

"I see," Julien said pleasantly. He took a sip of sherry, which was not nearly as good as the St. Clair sherry. It occurred to him again that perhaps Sir Oliver's finances were in need of a healthy settlement.

Not at all a stupid man, Sir Oliver had seen the earl's eyes on Kate as Filber served the sherry. Had his lordship already fixed his interest in her? The thought seemed ludicrous to Sir Oliver, but nevertheless he decided to test his observation.

He cleared his throat and addressed the earl: "Perhaps your lordship would like to see the Brandon gardens. They are not, of course, at their full beauty, but still are not to be despised." He turned and bent his gaze full upon his daughter. "Kate, conduct his lordship to the gardens."

Kate looked at her father with blank surprise. What ever can he be thinking of? she asked herself.

Julien rose, placed his glass on a table, and said with gentle kindness: "I would enjoy seeing the gardens, Lady Katharine, if you would not mind."

Kate rose somewhat unsteadily, nearly bumping over the small table beside her. She could almost hear her father cursing her for her clumsiness. She raised a pale face to the earl and replied in a small voice: "I would be delighted, my lord. Please come with me."

Sir Oliver also rose and extended his hand to the earl. "If your lordship would deign to take dinner with us . . . say, tomorrow evening, I would count it a great honor."

A slight smile hovered over Julien's lips as he shook Sir Oliver's hand and replied: "The honor is mine, sir."

"Then I bid you good afternoon, my lord." With those words Sir Oliver darted a sideways glance at Kate and removed himself from the drawing room, quite pleased with himself.

Kate frowned after her father, gave her head a tiny, perplexed shake, and walked to the side door beside the windows. As she opened the door, she said over her shoulder: "The gardens are wretched. I cannot imagine why my father would wish you to see them."

Julien smiled at her naiveté and forbore to comment. It had been quite some time since he had been treated to such blatant tactics as Sir Oliver's.

Kate said nothing more as they walked through overgrown ill-kept bushes and brambles. She finally drew to a halt and seated herself on a stone bench that stood in the middle of what must have been at one time a lovely rose bower.

Kate was certainly no gardener, Julien thought with a wry grin. He sat down beside her and gazed at her lovely profile. He very much liked the straight, proud nose and her firm chin. Tendrils of soft hair blew gently against her cheek, and he felt a fleeting urge to smooth them away.

Kate turned to him suddenly and said in a wondering voice: "However did you manage to turn him so sweet? I have never seen anything like it in all my life!"

Julien arched an elegant brow and replied in his haughtiest manner: "My dear Lady Katharine, would you accord any less treatment to the great Earl of March?"

She pondered his words for a moment before giving a crow of laughter, the dimples he so dearly loved making her whole face alight with amusement.

"But you know," she said seriously, "he was positively . . . toad-eating you. I found it unnerving!" She continued with undisguised wonder in her voice: "And dinner tomorrow evening! Cook will be in such a flutter of nerves. I shall probably have to spend the greater part of my day tomorrow polishing silver so our noble neighbor will not be disgusted!"

"I trust you will do a good job, for I will have you know that I am very high in the instep and will not lower myself to eat if the silver does not sparkle."

"You are quite horrid," Kate retorted in high good humor.

Quite at her ease now, she asked without preamble: "Have your guests left?"

"Yes, Sir Hugh and Sir Percy departed just after lunch to return to London."

"Why did you not go with them?" she asked politely, without guile.

Julien was jolted for a moment, for he had not expected her to be so completely ignorant of the intent of his visit.

He answered smoothly: "I do have quite an estate here and there are matters which require my attention."

"Oh," she said, pondering his answer.

He added in a teasing voice: "It is also possible that I wish to further my acquaintance with the Lady Katharine."

"I cannot imagine why," she said frankly. "The Lady Katharine is but a graceless provincial, quite unworthy of the great Earl of March's attention."

"Do not ever say that, Katharine," he said harshly.

Kate could not imagine why he was so incensed by the simple truth. With disarming candor she said: "One should never be blind to what one really is. I do not see why it should anger you. After all, it is I who am the subject of my own stricture, not you."

Julien found that he was losing rather than gaining headway. Kate relieved him of the burden of finding suitable words to express his feelings by smoothly changing the topic.

"Harry will be sorry to have missed you. He thought you a great gun, you know. Well," she temporized, never one to speak half-truths, "he did think you might be arrogant and conceited, but of course, he did not have the benefit of fishing with you!" She chuckled. "Harry was afraid that you would expose me and thus kindle Father's wrath. And I must say," she reflected, "I found myself quite on tenterhooks when Father asked me where I had met you. Thank you, my lord, for your kindness."

She smiled and reached out a slender hand and laid it lightly on his arm.

Julien took her hand in his and pressed her fingers. He looked tenderly into her eyes but saw only openness and, yes, trust. She did not yet understand, nor did it appear to him that she felt anything for him but friendship. It rankled a bit. For all her independent ways, she was innocent of the ways of the world. He curbed his impatience; he decided that he must give her time.

He rose and helped Kate to stand. "I must be going now. I have kept you overlong as it is."

She looked disappointed, like a child who had lost a coveted treat.

"Will you ride with me tomorrow morning, Kate?" His voice was warm, but not overly so.

She frowned. Seeing that he waited for an answer, she hurriedly said: "Oh, yes, I would very much like that. It is only that I must have my father's permission."

"Do not fear on that score. Sir Oliver will not mind."

She smiled saucily at him. "How true. I had forgot how you have quite won him over."

As the remnants of the frown still furrowed her forehead, Jullien asked: "What else troubles you, Kate?"

The frown vanished and she turned laughing eyes to his face. "It will be such a bore! Oh, it has nothing to do with you, my lord," she cried playfully, "it is just that I will have to wear a riding habit and not my breeches!"

"I am most honored that you make that sacrifice, Lady Katharine."

"But my riding habit is much outdated and quite tight. I do but pray that I will not pop my buttons!"

Julien laughed aloud and in an unthinking swift movement brought his hand up and cupped her chin. She made no resistance whatsoever and merely looked up at him, her eyes shining with innocent humor.

"You are an outrageous chit, Lady Katharine!" He drew her arm stiffly through his, and looking straight ahead, walked back to the hall.

Kate awoke slowly from a dreamless sleep. She stretched luxuriously under a mound of covers, savoring the warmth of the August sun upon her face. Her body felt light and as she turned to look at the clock on the table beside her bed, as she had each morning for the past week, her lips curved into a smile of anticipation. She would be riding with the earl in but two hours.

She slipped quickly out of bed and winced slightly as her bare feet touched the cold wooden floor. Hurriedly she stripped off her nightgown and bathed in the basin of cold water, scrubbing and splashing the water over her until her skin tingled. She shivered and looked at the empty grate with displeasure. It was a chilly summer and she wished that her father would break his rule, just once. As far back as she could remember, he had allowed no fires in the bedrooms until after the first snow.

She was tugging on her stockings when a light knock sounded, and a moment later, Lilly peered in. She bobbed a slight curtsy and said with an arch look: "Squire Bleddoes is downstairs and wishes to see you."

"Good Lord," Kate cried, annoyed. "Whatever can Robert want at this hour?"

"He is probably here for the usual reasons, my lady," Lilly said smugly.

"Well, you needn't look like the cat that swallowed the canary! I suppose I must see the man. Do help me into my riding clothes, Lilly. The earl will arrive in little more than an hour."

Lilly's face took on a rapturous look at the mention of the earl.

"Oh, Lady Kate, whatever will you do if the two men meet?"

"Don't be a goose, Lilly," Kate said sharply, wondering how she could be so nonsensical.

Kate sat herself at her dressing table and began to vigorously brush her hair. In the mirror she saw that Lilly was still in blissful contemplation over this imaginary scene. She halted her brushing and said matter-of-factly: "Lilly, the earl honors us with his friendship. That is all. As for Robert Bleddoes . . . well, you know as well as I do that the poor man expects all females to swoon at his feet. Why he must needs continually pester me—and with no encouragement—is more than I can fathom!"

Having clarified the situation to her own satisfaction, Kate turned back to her mirror and continued brushing the tangles from her hair.

Lilly shot her mistress an incredulous look. If only Lady Kate knew the servants' gossip! It was plain as a pikestaff that the earl was smitten with Lady Katharine Brandon. Why, he had called at Brandon Hall no fewer than four times during the past week! Everyone knew it, save, it seemed to Lilly, her mistress. As for Squire Bleddoes, that pompous windbag, Lilly would be quite content to see him routed. Quite a nuisance he had become, presenting himself at the hall with only the flimsiest of pretexts.

Kate harbored very close to the same opinion of Robert Bleddoes as did Lilly. She had met him by accident nearly six months ago when she had ridden a far greater distance than she had intended. She thought him at first to be a rather overly serious young man, but quite unexceptionable. She soon realized that his stolid, prosaic opinions, uttered invariably with monotonous precision, masked a feeling of self-importance that made her grit her teeth. After his first visit to Brandon Hall, Kate was convinced that he was a total bore.

She said as much to her father and stared at him with disbelief when he rounded on her in fury. "You discourage him, my girl, and you will feel my hand on your back!" He snarled with blatant derision that made Kate flinch. "You think yourself so puffed up, my *lady*. Let me tell you, if Bleddoes offers for you, it will be much more than you deserve! That any man would want you is more than I can imagine."

Mindful of Sir Oliver's warning, Kate did not openly discourage Robert. She forced herself to learn tolerance and tried to treat him as kindly as she treated Flip, the pug.

She had played a dangerous game the past three months, holding Robert off as best she could with soft, vague words, and skirting the issue of marriage whenever Sir Oliver chanced to broach it.

Sir Oliver, happily not aware that Robert had declared himself on several occasions, blamed Kate for her failure to bring the squire up to scratch. He had commented to her sourly one evening at dinner: "I might have known that you could not attract a man. You are a witless, unnatural girl!"

Kate did not think of herself as being witless or unnatural, but she wisely forbore to reply. She kept her head down and concentrated her attention on forking a lone pea that lay in the center of her plate.

It occurred to her now, as she handed Lilly a ribbon with which to secure her hair, that Sir Oliver had not mentioned Robert Bleddoes for the past week. She tapped her fingers on the tabletop. No, it was true, there had been no mention of the squire since the Earl of March had come to call. She went pale at this realization. Dear God, Sir Oliver could not possibly think the earl was interested in her!

Kate rose somewhat unsteadily and raised her arms for Lilly to slip the riding skirt over her head.

"Draw a deep breath, Lady Kate, the buttons won't meet elsewise," Lilly instructed.

Kate sucked in her breath and felt the buttons dig into her skin through the thin material of her chemise.

Her jacket followed, but as it did not meet over her breasts, she was forced to leave it open, revealing a well-worn white blouse.

"I am not exactly the height of fashion, am I, Lilly?" Kate remarked as she stepped back and regarded herself ruefully in the mirror. She made a moue at herself. "Well, it will just have to do!"

Lilly felt a stab of indignation. It was disgraceful how the lovely Lady Kate was kept by her father.

"You look just fine, Lady Kate," Lilly said stoutly, twitching an errant pleat into place.

"You are quite kind to say so, Lilly. But so untruthful!" Kate teased. She gave Lilly an affectionate hug, picked up her riding gloves of York tan, and made her way with a light step downstairs.

She took a deep breath, planted a smile on her face, and squared her shoulders.

Robert Bleddoes rose with alacrity and hurried over to greet her. He was dressed in his usual brown broadcloth, eminently suitable for country wear, as he had once informed her. Harry, who now affected the "windblown" fashion made stylish by Lord Byron, had sniffed disdainfully at Robert's close-cropped brown hair, declaring him to be the complete flat.

"Good morning, Robert," Kate said calmly, extending her hand. "To what do we owe this pleasure?"

Robert bowed ponderously and clasped Kate's proffered hand in his. He held it a trifle overlong and she pulled her hand firmly away.

"Good day to you, Lady Katharine. May I say that you are in great looks today."

"I would prefer that you did not, Robert, but since you have already, I suppose that it would be inhospitable of me to cavil," she stated flatly. She watched him closely as he blinked in an effort to understand her words.

He brightened. "Ah, Lady Katharine, you have such a ready wit! I see that you are funning me."

Kate curbed her exasperation. "Do take a seat, Robert. What news of Bonaparte do you have for me today?" With Napoleon's defeat and his subsequent departure to Elba, Robert in the past six months had never arrived at Brandon Hall without some bit of news to give credence to his visits.

He cleared his throat and beamed at her. "I had thought that you and Sir Oliver, of course, would find it of great interest that the Allies will convene this fall in Vienna to determine the fate of France."

Kate did not tell Robert that the earl had already discussed this interesting topic with her and that as a result, she found his news to be not entirely accurate. "It is a critical step in restoring a balance of power," the earl had told her. "Lord Castlereagh, our ambassador, has a mightily difficult task facing him, particularly after the bad will resulting from the tzar's visit to England in June."

Kate responded to Robert's statement with only a ghost of humor in her voice: "How very kind you are to ride such a great distance to so enlighten me. Why, I wish I could pack my bags this instant and accompany our ambassador to Vienna!"

Robert pondered her words with great seriousness and finally announced: "Ah, you are quizzing me again, Lady Katharine. You would, of course, have no desire to travel out of England. Foreign travel is not at all the thing for well-bred English ladies!"

Kate returned a forced smile and allowed the veil of boredom to close over her. She listened politely as Robert regaled her with the happenings of the past week. His mother was in fine health, barring, of course, her anxious concern for the chill he had contracted.

Kate, knowing her duty, asked: "Nothing serious, I hope, Robert. You seem to be quite well now."

Robert was delighted with her expression of concern. Though he thought the Lady Katharine to be a bit too vivacious upon occasion, he had always dismissed it as girlish spirits. Now, for instance, the true womanliness of her nature would be apparent to anyone.

He expanded most willingly upon the topic of his health, anxious to allay her concern about his illness.

Kate was near to screaming with vexation when Robert's commentary was halted by the entrance of Filber, announcing the Earl of March.

Kate rose quickly from her chair, a radiant smile on her face. Rescue was at hand. She walked swiftly to the earl and stretched out her gloved hand.

Julien lifted her hand to his lips and murmured softly so that only she could hear his words: "My poor Kate. My timing is exquisite, is it not?"

She bit her lips to keep from laughing aloud and raised her eyes to him in silent warning.

"Humph!" Robert had risen and stood alarmingly red-faced, his eyes shooting daggers at the unwelcome intruder.

"Oh, do excuse me, Robert," Kate cried, pulling her hand away from the earl's. Somehow she had not noticed that the earl had held her hand overlong, much less kissed her fingers lightly.

"Mr. Robert Bleddoes . . . this is the Earl of March." She added smoothly, "The squire has been good enough to bring us news of Napoleon this morning."

A strange transformation came over Robert. He appeared to visibly shrink in size and he was able to murmur only a strangled greeting to the earl.

Julien seemed not to notice the stumbling phrases that were proffered and performed his "how d'ye dos" with his customary grace. He found himself being scrutinized from his exquisitely tied cravat to his polished Hessians. He bore up under this well, quelling the set-down that rose automatically to his lips for such gauche behavior. He thought wryly that much could be forgiven a man who was so obviously smitten.

Julien was glad that he remained silent, for a chance glance at Kate's face showed her to be in an agony of apprehension.

Robert managed to recover a modicum of self-assurance and observed in a tight voice: "I did not know that your lordship was acquainted with Lady Katharine." He realized that he did not show to advantage next to the earl, that somehow his serviceable brown suit seemed awkwardly out of place. His lordship wore a superfine light baize coat that fit so well that it seemed a part of him. Robert cast a surreptitious glance at Kate to see if he could read her feelings about her noble guest. What he saw sent red flashes of danger shooting through his mind. He reluctantly pulled his eyes away when he became aware that the earl was answering his inquiry.

"Yes, the Lady Katharine and her brother were riding in the village. We met there."

Kate seemed to have lost her tongue and Robert was tugging unconsciously at his cravat. Julien felt laughter bubble up but sternly held his amusement in check. He shifted his attention back to the squire and inquired blandly: "What news have you of Napoleon?"

Robert drew himself up at this opportunity and began in ponderous tones: "I was telling Lady Katharine that

Bonaparte is safely secured on Elba and that the Allies will convene in Vienna this fall to determine his fate."

"How very interesting."

Thinking that he had impressed the earl, Robert proceeded to favor the company with his opinions on Napoleon, Tallyrand, and the restoration of the Bourbons. After all, his mother had always assured him that his political knowledge was unrivaled; it never occurred to him to doubt her assessment.

"Why, Robert, you constantly amaze me," Kate cried, throwing herself into the breach. She was well aware that the earl's forbearance was stretched to the breaking point. "You never lose yourself in a tangle of words! How you contrive to remember so much is astounding!"

Robert's chest expanded under this ambiguous praise and he seemed quite content to take Kate's words at their face value.

Kate eyed Robert for a moment and said, not unkindly: "I regret, Robert, that his lordship and I must leave now. I have promised to . . . inspect a new hunter and must indeed keep my word! I know you will understand, for you are so . . . sensible!" With those words Kate firmly shook the bewildered squire's hand, turned quickly, and rang the bell cord. Filber entered but a moment later. She hoped he had been vastly entertained at the keyhole.

"Filber, do show Squire Bleddoes out. He must be taking his leave now." She spoke firmly, flashing a brilliant smile at Robert. She propelled him to the door, her hand on his arm.

Robert found himself in a quandary. He would not have minded leaving were it not that Lady Katharine would be left alone with the earl. Though he knew his own worth, he had heard that females were highly impressed by a man's rank and fortune. The earl was undoubtedly a dangerous marauder. But for the moment there seemed to be nothing he could do about it. As he reached the open doorway, he turned and said with as much calm as he could muster: "A pleasure, my lord." He executed a quick bow and followed Filber from the room.

Kate waited a moment until she heard the front door close. She closed the door to the drawing room and leaned against it, heaving an undisguised sigh of relief.

Julien said meditatively: "I do hope that he will not call me out. I have no one available to act as my second."

"Perhaps Filber . . ." Kate giggled.

Julien continued in the same meditative tone: "I suppose that now I must purchase a new hunter and make you promise to inspect him."

A slight blush rose over her cheeks and she said defensively: "What would you have me do? Tell him he is a prosy bore and demand that he leave?"

"Something of the kind, I imagine," Julien retorted. "You are, after all, Kate, quite gifted with words and never one to draw in the clutch!"

"It is something I cannot do," she said slowly.

"Why?"

"My father would not like it," she said quietly.

Good Lord, he thought, had Sir Oliver envisioned that country bumpkin as a suitable groom for his daughter? The thought was appalling.

He stepped forward and gently placed his hands on her shoulders. "Kate, forgive me. I should not have spoken so. I would not for the world cause you discomfort."

Kate raised her eyes to his face and saw a good deal of kindness and concern written there.

She broke the power of the moment by giving her head a tiny shake and said ruefully: "You might well wonder why Robert is allowed to run free in Brandon Hall. But now he is gone and I do not wish to think any more about him. That is, my lord, if you do not mind," she added with great humility.

"Little liar," he said. "As if you would care!" With some effort he forced himself to remove his hands from her slender shoulders.

He noticed the shabby riding habit, the same one she had worn on the several occasions they had gone riding together. Damn Sir Oliver!

Kate caught the brief look of anger in Julien's gray eyes. Perplexed, she asked: "What troubles you, O most noble neighbor? It cannot be something I have said, for I swear that I have been most guarded in my speech."

"I cannot seem to think of a place in the neighborhood that would have a hunter for sale," he replied.

"I can see that from now on I must be more careful in my choice of fibs," she said with a gurgle of laughter.

"Particularly when it involves my pocketbook!"

A tiny frown appeared immediately, and Kate felt instantly contrite. "I do beg your pardon! Are you short of funds?"

Her ingenuous question, so ridiculous to anyone with even the slightest knowledge of the Earl of March, left him speechless for a moment.

Kate misread his silence and said kindly: "I can truly commiserate with you, for we are forever short in the pocket."

"Kate!" he exploded. "How dare you so impinge my consequence!"

Words of apology died in her mouth when she saw the laughter in his eyes. "I might have known that you are disgustingly wealthy!" she cried indignantly. "As if you would care about buying a new hunter!"

"Before I am forced to give you a full reckoning of my holdings, curious Kate, let us go for a gallop."

She shot him a saucy look, the impish dimples dancing on her cheeks.

As was her custom, Kate patted Astarte's silky nose and whispered endearments that were quite unintelligible to Julien, but not, apparently, to his horse. Astarte nodded her great head in seeming agreement with the compliments and gave a snort of impatience.

"She is such a beautiful creature." Kate sighed, turning to mount her own mare, a docile swaybacked bay that was known to all at Brandon Hall as the "ladies' hack."

Julien cupped his hand and tossed her into the saddle. He looked forward with great anticipation to the day he could provide a suitable mount for Kate, His own Astarte, he thought, would suit her to perfection. He pictured her fleetingly in a rust-colored velvet habit and a riding hat with gauzy veils to float behind her in the wind.

"Come, my lord," she chided him from his inattention. "Astarte grows quite impatient."

"What, a shrew already, Kate?" He spoke without thought and instantly regretted his words. In an effort to distract her attention, he turned to his horse and vaulted into the saddle.

"How dare you call me a shrew," she exclaimed, turning quite pink.

He appeared to consider the matter with great seriousness as he turned Astarte about. "My apologies, Lady Katharine, I fear that I have read my Shakespeare quite recently and was unjustly influenced."

Kate puzzled over this for a minute, mentally dusting off his innumerable plays. Her eyes widened and she declared, very much incensed: "It is very ungallant of you to compare

me to Shakespeare's Kate! Furthermore, I did not like at all
the way she ended up. Can you really imagine her falling at
her husband's feet and vowing that she lives only for him?"

"Being irreparably a male, Kate, I must confess that I do
not find the idea entirely repugnant!" he declared. To
forestall further comments, he flicked her mare's rump with
his riding crop, and both horses broke into a comfortable
canter.

As they turned their horses into the country lane just beyond the park to Brandon Hall, Julien shot Kate a sideways
glance. Much to his relief, her attention was drawn to the
brilliant riot of leaves. She seemed not to have noticed that
his comment to her had given away his amorous intentions,
for which he was profoundly grateful.

He was painfully aware that it was too soon for him to declare himself. He was quite certain when he entered the
drawing room that morning that her eyes lit up at the sight of
him, but he could not be sure that her obvious joy denoted a
more serious sign of affection. Just the day before, while they
sat fishing on the soft grass beside St. Clair lake, she had confided to him in her open, unaffected way: "It is so very nice
to have a friend. You know . . . someone you can feel perfectly at ease with and say whatever comes to your mind."
She had continued happily: "You are the only person that I
can laugh with, save, of course, for Harry."

He had looked at her searchingly for a moment, hoping to
see something more in her words. A friend . . . He was momentarily taken aback by her innocent declaration, but upon
brief reflection he found much to his own surprise that she
had spoken the truth. Indeed, she was also his friend, an experience with a woman that he had never known until now,
with Kate.

"It is a . . . new experience for me, Kate," he replied seriously, carefully choosing his words. "You see, I have never
before met a woman with whom I did not have to . . ." He
paused, biting his tongue, for he had been on the point of
saying "offer gallant compliments in exchange for her favors."

Kate had no idea why he had faltered and she waited patiently for him to finish. Somehow, she wanted very much for
him to agree wholeheartedly with her.

Julien looked at her and his mouth curved into a twisted
grin. She was gazing at him expectantly, like a child waiting

for a long-treasured treat. He said simply: "I have never met a woman who is so excellent a companion. You are a treasure, Kate," he added softly.

Her eyes sparkled happily. She took his words at their face worth and was quite pleased at his response. It did not occur to her that no other woman in the earl's acquaintance would be overly pleased to be called an "excellent companion."

They rode for a time side by side in comfortable silence, each thinking private thoughts. Julien chanced to look up and gazed around him, unsure of where they were.

"Let us try down this path, Kate," he called, giving Astarte a gentle tug on her reins.

Kate nodded her agreement, and their horses continued in an easy canter for some time until they emerged into a small meadow, bordered on one side by a wooded copse. The full, lush green foliage gave Julien the inclination to spend some time exploring.

He dismounted and called to her: "Come, Kate. This is a lovely spot. Let us commune with nature for a while."

It was several moments before he realized that she had not moved to dismount from her horse.

"Kate . . . ?" He stopped abruptly at the sight of her face. She sat rigid in the saddle, her face a deathly pallor. Her eyes were riveted toward the small copse.

He strode quickly to her. "What the devil is the matter?" he demanded sharply.

Her lips moved but there was no sound. As if with great effort she tore her gaze from the copse. "I . . . I do not like this place." Her voice was so low that he could barely make out her words. She was trembling visibly and she looked at once frightened and bewildered.

"I do not like this place," she repeated haltingly, averting her gaze.

Before he could respond to her, she turned her horse and dug in her heels fiercely. Her hack gave a snort of surprise and plunged into an erratic gallop. She did not look back.

Julien swung himself into the saddle in one swift motion and urged Astarte forward. Good God, what had upset her so? Had she seen something that he had not? He felt at once perplexed and fearful for her. In but a few moments he drew alongside her panting horse. She seemed not to see him, her eyes fixed on the road ahead.

His first thought was to grab her reins and forcibly pull

her to a halt. But she appeared to have her horse well in control, and he contented himself with keeping pace with her.

She swung off to the left to another path that Julien had not noticed on their ride. Without hesitation she soon veered from the path and skirted a large meadow. Several minutes later Julien saw that they were quite near to Brandon Hall. He would never have thought that they could return so speedily.

The instant her horse's hooves touched the gravel of the drive, she pulled to a halt and blinked in rapid succession as if awakening from a dream.

He reined in beside her and demanded more sharply than he intended: "Kate, what the devil is the matter? What did you see back there?"

She turned a pathetically white face to him. It was a moment longer before she answered him. "I do not know. It is simply a . . . place that makes me very uncomfortable." Her voice was surprisingly calm, almost devoid of emotion.

"Don't give me that flummery, Kate! If that is your notion of discomfort, it is certainly not mine!"

She flinched at his harshness. He felt contrite and softened his words. "Forgive me, I did not mean to shout at you. But I would like to know what upset you so back there." He gestured in the direction they had ridden.

She managed a stiff smile and replied in a too-hearty voice: "I have behaved quite foolishly! I assure you, sir, that it is nothing. And if you please," she added, her voice now almost pleading with him, "I would wish to forget it."

He looked searchingly at her, trying to probe her mind. She returned his gaze almost defiantly.

"Very well, Kate. If that is what you wish . . ." His voice trailed off.

She fanned her hands in front of her in a helpless gesture. She realized that he wanted her to confide in him, but how could she explain something that she could not even now understand herself? She had the lingering certainty that the place was evil. Just exactly what the evil entailed, she did not know, for it seemed closed behind an impenetrable wall. Her eyes pleaded with him silently not to question her further.

Julien curbed his frustration at her silence and lifted his arms to help her down from her horse. It was a gesture he normally proffered, but one that Kate usually ignored, alighting unassisted, as would a man. This time she responded and touched her hands lightly on his shoulders as he circled her slender waist. He swung her down but did not immediately release her. To his infinite joy, she did not draw away but gazed up at him, an unfathomable expression on her pale face. Without thought and with great tenderness, he bent down and gently touched his lips to hers. He knew that he was not mistaken in her response: her soft lips parted ever so slightly and he felt her hands press against his shoulders.

But the brief moment was over as quickly as it had begun. She tore herself free of his arms and jumped back, her breath coming in short, jerky gasps. She raised her hands to her lips in a protective, bewildered gesture, and her eyes seemed to grow larger and darker as she stared at him.

He took a quick half-step forward, his hand outstretched to her. "Kate . . ." He murmured her name tenderly, his voice husky with passion.

She backed away, shaking her head. "No . . . I don't . . . I cannot . . ." She spoke as though the words were wrenched out of her. She turned on her heel, grasped her riding skirt, and fled from him without a backward glance.

This time he did not attempt to follow her. He stood motionless, watching her retreating figure, feeling not at all disconcerted by her abrupt, confused flight. On the contrary, it pleased him that he was obviously the first man who had touched her. He touched his fingertips to his own lips and fancied that he could still feel the soft, trembling touch of her mouth. A confident smile flitted over his face. She was an innocent girl, a virgin, and her maidenly display of confusion delighted him. Could he not now be certain that she cherished for him the most tender of affections?

Julien turned to see her horse lazily chewing some errant blades of grass at the side of the drive. "Well, I hope you know your way to the stables, you slope-shouldered old hack." With a lighthearted laugh he flicked the animal's rump with his riding crop and aimed the horse in the direction of the hall.

Astarte nuzzled his shoulder with her nose as if she were jealous of his attention. He patted her nose and swung up into the saddle.

"An excellent morning's work, Astarte. You may offer me your congratulations!"

Obligingly, she neighed, and at the light tug on her reins, broke into a canter.

He had not ridden far when Kate's strange behavior at the copse came into his mind. She had been afraid of something, yet strangely confused. But his buoyant spirits would not let him long dwell upon the unusual incident; in all truth, the experience paled beside the promising response of her soft lips. As her husband, he would, of course, have her trust and her confidence.

He willingly let his mind race ahead: this very afternoon he would draw up an exceedingly handsome marriage settlement, a settlement that Sir Oliver could not refuse.

5

Filber tapped softly on the door and entered the small, rather airless bookroom where Sir Oliver spent the greater part of his day. His master sat hunched over a large tome, oblivious of his presence.

Filber cleared his throat. "My lord," he began.

"Yes, yes, what is it, Filber? You know I do not like to be disturbed!"

Sir Oliver wheeled around in his chair and glared at his butler, but to his surprise, Filber did not flinch or embark on a round of apologies. Sir Oliver's bushy brows snapped together as he noted the rather smug, complacent look on Filber's face.

Filber stood his ground, even under the frowning scrutiny of his master, and replied confidently: "His lordship, the Earl of March, is here to see you, my lord."

This information carried a wealth of meaning, and Sir Oliver eyed Filber a moment before replying. Filber noted with satisfaction the myriad of emotions that crossed his master's face, particularly the speculative glitter that finally narrowed Sir Oliver's eyes. He knew that he had not been mistaken about the importance of his announcement. The Lady Katharine had obviously succeeded in capturing the regard of the wealthy and powerful Earl of March. Undoubtedly Sir Oliver was at that moment busily calculating some vast sum of money that he would try to extract from his future son-in-law. Filber could not help but feel pleased with himself, for it had been he who had announced to Cook and Lilly, not long after the earl's first visit to Brandon Hall, that the earl was taken with Lady Kate. Not altogether surprised by this revelation, Cook and Lilly had given free rein to their condemnation of Sir Oliver—whom they thought a vicious despicable man despite his puritan ways—and heartily toasted Lady Kate's good fortune from Cook's bottle of cowslip wine.

Filber shifted from one foot to the other as he watched Sir Oliver expectantly.

Sir Oliver's mind reeled at the implied nature of the earl's visit to him. He had been very much aware of the earl's constant attention to Kate during the past week, and simple avarice had led him to nurture some fantastic notions that the earl might offer for her. But the earl was here, now, and wanted to see him! He cursed himself, remembering how he had forced Kate to receive the attentions of Robert Bleddoes. But how could he have imagined that the miserable little creature would do better for herself? Good God! She would be a countess. The Countess of March! It was fortunate that his need for money was greater at the moment than his abhorrence of his daughter, for the mere thought of her queening and pluming herself about him was nearly enough to dampen his enthusiasm.

He became suddenly aware that Filber was covertly observing him and quickly decided on what he considered to be a suitable settlement from the earl. He rose from his chair and said: "Filber, tell his lordship that I will be with him directly. And don't tarry, man!"

Filber obligingly scurried from the room, and Sir Oliver stepped to a small mirror on the mantelpiece and tugged his cravat into more acceptable shape. His face was pale with suppressed excitement and he shook his head in sheer wonderment as he left the bookroom to greet his future son-in-law.

When Julien was informed by Filber that Sir Oliver would join him directly, he inquired: "Is Lady Katharine about, Filber?"

Filber noticed the softening of his lordship's voice at the mention of Lady Katharine's name, and he allowed a slight conspiratorial smile. "No, my lord." He leaned closer to the earl and added: "I believe, though, that the Lady Katharine is walking in the grounds. If your lordship wishes to see her, it is possible that she is by the small pond behind the gardens."

"I thank you for the information, Filber," Julien replied warmly, amused at the butler's matchmaking intentions.

On the threshold of making his first offer of marriage, Julien found himself unusually calm. He felt at his ease, and confident, particularly about the interview he would shortly have with Sir Oliver. He had taken the man's measure and had determined that despite his preachy, sanctimonious ways, Sir Oliver was anxious to see Harry well placed and Kate off his hands as quickly as possible. Since he seemed as solitary as he was cheerless, and appeared to nurture for some curious inexplicable reason a profound dislike for his own daughter, it was unlikely that he would thrust himself upon them after their marriage.

"My lord!" Sir Oliver executed a formal bow and advanced toward Julien with his hand outstretched.

Julien returned his greeting, aware instantly that his purpose was quite evident to Sir Oliver.

"Please do be seated, my lord."

Julien obliged and eased his long frame into a worn leather chair next to the fireplace. Sir Oliver seated himself opposite and looked at him expectantly.

"I would imagine, sir, that you can easily guess the nature of my visit."

Sir Oliver could not repress the gleam of anticipation in his eyes, and Julien realized that he could dispense with any further formalities.

He said smoothly: "As you know, sir, I have developed a great regard for Lady Katharine and cherish hopes that she returns my affection. I have taken the liberty to have a marriage settlement drawn up." He paused a moment and pulled a folded sheet of paper from his pocket. "You will notice, sir, that I have included the promise to buy Harry a pair of colors and see him admitted to an elite cavalry regiment." Julien was pleased with himself that he had thought of this, for the pleasure was evident on Sir Oliver's face. "As you see, the sum to be presented to you, sir, upon my marriage to Lady Katharine, is named, I believe, in the third paragraph."

As Julien had anticipated, Sir Oliver's eyes widened and he

was voluble in his expression of gratitude. "Very . . . very generous of you, my lord!" he exclaimed, unconsciously rubbing his hands together. "I count it a rare privilege that our two families will be united. Of course," he added hastily, "my daughter is a fine young lady and worthy of the exalted position your lordship offers."

Julien controlled the stab of anger at Sir Oliver's belated and unwilling praise of Kate. Though Sir Oliver was an irritating and pious nip-farthing, he was an older man and Kate's father.

Their business concluded, Julien immediately rose and sealed their bargain with a handshake. Sir Oliver thought to ask, "I presume your lordship has already spoken to my daughter?"

Julien shook his head. "No, sir, I deemed it proper to secure your permission first."

"Very proper . . . quite right, my lord." Sir Oliver nodded his agreement.

"I suppose your lordship would like to speak to her now," Sir Oliver offered.

"Yes, I think it now appropriate," Julien replied, walking beside Sir Oliver from the room. "Filber informs me that she is most likely near the pond . . . behind the gardens?"

"Yes, my lord. Shall Filber show you the way?" His eagerness was becoming an irritant, and Julien quickly disclaimed.

"No, no, I know my way."

Julien strode out of the hall into the overgrown gardens and shaded his eyes with his hand from the bright sunlight. He scanned the gardens and, not seeing Kate, walked toward the pond.

He found her seated on the mossy bank, her arms clasped around her knees, a pensive, faraway expression on her face. Her hair was unbound and hung down her back in soft waves, reaching nearly to the ground. His calm assurance did not falter as he approached her. He knew exactly what he wanted to say, and he had spent much of his day visualizing her response. She would be surprised at how soon he was declaring himself, but she would be prepared, for his feeling for her was obvious. Her face would flush slightly and she would softly declare her own feelings for him. The altogether delightful vision ended with a gentle, yet promising kiss.

As Julien drew nearer, he could hear Kate softly singing a Scottish ballad. He grinned, for she had a small wooden voice. He rather hoped that she did not play the pianoforte, for he had had to endure the painfully accurate performances of too many nervous debutantes.

She did not notice his presence until he dropped down on his knees beside her. Kate looked up, not at all startled, and said cheerfully: "Good morning, sir. You are up and about quite early."

"What is this? You think me a lazy sluggard, Kate?"

"Well," she temporized, the irrepressible dimples peeping through, "not exactly. a . . . sluggard! Being one of the— what is it you fine gentlemen call it?—ah, yes, being a Corinthian, I would naturally expect your lordship to be at his dressing table until at least noon!"

"Little baggage!" The tone in which he spoke robbed his words of any offense, and Kate laughed in delight.

He looked at her searchingly for a moment, thinking suddenly of the way they had parted the day before, of her fear at the copse and her undeniable response to his kiss. Neither of these incidents appeared to be disturbing her now. She was perfectly at her ease, the pensive expression he had observed on her face vanished.

Kate saw that the earl was regarding her with a very serious expression on his face.

"What . . . can you still not find a suitable hunter to buy?" she quizzed him. She laid her hand on the sleeve of his light blue broadcloth coat, thinking fleetingly how very exquisite he looked. His cravat was snowy white and arranged with such subtle perfection that she wished that Harry could see it.

Julien looked down at her hand and clasped it in his own. She made no move to pull away, but simply cocked her head to one side and gazed at him inquiringly. With supreme confidence, emboldened by her gesture, the earl embarked on his first proposal of marriage.

"Kate, I have spoken to your father. In fact, I have just come from meeting with him."

"Good heavens!" she exclaimed, taken aback. "What ever would you have to say to Sir Oliver?"

A bit daunted by her naiveté, he hesitated a moment, carefully choosing his words. "I of course wanted to . . . make a suitable agreement with your father before speaking with you. In short, Kate, my dearest Kate, I asked his permission to pay you my addresses. I want you to be my wife, Kate. Will you do me the honor of marrying me?"

"Marry you," she repeated blankly. Her eyes widened and her hand tensed in his.

"That is correct, Kate," he said gently. He was quite pleased at her response, for it fitted to perfection the reaction he had expected from her at his declaration. He could almost imagine now the softness of her lips and the feel of her silky hair in his hands.

"You are not quizzing me, my lord?" she asked in a low, barely audible voice.

It occurred to Julien that perhaps she could not quite believe that she would become a countess. "It is a serious matter, Kate. I have already spoken to your father, as I said, and he gives us his blessing."

"My father has agreed to this?" Her voice was a whisper, and he had to strain to make out her words.

"Yes, Kate," he affirmed.

With an effort she wrenched her gaze from his face, terribly aware at that moment of his nearness to her. The day before, when he had kissed her, she had known an instant of tingling excitement, an altogether new sensation that was quite pleasurable. But the brief moment passed so quickly that she could not be certain that it had happened at all; what she remembered was that she had felt at once so consumed with an unexpected, deadening fear that had caused her to flee from him in confusion. She had been unable to understand either her sudden fear or the unwanted feelings that had surged through her at his touch. She had decided later that she had behaved most foolishly and that the earl had merely given way to a moment of capriciousness. She realized now that she had been mistaken not only in her final dismissal of her own feelings, but in the earl's motives as well. His had not been the action of a capricious nobleman. He wanted her. She felt the strength and possessiveness of his hand and jerked hers away. Her chest tightened painfully as it had the day before, and she felt an overwhelming desire to run. But she did not move; her body seemed leaden, weighted down by a strange lethargy. Her mouth went dry and she licked her lips nervously. Without wishing to, she pictured his powerful, muscular body barely held in check by his elegant clothing. The inexplicable terror that had consumed her at the copse now descended, cloaking her mind in a pervasive and dreadful blackness.

"Kate . . ." Julien's voice penetrated the darkness.

Her mind cleared suddenly at the sound of his voice, and the full realization of what he wanted broke over her like a massive wave of freezing, numbing water. Marry him! He would be her husband . . . her husband! Her father had given him his blessing!

A bitter fury gripped her and she encouraged her rage, for it gave her mind direction. How dare he be so presumptuous, so very sure of himself! She cried between gritted teeth, "How dare you! You bargain with my father like . . . stocks on the exchange! Did it never occur to you, O most noble lord, that I find your sly maneuver repugnant and despicable?"

She paused for breath, her breasts heaving.

"I . . . I do not understand you, Kate," he stammered. Surely, he thought, there must be some mistake!

She fanned her fury and taunted him, "How odd! To this moment, I have always found your understanding to be quite superior!"

He gazed at her, stupefied, and she could not hold to her anger. Brokenly she whispered, "I thought you were my friend, that you held me in equal esteem. I cannot believe that you have done this. . . ."

He had been incredulous at her sudden fury, and was now appalled at the anguish in her voice. He leaned close to her and said earnestly, "Kate, surely you must see that it is only proper for me to seek out your father first. That you are angered by my action, I am sorry. No, don't look away from me," he said in an urgent voice. "Of course I am your friend. My esteem and respect for you cannot be in dispute. It is just that I wish to be much more to you, in truth, I want to be your husband."

She closed her eyes tightly as each of his words burned deep into her. She knew of a certainty that she could not escape him as she had done the day before, that he would pursue her and demand an explanation. But she had no such explanation, even to herself. She drew a deep breath and said in a voice of determined calm, "Pray forgive my anger, my lord. I was . . . unprepared and therefore shocked by your proposal. I . . . I am aware of the great honor you do me." To her own ears she sounded stilted, and she finished in a rush, "But I do not wish to wed you, nor any other man, for that matter."

Julien grabbed her arm, his own gray eyes darkening with

anger. "What game are you playing, Kate? Surely you cannot expect me to believe that you are indifferent to me, that you do not care! Indeed, I have waited until I was certain of your feelings."

She looked down dispassionately, thinking it strange that she felt no pain, for he was holding her arm in an iron grip. She replied calmly, "What you wish to believe is your own affair, my lord. That I do not wish to wed you is a fact." She softened her voice. "I am sorry if it causes you pain."

"Surely you cannot wish to marry that bumptious ass Bleddoes!" he thundered at her. Before she could reply, he jerked her to her feet and tightened his grip on her arm.

"If you would like to beat me, my lord, my father finds a cane to be most efficacious." She stared at his angry face, her chin thrust up defiantly.

It was as if she had struck him full in the face. Appalled at his lack of control, he released her abruptly.

She did not move or attempt to back away from him. "There is no one else, my lord, nor will there ever be. I . . . I do not wish to be wed with any man," she said in a very low voice.

He looked at her blankly and repeated vaguely, "No one else, Kate?" This gave him rational direction and he asked slowly, "Then what is it you want, Kate? I offer you all my wealth, the protection of my name, and above all, I offer you the chance to escape from the intolerable life with your father. That I love you is without question."

Kate looked down and began to unconsciously rub her arm. What he said was true, though she could not fathom why he should possibly profess love for her. She knew a brief moment of doubt before the strange fear gripped her and she knew that she could not marry him.

She raised her eyes again to his face and saw that he clearly expected an answer from her. His gray eyes were clouded with confusion. He was her friend, her only friend save Harry, and now she would lose him.

"What you say is true, my lord. It would be absurd to deny that my father and I do not . . . deal well together. But I cannot, indeed, I will not marry you for such reasons as you have listed."

"I see." Julien's voice was flat, emotionless. His eyes bore into hers for one long, silent moment. He wanted desperately to see some change, some hesitance in her, but she met his gaze without flinching or turning away. He did not know the effort it cost her, for absurdly, she wanted to cry.

He had no more words, no more arguments to present to her. He had only a shred of his pride. He executed a brief, ironic bow and strode away from her. He turned back after a few steps and flung at her over his shoulder, "Pray forgive me, madam, for my impertinence!" An inward voice mocked him.

He turned again and hastened away from her. He did not again look back. Kate, in an unconscious gesture, raised her hand toward his retreating back. The overgrown garden soon blocked him from her view. Slowly she lowered her arm, and finding herself quite unable to support her own weight, she sank down onto the mossy bank. There were no tears, only a deep sense of loss.

6

Mannering was aghast when he opened the great oak doors to admit his lordship. The earl said not a word; his face was pale and his gray eyes glazed. The words of congratulation died on Mannering's lips and he stepped quickly aside. Mannering watched his master walk the length of the hall, fling open the door to the library, and slam it behind him.

A sense of unreality seized Mannering. Good God, he thought, Lady Katharine has refused him!

Mrs. Cradshaw, who had been waiting impatiently in the parlor for the earl's return, came bustling out. Her smile vanished as she approached Mannering and saw the pained expression on his face.

"Edward, what has happened!" she exclaimed, shaking his coat sleeve.

Mannering drew a deep breath to steady himself. "I fear, Emma, that there are to be no congratulations for his lordship. It would appear that Lady Katharine has turned him down."

Mrs. Cradshaw drew back in stunned surprise. "Edward . . . surely not . . ."

Mannering seemed not to have heard her. She was suddenly indignant, her motherly instincts aroused. "How dare Lady Katharine serve his lordship such a turn! I would not have thought it possible. 'Tis disgraceful, that's what it is!"

Mannering felt tired. It was with an effort that he pulled himself up straight, his shoulders squared. He patted Mrs. Cradshaw's arm in a soothing gesture. "I am afraid, Emma, that there is little we can do about it, save wait and see what will happen. We will have to be very understanding with his lordship," he added, realizing that it was his duty to protect the earl from the curious glances of the servants and any embarrassing questions that Mrs. Cradshaw might take it into her head to ask. He began to silently rehearse his speech to the servants.

Mrs. Cradshaw nodded slowly. That such an unbelievable turn of events should happen to the St. Clairs! Arm in arm, the two old friends walked across the hall to the servants' quarters. Mannering thought fleetingly of the vintage champagne that he had unearthed from the wine cellar. He must remember to put it back.

Julien stood in the middle of the library, staring blankly ahead of him. His body felt curiously detached from his mind, and neither seemed capable of functioning. He had managed to nurture anger at Kate for the greater part of his ride home, only to find that he could not sustain it. A great sense of loss had descended over him.

He flung himself into the large chair and sat brooding for a time before a deep sense of humiliation stung him to action. God, what a fool he had been! He mocked himself bitterly as he remembered how he had been so certain of her; how he had even gone so far as to envision her every response to his gracious offer of marriage. And he had been mortally insulted when she flung his declaration in his face! He could find no excuse for himself. Though he had never thought himself a paragon, it was painful to realize that he had behaved in the most reprehensibly conceited manner possible. "Dammit to hell!" he cursed aloud. "If ever a man needed a drink . . ." He grabbed a bottle of brandy from the sideboard, carried it back with him to his chair, and hurled himself down again.

Mannering hurried to the library when he heard the ring of the bell cord. He hoped that his lordship would be wanting his dinner, for it was growing quite late. The sight that greeted his eyes when he opened the door made him wince. The earl was sprawled in the large stuffed chair, his late father's chair, an empty bottle dangling in his outstretched hand. His cravat was askew as if he had unsuccessfully tried to pull it away, and his fair hair was decidedly disheveled.

"My lord!" Mannering was shocked. He had never before seen his master so obviously foxed.

Julien turned his blurred vision to his butler. "Get me another bottle of brandy, Mannering. And don't give me one of your looks—there are times in a man's life when brandy is not at all a bad thing! Do be quick, man, I have no intention of losing my hold on a world that is for the moment altogether tolerable!"

"Yes, my lord, as you wish, my lord," Mannering murmured unhappily. He left the room with dragging steps to do his master's bidding.

As he closed the library doors, he heard a curse and the sound of glass breaking. He glanced hastily around, hoping that no servants, particularly Mrs. Cradshaw, were in hearing distance.

Upon his return, he saw that the earl had thrown the empty bottle, shattering it against the marble fireplace.

"My lord . . ." Mannering stammered.

"Don't you dare prose at me, Mannering!" Julien rose drunkenly from his chair and grabbed the bottle. "And don't stand there gaping like a black crow, man! I'll call you if I have further need of you."

Mannering stiffened at the harsh words but almost instantly forgave his master. He bowed, and with as much dignity as he could manage, walked from the library, closing the door softly behind him.

With considerable effort Julien forced his eyes open and looked about him. He was lying in his bed, fully clothed, a cover partially pulled over him. He winced at the bright sunlight and turned his head away, only to find that this simple movement brought on excruciating pain. He lay very still until the pounding in his temples lessened. He had no memory of how or when he had left the library to come to his room. He gave a loud groan upon seeing a half-empty bottle of brandy standing precariously on the night table, and wondered how much he had consumed before falling into a drunken sleep.

Too soon he remembered the events of the previous day, and he found himself almost welcoming the physical pain in his head, for it forced his attention away from less pleasant thoughts.

He lay quietly in the silent room until finally with a determination born of despair he rose unsteadily. He glanced at the clock on the night table and was surprised that it was quite early, in fact, only seven o'clock in the morning. He began to feel disgusted with himself, for he had always scorned those gentlemen in his acquaintance whose sole purpose for getting drunk was to escape and forget their misery. He cursed long and fluently, and it made him feel better. He wanted to cleanse himself, to clear both his mind and body from the effects of the brandy.

He hurried from his room, not even thinking of the odd appearance he presented, made his way downstairs, and flung open the front doors. He strode past two startled footmen, who had barely enough time to bow, and broke into a run across the front lawn toward St. Clair lake. The rapid movement made the pain in his head near to unbearable, but he gritted his teeth and never broke his stride until he reached a large rock that formed a cliff of about six feet above the lake. He quickly pulled off his clothes and poised himself naked on the edge of the rock, panting a moment from his exertion, and dived into the water.

He gasped with the shock of the icy water. His pounding head protested and his skin tingled, smarting at this outrage, but he ignored his body's protestations and set out with long, firm strokes. He swam at a furious pace until he reached the opposite shore and then turned himself about and swam back. He found his footing and waded through the water reeds to the grassy bank. His heart pounded with the exertion, but he felt exhilarated, somehow renewed. He stretched out his arms and embraced the cold air against his wet skin.

He turned and gazed out over the lake, a strange smile flitting over his face. He said half-aloud to the calm blue water: "What a fool to think of giving up! I will tame my Kate and wed her, just as I planned. And I will not pay her court as does that fool Bleddoes!" As he dressed himself, he let his mind nurture the idea until it burst forth. He announced again to the silent lake: "Damn, I shall have her! I will make her love me." Not bothering to tie his cravat, he strode with confident steps back to the mansion.

Sir Oliver found that his arm ached. He considered himself a pious man, and it angered him that Kate had made him curse to vent his spleen. "Damn the girl," he snarled fiercely, turning to his Bible for epithets. "I've nurtured a viper to my bosom, an unnatural, willful child!"

He massaged his arm. He had been fair, of course he had been fair, he told himself stoutly. When she had calmly informed him that she did not wish to wed the Earl of March, he controlled his anger and presented her with innumerable advantages to such a match. But she had stood stiffly before him, in that contemptuous silent way of hers! And when he threatened her with Bleddoes, she told him quietly that she had already refused the squire! Obstinate, that's what she was! The little slut did not even cry, nor did she beg for mercy when he raised his cane and shook it in her face. She pulled her long hair away from her back and covered her head with her arms. When he stopped beating her, she rose unsteadily to her feet, gazed at him with hatred in her green eyes, and staggered to the door. He realized full well that the beating had not made her change her mind. At least, he reflected, it had made him feel better.

As he sat pondering his ill fortune, he was informed by Filber that the Earl of March had called to see him. A flicker of hope widened his eyes and he exclaimed: "Well, don't just stand there like an idiot, Filber, show his lordship in!"

Hastily he rose and removed the cane. There was dried blood on it and it did not seem politic for his lordship to see it.

Filber returned to the earl and took his hat and cloak. "Sir Oliver will see your lordship in the bookroom, my lord."

"Thank you, Filber." Julien added softly, "Filber, just a moment."

"Yes, my lord?"

"Is Lady Katharine here?"

Filber's calm facade nearly broke and as he replied he was aware of the hardness of his own voice: "Lady Katharine, my lord, is . . . physically unable to see anyone."

Julien asked, his words so softly spoken that Filber had to strain to hear: "Has he hurt her, Filber?" To anyone who knew the earl well, the quietly spoken words would have been an instant signal that his lordship was in a dangerous mood. Filber, who did not know this, felt emboldened to say reproachfully: "Yes, my lord . . . very badly."

There was an infinitesimal pause before Julien said in a deceptively cool voice: "Thank you, Filber, for your honesty."

Julien stopped him again as he turned to go. "I will contrive to see that Sir Oliver never touches Lady Katharine again."

Filber gazed at the earl with a thoughtful, arrested expression. He realized that he had been wrong about his lordship. The servants had been surprised at Lady Katharine's refusal of the earl, but that Sir Oliver had dared to try to beat her into submission had left them all enraged. The baronet had suffered sullen looks and indifferent food prepared by Cook since that time.

Julien was closeted with Sir Oliver only briefly. He stated his business in a concise, controlled voice. Sir Oliver stammered and fussed but ended by agreeing to Julien's demands. Julien rose as soon as they had reached an agreement and concluded: "Very well. I will expect to see Kate installed with Lady Bellingham in London within two weeks. Not longer, mind!"

"As you say, my lord, within two weeks," Sir Oliver agreed.

Julien could not bring himself to shake Sir Oliver's outstretched hand, and turned abruptly toward the door. He stopped and again faced Kate's father, his gray eyes cold and hard as agates.

"If you dare to harm Kate again, you can be assured that she will be an orphan before the day is through! Do you understand me?"

Sir Oliver paled. It did not occur to him to question how his lordship knew of his beating of Kate. He tasted real fear for the first time in his life. He nodded his head vigorously and managed to whisper in a strangled voice: "I quite understand you, my lord."

"It is well that you do!" With these words Julien left the room.

It was some moments before the hammering of fear lessened and Sir Oliver was able to walk slowly to a chair and sit down. He sagged against the back and closed his eyes. He could see Kate's bloodied back, her dress shredded as she staggered away from him. Fleetingly he wondered if he had scarred her. He brightened as he realized that his overbearing son-in-law would perhaps not be so pleased with his bride. Indeed, he reflected with satisfaction, there would be much to displease the earl!

7

Kate chewed absently on her thumbnail as she sat gazing out her window overlooking Berkeley Square. She marveled that the peaceful scene below was yet another face of London. The Pantheon and Bond Street, where she had shopped with Lady Bellingham, were filled with the clatter of carriages and horses, the shouts of coarse vendors in words that she barely understood, and the bustle of link boys clearing the way for their masters and mistresses. It had been difficult to believe that so many different kinds of people contrived to make their way in one city.

There was a light knock on her door and Eliza stepped into the room and swept Kate a slight curtsy. Kate rose slowly from the window seat, mindful of the red weals on her back that were healing, but still brought pain if she moved suddenly. She was unable still to face her maid without embarrassment, since Eliza had attended her first bath and without a word produced an ointment and gently rubbed it into her tender skin.

"What is it, Eliza?" Kate asked.

" 'Tis Lady Bellingham, my lady. Some of your gowns have arrived and she requests you to come to her sitting room," Eliza informed her in her polished London voice.

"That is good news indeed," Kate exclaimed, her embarrassment forgotten and her eyes sparkling with excitement. "Good heavens . . . it has been but three days!"

"Lady Bellingham is never one to be put off," Eliza observed, as Kate straightened a flounce in her old gown and patted her hair into place. She thought fleetingly, and with no regret, of Harry's old breeches folded from sight at the bottom of her trunk. Her disreputable leather hat she had carefully hidden with her fishing pole in a dark recess of the stable.

Kate made her way down the carpeted hallway to Lady Bellingham's sitting room and tapped lightly on the door. She heard a muffled "Come in!" and opened the door to see her hostess pacing back and forth in obvious agitation, her brow puckered and her plump beringed hands clasped to her bosom.

"Ma'am?" Kate inquired, concerned.

"Oh, my dear Kate. Do come in, child! But see, your new gowns have arrived. Madame Giselle has performed marvels with the materials we selected. Just look at the evening gown, my dear!"

Kate wondered briefly at the good lady's upset manner, but seeing her now in high good humor and quite as excited as Kate over the new dresses, she moved quickly to the several tissue-swathed garments. There was a severely cut gold velvet riding habit with a plumed, high-poked hat to match, a morning gown of soft yellow muslin with laced frocking, and the most beautiful dress she had ever beheld—a pale blue velvet evening gown, fashioned high in the back in the Russian style, with plunging neckline and long, fitted sleeves sewn with tiny seed pearls on the cuffs. Kate drew the gown from its silver tissue paper and held it in front of her.

"My love, it suits you to perfection!" Lady Bellingham exclaimed in delight. "How very elegant you will be tonight, to be sure."

"Tonight?" Kate ceased her pirouette and gazed inquiringly at her hostess.

Lady Bellingham's eyes flew to Kate's in consternation. She sat heavily down on a setee and began to wring her hands together.

"My dear ma'am, whatever is the matter?" Kate quickly sat down beside her and clasped her fluttering hands in her own.

Lady Bellingham embarked on a somewhat tangled explanation of what she had unwittingly let slip: "Oh, dear, I had not intended . . . that is, dear Kate, of course I was going to tell you . . . the earl, you know . . ."

Kate stiffened and pulled her own hands away. So that was why Lady Bellingham appeared in such an agitation of the nerves. The good lady did not have to finish, for Kate knew that tonight, dressed in her beautiful new gown, she was to be escorted by the Earl of March to some occasion. Did Lady Bellingham think her dim-witted? From her first day in London when her hostess had begun making oblique yet complimentary references to the Earl of March, she had realized that it was he who was responsible for her presence in London. She had cursed her stupidity for not realizing from the first that it was the earl's doing when her father had been so adamant that she visit the fashionable Lady Bellingham, whose relationship to her own family was so tenuous as to be laughable. She had passed from shock at the earl's high-handed maneuvering to outrage at her discovery that even the lowest scullery maid considered her all but betrothed to the earl. She felt even now, as she gazed with a hard look at Lady Bellingham's crumpled features, that he had taken ruthless advantage of her. She had known that it was just a matter of time until he came to pay her court, and there was absolutely nothing she could do about it.

"Kate, my dear, I . . . realize that you and the earl have had some sort of misunderstanding. Surely you must see that your marriage to him would bring you the greatest advantages. Come, child, do not look so upset," Lady Bellingham pleaded. Lord, how did she ever let Julien embroil her in such a tangle!

Kate turned away, angry at herself for being such a fool and at the earl for placing her willy-nilly in such an untenable position. It was on the tip of her tongue to unleash her anger and frustration at Lady Bellingham, but she realized the good woman really had as little to say in the matter as did she.

At the sound of Lady Bellingham's pained breathing, she turned quickly back.

"Please, ma'am, I am truly sorry that you are to be so upset by this . . . matter. Here, let me fetch you your vinaigrette."

Lady Bellingham ceased her sobbing at last and leaned back against the pillows Kate had carefully placed behind her head. She managed to say with some semblance of calm:

"Kate, I vow you will much enjoy yourself. We are to see John Philip Kemble perform *Macbeth* . . . at Drury Lane. The earl will arrive at eight o'clock this evening, and after the play we shall have a late supper at the Piazza; a most delightful place, my dear. . . ." Lady Bellingham halted her monologue, for Kate was staring blankly ahead of her, seemingly oblivious of what Lady Bellingham was saying.

Drat Julien! Lady Bellingham thought. Why could he have not chosen a girl to wed who was, at least, not averse to his suit? Why must he have a girl who positively loathes him?

"At eight o'clock, did you say, ma'am?" Kate asked quietly.

"Yes, my dear." Her hostess smiled. Finally, she thought, relieved, Kate was coming around to accepting the situation. And although she was quite pale and her green eyes looked enormous against her white skin, she now seemed quite composed.

"Very well, ma'am," Kate said as she bundled the gowns in her arms. "I do suppose I shall very much enjoy seeing Kemble."

Lady Bellingham did not notice the tinge of controlled bitterness in Kate's voice and silently congratulated herself on her deft handling of the situation.

Julien rose from his dressing table, satisfied with the exquisite result he had achieved with his cravat, and allowed Timmens to remove an infinitesimal speck of dust from his black satin evening coat.

"Does my appearance meet with your approval, Timmens?" Julien quizzed his Friday-faced valet.

"There can be no one to outshine your lordship," Timmens affirmed. He had discovered long ago that if he attempted to respond to his master's little jokes, he fell into such a floundering tangle of words he was quite discomfited for days afterward. It appeared to him that the earl was quite amused if he simply pretended ignorance at his lordship's humor and treated his every utterance with the utmost seriousness.

"Let us hope that you are right, Timmens," Julien remarked as he drew on his evening gloves. "Oh, Timmens, you need not wait up for me," he added as he left the room. Julien knew Timmens would be waiting no matter the lateness of the hour, but he never failed to remind Timmens that he did not take this extra service for granted.

It was with a light step that Julien descended the carpeted

stairs to the elegantly marbled front hallway. He looked about him for a brief moment before nodding to a footman to open the front doors. It would not be long now, he thought with satisfaction, before he would know if Kate found his town house to her liking.

Bladen, elegantly clad in the St. Clair livery of scarlet and white, hurried to open the door of the carriage for his master.

"Bladen, I find that I am somewhat early. Pray inform Wilbury that he need not hurry." Julien sat back comfortably against the red velvet cushions, stretching his long legs diagonally to the seat opposite him.

Wilbury was surprised by this instruction, being used to driving at a spanking pace no matter the occasion. He shrugged his shoulders and with a gentle click-click allowed the horses to slowly move forward.

Julien smiled in anticipation of his long-awaited meeting with Kate. It had been with some difficulty that he had forced himself not to pay her a visit upon her arrival in London. He had realized that he must give her time, time primarily to discover that it was he who was responsible for bringing her here, and time to adjust to the idea that he had no intention whatsoever of letting her go. He knew full well that he had placed her in a situation where her choices were most limited. She could not return to Brandon Hall, and he guessed that she was far too well-bred to behave in an openly churlish manner toward Lady Bellingham. He knew she would be furious at his treatment, but he quelled any pangs of conscience, certain that he was acting in her best interest, and, of course, in accordance with his own wishes.

He did, however, reproach himself momentarily about his devious maneuver of placing Eliza in Lady Bellingham's household to act as Kate's personal maid. He smiled in the dim light of his carriage at what Eliza had told him about Kate's behavior after her meeting with Lady Bellingham. Kate had been a caged tiger, Eliza had informed him, pacing her bedroom, hurling invectives at his head, until finally, her anger spent, she had grown quiet. "An ominous quiet," Eliza had declared. Actually, Eliza's description had fit well with his own prediction of Kate's reaction. Well, he would soon see. He had chosen Kemble's *Macbeth* deliberately for their first meeting, fairly certain that Lady Bellingham would drop off to sleep by the second act, leaving Kate for all practical purposes alone with him. She would not be able to rail at him for fear of waking her kind hostess, nor would she be able to leave the box, for she was well aware that such behavior would cause endless speculation from the polite world.

He grinned now quietly to himself at the speculation he himself had caused when he had invited Hugh and Percy to dine with him upon his return to London. That they had thought his scheme a little mad, in fact, became obvious as the evening wore on.

Hugh had finally given utterance to this thought. "You must forgive us, Julien, for appearing to think your behavior . . . odd," he said frankly.

"Damned odd, if you ask me," Percy agreed.

Thinking that Julien might be offended, Hugh hastened to add by way of explanation: "It is just that I . . . we, have never seen you go to such lengths over a lady."

Hugh's mildly spoken observation brought a quick smile to Julien's face. "Do not trouble yourselves," he said cheerfully, "for I have quite given up trying to explain my . . . odd behavior. Perhaps it is old age and advancing senility."

Hugh grinned and turned to Percy. "Well, it appears that we must again offer Julien our congratulations."

Both men raised their glasses and Percy declared: "To a well-fought and successful campaign. May the best man—or lady—win!"

Julien roused himself and pulled the white satin curtain from the carriage window. Lord, he thought, Wilbury was certainly taking him at his word. He settled back again against the luxurious cushions and let his mind wander to Yvette and Lady Sarah, reflecting with a certain degree of relief that he had no more to worry about in regard to either of them. He had most willingly given his blessing to Lord Riverton in his pursuit of Yvette. But the Lady Sarah had been a more serious matter.

"Julien, my love! I had quite thought that you had decided to immure yourself forever in the country!" Sarah greeted him in her high, breathless voice. Always aware of gossiping servants, she met him in a small parlor on the second floor of Lord Ponsonby's mansion. She was elegantly dressed in a riding habit of blue velvet, and looked to be on the point of leaving.

"You are going out?" he inquired, taking her small hand for a brief moment and raising it to his lips.

She made a small, fluttering gesture, fanning her hand in

front of her, and gave him an arch smile. "It will do Lord Davenport no harm to wait a half-hour," she said softly.

Julien realized that she hoped to provoke him to jealousy, but he felt only relief at the mention of Lord Davenport. A man of great address, was Sir Edward. Julien had never before thought of the affected viscount with such fondness.

Sarah moved away from him and sat down gracefully on a small sofa, patting the place beside her.

"Come, Julien, sit down. You make me quite nervous standing there like a great silent bear."

"Good Lord, Sarah. A bear?" He grinned at the unlikely simile. One of the lady's greatest charms lay in her ability to make peculiar, yet delightful comparisons.

"That is not at all important," she chided gently. "Come, my dear, what is on your mind?"

Julien did not answer immediately, and he was rather taken off guard when she filled the silence in a rather flat voice: "You have met another lady."

"You are astute, Sarah," he said. "Indeed I have come to tell you, and hope," he added gently, "that you will wish me happy."

Her blue eyes widened and she stared at him open-mouthed. "You . . . you plan to marry?" she asked disbelievingly.

He nodded slowly, and he saw the hurt in her eyes before she turned her head away. He did not wish to admit it, but he knew that this abrupt ending of their liaison was not only a blow to her pride but also to her heart.

"Sarah . . . I am indeed sorry." He spoke gently but was aware of a tugging impatience to be gone. Although Sarah tended to become romantically involved with her lovers, she knew as well as he did that their affair would end in time. He was only sorry, knowing Sarah as he did, that it was not she who broke off their relationship.

"What is her name?" Sarah asked in a choked voice.

"You do not know her. She has lived all her life in the country. In fact, her father's estate lies near to St. Clair. She will be coming to London to stay with Lady Bellingham." Realizing that he had not answered her direct question, he added, unaware that his voice softened: "Her name is Katharine."

Sarah heard the tenderness in his voice and turned back to

him. There was wonder written on her face. "My God, Julien, you are in love," she cried with a gasp of surprise.

An odd light flickered in his gray eyes before he said softly: "Yes, Sarah, I suppose that I am."

"And you have come to end our . . . affair," she stated flatly.

"Yes, Sarah."

She rose abruptly and pressed her fingertips against her temples. "Well . . . it seems that we have little else to say to one another."

Julien also stood up. In a swift motion he leaned down and kissed her gently on the forehead. He gazed deep into her china-blue eyes and said quietly: "I hope that you will be . . . kind to Katharine. She knows no one in London."

She seemed to force a smile and replied airily: "Of course I shall be kind to her, Julien. I wish you the best, you know that. And your Katharine. You had best go now before I become the fool."

It was not lost on Julien that she glanced covertly at the clock as she spoke.

Julien sat up with a start and saw Bladen patiently holding open the door of his carriage for him to alight.

"Thought you had fallen asleep, my lord," Bladen observed.

"Very nearly," Julien replied, stepping down on the flagstone in front of the Bellingham mansion. He called to Wilbury: "Walk the horses, Davie, I cannot be certain how long I will be."

Julien was quickly admitted to the Bellingham mansion and shown to the drawing room.

"Oh, Julien . . . dear me, you have arrived!" Lady Bellingham straightened her dowager's lavender turban over the small crimped curls and turned distractedly to him.

"I hope I find you well, Lady Bella," Julien said suavely, crossing to where she sat and lightly touching his lips to her gloved fingers. He raised his eyebrows inquiringly.

"Don't stare down your nose at me, Julien! I vow I cannot help it if Katharine must needs spend . . . hours getting dressed! And I thought that she had changed her mind toward you . . ." the good lady moaned.

Julien laughed and moved over to stand next to the fireplace. "Do forgive me, Lady Bella."

"A more ill-matched pair I have yet to see," she grumbled.

"Do help yourself to a glass of sherry, Julien. Lord knows what the girl is doing!"

Julien did as he was bid, careful to pour a very full glass for Lady Bellingham. She was fond of her sherry, particularly when she was undergoing an agitaiton of the nerves.

He handed her a glass and eased himself down in a chair opposite her. "Have you been waiting long, ma'am?" he asked.

"You were expected at eight o'clock," she snapped. "It is now eight-thirty."

"The performance does not begin until nine-thirty," he soothed.

"That is not the point, as you well know, young man," she declared, downing a sizable gulp of sherry. "What ever would your dear mama say to your antics!"

"Actually I have not yet spoken to her," he replied frankly. He added quickly at the look of surprise in Lady Bella's eyes: "Never fear, ma'am, I shall pay her a visit as soon as our engagement is to be announced in the *Gazette*."

"At the rate you're proceeding, your hair will be as gray as mine!" She heaved a deep sigh and swallowed the rest of her sherry.

When Julien had paid Lady Bellingham his unexpected visit almost three weeks ago, she had been eager to fall in with his plan. She had proudly seen her dear Anne, the last of her numerous brood, wed to the young Viscount of Walbrough during the past summer, and had grown quite bored resting her bones at home in the evenings. She had known Julien's mama before her marriage to the Earl of March and she had watched Julien over the years politely but disinterestedly turn away from each new season's debutantes, including her own dear girls. The thought of again being involved with a courtship, and particularly the idea of meeting the girl who had finally managed to turn his lordship's head, had made her quite animated. As for the tenuous connection she shared with the Brandon family, that bothered her not at all. Her only concern had been that Katharine would speak with that horrible northern accent and thus make both of them a laughingstock among the ton.

When Katharine arrived on her doorstep, clad in the most horrid and outdated of clothes, she had groped for her vinaigrette, believing that the worst of her fears had been realized. The girl spoke in a soft, cultured voice, which was somewhat of a relief, but Lady Bellingham did not set aside her vinaigrette until Kate proudly announced that she had a thousand guineas with which to purchase a new wardrobe. Her enthusiastic response was catching, and Katharine herself unbent considerably. But what a surprise it had been to Lady Bellingham when at every mention of the earl's name, the girl's green eyes flashed daggers!

Julien asked Lady Bellingham matter-of-factly: "Has Katharine been a sad trial to you, ma'am?"

Lady Bellingham hastened to deny such a thing: "Good gracious no, Julien! It is just . . . well," she stammered, groping for safe words, "she is quite . . . independent, but a dear girl. She will lead you a merry chase, Julien, that's for sure," she finished, gazing at him earnestly.

"Believe me, ma'am, she has done that since the first time I met her!" Julien grinned ruefully.

"Lady Katharine, his lordship and Lady Bellingham are awaiting you," Eliza said as she pulled nervously on her mobcap. She did not relish having to remind her mistress a second time.

"Yes, Eliza, I am aware of that fact. Pray inform his lordship and Lady Bellingham that I will be down directly," Kate replied, not looking up.

"Yes, my lady." Eliza sped toward the door, thought better of it, and turned. "Perhaps I can help?" she asked in a faltering voice.

Kate cut her off. "No . . . no, I have just to fetch my gloves and cloak."

She did not move from her dressing table until Eliza had closed the door behind her. Kate stared for a moment into the mirror at her pale, set face. She did not look at all like herself, her hair fashionably dressed, and the blue velvet gown plunging low over her bosom, and revealing, she thought, far too much white skin.

She realized that purposefully dallying was a rather childish style of retaliation, but she was unable to think of a more comprehensive revenge at the moment. She had decided only a short time before that she would suffer the earl's presence, for she appeared to have no other choice in the matter, but she would not give him the satisfaction of showing overt distress or anger. She would face him with a cold hauteur that would show him what she thought of him, and keeping him waiting was a very good beginning. He had turned from being her friend to being now more in the nature of an enemy, and she would see him routed!

She picked up her gloves and cloak and slowly made her way down the curving staircase. Smithers, the Bellingham butler, stood awaiting her at the door of the drawing room. Kate forced herself to halt a moment, schooled her face into an impassive expression, and waited for her heart to stop pounding uncomfortably against her ribs.

Kate finally gave Smithers leave to open the door, and he observed her nose rise a good three inches as she sailed past him into the drawing room.

It was with a distinct effort that Kate maintained her imperious demeanor, for the earl stood quite at his ease, leaning negligently against the mantelpiece. Her anger flared and her eyes flashed at the barely suppressed gleam of amusement in his eyes.

She remarked, without wishing to, that he looked his usual elegant self, his black satin evening clothes fitted to perfection.

Julien did not immediately move toward her but watched her closely as she swept into the room, the train of her velvet gown trailing behind her. How very beautiful she looked, he thought appreciatively, the gown fitted to her slender figure, accentuating the soft curve of her breasts. Her thick auburn hair was piled artfully on top of her head and two long tresses lay gracefully over her bare shoulder.

"Oh, there you are, my love . . . at last," Lady Bellingham greeted Kate, her voice a mixture of relief and reproach.

Kate swept a haughty curtsy to the earl and proceeded to pay him no further notice. She turned to Lady Bellingham and gave her a warm smile.

"I do hope, ma'am, that I am not too late." She shot a defiant challenge toward Julien and added mendaciously: "Eliza had some difficulty with the . . . buttons on my gown." She stood proud and stiff in the middle of the room, not displeased at her performance.

Lady Bellingham wished that she had another glass of sherry.

Julien, however, seemed to think nothing amiss and moved gracefully toward Kate.

"Good evening, Kate," he said calmly. "It is indeed a pleasure to see you again. I hope that you had a pleasant journey to London and have been enjoying the sights." He took her hand and brushed his lips lightly over her fingers.

She felt a dull flush spread over her face and snatched her hand away. "Indeed!" she replied.

"I trust your . . . buttons are now adequately arranged," he said gently.

"I said I was sorry that I am a . . . trifle late."

"I did not ask you for an apology. In fact, I quite understand."

"Do we continue this nonsense, my lord, or do we leave to see the play you have so graciously chosen?"

He leaned close to her and said softly: "Cold Kate. Indifferent Kate. Surely there must be something written somewhere about such a Kate."

Julien turned before she could answer and addressed Lady Bellingham: "If you are ready, ma'am, I think that we should be leaving. I am certain," he added, glancing at Kate, "that you would not wish to miss the first act of *Macbeth*."

Julien helped Lady Bellingham to her feet and arranged the silk paisley shawl around her plump shoulders.

Lady Bellingham watched Kate turn on her heel and sail from the room. She turned a troubled countenance to Julien. "Oh, dear. Perhaps I should speak to her, Julien. She is being quite provoking, you know."

"On no account, ma'am, I beg of you," he replied firmly, taking her arm and steering her after Kate.

As they passed through the front door, Julien leaned down and said softly: "Believe me, Lady Bella, I have the situation well in control."

She looked up at him doubtfully, but seeing the calm look of self-assurance on his face, thought that perhaps he did. She felt a momentary twinge of concern over Katharine. Although she was an ambitious mama, well versed in the art of matchmaking, she would never have dreamed of pushing her offspring into marriages that were distasteful to them. She shook her head wonderingly; how any woman would not wish to marry the Earl of March was more than she could fathom!

As Julien helped her into the carriage, she cast an uncertain glance at Kate, who was sitting ramrod-stiff, gazing out of the carriage window. She would have given up her medicinal dosage of sherry for a week to know what was going on in the girl's head.

Julien swung himself into the carriage and seated himself

opposite Kate and Lady Bellingham. He tapped his cane on the roof of the carriage and Wilbury whipped up the horses.

"So we are to see *Macbeth*," Lady Bellingham said brightly.

"Yes, ma'am. I do hope that you approve my choice."

She was not particularly enthusiastic about seeing a Shakespeare play for she found the dramatic lines, delivered with wild gesticulations, beyond her comprehension and thus rather boring. Her thoughts leaped ahead to the sumptuous supper they would enjoy after the play. Even Katharine at her most glacial would not spoil that part of her evening!

Though London was rather thin of company this time of year, many of the ton having followed the regent to Brighton for the summer, there was still a sizable crowd to attend Kemble's performance. Lady Bellingham was able to wave to several acquaintances as they took their seats in the elegant box that Julien reserved each season.

Kate was not quite sure how it happened, but she found herself seated between Lady Bellingham and the earl. She turned her shoulder stiffly toward Julien and fastened her eyes on the stage. Despite her best efforts, Kate forgot herself and became quite involved in the great actor's rendition of *Macbeth*.

When the curtain fell after the first act, Kate was dismayed to see that Lady Bellingham was gently dozing in her chair. She was uncomfortably aware of how close the earl was sitting to her. She tried to draw away, for his thigh was but an inch from hers, but Lady Bellingham's ample figure prohibited it. She felt the earl's eyes upon her, and to her chagrin, she felt her face flush with color.

"Are you enjoying the play, Kate?" he asked politely, leaning close to her.

She could feel the warmth of his breath on her cheek and was uneasily aware of a certain tingling of her senses. Her heart seemed to be beating inordinately loudly. Without turning to him, she replied in a low, tense voice: "It is quite tolerable, thank you, my lord."

"Only tolerable, Kate? You surprise me, for I thought you quite animated over Kemble's performance. I really do wish you would face me, Kate," he added pensively. "Although you have a lovely back, I would much prefer conversing to your face."

She tossed her head and he remarked provokingly: "I had not thought you a coward, Kate."

She turned quickly in her seat and glared at him.

"That is much better. You really must cultivate that look of innocent outrage, it makes your green eyes sparkle quite attractively, you know. Please do not turn away again, Kate, for I will think you . . . afraid of me."

"I am not afraid of you, my lord," she hissed. "It is just that I find that your perfidy passes all bounds. Afraid of you indeed!"

"That is much better, Kate. I had feared that your wit had grown dulled during my absence. Poor Bleddoes . . . he had not the wherewithal to keep pace with you! Rest assured, my dear, that I will keep you properly . . . amused, when it pleases me."

Kate felt that her carefully planned strategy to maintain a haughty silence was fast crumbling. He was deliberately provoking her! Well, she would not let him succeed. She shrugged her shoulders as if in only slight irritation and turned her gaze to the elegant audience. She was immediately diverted.

"I do wish you would tell me who that oddly dressed man is who is waving at us. How very curious—he is wearing a yellow-and-green-striped waistcoat!"

"That is Mr. Fresham, Kate. He has always fancied himself Brummell's greatest rival. You must see him walk, his heels are so high that one fears him to topple over at any moment."

"How altogether ridiculous!" Kate said with scorn. "Men should appear as men, and not as painted peacocks!"

"Shall I take that for a compliment?" Julien reflected aloud as he returned the wave of Mr. Fresham.

Kate shot him a look of pure dislike and raised her nose in the air.

"You must take care, Kate, else you will not see the view of the world that we ordinary mortals have," he advised her serenely. "Would you care for refreshment, Kate? Perhaps some champagne?" Julien asked.

"No," she replied curtly.

Julien changed his topic: "I believe you evinced a desire to Lady Bellingham to enter the hallowed doors of Almack's. I have secured vouchers and will escort you, and, of course, Lady Bella, tomorrow evening."

Kate made a choking sound and clenched her gloved hands. She needed to be in London less than a week to know that his escort to Almack's would be tantamount to announcing their betrothal! Indeed, an announcement in the *Gazette* would be expected to follow but a few days after such an appearance.

She turned on him, her eyes flashing indignantly. "How dare you!" she hissed, careful to keep her voice low so as not to wake Lady Bellingham.

Julien raised inquiring eyebrows. "I beg your pardon?" he asked, a picture of bewildered innocence.

It was difficult to convey the depths of her anger in a whisper, but her heaving breasts, which Julien remarked with pleasure, bespoke her outrage.

"My lord, I do not recall ever having evinced a desire, as you phrased it, to attend the dancing at Almack's! And you know quite well what your escort would imply, indeed promise to all present!"

It seemed to Kate at that moment that flickering lights shaped like tiny devils danced in his gray eyes. Her hands formed into fists. How she would have loved to strike that complacent look from his face!

She was disconcerted when he appeared to have read her violent thoughts. "Now, dear Kate," he soothed, "it would be unseemly for a lady to strike a gentleman in so public a place."

"I am not your 'dear' Kate," she snapped.

"Ah, but you very soon will be, my dear." He spoke the words quietly, but she could feel the strength of purpose behind them.

She bit her lower lip and quickly averted her face. With an effort she forced herself to say in a calmer voice: "Why will you not leave me alone? Do you think me such a fool that I would not quickly guess that it was you who are responsible for my visit to London? What is it you want of me?" As if she found her query absurd, she hastened to say: "I have told you that I have no wish to wed anyone! Why can you not leave me in peace?"

He answered her in a low voice, without hesitation: "I love you, Kate. If I really believed that you do not care for me, I would withdraw, though unwillingly, for it would mean a continued life of unhappiness for you with your father. But I cannot and I will not believe that you are indifferent to me,

Kate. I have watched you when you were not aware of it. Your eyes give you away . . . and, your response to my kiss."

"I do not wish to wed you, Julien, no matter the . . . arrogant assumptions you have dared to make about my feelings!"

"But you will wed me, Kate." His voice was gentle.

"Your choice is a foolish one, Julien. You lie to yourself. It is only because I rejected you that you now want me. It is only your wounded pride. Oh, why do you look at me so? How can you want a wife who does not love you?"

He pulled her hand unwillingly from her lap and held it in an iron grip. "You must wed me, Kate, if for naught else to escape the cruelty of your father."

Kate looked down at his long fingers closed tightly over her gloved hand. She heard her own voice as if from a great distance: "I do not wish to marry any man, Julien."

"That is unfortunate, Kate, and, I think, untrue. But you now have no choice in the matter."

"You cannot bend me to your will, Julien. You have evidence that my father has tried."

He reeled back as though she had struck him and said harshly: "My God, Kate, do you think I would ever hurt you?"

"You have humiliated me, Julien. That is worse than the physical pain of my father's cane."

"Humiliated you," he repeated blankly, his grip loosening on her hand.

She saw that she had upset him, and pressing her advantage, she said with cutting sarcasm: "You must beware, my lord, that someone does not place a higher bid with my father!"

Julien had a great urge to shake her until her teeth rattled. He said savagely: "Do not be a fool, Kate! I have borne with your antics quite long enough! If you push me further, I will forcibly drag you out of here, perhaps to my yacht in Southampton. After several days in my company, my dear, you will be quite willing to accept me as your husband!"

Kate gave him a look of pure disdain and said blightingly: "Since you are a . . . licentious rake, I suppose that would be in your style! Let me tell you, you odious, conceited . . . arrogant . . ." As she could think of no more suitable epithets, she faltered a moment and finished in a rush: "I would sooner marry a . . . a . . . toad! Your threat is laughable, my lord!"

Julien took a firm grip on himself. He could not help but admire her courage and spirit. He had failed to intimidate her. God, but she was beautiful, he thought, her breasts rising and falling, her vivid green eyes flashing her outrage.

Kate took his silence for defeat. At last she had bested him! Unaccountably, she found herself swallowing convulsively, tears very near to the surface. Her victory seemed a hollow one.

"Good evening, Julien, Lady Katharine. I hope that you are enjoying the play. And you, Lady Katharine, I trust you are enjoying London?"

The tension between them was broken by Sir Hugh's words. Kate was overcome with embarrassment and found that her tongue was thick and unmoving in her mouth.

Julien cursed silently under his breath, forced a smile of welcome on his face, and said easily: "Good to see you, Hugh. Won't you please join us?" He shot Kate a look of mischief and added: "Kate and I have just been discussing the merits of . . . yachts!"

"Oh, I see," Hugh responded uncomfortably. He noted Kate's flushed face and quickly came to the conclusion that his presence was *de trop*. He raised his hand and said hurriedly: "I believe I see someone waving to me. I will take my leave now. Indeed a pleasure, Lady Katharine, to see you again."

He took a step backward, freedom within his reach, when, to the chagrin of the entire company, Lady Bellingham jerked up her head, blinked her eyes, and announced in a flurry of words: "Oh, dear. I declare I must have dropped off for a moment. Sir Hugh . . . how charming to see you, dear boy! Have you been keeping Julien and Katharine company?"

Hugh took a deep breath, cast an apologetic glance at Julien, and bowed low to Lady Bellingham. "Your servant, ma'am. Actually, I was just about to take my leave."

"He noticed a friend . . . waving to him," Julien added, his white teeth flashing.

Kate glared at Julien, and having found her tongue at last, said to Hugh with honeyed sweetness: "We would count it a great honor, sir, if you would deign to stay awhile with us. Surely your friend will understand."

"Well-said, Katharine," Lady Bellingham agreed. "Come,

Hugh, sit beside me." She patted the empty chair beside her, and Hugh, defeated, sat down.

Kate knew but a fleeting moment of victory, for the box was small, and although Hugh was slender, they were forced to move their chairs even closer together. She felt Julien's thigh pressing against hers, and the gentle pressure sent again the tingling sensation coursing through her body. She cursed him silently for having such a confusing effect on her. Fortunately the lights were dimmed at that moment and the curtain rose for the second act.

Julien felt her reaction and sat back, a self-satisfied smile on his face. For the remainder of the play he indulged in various pleasurable fancies.

Had anyone later asked him to discuss the merits of Kemble's performance, he would have been quite unworthy of the task.

Kate did not awake until nearly noon of the next day. She felt surprisingly well rested and alert despite the fact that she had not fallen into her bed until well after two o'clock in the morning. She rose, eased her feet into slippers, and pulled on a wrapper. She thought of Julien and jerked the bell cord with more violence than was necessary.

Eliza appeared but a few moments later, carrying a tray with crunchy rolls and hot chocolate. "Good morning, my lady," she said brightly. "Cook just baked the rolls for you. Piping hot, they are!"

"Thank you, Eliza," Kate replied with a smile, forcing Julien momentarily from her mind. She took a sip of the chocolate, savoring its sweetness.

"Your new green velvet gown has just arrived, my lady, in time for you to wear to Almack's this evening. I went around to Madame Giselle's myself this morning to fetch it, Lady Bellingham being in quite a taking that it would not be ready in time."

Eliza felt rather deflated that this news did not appear to excite her mistress.

The crunchy roll seemed to revert to dry dough in Kate's mouth. She lowered her head so that Eliza would not see her discomfiture. Almack's. She could envision the curious stares and the smug glances; the whispered comments behind gloved hands.

"I thank you, Eliza, for your trouble," Kate finally answered, not wishing to appear churlish to her maid. "Then you know that Lady Bellingham is planning to attend Almack's this evening?"

"Oh, yes, my lady. Walpole is in quite a tizzy about how to best arrange her ladyship's hair," Eliza replied. She picked up a brush to comb out the tangles from Kate's messed hair. She fancied that Walpole was jealous of her attending the beautiful Lady Katharine.

Damn him, Kate thought furiously, thumping down her cup of chocolate on the tray. He had told her himself about their attendance to Almack's this evening so that she would not have the opportunity to refuse Lady Bellingham, were the good lady the one to suggest it.

Still glorying in Walpole's jealousy, Eliza brushed the long silken tresses, oblivious of her mistress's anger, and said enthusiastically: "If you would not mind, my lady, I would like to dress your hair high on top of your head, in curls. You will be the most beautiful lady present!"

"As you wish, Eliza," Kate responded distractedly. She added quickly, seeing the hurt look on her maid's face: "Do forgive me. Eliza, it is just that . . . well, I have many things on my mind."

The day was already half gone and the remainder passed much too quickly for Kate. She restlessly paced back and forth in her room, alternately shaking her fist in the direction of Grosvenor Square and cursing herself for her inability to find a solution to her most immediate problem. She felt that she might as well be an actor on the stage saying lines and going through motions provided solely by the earl. If only there were some way she could spike his guns!

Eliza interrupted her rantings to announce that a young gentleman was downstairs asking to see her.

"A young gentleman?" Kate asked, surprised.

"Yes, my lady," Eliza affirmed. "He did not give his name, saying that you would want to see him."

Puzzled at this, Kate quickly patted some strands of hair into place, smoothed her gown, and hurried downstairs to the drawing room.

"Harry!" Kate stood poised an instant in the doorway before running into her brother's arms. "Oh, my dear . . . what ever are you doing here? I had no idea . . . oh, it is so good to see you!" She buried her head against his shoulder and wrapped her arms tightly around his neck. At last! An ally who would help her escape!

Harry hugged her briefly and replied with a touch of embarrassment: "Lord, Kate . . . of course it's me!"

He firmly took her shoulders and pushed her back. He looked down into her glowing face and said cheerfully: "What looks you are in, sister. I see that town life agrees with you! You must be cutting quite a dash!" He held her at arm's length and critically surveyed her modish yellow muslin gown, an appraising gleam of appreciation in his eyes.

"Oh, the gown . . . it is nothing!" she exclaimed, hugging him again.

"Now, old girl, you mustn't ruin my new waistcoat," he reproved.

Kate laughed and stepped back to regard her brother. "Well, I say, Harry, it is you who are looking . . . terribly smart! Those yellow stripes are quite dazzling!"

Harry beamed at her proudly. "Now, don't sidetrack me, Kate! You certainly know why I am here—you sly puss! My congratulations to you, little sister. I must say, though, I was surprised to hear from Father that you had attached the Earl of March. Quite a feat, my dear!" In truth, Harry was very nearly speechless at the news. His Kate getting married—his little sister! But now as he looked down at her, he realized that she was quite beautiful, certainly lovely enough for an earl. Dressed in the height of fashion, she looked already like a countess.

"Father wrote you?"

"Don't look so surprised, Kate. Of course he did. Quite right of him to do so, you know. Come, let us sit down . . . you can't leave a guest standing in the middle of the room! I will tell you all about it, and then you must tell me how you managed to trap the earl!"

Kate gritted her teeth. She gazed at her brother's open, smiling face for a moment, bit her lower lip, and held her tongue. Neither of them talked of anything of consequence until she had served Harry a glass of sherry and sat herself down beside him.

"Now, Harry, tell me what our father wrote and why you are here." Her voice was a trifle hard, but she could not help it.

"I got a letter from father just last week. Told me in great detail how the earl wanted you to gain some town polish before your wedding."

Kate made a choking sound into her sherry.

"There, there, Kate," he continued kindly, "I know that you must have difficulty believing your good fortune—"

"Yes, yes, Harry," she interrupted. She had to hear from her brother's own lips the depths of the earl's and her father's perfidy.

"I must say, Kate, the settlement made my head spin! Father wrote that the earl is not only settling his debts but that he also wished to buy my colors. Lord, Kate, I never hoped for this!" Harry's eyes were shining in excitement, and Kate fancied she could picture what was in her brother's mind. Harry astride a magnificent black charger, dressed in a dashing hussar's uniform.

Indeed, she was very nearly right, and Harry pulled himself away unwillingly from his delightful vision. He continued happily: "Father also sent me some money. So I got myself rigged up and came to London. I got here just this morning."

"But it is afternoon, Harry. Why did you not come to see me when you arrived?" She spoke quickly, in an effort to give herself time to think. Harry as an ally, as a rescuer, was fast fading as a possibility. Lord, did the earl think of everything? He had bought her father, and now he had made Harry's fondest wish come true. It seemed that she was quite alone in manning her defenses.

Harry leaned over and patted her hand with brotherly affection. "Now, Kate, don't be offended. You must know that it was only proper that I pay my respects first to my future brother-in-law."

It was with some difficulty that Kate remembered her question to Harry. "You what?" she asked uncertainly, unwilling to believe her ears.

"I went to see the earl," Harry repeated with great patience. "Lord, what a mansion he has in Grosvenor Square! But of course you have been there. . . ."

As Kate did not deny this, being quite unable to fit two words together at the moment, Harry continued serenely: "You know, Kate, I was certainly wrong about his lordship. Dashed nice fellow . . . not at all puffed up! Why, we spent quite four hours together discussing the regiment I wanted to be in and, of course, other things."

Harry paused and looked at his sister. She was no longer

the wild hoyden, dressed in boy's breeches, ready for any lark. She looked positively regal. He wondered at her quietness, for it was quite unlike her. But having spent the entire morning with the elegant Earl of March, he decided that her silence was properly due to her modesty.

"You are . . . in favor of this match, Harry?" Kate asked in a leaden voice.

"Don't be a widgeon, Kate!" he exclaimed. He eyed her warily for a moment. "What is wrong with you, sister? . . . never known you to ask stupid questions before."

Kate saw the happy flush on her brother's handsome face and gave her head a tiny shake. Harry would think her mad if she were now to tell him that she found the very idea of marriage to the earl abhorrent. And how could she tell him? The earl had swooped down into Harry's life and granted him his greatest wish!

"Never seen you succumb to womanish vapors," Harry observed, frowning. "Lord, Kate, you will make the perfect countess! You mustn't think you are not up to snuff!"

Kate clutched her hands together in her lap and gazed at her brother, the only person she loved in the world. She would not, indeed, she could not risk losing his affection. She forced a smile and continued instead: "Do not bother yourself, Harry."

To forestall further comments on her marriage to the earl, she said hurriedly: "We go to Almack's tonight. Will you accompany us, Harry?" She spoke the words lightly, but in a flash she realized that if Harry were to also be her escort, it might perhaps lessen the impact of Julien's presence with her.

Harry stared incredulously at her and exclaimed in a voice of loathing: "Almack's? You must have rust in your brain box, Kate! Isn't at all my style, as you well know!"

Seeing her disappointment, Harry added more gently: "I will come by tomorrow, Kate. The earl offered me one of his hacks, and we can go riding in the park."

Kate's breasts heaved in indignation at this final blow. "You would not use one of the earl's horses, Harry!"

"Don't be a nodcock, Kate! It's quite proper, my dear. After all, he will be my brother-in-law in a week's time."

"I . . . I see what you mean, Harry," she replied in a low voice. The earl had told Harry they were to be married in a week! Words of bitter recrimination stuck in her throat, but she said nothing.

Harry clasped her hand and exclaimed happily, "Good Lord . . . my sister a countess! Only one more week, Kate!"

Kate had not yet been to King Street and she found the rows of buildings, including Almack's, not to be as grand as she had supposed. Almack's had been so touted that she had half-expected to see a structure as impressive as Carlton House. She had to admit, though, once they entered the enormous entrance hall filled with branches of glowing candles and lined with very superior-looking footmen, who gave the impression of conferring a favor by admitting guests, that she seemed indeed to be stepping into the very inner sanctum of society. As Julien divested her of her cloak, she heard strains of a waltz coming from one of the rooms that branched off the hall, and wondered with a sinking in her stomach how many people would be there to witness her arrival on Julien's arm.

She knew she looked in particularly fine fettle this evening in her high-waisted green velvet gown that hung straight to the floor, accentuating her slender figure. The yards of green velvet were broken by rows of white Valenciennes lace delicately sewn to fit snugly under her breasts. She unconsciously fingered the exquisite emerald necklace with its intricate gold setting that circled her neck. It was indeed kind of Lady Bellingham, she thought, to have lent her the beautiful emerald set. There were also a bracelet and earrings. The jewels sparkled with strange green lights, enhancing the whiteness of her skin and matching perfectly the color of her gown.

As Julien turned back to her, she was aware of the open expression of admiration on his face, and she felt a moment of power over him. She met his gaze with a cold stare. Let him admire her as much as he wished, she thought with a pettish shrug of her shoulders; she would show him that he was not one whit closer to achieving his ends.

She graciously gave him her arm, and Julien guided her and Lady Bellingham down the long hall and into a noble, high-ceilinged room where the glitter of the candles was rivaled by the sparkling gems and bright-colored apparel of the assembled company, who were dipping and bowing in the steps of a country dance. Rows of burgundy brocade-covered chairs lined stark white walls, and were occupied, for the most part, by turbaned dowagers, who formed small chattering groups.

It seemed to her when the portly white-haired announcer cleared his throat and called out each of their names that the music grew softer and many eyes turned in their direction. Julien leaned toward her and said softly: "Well, my beautiful shrew, did I not tell you that you would outshine all the lovely ladies present?"

"If I am such a shrew, my lord," Kate hissed, ignoring his compliment, "then you must be quite mad in your intentions!"

"Quite mad, Kate," he agreed. "We are well-matched."

In a calculated gesture, Julien drew her arm through his and escorted both ladies to the far side of the room to where the patronesses of Almack's held their court. He realized that their arrival was causing an instant sensation, as the rumors of his imminent marriage to an unknown girl from the country had provided polite society with choice conversation for the past week.

Of the four patronesses, only the Countess Lieven and Mrs. Drummond Burrell were present this evening. The raven-haired Countess Lieven, wife to the Russian ambassador, raised her dark eyes and gazed at Kate with open curiosity. Lady Bellingham, long acquainted with both patronesses, greeted them and moved aside for Julien to present Katharine.

Himself a favorite with both ladies for some years, Julien said with easy familiarity: "Countess, Mrs. Burrell, I would like to present Lady Katharine Brandon."

Kate repeated polite words to the Countess Lieven, who made a rather startling picture in pink satin and gauze. The countess smiled at her, not unkindly, and Kate turned to Mrs. Drummond Burrell. The lady was appraising her coldly, her hawklike nose thrust upward to a height that even Kate had not achieved. An idea burgeoned in her mind, and she executed it without further examination.

Proffering only an infinitesimal curtsy, she observed to Mrs. Drummond Burrell in her coldest and most distant voice: "Almack's is not as elegant as I was led to believe."

Lady Bellingham froze in shocked silence and stared aghast at Katharine. She would have been thankful had the floor opened beneath her feet and dropped her into oblivion.

Julien gave no sign of having noticed anything extraordinary in Kate's remark and stood quite at ease waiting to see what would happen.

The Countess Lieven gasped aloud and darted an expectant glance at Mrs. Drummond Burrell. Mrs. Drummond Burrell, however, moved not a muscle in the tense moment of silence that followed.

Kate thrust her chin higher and waited to see the result of her outrageous comment. Surely Julien must be acutely embarrassed at her behavior. Well, she would show him that she was not a helpless female, a puppet to be dangled willy-nilly on his strings! Perhaps he would realize that he was mistaken in her character and pack her back to the country.

To the infinite surprise of all present, the haughty mask Mrs. Drummond Burrell presented to the world loosened and her thin lips parted in a slight smile. Reputed to be the most insufferably proud lady in London society, which indeed she was, she realized with a flash that at last she had found a kindred spirit. She dismissed the scathing set-down that had instantly come to her lips. Long used to simpering debutantes and ladies of her own rank who were openly terrified of her scathing tongue, she saw with something of a shock that here was someone, indeed a mere girl, who was not in the least afraid of her. A girl, in fact, who was openly provoking her.

A sense of humor that she thought long dead was resurrected and she replied with a hint of amusement in her voice: "Indeed you are right, my dear, but you see, Almack's is considered almost a shrine, an old revered meeting place for society. Though the rooms are not as . . . elegant as one could wish, we hope that you will not quite disdain it, and turn your attention rather to the people you will meet here."

Kate, who was not aware of the terrifying rule over society held by Mrs. Drummond Burrell, decided after a brief moment of disappointment that the lady was but another supporter of the earl's. Thus she did not unbend and flush to the roots of her hair at her rudeness, as those present expected. Rather, she turned and gazed briefly with a distinct air of boredom around the room. Very slowly she raised incredulous eyebrows, turned back to the lady, and replied with careless indifference: "Indeed, ma'am, I suppose that what you say may prove to be true."

She would have said more, but she chanced from the corner of her eye to see the obvious agitation on Lady Bellingham's face. As she did not wish what she hoped to be her own social ostracism to descend on the hapless Lady Bellingham, she merely stared with an unconcerned gaze at the two patronesses and started to turn away.

Mrs. Drummond Burrell found herself vastly entertained by this unconventional girl. She commanded Kate in a not unkind voice: "Stay for a moment and converse with me, my dear." She looked briefly at Julien for confirmation. "The earl will, I am certain, not begrudge me your company for a few moments."

Julien wanted to laugh aloud at the look of puzzled confusion on Kate's face but managed to bow deeply and say with great aplomb: "Lady Katharine finds herself honored, ma'am. I gladly relinquish her to you."

"My dear St. Clair, I am quite certain that you do not relinquish your betrothed willingly," she remarked acidly, "but five minutes without her . . . most interesting company should not leave you quite downcast."

Julien met Mrs. Drummond Burrell's eyes with a distinct gleam in his own, turned to Lady Bellingham, who stood with her mouth unbecomingly open, and said with a quiver in his voice: "Come, ma'am, we will leave Katharine and refresh ourselves with a glass of orgeat."

Lady Bellingham cast Julien a rather bewildered glance and promptly thrust her arm through his. It was she who bore him off.

Kate felt completely at sea. It did not seem possible that she had not managed to disgrace herself. She was being asked to enjoy a comfortable prose with a forbidding lady whom she had grossly insulted! Defeated, she dropped her cold disdain and seated herself gracefully in the chair next to Mrs. Drummond Burrell. As she felt no fear of the lady, she spoke openly, and had she but realized it, quite charmingly. She noticed the look of awe on the Countess Lieven's face, but not understanding, she dismissed it, and gave her full attention to the questions of Mrs. Drummond Burrell.

She relaxed and responded after a few moments with friendliness to the lady's inquiries about her family. It was like a dousing of cold water when Mrs. Drummond Burrell remarked appreciatively: "The St. Clair emeralds look as if they had been made especially for you, my dear." She added with cutting humor to the Countess Lieven: "They always reminded me of heavy colorless green stones on Caroline's unprepossessing neck!

"Caroline is, of course, to be your mother-in-law, the late

earl's wife," she added, turning back to Kate. She did not notice that Kate's color had mounted, and continued to enthusiastically enumerate the shortcomings of the dowager Countess of March.

It was just as well that Mrs. Drummond Burrell did not expect any interruptions in her monologue, for Kate was so furious at the earl's latest underhanded trick that it took all the control she could muster to cloak her anger from the patronesses. How very devious of Lady Bellingham to conveniently forget to mention that the emeralds belonged to the earl!

Mrs. Drummond Burrell smiled with great understanding at Kate's distractedness.

She looked up to see the earl approach and leaned over and patted Kate's hand. "Your betrothed approaches, my dear." She added with great sincerity, "Although the Earl of March has been the object for many years of matchmaking mamas and indeed is a charming young man, I confess that I think him more the lucky one."

Julien heard her last words and smiled with undisguised tenderness at Kate. The look was not lost on the two ladies, and for a brief instant they were drawn back into time, to such magic moments of their own.

"I am, of course, in absolute agreement with you, ma'am. I count myself the most fortunate of men."

Julien offered Kate his arm, and she rose and stood beside him.

Mrs. Drummond Burrell nodded her dismissal and said to Kate as she turned to go: "We will talk again, my dear, after you return from your wedding trip."

Kate did not realize it, but from that moment, her success in the ton was assured. Her intimate conversation with Mrs. Drummond Burrell was remarked by all present, and as Julien led her on the rounds of introductions, she was treated with a respect bordering upon awe. Because she was seething with anger, she responded with the most brief and clipped of phrases. Ladies and gentlemen vied to meet the seemingly proud but, of course, interesting Lady Katharine Brandon.

When the band struck up a waltz, Julien turned in the direction of the two patronesses and arched his brow upward in a silent question. Mrs. Drummond Burrell waved her hand and nodded, a benign smile on her face.

"Come, Kate, dance with me. As you have observed, it is mandatory that you have the consent of the patronesses to dance the waltz. I have just secured that permission."

Still fuming with unspoken anger, Kate allowed him to lead her onto the dance floor and encircle her waist with his arm. As he whirled her around to the slow German music, he felt her body slowly relax against him as she gracefully followed his lead. He bent down and felt her soft hair tickle his chin. "What, little termagant, no words of abuse this evening?" he asked.

Kate jerked her head up at his words and her eyes smoldered darkly. "This is not a play, Julien. I am not so easily won as Petruchio's Kate!"

His response was to tighten his grip about her slender waist. He was pleased to see a dull red flush creep over her pale cheeks.

"You see, Kate," he whispered close to her ear, "though you are but a girl, we both know that you are all fire and passion beneath that cold facade. Admit this to yourself, my dear. Stop fighting me. You must not be afraid, Kate . . . I will teach you."

But she was afraid, sickeningly afraid. Never before had he spoken to her with such ill-disguised intent. She suddenly felt very weak, and she could sense the color drain from her face. She tried to pull away from him, but he held her fast.

"Do not give the world cause for comment," he chided gently. "We are betrothed, and in their eyes, the happiest of couples."

"Would that I had a whip, I would take it to you willingly!" she hissed.

"When we are married, I will give you that opportunity," he retorted swiftly. He bent his head close to hers and added in a caressing voice: "I shall very much enjoy wresting it from your hands."

"I hate you, Julien," she gasped, her voice tight with fury. "And do not think I am such a fool . . . I know now that these are the St. Clair emeralds! Oh, how I hate you!"

"You must take heed, dear Kate, not to become repetitious in your conversation. You would not wish to bore your husband," he replied calmly.

Bereft of speech, Kate narrowed her eyes and gave him a look of loathing. He returned her stormy look with one of amusement.

"Do allow me to congratulate you on your most . . . unusual performance for Mrs. Drummond Burrell. Unfortunately, you picked quite the wrong person on whom to try your antics. Ah, yes, you hoped to disgrace yourself, did you not, Kate? Let me tell you, my dear, that the good lady finally met someone more cold and haughty than herself! A strange coincidence, is it not?"

Kate wondered at that moment if she had been born under an unlucky star. Everything seemed to go awry. She looked up at him, her eyes filled with misery. "Why do you torment me?"

She was looking up at him with such pained confusion that Julien was sorely tempted to throw his masterful stratagem to the winds and comfort her, perhaps even to plead his case with her again. But he caught himself, realizing that it would be a fatal mistake.

"What would you, Kate? Shall I languish at your feet like that fool Bleddoes?" He shook his head, his strong white teeth flashing. "No, dear Kate, it is a strong hand you need, and I am the only one to suit you!"

"I will surely make you sorry for this!" she cried, her words sounding even to herself like the hollow threat of an angry child.

He merely arched an elegant brow and whirled her faster and faster until she was panting for breath.

When at last the interminable waltz ended, Kate looked up to see herself being regarded with shy admiration by a young man clad in colorful regimentals. He reminded her of Harry. She shot Julien a disdainful look and smiled most beguilingly at the young man. He began a tentative approach.

"Another Bleddoes, Kate. I pray that you do not break his heart to spite me." He smiled down at her and enthusiastically waved the young man forward.

Kate growled under her breath and tossed her head. She smiled charmingly and stepped forward, her hand outstretched.

The young man coughed and asked shyly: "If you do not mind, my lord . . ."

"Not at all. My betrothed is very much taken with young men in uniform, as her brother is shortly to join the cavalry."

"I believe, sir, that it is from me you should seek your permission," Kate interrupted sharply.

"Do not lead him a merry dance, Kate," Julien said as Kate firmly took hold of the young man's arm.

He stood quietly for a moment as he watched her look with the most appealing expression at her young gallant. She was flirting outrageously to spite him. His mouth curved into a rueful smile. He could not imagine ever being bored by Kate.

"So that's the girl you're going to marry, eh, Julien?"

Julien turned to see his aunt, Lady Mary Tolford, standing at his elbow.

"Good evening, Aunt. Yes, that is Lady Katharine Brandon," he replied.

"Well, I'll say this for you, Julien, your taste in women, like that of your grandfather, is impeccable. But you know, my boy," she added thoughtfully, gazing at Kate, "the girl doesn't look much of a breeder to me. Far too slender! Look at those long legs . . . like a boy's!"

"Really, Aunt, you shock me!" He looked down at her in amusement. "I am not even married, and you are already planning to fill my nursery with future earls."

Lady Mary tapped her fan on his sleeve and replied sternly: "The St. Clairs are a long, proud line, Julien. You've picked a lady of quality, no doubt about that, but there are heirs too, my boy. It's your duty, and about time, too, I might add!"

"My dear Aunt, you need have no fears," Julien assured her gravely. "I promise you an heir within the year."

"I suppose you've informed your mama that she is about to become a mother-in-law. I'll wager she became hysterical," she said with relish.

Fortunately Julien had just that afternoon paid a long-overdue visit to his fond parent and informed her of his imminent marriage. She did resort to her smelling salts upon hearing he was to wed a Brandon, and it had taken him a good half-hour to soothe her ruffled sensibilities.

"Yes, Aunt, I have seen Mama, and no, she did not have hysterics." He smiled wryly at the look of disappointment on his aunt's face and hastened to add, for Lady Mary Tolford was quite his favorite relative: "She did rely, however, on very strong smelling salts."

Lady Mary gave a crow of delight, envisioning with some satisfaction the look of shock on her sister-in-law's face. She had always thought Lady Caroline a widgeon, and now that the dowager countess was getting older, she had taken to dosing herself with every conceivable medicine. As the state of her health was also Lady Caroline's favorite topic of conversation, Lady Mary had found her own nerves near to the breaking point, and thus, recently, had paid fewer and fewer visits to Brook Street.

"Now, my dear Aunt, if you will excuse me, I must detach my betrothed from that gay young buck. It is my duty, as you said."

Lady Mary gave Julien a light rap on the arm with her fan. "Be off with you, rogue," she admonished fondly.

Julien was careful to ensure that he danced three waltzes with Kate. Two waltzes between an unmarried couple caused wild speculation. Three placed the gold band on her finger. He wondered when Kate would discover this fact and rip up at him.

Evidently she was not informed, for the remainder of the evening she maintained a stony silence in his presence, pointedly ignoring even the most provoking of comments. Even when he informed her matter-of-factly that he had procured a special license so they could be wed within the week and that her trousseau would be arriving at the Bellingham mansion on the morrow, she kept her eyes downcast and refused to favor him with a reply. He thought at first that she was employing a new tactic, but as the evening continued, he wondered if she was finally coming to her senses and had given up her losing battle with him. It was very late when he deposited Lady Bellingham and Kate at the Bellingham mansion.

Only later, as he lay comfortably in his own bed, did it occur to him to worry about her behavior. She had been too pliant, too docile, her surrender almost too immediate and complete. He did not sleep well that night.

As for Kate, she did not sleep at all; she was far too busy packing her portmanteau and making her plans. Had the dashing young officer in his colorful regimentals known of the daring idea he was giving Kate, he would not have been so voluble in his praise of Paris. Kate was but half-listening as they danced, too aware of Julien's eyes following her around the dance floor. But she smiled prettily up at the young man and he felt emboldened to speak of his adventures in a Paris now freed from Napoleon's influence. He had been astounded at the gaiety of the French people, the prosperity that was restored under Louis, and above all, the enthusiastic attitude of the Parisians toward the English, whom they now regarded as their liberators.

It was a short time later, as she stood drinking a glass of orgeat, that the promise of the young officer's words struck her forcibly. Smarting from her successive failures to rout the earl, and seeing help from no other quarter—Harry now being in the ranks of the earl's ardent supporters—she decided that it was time she took matters into her own hands. She had danced to the earl's tune long enough!

Why should she not go to Paris? She had always told herself that she wished to be her own mistress. Surely she would be the most despicable of hypocrites if she did not jump at the chance to be free forever of her father's influence and the earl's autocratic person. It required not much mental struggle on Kate's part before she convinced herself that only a coward would let such an opportunity slip by.

As she sat now in her darkened room, she recalled the earl's last words to her about her trousseau. Conceited man! He had not even bothered to consult her! A smug grin lit up her face. He could take his special license and his trousseau and go to the devil! She would be far away, free . . .

But to do what, to be what? A vision of herself in a foreign land, alone, rose in her mind. She felt a wave of apprehension and a taste of fear. "I shall find employment and be quite comfortable," she told herself stoutly. She shook her head vehemently to blot out further unpleasant thoughts of her future. Surely she could make her way well enough. She spoke French passably well and had sufficient accomplishments to make a position of governess not altogether ridiculous!

Kate folded a pair of stockings and stuffed them into the portmanteau. It occurred to her for the first time that her venture would require funds. She lit a candle and searched methodically through her dresser and reticule. After some moments she scooped up her small fortune and sat cross-legged on her bed, sorting the coins into different stacks. Uncertain of the cost to reach Paris, she decided it best to be overgenerous in her estimates. This deduction made, she was left staring with some dismay at four guineas. She frowned and dismissed the problem, telling herself with more bravado than she felt that she would simply have to find employment very quickly.

She drummed her fingers and thought of how she would reach Paris. Though she knew nothing of coach schedules from London to the coast, she reasoned that surely there were such vehicles leaving early in the morning. Once at the coast, there could be no problem finding a packet to take her to France.

Having resolved such mundane problems to her satisfaction, she sat back and closed her eyes. She thought of the scandal that would result from her disappearance. And Julien. He would finally receive his just deserts! He would no doubt despise her and curse her soundly for making him look the fool. But a fool he was for thinking he could snap his fingers and believe she would docilely submit to his commands!

But Harry was quite a different matter. For him, her marriage to the earl meant his colors, a career in a crack regiment. It would be, doubtless, a severe blow. Perhaps he would never wish to see her again. Tears stung her eyes and spilled onto her cheeks. For a brief moment her determination faltered. She thought about her own life, how all choice had been wrested from her. Sir Oliver would manage somehow to buy Harry his colors, for Harry was, after all, his favored son.

She angrily dashed her hand across her cheeks. She had no use for tears.

Just before dawn she slipped quietly out of her room and sped lightly down the stairs. The front door groaned in protest, and the sound was so loud to her own ears that she stood frozen, waiting for the servants to descend upon her.

The house was silent. She pulled her cloak closely about her shoulders and over her head and stepped out into the night. She gazed a moment up and down the empty square, clutched her portmanteau tightly, and walked quickly away from the Bellingham mansion.

8

Kate Brandon made her way with forced enthusiasm to the Luxembourg Gardens after quitting her rather dismal room on the Rue Saint Germain. She sat down on a wooden bench and drew the journal from her pocket, when her attention was drawn to the sound of a child's voice. She looked up to see a small boy skip past her with his nanny in pursuit. A gentleman and lady strolled by, their heads close in intimate conversation. There was a gentle smile in the gentleman's eye and a shy look of confidence on the lady's face. She silently cursed the romantic gardens, heaved a deep sigh, and forced herself to turn back to her unopened journal. She assiduously thumbed her way through the pages until she found the advertisements for positions. It seemed to her that no one ever filled the various posts, for the same ones appeared day after day. A butcher's assistant, a link boy . . . a governess. A dark look came over her face on seeing the post.

She had applied for it with alacrity but a few days before. Outfitted in her most subdued gray high-necked gown, her hair drawn into a severe bun at the nape of her neck, she had sounded the knocker at the solid brick residence in the heart of a very respectable bourgeois area of Paris. After a few moments the front door swung open and she confidently faced a rather pinch-faced butler who demanded without preamble what the "young person" wanted. Upon being informed in rather halting French, punctuated with gestures to the post in the journal, the butler allowed a flicker of surprise to pass over his cadaverous face and cast Kate a look that made her feel as if she were some sort of oddity. He said quite unnecessarily: "Mademoiselle is English. I will see if Madame wishes to see you."

She bore this with fortitude and was admitted not many minutes later into a large *salle* that struck her as being furnished in less than the first stare of elegance. Like the *salle,* the large, somberly dressed Madame Tréboucher looked to be a bastion of respectability.

"You are English," Madame announced frostily.

Finding this statement to be unarguable, Kate replied simply and proceeded to inform Madame of her aspirations. Madame was silent for a moment, her thick lips pursed. She looked Kate up and down with cold appraisal and finally announced with the utmost disdain that Mademoiselle was far too young for such a responsible position, and furthermore, she wanted no red-haired Englishwoman running free in her house to seduce her son and her husband! Kate stared at her openmouthed, and finding herself unable to vent her outrage in the French tongue, stiffly rose and stalked out without a word. Once outside, she raised her fist to the heavens and demanded that God strike down the ill-bred bourgeois Madame Tréboucher.

Kate sat back on the bench, the journal lying in her lap, and stared for a moment ahead of her. Her flight to Paris had been so utterly undramatic that she had quite decided that her luck had changed, that perhaps she had not been born under the wrong stars after all. But now, after more than a week in Paris, her small hoard of coins practically gone, she felt near to panic. A growl of hunger in her stomach reminded her sharply that panic over her situation would not buy food, nor would it pay the rent for her room for the next week. She scanned the remainder of the positions on the page with fierce intensity. A milliner's assistant on the Rue de la Bourgoine. What a paltry wage, barely enough to maintain the small room! She curled her lips and with a determined effort repeated aloud the street number.

She looked up, the street address on her lips, when she saw a tall, elegantly dressed gentleman walking purposefully down the hedged walk towards her. Her eyes widened in disbelief. The earl . . . Julien! All her careful planning . . . for naught!

"Damn him!" she cried. She jumped to her feet, the journal gliding unnoticed to the ground, and took to her heels in the opposite direction. Her breath came in quick gasps and her violent exertion on a very hungry stomach made her dizzy. She pulled up short, weaving back and forth. The gardens blurred before her eyes; she took another uncertain step forward, only to find that two strong arms were around her and that her head was against his chest.

Julien held her against him none too gently and said in a hard, uncompromising voice: "Hold, Kate. Your game is over!"

She looked up unwillingly into his set face, and to her own chagrin, felt tears of frustration spill onto her cheeks.

"Oh, God, no! Please, please let me go, Julien!"

She sobbed in earnest, and brought up her fists to pound impotently at his chest.

His features softened, and a look of great tenderness came into his eyes. He tightened his arms about her and gently touched his cheek to her hair.

Finally so wearied and exhausted by her hunger and by her unwelcome relief at being pressed so close to him, she flattened her fists and lay weakly, even willingly, against him.

After a few moments she drew her head back from the circle of his arms and gave a watery sniff. She said in a matter-of-fact voice: "I am so hungry."

A smile lit his eyes and he raised a gloved hand to brush away the tears from her face.

"That is, at least, something I can remedy to your satisfaction."

There was no mockery in his voice, but Kate's own intense pride made it to be so, and she tried to wrench herself free of him, her cheeks flushed with sudden anger.

"I will not be made mock of!" she cried, glaring at him.

Julien arched his eyebrows and regarded her with mild surprise.

"I do not mock you, I merely offer you breakfast. Come, Kate, cry peace, at least until after you have eaten. You are not a worthy opponent on an empty stomach."

She would have liked very much to yell at him, to call him such names that he would take her in profound disgust, but she could think of no worse epithets than those she had many times before hurled at his head. It dawned on her with a good deal of force that she had finally lost.

"I should have gone to India."

Julien bit back sudden laughter and said instructively: "No, not India, I think, my dear Kate. There you would serve many men, being a beautiful woman without protection." He added reflectively: "Indeed, you are fortunate, my love. You need to serve but one man."

He ignored her growl of anger and took her arm. "Come, Kate. Let us go."

She fell into a stiff step beside him. As they emerged from the gardens, they passed once again the lady and gentleman and Kate saw the lady gaze at Julien coyly from beneath her lashes.

She heard herself mutter in disgust: "She deserves to be whipped."

"On that point, Kate, we find ourselves in complete agreement."

Her eyes flew to his face, her own blushing hotly. "I did not intend, that is, I . . ."

"What more could a man ask for?" he mused aloud. "I presume you will be a fiercely loyal and faithful wife." His eyes twinkled and he squeezed her arm possessively.

"Oh . . . how I hate you!" she cried. "You cannot force me to wed you, Julien!"

"We shall see, my dear, we shall see."

She flung away from him and looked doggedly ahead. Julien looked down at the beautiful face beside him. She was so very proud, and he admired her indomitable courage. Even when he wanted to shake her for her stubbornness, he could not but respect her.

When Eliza had come panting into his breakfast room the morning of Kate's flight, his first response was to want to spank her soundly the moment he got his hands on her. But then he grinned, for he had suspected that her docile behavior was anything but an indication that he had finally brought her to heel. She had certainly succeeded in making him feel the fool. He commanded Eliza not to say a word to Lady Bellingham and immediately dispatched several of his retainers to the posting houses in London. He was informed within two hours that a young lady answering Kate's description had taken the mail coach to Dover. So she was off to France, was she! Were he not certain in his own mind that she cared for him, he would have readily drawn the conclusion that such an outrageous and even dangerous venture by a young lady of breeding was an evident sign of loathing. But he was certain that somewhere Kate did harbor more tender emotions toward him. He looked impatiently toward getting this damned marriage over with!

He met briefly with Percy, Hugh, and Lady Bellingham. By that evening, the announcement that he and Lady Katharine Brandon were to meet in Paris and there to be wed was being circulated to all the appropriate quarters. He himself dispatched an announcement to the *Gazette*.

As he now guided Kate down the boulevard, his steps shortened to match hers, he wondered if she knew how much she had simplified his plans.

When he first arrived in Paris, he had thought to bring her to heel immediately. Upon reflection, however, he decided to give her free rein, hoping perhaps foolishly that when he came to her she would joyfully welcome him. Actually, he thought, she had, in her own way, welcomed him. Her eyes always betrayed her, and for a fleeting instant her pleasure and relief at seeing him were obvious. Had he truly wished to break her spirit, he would have held away from her longer; but he knew too well of her straitened circumstances, and he could not allow her to be alone any longer. His lips twisted into a grudging smile as he thought of her honest admission to being hungry. Lord, she was stubborn . . . but charmingly so.

Julien guided Kate into a small café off the boulevard. He quickly dismissed the idea of taking her to his lodgings. She had to eat, else she would never have the strength to go through the activities he had planned for the day and evening. He did not wish to chance her throwing the food at his head, and thought it less likely she would refuse to eat in a café than in his rooms.

The owner, observing that Quality had entered his modest establishment, bustled forward to provide his best service. He assisted the lady into her chair at the choicest table and hovered as the gentleman disposed himself gracefully across from her.

Julien ordered Kate a most liberal breakfast and for himself a cup of coffee. Kate seemed to find the checkered tablecloth of great interest. She removed her gloves and began with the greatest concentration to trace the red checks.

"The design is most fascinating," he said dryly after she had been engrossed in this activity for some time.

"Is it not?" she affirmed, keeping her head strictly down.

The owner returned shortly, laden with covered dishes. Julien applauded his decision to bring her here, for her eyes rested longingly on the plates of eggs, toast, kidneys, and the rasher of bacon. She ate quickly at first and then more slowly as the gnawing in her stomach eased. Abruptly she laid her fork down, sighed in contentment, and leaned back in her chair.

"You would have an instant friend in Sir Percy Blair-stock," Julien observed.

She looked at him blankly.

"A friend of mine who very much enjoys a good meal," he explained.

"I was hungry," she said defensively.

"Kate, when will you acquit me of malicious design? I was merely indulging in light conversation."

Kate's confidence had returned with each bite of food, and now she felt strong and self-assured. How could she have been such a weak fool as to cry?

She daintily passed her napkin over her lips, took a final sip of coffee, and made to rise. "I thank you, my lord, for the excellent repast. Perhaps when you are in Paris again, we can breakfast together."

Julien's hand shot out and he grabbed her arm. "Be seated, Kate!" he commanded. He tightened the pressure on her arm until, finally, she eased herself back into the chair.

"It appears that I must starve you if I wish a docile wife," he observed lightly.

She tried to pull away from him again, but he held her fast.

"If you try such a stunt again, little shrew, I shall apologize to our good owner, throw you over my shoulder, and carry you out! Do I make myself clear, Kate?"

His voice sounded menacing to Kate, and she found herself believing that he would do exactly as he said. In any case, she was unwilling to risk such a humiliating eventuality. She sat rigid, waiting to see what he would do.

"That is much better. Now, my dear, I have something of the utmost importance to say to you and you will attend me or it will be much the worse for you. For over a week now I have watched you try to make your way and have seen you fail time after time. Don't look so startled, Kate. Did you truly imagine that I would have difficulty in locating you? In any case, I did not come to you immediately because I wished you to discover for yourself that a young woman with no money, regardless of her breeding and talents, has little if any chance of earning an honest wage. I had hoped that after your experience with Madame Tréboucher you would come to your senses."

"How . . . how did you know of Madame Tréboucher?" she stammered.

"Dear goose, I have had you closely watched. Could you ever believe that I would leave my future wife alone, without protection, in such a city as Paris? As a matter of fact, I myself observed you leaving that woman's house." He looked faintly amused recalling the scene.

Kate found that she was trembling from humiliation. He had stood by and witnessed her chagrin! Unaccountably, the fact that he had not come to her sooner rankled; that he had waited and watched while she had made a total and utter fool of herself was too much to bear. "How could you!" she cried in a strangled voice.

"How could I what?" he asked, regarding her steadily.

Kate turned away quickly from his gaze and swallowed the rising lump in her throat. She could think of no reasonable answer.

"You do not wish to answer my question, Kate?"

He watched one slender hand form a fist and thought it politic to rescue her from her plight. He thought her utterly adorable at that moment. If only she would admit to herself that she cared for him, that she had wished wholeheartedly that he would come to her in Paris.

He said gently: "I believe we have sufficiently abused the topic. Let me return to what I have to say to you, Kate. We will presently go to Mademoiselle Phanie's, a most elegant milliner's shop. Then we will purchase the proper shoes for you. I have already acquired your gowns and other personal articles, but I found it quite beyond my ability to recall your size in shoes and to determine what kinds of charming confections look best on your auburn hair."

"I . . . I don't understand you," she stuttered, looking quite at sea. "You have bought me clothes?"

He nodded. "Yes, that is right. Morning dresses, evening gowns, riding clothes, chemises, shifts, ah, let me see, wrappers, nightgowns, and the like."

"But why?" she asked in a small voice.

"Patience, my Kate, and I shall tell you." He held her gaze steadily and continued matter-of-factly: "After we have suitably outfitted you, we shall proceed to my rooms and there you will be attired in your bridal clothes. Don't look so surprised, Kate. Could you doubt that I would not bring your trousseau with me? Promptly at five o'clock we are expected at the embassy, where we will be married by an English divine."

Julien had thought that she would scream at him like a fishwife. But she simply stared, pale-faced, her fingers clutching the edge of the table.

Kate felt Julien's eyes upon her, so arrogantly self-assured. She saw no signs of affection for her, no gentleness; merely this conceited man who had run her to ground as if she were a fox in the hunt. He had shamed her, humiliated her; he wished only to own her and add her to his worldly possessions. He was utterly ruthless.

She gathered her scattered remnants of pride together and raised her face to his. She said contemptuously: "I am not a piece of property or a possession to be sold to the highest bidder, my lord! I fear you have made a poor bargain with my father and are now out some guineas! You act as though I were some sort of prized animal . . . a . . . a . . . horse to be sold!"

"A filly, Kate, a filly," he corrected kindly.

Kate felt as if she were struggling against an invisible but impregnable wall.

Julien leaned toward her in a conciliatory gesture to take her hand in his, but she snatched her hand away and drew back away from him as far as she could in her chair.

"I am sorry, my dear. It was a jest, no more."

As his attempt at an apology met with a fierce glare, he said in clipped tones: "I have no intention of prostrating myself at your feet! Now, Kate, it is time that we did your shopping. You would not wish to be late for your own wedding, now, would you?"

"I am not so poor-spirited, Julien. I will not go with you! And you cannot force me!" She shot him a cold challenge, reasoning to herself that they were, after all, in a public place.

Julien countered in a precise, calm voice: "Very well, Kate. Allow me to outline the alternative. If you do not come willingly with me, this is what I shall do. I shall take you forcibly to my lodgings, or if you prefer, I shall simply render you unconscious and carry you there. If you choose to continue in this obstinate manner, I shall force a certain drug that I now have in my possession down your throat. It is very efficacious, I assure you! It will make you very pliant, like a puppet, Kate."

He paused a moment to ensure she understood his threat.

"I will then, myself, dress you in your wedding finery and take you unresisting to the embassy."

"You . . . you would not!" she gasped, quite white about the mouth.

"Most assuredly I shall, if you force me to, Kate. I have been a patient man, but I have had quite enough of your antics!" Perhaps Hugh and Percy were correct, he thought, I am quite mad. Had someone told him even a month ago that he would force a young lady of quality to marry him, he would have thought it a ludicrous joke. Damn Kate for forcing him to go to such lengths! Why would she not simply admit that she wanted him?

He was beginning to feel rather impatient with her and drummed his fingers on the table.

"Oh, if I were but a man!" she cried.

"That is the stupidest thing I have yet to hear you say! If you were a man, this conversation would never take place! Now, Kate, will you or will you not obey me?"

Kate felt suddenly very tired, all emotion drained out of her. Even her fear of marriage to this man, never far away from her thoughts, was now effectively quelled. She raised her eyes to his, perhaps hoping to find some weakness, some uncertainty written there. But there was none. He was implacable and she knew it.

"Very well," she said finally, her voice flat. "Let us get it over with."

Julien merely nodded, rose, pulled on his gloves, and helped her to rise from her chair. He drew her unresisting arm through his and led her to the door of the café.

The owner was rendered almost incoherent with gratitude when the gentleman pressed a louis in his outstretched hand. He stood in the doorway of his small establishment and watched the lady and gentleman step into a hackney. He had thought their behavior odd, but not understanding a word they had said, shrugged his shoulders in expressive indifference. The English were, after all, quite mad.

Kate spoke scarce a word as Julien guided her to various milliner shops and booteries throughout the remainder of the morning and into the afternoon. She appeared uninterested, coldly withdrawn, and acquiesced to whatever Julien directed her to do. It was he who chose the dainty kid slippers, and the colorful assortment of bonnets. Julien retained a certain degree of skepticism at her seeming capitulation but allowed himself for the moment at least to let his nerves enjoy their first respite in over a week.

Later in the afternoon, their shopping completed, he led her, still unresisting, to his lodgings.

"This is your room, Kate," he said as he propelled her inside. He felt her stiffen beside him and he saw her eyes fly to the bed in the center of the room. She took a step backward, but he stopped her with his arm against her back. He chose for the moment to ignore her gesture and said crisply: "Here is your maid to help you bathe and dress. If there is anything you require, you have but to ask."

Julien walked away from her and gave the maid her instructions in a low voice. He nodded to Kate and left her room through an adjoining door.

Julien stood quietly for a moment in his own room. He was not displeased by the fear he had seen on her face. He knew he was a gentle, skilled lover and he felt confident that he would make her forget her natural fear and virginal modesty. He had, after all, felt the quickening response of her body whenever he was close to her. His main problem would not be her fear, but her pride. In all likelihood she would view pleasure at his hands as a final capitulation to his dominance over her.

Kate forced herself to turn away from the bed. Beads of perspiration broke out on her forehead. She watched the maid bustle toward her after giving Julien a deep curtsy as he left the room. In sudden panic she started toward the door, only to realize that she would not get beyond the stairs.

With a dragging step she returned to the waiting maid, who was regarding her with some astonishment. She stood silently as the maid helped her out of her dress and into her bath.

It seemed but a moment had passed when she heard the maid breathe reverently: "How beautiful you are, my lady."

For the first time that afternoon, Kate focused her attention on the maid's words and looked to see herself in the long mirror. She stared at her reflection unwillingly as the maid smoothed an invisible wrinkle from the skirt of the white satin-and-lace wedding gown. She was not a vain woman, but she realized that she looked quite well, and her fear grew. Julien too would think her beautiful.

She thought of the drug that Julien had in his possession.

She had now no doubt that he would use it if she attempted to again escape from him. Tears welled up and rolled heedlessly down her cheeks. She turned her back to the mirror.

"Give me a handkerchief," she said brokenly to the maid.

There was a light tap on the adjoining door, and Julien entered just as Kate finished dabbing the tears from her face.

He turned to the maid and said curtly: "You may go now. You have done excellently."

Julien walked to where Kate stood. He saw the wadded handkerchief in her hand, wet with her tears. He smiled at her gently and held out his arm to her.

"Come, Kate, it is time. We are expected at five o'clock."

As she raised her pale face to his, he added tenderly: "My love, you must trust me. I do what is best, you must believe that."

Her expression did not change, and without a word she placed her hand on his arm.

They were welcomed at the English embassy with all deference accorded to a peer of the English realm. Mr. Drummond, the English divine, was properly effusive in his compliments to the bride; he was well aware that his consequence could not but be enhanced by officiating at the wedding of such prominent personages.

As he had been led to expect, the Earl of March was indeed an elegant and charming nobleman, and he seemed to radiate an aura of quiet confidence. He wondered at the pallor and unremitting silence of the bride. She appeared withdrawn, even uninterested in the proceedings.

As Mr. Drummond reached his final words, he gave the earl a signal, and Julien turned to Kate and commanded gently: "Give me your hand, Kate."

Mr. Drummond watched with growing alarm as the lady hesitated for what seemed an eternity before finally extending her hand. He watched with relief as the earl withdrew a narrow gold band from his pocket and with quiet dignity slid the ring on her third finger.

With dramatic emphasis Mr. Drummond pronounced them man and wife. Julien leaned down to Kate and kissed her lightly. Her lips were cold. He wondered fleetingly if such a drug as the one he had threatened her with was really in existence. If indeed there was such a drug, he could not imagine that it would render her more deadly cold than she was now.

9

———•••————

Kate nodded silently to the footman, gathered up the train of her wedding gown, and seated herself across the table from her husband. They were in the small sitting room that adjoined Julien's bedchamber, waiting for the sumptuous wedding dinner Julien had ordered. The smells of gourmet cooking assailed Kate's nostrils and sent her stomach churning uncomfortably.

The renowned chef Monsieur André was seen to follow closely behind his creative efforts, a rather startling vision all in white. Consigning a flunkey to serve less important persons, Monsieur André served them himself, his voluble presence preventing any conversation between them.

Kate observed with a feeling of vague ill humor that Julien seemed to be enjoying himself, his fluent French blending with that of the small, dark-mustached chef. She did not particularly find favor with the innumerable references to *la belle comtesse* and remained silent and aloof, her lips curled disdainfully. The two men laughed; in all probability, they were exchanging ribald jokes.

When Monsieur André bowed himself out of the room, an undisguised knowing look in his black eyes, Kate felt the urge to fling her delicate fillet of fish with wine sauce in his face. She did not, however, execute this display of violence, but rather lowered her head in seeming concentration on her dinner.

Julien looked across the table at his wife. She looked exhausted, the pallor of her skin emphasized by the white of her wedding gown. As he savored a bit of the light, flaky fish, he said more to himself than to Kate: "It would be interesting to pit Monsieur André's skill against that of François."

"Yes, it would be a fierce competition."

Surprised that she would deign to speak to him and that

she knew of François, Julien inquired: "You are acquainted with my temperamental chef, Kate?"

"Yes, but only through the colorful picture painted by Mannering and Mrs. Cradshaw." She lowered her head quickly again to her plate. It was somehow a betrayal of herself to indulge in the light banter she had enjoyed—so long ago, it seemed—when he had been her friend.

"When we return to London, François can prepare the same dish and you can judge the winner."

She made no answer and kept her head doggedly down, refusing again to meet his eyes. Their meal continued in silence, and though Julien ate well, he noted with some perturbation that Kate merely picked at her food, her downcast face strained and her hand none too steady.

He began to think of how he would approach lovemaking with her. He could not but dismiss the thought after only a moment of weighing her evident exhaustion against his ardent desire for her.

As if she read his thoughts, Kate raised her face, and he saw such apprehension in her eyes that any faltering in his determination was effectively stilled.

Once the covers were removed and a bottle of chilled champagne was set in front of Julien, he dismissed the footman.

Kate looked up as the door closed, and warily met her husband's eyes. She simply could not believe that she was now married to this man. It seemed as though the footman had locked the door to her prison cell. She had little knowledge of lust and desire, her experience confined primarily to the stilted restrained declarations of love proffered by Squire Bleddoes. But she was certain that she read both of these on Julien's face. Unconsciously her hand stole to her neck in a nervous, protective gesture.

"Kate, here is your champagne." Julien extended a glass of the sparkling liquid to her, and he was somewhat annoyed that her hand shook visibly as she took the glass from him. As he could think of no toast that would not in all likelihood upset her, he simply clicked his glass to hers.

Kate took a long, deep drink of the champagne and barely managed to restrain a sneeze from the frothy bubbles. Julien refilled her glass. Kate began to think that champagne was not at all the nasty sort of drink she had once believed, and confirmed her new opinion by quickly downing the second glass. The third glass gave her a certain sense of warmth and lightheadedness that dissolved the gnawing fear and the shaky feeling in her stomach. Her taut nerves began to loosen, and the room, indeed Julien's face, took on a pleasant blur.

· Julien had never before witnessed Kate drink more than a few sips of any drink, including the mild orgeat at Almack's, and as he watched her finish her fourth glass, he grew concerned that she would make herself ill. He gently leaned forward and removed the glass from her fingers.

"Surely you have had enough, Kate, and it is time for you to retire. It has been a long day."

Kate very much disliked being disturbed from her foggy haze, and once his gently spoken words penetrated her mind, she could not but feel that they cloaked a baser intent. She felt his hand firmly take her arm and pull her to her feet. She weaved uncertainly from the effects of the champagne, and to her horror, leaned heavily against his chest.

"I can see that you are in need of some assistance," he remarked wryly. He ignored her slight flutter of protest and gently lifted her into his arms.

"I am not," she said ineffectively.

He carried her through the adjoining door to her room and set her down on a chair. "Do try not to fall off the chair, Kate," he said over his shoulder as he pulled the bell cord.

Kate huddled in the chair and watched tensely as Julien spoke in a low voice to the maid. But a moment later, the maid curtsied and Julien left the room.

A small voice deep within her told her that now was her chance to escape. She could render the maid unconscious and flee. But her mind seemed strangely befuddled, and the door seemed such a great distance away.

The maid approached her and asked her shyly to rise. Kate stood quietly as the maid began to unbutton the many tiny hooks of her wedding gown. The dress dropped to the floor. Next came her chemise, stockings, slippers, until finally she stood with only her shift covering her body. As if from a great distance, she heard the maid ask her to sit at the dressing table. Her body obeyed the request and she sat down. The maid unfastened her long hair from its pins, and soft tresses fell down her back. As the maid brushed out the long curls, she thought that the lovely English lady was acting even more strangely than she had this afternoon. With her French common sense, she could see no reason why the lady should not be excited about the prospect of being bedded by such a handsome gentleman. But the lady was quite young, and in all likelihood innocent. Her maidenly display of modesty was probably just what the English gentleman would wish.

The maid finished brushing out the long, thick tresses, slipped the shift efficiently over the lady's head, and stood for an instant in admiration of her lovely body. She thought it far more the thing for the lady to await her husband naked in her bed, but the English gentleman had given her explicit orders to put her in her nightgown. This she did, fastening the ribbons around Kate's throat and straightening the long hair. Finally, according to her instructions, she walked to the adjoining door and lightly tapped on it.

She turned and curtsied to the lady, who was standing like a statue in the middle of the room where she had left her, seemingly oblivious of her presence. The maid felt a stab of pity, for she was certain that there was real fear on the lovely pale face, not simple maidenly shyness. She sped quickly to Kate and whispered softly: " 'Twill not be so bad, my lady. Your husband will be gentle and kind, I am certain of it." She heard the gentleman's approaching footsteps, darted one last glance at the lady, and fled the room.

Julien opened the door and entered Kate's bedroom. He pulled up short at the sight of her. She stood quite still where the maid had left her, covered from her chin to her feet in the fine white lawn gown. Her hair fell like soft clouds of rich auburn down her back and over her shoulders. The nightgown was a bit large for her and it made her appear more like a frightened child than a bride.

He strode over to her, cupped her chin in his hand, and forced her to look up at him.

"You are tired, Kate, are you not?"

She nodded mutely, her eyes huge and dark against her white face.

"Then come, my dear. I'll help you to bed."

She did not move, and he could feel her body tense even though he had not touched her.

"Come, sweetheart," he repeated softly, pulling her arm through his.

She was trembling violently, although the room was quite warm. She tried to still her shaking body, but to no avail. She thought inconsequentially that Julien's brocade dressing gown was very soft to the touch. Her fingers twitched nervously on his sleeve.

Julien wondered what thoughts were going through Kate's mind. Her face was chalk white, and he felt her fingers clutching at his arm. He gently disengaged her hand and lifted her onto the bed. His desire flamed as he felt the softness of her body through the flimsy gown. She turned her head away from him on the pillow, and without intending to, Julien sat down beside her. He reached out an unsteady hand and stroked the rich auburn hair. It felt like silk, smooth and soft in his hand. She did not move. He saw the outlines of her full breasts, made more prominent by their rapid rise and fall.

Tentatively he laid a hand on her breast and began to caress the round softness.

Kate rolled suddenly away from him, a low cry of panic escaping from her throat. Julien froze, his hand still outstretched. He drew a deep breath, and with a strong effort drew back his hand. He had wanted her too much and for too long to blunder now by frightening her.

Her shoulders shook with low convulsive sobs. Slowly he rose and mechanically pulled the covers over her. He could think of no way to comfort her, to reassure her. He said only, "Sleep now, Kate."

He had meant his words to be calm, but even to his own ears there was a tremor of passion. He drew a deep breath, turned from her bed, and walked slowly to his own room.

Long after Kate heard Julien close the door behind him, her low sobs diminished into watery sniffs, she drew her knees as close to her chest as she could and burrowed into the covers for warmth. Her hand stole to her breast—the breast he had touched. For the first time in her life she became aware of her own womanness, of the softness of her body. She could still feel his hand upon her, stroking, wanting her.

A shock of fear ripped through her, and she sobbed aloud. The sound of her own voice brought with it a certain calm, and with forced detachment she tried to examine her fear. She knew that men took total possession of women's bodies, an admission that brought the telltale red flush to her cheeks. She thought of Julien's hands on her hair, her breasts, and then moving elsewhere on her body. She pressed her thighs tightly together.

Strangely, she thought about Julien's French mistress. Lady Bellingham had let her name slip; what was it? . . . Yvette. How many other women had Julien possessed? Unbidden, innumerable faceless women rose in her mind, and she pressed her fists against her temples to blot out their images. There was an unaccountable bitter taste in her mouth, and for the moment she encouraged a contemptuous disgust. Unable to determine a precise cause of such violent emotions, she turned the contempt back onto herself. Had she not allowed Julien to do just as he had wished with her? Even forcing her to wed him against her will? She saw herself as weak and despicable, capitulating to a will stronger than hers. In vain she tried to excuse herself on the grounds of Julien's physical threats. She should have fought him, forced him to rely on the drug. Anger at herself welled up within her. She had been a contemptible, simpering female, and now she hated herself for it.

Kate forced herself to be calm again. She sought to understand why she had lost all will to fight him, why indeed she had executed his every command. The thought that she had wanted him to force her took a foothold in her mind, and anger surged through her again. She forced herself to relive the moments when Julien carried her unresisting and laid her on the bed; when he had stroked her hair; when he had caressed her breast. She sat up in her bed and shook her head in blind confusion. Surely she could not be so uncertain about her own feelings.

Her thoughts flew again to Julien's French mistress. How was she different from that woman? After all, Julien had bought her just as he had Yvette. He would tire of her, just as he had tired of Yvette. That he had married her did not count to his advantage, for Kate was not so naive as to believe that even the Earl of March would attempt to seduce an unmarried lady of quality. No, he had been forced to wed her. Her own destiny, whatever that might have been, had been wrested from her control the moment he had decided he wanted her. He had won, and having won, she wondered bitterly how long it would be before he left her to preside alone over his household and search out his next quarry.

A twisted smile passed over her face. Undoubtedly Julien now thought her cowed and submissive. Her jaw set itself into a stubborn line as she resolved never again to show weakness. He had compared her to Shakespeare's Kate. Very well, she would be a shrew, a termagant. She would thwart him at every opportunity.

She pulled up short after a moment of savoring this satisfying revenge. Possession of her body would be his next object. With determination she fought back the unreasoning fear that accompanied this thought. Damn him, no! He had made a very expensive purchase, but she would see him in hell before she would allow him to enjoy it. Her life had become a continuous battleground since she had met him, and it did not seem likely to her now that anything would change. Nay, she would not let it change. With this resolve she fell into an exhausted sleep.

As Julien lay in his own bed, his head propped up on his arms, he reviewed the day's events with some satisfaction. He was pleased with himself that he had forced Kate to wed him as soon as he had, for he had allowed her to hold on to her pride. He could have waited another week, but he had not been able to bring himself to do it. He had not wanted an admission of failure from her; he had not wanted her on those terms. In all truth, to Julien their marriage was not a victory over her, but rather a natural course of events.

He raised himself on one elbow and blew out the candle beside his bed. He lay back wondering how long it would be before she would admit to her love for him. At least now she appeared to be more reasonable, and having her at his side continually, he felt confident that she would learn to trust him. He planned to begin by explaining his high-handed treatment of her. He would become her friend again. He mentally added to this list that he must speak openly to her of lovemaking, for they were, after all, now man and wife. He had acted precipitately this evening; he must remember that Kate was young, innocent, and quite vulnerable, despite her bravado.

Before dropping off to sleep, he decided to quit Paris on the morrow and remove immediately to Switzerland, to the villa he had hired in the mountains near Geneva. They would be alone, save for two servants. There they would have time to come to an understanding.

Julien awoke the following morning, light of heart and full of confidence. He patiently bore with a valet provided by the hotel, having given Timmens a *congé* until his return to England. His coat, at least, was properly pressed. He was impatient to see Kate, and so contented himself with the first result achieved on his cravat. A hotel lackey arrived just as he finished dressing, bearing the hearty English breakfast he had ordered to please Kate.

With a light step and a gleam of anticipation in his eyes he tapped on the adjoining door. Receiving no immediate answer, he opened the door and stepped into the room.

Kate was seated at the dressing table, engrossed in the coiffure the maid had achieved. She did not turn immediately, but rather patted her hair here and there, straightened the collar of her gown, all in all making a fine show of ignoring his presence.

Julien approached her and stood behind her chair so that she could see his reflection in the mirror.

"Good morning, Kate."

She turned slowly in her chair, gazed at him with great indifference, and replied, "Good morning, sir. I trust you have slept well."

Kate silently congratulated herself, for even to her own critical ears she had spoken with a marked lack of concern, as if his presence were a mundane occurrence, not at all above the commonplace. She held his gaze and noticed with satisfaction that his brows arched in fleeting surprise, and it seemed obvious to her that he had expected her to behave quite differently, perhaps with docility, perhaps with anger; but certainly not with a sublime indifference.

After a moment Julien replied, "Yes, Kate. I slept quite well. Did you?"

Kate patted her hair again, quite unnecessarily, and said cheerily: "Give me but a moment longer, sir, and I shall join you for breakfast. It does seem to be a very lovely day, does it not? That is very fine, Nicole, you have performed wonders with my hair!"

Kate rose and shook out her skirts, all the while watching him carefully. She was rewarded with a frown on his brow, for instead of wearing one of the elegant gowns he had bought for her, she had insisted on donning her own gown. It was sadly in need of pressing, and she delighted in each wrinkle.

Julien pursed his lips and turned abruptly to the maid. "You may go now. I think you have done quite enough for her ladyship."

He did not turn back to Kate until he had carefully

schooled his features. She had wanted to anger him and he had most willingly obliged her. Gentle, reasonable treatment from a loving husband was not, at least for this morning, what his Kate would tolerate.

He proffered her his arm and remarked in a bland voice: "How very charming you are this morning, my love. Marriage obviously agrees with you. Come, your breakfast will get cold. As you said, it is a lovely day. You would not wish to waste it."

Kate merely shrugged her shoulders and lightly laid her hand on his arm.

Once seated at the table, she gave her full attention to her breakfast. After eating her fill, she spent an extraordinarily long time in pushing her food back and forth on her plate. Bored with this pastime, she chanced to look up and saw Julien gazing at her, his eyes alight with amusement.

"Oh, dear! Do forgive me, sir! I have always thought it unforgivably rude to stare at others who have not yet finished their meals, but then, perhaps you are in a hurry to quit these rooms and think that I am much too slow at my breakfast. Do allow me but a moment longer!"

"In many ways, you are such a child, my dear wife. Watching you grow up will give me infinite pleasure. As to the urgencies of your breakfast, dear Kate, I fear that your toast is by now like dried leather and your bacon stiff with age!"

"Did it never occur to you, sir, that I might find even stiffened bacon and dried-up toast more to my liking than your nonsensical conversation? But here I am quibbling over such a small matter! I now count my breakfast finished, sir, and await to hear your pleasure. What delights have you planned on this altogether lovely day?"

Julien drew out his watch and consulted it. He remarked in a voice of affability that she found exasperating: "My pleasure, Kate, is that you are packed in an hour. Why the look of surprise, wife? We are, after all, on our wedding trip. I wish that we leave for Switzerland this morning."

"I have never cared for Switzerland."

"How very curious . . . I was not under the impression that you had ever traveled to that country."

"I have not . . . but I understand that it is quite inferior to England."

Julien allowed a look of astonishment. "I thought that you

were singularly undisturbed by other people's opinions, Kate. I must confess that I find myself somewhat disappointed that you do not wish to form your own independent judgment." He sighed pensively. "I had hoped that unlike most other women you would not be content to merely parrot words. I fear I hear the sound of poor Bleddoes' staid pronouncements!"

"That is not true, as you well know! Even though Robert has said on occasion . . . Oh, how very odious of you to draw such an unbecoming picture!" Kate rose in agitation, her face charmingly flushed.

"An hour, Kate?"

She flung her napkin on the table, turned on her heel, and flounced from the room.

Julien remained seated for a moment longer, looking at the recently slammed door. It had never before occurred to him to bless his quickness of wit. It came to him with something of a shock that she was behaving more arrogantly than he had done himself when trying to bring her to heel in London. That she would ride roughshod over him given the least opportunity, he did not doubt. For a fleeting instant he envisioned his life as a marital battleground.

As he rose to ring for a lackey, he wondered idly how long she would insist upon wearing the same gown.

The post chaise Julien had procured for their trip to Switzerland was well-sprung and elegantly furnished with blue satin cushions and squabs and warm blue velvet rugs. Though the horses stood over fifteen hands and were blessed with broad chests and powerful thighs, Julien found that they did not possess the speed of his own bays.

Julien watched Kate with some amusement as she tried valiantly not to appear overly interested in the French countryside. He well understood her dilemma and thought her altogether adorable.

They ate their lunch in the small town of Brayville, drinking the local cider and feasting on cold chicken, cheese, and crunchy warm bread. Feeling fortified by the heady cider, Julien found himself, not long after their return to the carriage, clearing his throat to gain Kate's attention.

"Kate, I would ask that you listen to me for a moment."

"Yes?" She turned to face him unwillingly, steeling herself.

"My intention is to cease these meaningless hostilities between us. You thought me cruel, perhaps overbearing in my treatment of you in London. No, do not speak, let me finish. When you refused me, Kate, I was forced to admit to myself that I had rushed into the matter too quickly, that I had not given you sufficient time to judge your feelings for me. I never meant to insult you. Perhaps I am overly proud, puffed up in my own consequence as Harry said, but I found that I could not lose you."

He paused for a moment and looked searchingly at Kate's set face. His speech did not seem to be going as well as he had expected, but he pursued, speaking more rapidly.

"I knew that I could not continue to see you at Brandon Hall, for your father would force you to meet with me, and perhaps try to beat you into submission. You must understand, Kate, I could not allow you to remain under his roof any longer than necessary. That is why I arranged for you to go to London, to Lady Bellingham. There, at least, I knew I could control the situation. You thought me cruel, hard. I tell you now that I had no other choice in the matter! Kate, my intention was and still is to do what is best for both of us. That I forced you to marry me was not a reprehensible act. I had to wed you as speedily as possible after your flight to Paris, for had I not, had I left you alone to your own devices, you would have had to eventually return to England, your reputation ruined.

"As for my threat about the drug—I did not have such a drug, Kate. I simply could not think of any other way to secure your agreement."

"There was no drug?" She was appalled at her own gullibility.

"No," he replied shortly. "And I would not now have you think me a licentious rake, for I would have never forcibly taken you aboard my yacht."

"Either I am a fool or you have admirable sangfroid, my lord, for I did not doubt that you were utterly ruthless and implacable in gaining your ends!"

"Perhaps, Kate, it was merely that I felt compelled to use whatever . . . tactics I needed to secure you as my wife."

"You have paid dear for a wife who loathes you, Julien. I swear that you will never enjoy your purchase!"

A somewhat hard note entered Julien's level voice. "Do not rant nonsense at me, Kate. It now does you no credit! We are married and that is the end to it. You speak of my purchase—I will tell you, Kate, it is you who are now being arrogant and implacable!"

"How dare you to criticize my actions!" she cried.

He leaned over and dropped a hand on her shoulder and gripped it an instant. She tried to pull away, but he grasped both her shoulders and jerked her close to his face. He had meant to give her a good trimming, but found instead that his body quickened with desire for her. In a swift motion he cupped her face between his hands and pressed his mouth against hers. She tried to twist free of him, but he simply lifted her bodily and held her firmly in the circle of his arms.

At that moment the chaise lurched violently, throwing them both to the opposite seat. As they sprawled on the cushions, Julien automatically released her, and she scrambled away from him, clutching desperately at the door. He grabbed her hand and pulled her upright opposite him. All desire and anger left him as he stared at her white, shocked face.

Julien turned and looked out the chaise window. They were moving at a comfortable pace again. He methodically straightened his clothes and his cravat. He felt rather irritated at her damned missishness.

"I apologize for being rather overly . . . enthusiastic, Kate." He was beginning to feel the clumsy fool and thus spoke with a harshness of voice that he did not intend. He saw that Kate's eyes had darkened with sudden anger at his words.

He drew a deep breath and continued in a more controlled tone. "The fact is, Kate, we are man and wife. Can you not doubt that I wish to consummate our marriage, or, for that matter, that I wish you to bear my children? Although you cannot yet bring yourself to admit it, ours is a love match and not a marriage of convenience."

"I would rather die than let you touch me, do you understand, my lord? Ours is no love match, for I feel none for you, and your treatment of me has certainly shown none of the more tender emotions! You cloak your lust with words of love! You disgust me, Julien. Do you hear?"

Julien curbed his fury. To match her anger would achieve naught. She was overwrought, and his sudden passion for her had made her totally unreasonable. He said with surprising gentleness, "Enough said, Kate. Believe me, though, that I will make you my wife, in every way. I love you, and soon you will come to trust me."

"I fear you concoct a Banbury tale, Julien," she replied with scarcely a tremor to betray her agitation. "In truth, I would sooner trust any one of the Carlton House set than you, my lord."

"Very well, Kate," he said only, disregarding her most unflattering comparison to the regent's dissolute collection of rakes and hardened gamesters.

Kate rearranged her bonnet, which was sitting precariously atop her tousled curls, primly folded her hands in her lap, and looked out, unseeing, onto the French countryside.

They arrived in Geneva late the next afternoon, and Kate could not restrain her appreciation when Lake Geneva came into view. Though it was early September, the mountains surrounding the lake were snowcapped, and the setting sun cast á fairyland glow on the water.

"Oh, how very lovely it is," she exclaimed.

"Yes, it is beautiful, is it not?" Julien agreed, himself always taken with nature's magnificence in Switzerland.

Kate suddenly recalled her childish remark about Switzerland's inferiority to England. She drew back into the chaise and fastened her eyes on the cushions. "I suppose it is passable," she allowed coldly.

She could not prevent her eyes from going to his face, and saw his brows rise in ironic amusement. She flushed, mortified at her own churlishness.

She darted her gaze again out the chaise window and soon became absorbed with the endless rows of quaint shops that lined the cobblestone streets, each sporting colorful signs and displays. The Swiss themselves, not less colorfully arrayed than their shop fronts, bustled out onto the walkways, apparently hurrying to their homes for the evening.

The Coeur de Lyon was a two-storied, gabled brick building of some antiquity that stood back from the street, nearly hidden from view by giant elm trees. The courtyard surged with activity, and no sooner did their chaise pull to a halt than two ostlers appeared to grab the reins.

Kate allowed Julien to assist her from the chaise and was thankful that she did so, for her legs were weak from their long-cramped position. She looked up to see a very rotund, quite bald little man emerge from the *auberge* to greet them.

"My Lord March! What a long time it has been! A pleasure to see you again, my lord." He bowed, all gracious compliance and deference.

"Good evening, Perchon. Your establishment prospers, I see."

Monsieur Perchon beamed, bowed, and turned to give instructions in rapid French to two of his henchmen.

"Now, my lord, my lady, if you will please to follow me. Your accommodations, I assure you, are quite in order."

Kate was somewhat surprised that Monsieur Perchon spoke English so well. She was soon to discover that he spoke French, German, and Italian with equal ease.

A slender, brown-eyed maid who reminded Kate of a small, timid doe was assigned to see to her comfort, and as she prepared to follow the maid up the winding wooden stairs to her chamber, Julien called to her: "Put on a warm cloak, Kate, and let us explore before dinner."

It was on the tip of her tongue to declare pettishly that she had no such warm cloak, when Julien, apparently guessing her objection, quickly added: "You will find such a cloak in your large trunk, my dear. It is, I believe, blue velvet and lined with ermine."

Kate felt her hackles rise at the mention of the clothes he had bought for her. "The pelisse I am wearing will be perfectly adequate, thank you, sir!"

She felt rather deflated when he turned away from her and said over his shoulder, "Very well. As you wish, Kate. I shall expect you in the parlor in five minutes."

She was left standing on the stairs, a half-formed refusal on her lips. She turned petulantly and followed the maid to her chamber.

Kate untied the strings on her pelisse and tossed it, not without some agitation, onto the bed. She moved to the small blazing fire and warmed her hands for a moment before flinging down into a chair. So he had dared to order her! She gnawed at her thumbnail and tried to cool her anger, for she had learned through painful experience that such violent emotion dulled her wits and slowed her tongue. She forced herself to relax and settle back into the chair. She looked dispassionately at her chewed nail and thought, not without satisfaction, that the last day and a half had been more of a trial to Julien than to her, for after their brief and violent scene in the chaise, she had managed to treat him unerringly with a kind of indifferent civility. Instinctively she knew it was her best weapon against him.

"Excuse me, my lady, can I assist you to change?" the maid asked.

Kate jerked up her head, thought that she had dawdled a sufficient length of time, and rather proudly smoothed her travel-stained gown. She rose and said, "No, thank you. My pelisse is all that I will require."

There was a rather dubious look in the maid's soft brown eyes, for she had unpacked many of the lovely gowns. "Yes, my lady." She bobbed a curtsy and handed Kate her worn pelisse.

As Kate swept past the smiling landlord into the private parlor, she rather hoped that Julien would be irritated, as a good half-hour had passed. She pulled up short in the middle of the room, disappointed to find him seated comfortably before a blazing fire, engrossed in reading a paper. She grew quickly annoyed at being ignored.

Julien finally raised his eyes from the paper and said with some surprise, "Good heavens, that was indeed a short five minutes. How very impolite of me. My pardon, Kate, have you been waiting for me long?"

Kate's bosom heaved, and momentarily taken off her guard, she exclaimed, "You are the most . . ." She caught herself, yawned, and quickly changed her tone. "If you wish to continue with your paper, it would be quite shabby of me to take you away to what one might consider to be a boring pastime!"

"It would be ill-bred of me to prefer the company of a newspaper over that of my charming bride. Do allow me a few minutes to put on my greatcoat, Kate, and we will be off."

Julien rose and drew on his gloves and coat in a leisurely manner. He sauntered to where she stood and murmured ironically, "Do forgive me for making you wait, Kate. It takes such a damnably long time to pull on one's gloves. Shall we go?"

"As you wish," she replied indifferently.

As they stepped from the *auberge*, a gust of cold evening wind whipped up Kate's thin pelisse and chilled her to the bone.

"Perhaps it is a bit too chilly for a stroll," Julien began, his voice all gentle concern.

"On the contrary, it is a beautiful evening for a walk! I have always maintained that it is quite ridiculous to curb one's activities when the weather is not exactly what one would wish!"

She drew her pelisse closely about her and strode purposefully ahead of him.

Julien grinned at her back. He hoped that she would not catch a chill.

Kate soon found that she had to suffer another inconvenience. The uneven cobblestones cut into her feet through the soft kid shoes. She was forced to halt a moment and lean over to pick out an errant pebble that had worked its way to the sole of her foot.

Julien stopped beside her, but appeared quite unconcerned with her difficulty, seemingly engrossed in the contemplation of Lake Geneva. Perversely, she felt that he was treating her shabbily.

By the time they reached the water's edge, Kate was hard-pressed to keep her teeth from chattering.

"Look over there, Kate." He tugged at her sleeve and pointed her toward the mountains on the other side of the lake.

"That is Mont Blanc—White Mountain. Exquisite, is it not?"

"Most picturesque," she snapped. She would have most willingly traded the view of that awesome snowcapped peak for a pair of stout walking shoes and a warm cloak.

Julien turned to her in some surprise. "Why, Kate, I was under the impression that the racket of towns did not find favor with you . . . that you much preferred the openness and solitude of nature."

"That is perfectly true. But as you see, I am to be denied solitude!"

Julien slipped in quietly, "But, my dear wife, since we have entered the blessed state of matrimony, we must be considered as one—in spirit and in all things."

"It must be obvious to you, Julien, that these considerations of marriage do not apply to us!"

"Of a certainty they will, Kate. Did I not assure you of that fact? Do you grow impatient?"

She replied in a voice frigid with distaste, "How right of

you, Julien! I do find myself impatient . . . but only for my dinner."

Julien did not immediately respond, but leaned down and sought out a smooth pebble. Having selected a stone of the quality he desired, he flicked his wrist and sent the pebble jumping and careening wildly over the placid water. Seemingly satisfied with the number of jumps he achieved, he turned to Kate slowly, a thoughtful expression on his face.

"Impatient only for your dinner, dear Kate? I can give you much greater pleasure than a simple meal."

Were they not in the open, in a very public place, Kate would have fought down unreasoning fear at his words. As it was, color rose in her cheeks, and she allowed her anger full rein.

"Are you daring to taunt me again with your meaningless threats, my lord?"

"Threaten you? I do not recall having threatened you, Kate. Leastwise in the past few minutes," he added judiciously. "When you come to know me better, wife, you will discover that I do not make threats. I make but statements of fact."

"They are one and the same thing coming from you, Julien! I have told you that I hold you in . . . extreme dislike! I cannot believe you so unintelligent as to have so quickly forgotten my words."

She had hoped to provoke him, but was disappointed, for he only gazed at her impassively, a gleam of amusement lighting his eyes. She turned away and presented him with a stiff back.

Julien found himself hard-pressed to maintain the calm amusement she found so annoying. He had failed miserably with his so carefully thought-out speech to her the morning after their marriage in the carriage, and had but succeeded in providing her with more ammunition for her skirmishes against him. He wondered, somewhat pensively, what the devil he was going to do now.

"Come, Kate," he said after a moment, "it is time we returned. It will be dark in but a few minutes."

She did not reply, and hurried ahead of him.

He saw that she was shivering with cold. "Hold a moment, Kate," he commanded.

She stopped and looked at him questioningly, brows raised. To her chagrin, he removed his greatcoat and wrapped it around her shoulders. She drew back, uncertain whether or not to protest. She bit her lower lip and kept silent, deciding, for the moment at least, that warmth was more important than wounded pride. Julien made no comment, and they returned to the inn in silence.

Throughout their evening meal in the cozy private parlor, Julien spoke to her hardly at all, and it seemed to Kate that he appeared rather abstracted. She wondered suspiciously if he was employing a new stratagem. She was soon disabused of this notion, when, after their meal, as the landlord poured him a glass of port, Julien asked, "Would you care to join me, Kate?"

She shook her head vehemently, and he added smoothly, " 'Tis but one glass of port, Kate, not a half-bottle of champagne. Trust that I would not allow you to have more than one glass, for in truth, you are no fit companion when you are drunk."

She could only stare at him incredulously, momentarily speechless at his mocking, bald reference to their wedding night. But she saw the sardonic glint in his eyes and curbed her jumbled feelings of humiliation and anger, managing to reply with scarce a tremor, "You know, sir, you are quite right. One glass of port cannot be equated to . . . a half-bottle of champagne, as you so quaintly put it."

Unused to the heady port, Kate choked on her first drink and fell into a paroxysm of coughing. She quickly downed a glass of water, drew sputtering breaths, and leaned back in her chair.

Julien gazed at her with a pensive look. "You must really learn to conduct yourself with more grace, dear wife. It befits your new station, you know."

Without thought, Kate clutched her wineglass and readied to hurl the contents into his face. Julien read her intent and said sternly, "I warn you, do not do what you are thinking, Kate! I give you another statement of fact—if you commit such a childish act, I shall retaliate and treat you as a child."

Her resolve was shaken, but she did not lower the glass.

Julien said more harshly still, "In plain words, Kate, if you throw the wine at me, I shall throw you over my knee, bare what I am certain is a lovely backside, and spank you soundly!"

"You . . . you would not dare!"

"Try me, Kate!"

She set the glass on the table with a decided snap. She had been made to look very much the fool. Never again would she underestimate him. She rose stiffly and hurried without a word to the door.

"Running away? I did not think you so craven, Kate. Come, my dear, I do apologize."

He sounded perfectly sincere, and she stood uncertain, her hand on the doorknob.

Julien adroitly turned the subject, silently congratulating himself on this sudden inspiration.

"I have been given to understand that you play piquet quite well. Do you care to pit your skill against mine?"

Kate forgot her grievances, seeing her opportunity to best him. She felt a warm surge of confidence flow through her and turned back to face him, a glow of anticipation on her face.

"Of a certainty I would very much like a game with you," she said in a silky voice. Without thought, she added, "Would you care to lay a wager on the outcome? Say, perhaps ten shillings a point?"

She had no sooner spoken the words than her face fell ludicrously, for she realized she had no money.

Julien replied calmly, "Rather than guineas, why do we not set more interesting stakes?"

"What stakes do you have in mind?" she asked slowly.

He looked thoughtful for a moment. "Let us say, Kate, that if I win, you will ceremoniously dispose of the gown you are wearing and willingly wear the wardrobe I have provided for you." He felt quite pleased with himself, for the gown she had insisted on wearing the past three days was in lamentable shape. If she lost to him, which he was quite sure she would, her pride would be salvaged, for she would be merely paying a debt of honor.

"Yes, I will accept that condition . . . if I lose to you." Kate was suddenly aware of the gravy stain that had somehow managed to appear on the bodice of her dress during dinner.

"And what, Julien, is my prize if I win?"

"Have you something in mind, Kate?"

How could she tell him that if she won, she wanted nothing more than to have him vow not to touch her, to quit frightening her in that way? Her tongue seemed to tie itself into knots, and she stood in pained silence. Finally she managed to recall something that she very much wanted. Her words poured out in a rush: "If I win, Julien, I would that you teach me to fence—like a man!"

Julien grinned. "Ho, Kate, I was under the impression that you had already learned all men's sports from Harry."

"Harry!" she scoffed. "He is but a clod with a rapier." A predatory smile flitted over her face. "I butchered him at the second lesson," she said with satisfaction. "I do suppose you are somewhat skilled in the art?"

"Somewhat, my dear, somewhat," he said gravely.

"But as one of the dandy set . . ." Her voice trailed off in innocent speculation.

"Corinthian," Julien corrected softly.

"Dandy . . . Corinthian, be they not the same thing? You are only concerned with your own pursuits, your own pleasures."

"Now that you are my wife, I am very much concerned with your pleasure as well. But let us cry peace, Kate. If you do not mind, ring for our host."

At the hint of an order, she stiffened.

"A pack of cards, my dear . . . for piquet."

Once presented with a rather grimy, well-used deck of cards, Julien rose and held out a chair for Kate. She seated herself at the small table Julien had arranged near the fire, and began with a good deal of skill to shuffle the deck.

Julien seated himself across from her and found that he could not help admiring her vivid green eyes, glowing with excitement, and her auburn hair, shimmering with soft lights from the glow of the fire. He tore his gaze away from her face, only to find himself acutely aware of the gentle rise and fall of her breasts against the soft material of her gown. He did not notice the gravy stain.

"Three rubbers, Kate? We will total points at the end to determine the winner."

Kate nodded in agreement and extended the shuffled cards toward him.

"Would you care to cut for the deal, Julien?"

"Yes, certainly," he replied without pause, realizing that Kate would take the usual courtesy of allowing the lady the deal as an insult.

In a practiced move she fanned the cards on the table toward him. He turned up the jack of hearts. Kate perused the cards for a moment and withdrew the king of diamonds. Her eyes sparkled. "My king wins, sir!"

Julien inclined his head in agreement and watched her deal the cards. As she had been taught, first by her mother and then by Harry, Kate played the first several hands carefully, making a concerted effort to sum up Julien's skill. As a great deal of points were not scored, she found it difficult at the end of the first game to be certain of his abilities.

The rubber went to Kate, and although there was not much more than a hundred points to her credit, she began to feel more sure of herself. It seemed to her that Julien was an overly cautious player, particularly in his discards. She decided that he was much too conservative.

During the second rubber, the luck seemed to run evenly between them, and as Julien did not give her overt reason to change her opinion of his play, she began to take small chances, risking a gain of substantial points by relying on her instincts. The rubber went to Julien, but again the points were not great and she consoled herself that it was only a mild setback. But as she dealt the cards, she could not help but be secretly bothered, for she found that she was unable to pinpoint exactly why he had won. She decided that he had held the better cards after all. She allowed only a slight frown to pass over her forehead as she cut the deck to him.

"A glass of claret, Kate?" Julien offered, and reached for the decanter.

"No, I thank you not. I must keep my wits about me, I see," she returned lightly.

During the third rubber, Kate found, hand after hand, that she failed to defeat his major holdings because of his careful and studied retention of some small card. She quickly changed her opinion of his skill, for he seemed to calculate odds to perfection. He played his cards decisively, no longer ruminating over discards, and it appeared to Kate that he had the disconcerting trick of summing up her hands with an accuracy that made her wonder bitterly if he could see through the cards. She threw caution to the winds and began to gamble on slim chances, discarding small cards for the chance of picking up an ace or a king. Her confidence began to falter, and her nerves grew taut. It annoyed her that Julien appeared so abominably casual and relaxed. The third rubber ended quickly when, in the final hand, Julien spread out his hand, all save one card, and said gently, "I trust my quint is good."

"Quite good."

"And the four kings and three aces?"

"Also good," she said slowly, staring down at the impressive array of high cards and then back at the one card he still held in his hand.

"Oh, the devil!" she exclaimed. "I shall be fleeced shamefully if I cannot guess this discard. Drat, I have no idea what to keep!"

"No, I agree, there is nothing at all to tell you," he said calmly, sitting back in his chair, turning the lone card first one way and then another between his long fingers.

"Very well, a spade!" she cried, throwing down the rest of her hand.

"Sorry, Kate, but you must lose." Julien turned the card toward her and she saw that he held a small diamond.

She gazed at the card for a long moment, unwilling to believe that she had been trounced so thoroughly. How it galled her to lose to him when she had been so certain that she would defeat him! She fought with herself to take her loss gracefully.

"It appears that you have . . . bettered me," she managed to say with some semblance of good humor.

"I had no doubt of the outcome, Kate."

She recoiled from his quietly spoken words, and a shadow of hurt and surprise filled her eyes. She could not explain why, but it seemed very unlike Julien to make her feel her defeat more than necessary. "It . . . it is unkind of you to remind me."

He saw the hurt on her face and bit his tongue at his thoughtless words. "Kate, you are a fine player. You are weakest in your discards, and I fear that you do not play the odds as you should. Of course I would beat you, for I have at least ten more years of experience than you in the game. In time, if you attend carefully, your skill will equal mine."

"I . . . I see," she said quietly. She vowed silently that she would practice until she beat him.

As she gathered the cards together, Kate became painfully aware that Julien was regarding her steadily. She instantly forgot her vow to beat him at cards as she felt a surge of fear sweep through her. She dropped the cards onto the table and quickly squirmed out of her chair, her eyes fixed on the door.

"Surely you cannot wish to be gone from me so soon, Kate. Would you not care to perhaps discuss some of the finer points of the game?" Julien rose leisurely as he spoke and walked to the closed door, cutting off her only avenue of escape.

"I would go to bed now," Kate said with an effort.

"Precisely my idea, my dear. It is encouraging that you begin to read my wishes."

"That is not what I mean!" she cried hotly.

Julien walked slowly over to where she stood, like a panther, she thought, stalking his prey.

"But it is exactly what I mean, Kate. I let you have your way last night, but tonight I find that I am desirous of having my wife in my bed. Will you come with me, Kate?"

She whisked herself quickly behind the card table out of his reach. Though she was a scant three feet from him, the small barrier gave her courage.

"I will tell you again, my lord, I will have none of you! I find you inordinately dull-witted, for I have told you many times I find the thought of you . . . I find you loathsome!"

He drew nearer to her, and she read lustful purpose in his eyes.

"I will fight you with every ounce of strength, Julien! Never will I willingly let you touch me!"

Julien found himself torn between exasperation and a physical desire that was fast dying.

"Good God, Kate, I pray you, enough of your ridiculous dramatics! I find it refreshing that in these too liberal times virginal modesty still exists, but you carry it to an absurd point." He leaned over and spread his hands on the table, his eyes on a level with hers.

"When are you going to accept the fact that I am your husband?"

Kate found that she was trembling. Not wanting him to see her fear, she quickly whisked her shaking hands behind her back. "Oh, please, Julien, I beg of you . . . please let me alone," she whispered, wishing he were not so very close to her.

Julien drew up, baffled, for her face was as white as her collar. He had been certain that her refusal of him was due to her damnable pride, her anger at him for removing all choice from her. He saw fear now, stark and livid in her eyes, and he cudgeled his brain in an effort to understand. He remembered that her mother had died when Kate was but a young girl and that she had spent all her growing-up years with only her father and brother.

"Kate," he began, his voice now gentle, "I know that your mother died when you were quite young, in fact, at an age when a mother's advice and teaching cannot but be of importance and significance." he paused a moment to judge the effect of his words, but Kate was looking at him blankly, as if she had not heard him. He drew a deep breath and continued in a level voice: "A father and a brother are not, indeed, cannot be the same thing. Did your father perhaps warn you against men, Kate? Did he frighten you?"

A fragile image of her mother rose in Kate's mind, crooning gentle words to her, consoling her, stroking her hair. The fleeting picture brought with it an inexplicable panic.

"Kate," Julien repeated, "did your father frighten you?"

"No, oh, no," she cried quickly. She wished she had not spoken, for her words seemed to dissolve her mother's face, and with it the strange memory.

"Very well," Julien said, straightening. "Then I must assume that you are doing your very best to thwart me. I hope you do not choke on your pride, Kate. I would that you give it some thought, for I grow quite weary being your adversary." He turned away from her, strode to the sideboard, and helped himself to a glass of claret.

Kate gazed at him a moment, perplexed, and as he did not turn, she picked up her skirts and walked from the room.

Julien sat alone in the private parlor, his hands curled around a warm cup of coffee, waiting for Kate. He wondered if she would honor her lost wager and appear in a gown he had purchased for her. He had not long to dwell on this question, for soon the landlord opened the door and she swept into the room, dressed in the height of fashion, wearing a militant look. He silently applauded his taste, for the lavender muslin, secured below her bosom with rosebud lace, became her to perfection. He rose lazily from his chair and proffered her a deep bow. "How charming you are this morning, Kate."

"I am gratified at your compliment, Julien," she said as she seated herself at the breakfast table. Secretly she was quite pleased with the picture she presented, and impressed with the style and cut of the gown. She wished only that it had been she who had chosen it and not Julien.

"How did you know my size?" she asked without preamble.

A very accurate but unfortunately quite unsuitable response came to Julien, but he suppressed it. "A lucky guess, my dear," he said gravely.

She frowned at his inane reply and said sharply, "That cannot be true, Julien. I presume that you bribed my maid for the measurements."

His eyes twinkled. "As you will, Kate. I bow to your superior analysis."

"Rubbish! Do you think me such a ninny, Julien? It is quite obvious that you have gained such knowledge by purchasing such articles for your many mistresses!" She drew back, flushed, for she had not meant to say anything of the sort, and was appalled at the waspishness of her voice. If she thought Julien would be a gentleman and ignore her spoken thoughts, she was sadly mistaken.

"Ho, Kate, do I detect a note of jealousy? Do not trouble yourself, my dear," he continued, grinning broadly, "since my marriage, I have given all my *many* mistresses their *congé*."

"Perhaps that was a mistake, sir," she retorted swiftly. "It is quite possible that you will soon find yourself wishing for their amiable company."

"Do not, I beg you, Kate, hold yourself in such low esteem, for you are—and will be—all that I could ever desire."

"There you are quite wrong, Julien, for I hold myself in too high esteem for such as you."

"Tut, tut, wife, you are but a countess for three days. I fear that your lovely bonnets will grow too small if you puff your head with such prideful thoughts."

"Being the wealthy Countess of March, sir, I can change my bonnets as often as you change your cravats! Now, if you please, your pointless conversation has quite destroyed my appetite, and I would just as soon continue our journey."

"Our wedding trip," he corrected, rising.

They bowled out of the courtyard of the Coeur de Lyon not long thereafter, and as Julien wished to reach the villa by late afternoon, they maintained a smart pace throughout the morning, halting only once to change horses. To Kate's relief, she was relieved of Julien's company for the better part of the afternoon, as he decided to take the reins.

"We've a sluggish leader who needs a firm hand. I hope you do not mind being alone, wife."

Kate raised her brows and gave him a cold stare. As he stepped from the chaise, he remarked over his shoulder, "It is a sad trial. It appears that my firm hand is needed in so many things."

Kate did not reply, her attention being suddenly claimed by a very interesting rock formation by the side of the road. But it was not long before she found herself grinning somewhat ruefully. She was also forced to admit after the passage of but a few miles that he was good with horses, for the chaise was moving at a smoother pace, with fewer jolts and lurches.

She settled back and enjoyed the beautiful Swiss countryside that unfolded outside her window, and roundly chided herself for her childish condemnation of this scenic country. Such a short time ago, it would never have occurred to her to even consider such a boorish observation. So much had changed since the day she had first met the Earl of March. As she recalled the shocked look on his face when he realized that his duelist was a girl, her lips curled into a smile. How very pleasant too were the early days she had spent in his company. She had been so very comfortable with him, speaking her mind, never mincing words. He had been the most delightful of companions. Kate sighed and leaned back against the squabs, closing her eyes. He had destroyed those halcyon days and had robbed her of all comfort and peace of mind. She remembered unwillingly the day he had asked her to wed him, the suffocating fear that had risen unbidden to choke her. She understood her fear not one whit better than she had then. She knew only that it was deep within her, a part of her from which she could not seem to free herself.

Kate opened her eyes as the chaise lurched its way ponderously up a steep incline that cut its way through dense lush forest. A few minutes later the road widened and the chaise burst from the forest into a large triangular clearing atop a jutting promontory. In the center of the clearing stood a small, elegantly constructed white brick villa. Delicately wrought columns supported the overhanging balconies of the second floor. It seemed to Kate that in the fading sunlight the endless numbers of windows glittered like bright prisms. Snowcapped peaks were visible in the distance, and the well-scythed lawn seemed to melt into the green of the forest, as if blended into it by an artist's brush. It was an exquisite private mansion suited for royalty, Kate thought. She wondered from whom Julien had secured this place.

As Julien reined in the horses, Kate's attention was drawn to an older man and woman who bustled from the front doors toward them. Julien opened the chaise door and helped Kate to alight before turning his attention to the couple, who stood viewing Kate with lively curiosity.

"Good afternoon, James, Maria," Julien addressed the couple. "I would like you to meet the Countess of March, my wife."

The woman drew her stiff bombazine skirts into a curtsy, and the man gave a tug to a rather unruly spike of gray hair. "A real pleasure, my lady." He beamed at Kate, revealing slightly protruding teeth.

Kate inclined her head, conscious suddenly of the somewhat strange yet pleasing awareness of being treated with such deference.

"We weren't expecting your lordship and ladyship so soon," the man continued to Julien. "But Mrs. Crayton and I have everything ready for you, my lord."

"Excellent," Julien said in his easy way that so endeared him to those in his employ. "Her ladyship is quite fatigued from the long journey. Would you be so kind as to show her to her room, Maria?"

"I am not at all fatigued, Julien," Kate said frostily, her hackles rising automatically at his calm assumption of authority. She nodded graciously to Mrs. Crayton, and said charmingly, "However, I would very much like to see my room."

"Her ladyship has a great deal of stamina," Julien interposed. "Has the weather continued warm, James?" he asked.

"Yes, my lord, though the nights are quite chilly now. A peaceful place this is. Mrs. Crayton and I fancy that we can hear our hair grow, so quiet it is!"

Kate ignored Julien's laugh and followed Mrs. Crayton into a small entranceway. As she mounted the delicately carved staircase that wound in circular fashion to the upper floor, Julien halted her progress. "Kate, let us dine in an hour. Is that sufficient time for you to refresh yourself?"

"Perfectly adequate, my lord, though I do find that I grow fatigued . . . from our long journey."

"I do, of course, appreciate your efforts to please, my dear, despite your sudden feeling of weariness." Julien grinned, and she found the corners of her mouth tilted up at his sally. As this would never do, she quickly turned, hurrying after Mrs. Crayton.

She was shown into a small, delightfully furnished room, dominated on one side by a fireplace and on the other by long curtained windows of pale pink satin. The furniture was all white and gold, in the French style, blending with exquisite artistry into the delicate shade of pinks in the carpet. Her eyes alight with pleasure, Kate turned impulsively to Mrs. Crayton. "It is such a lovely room! I am surprised to find such elegance in so remote a place."

"Indeed, my lady, Mr. Crayton and I were quite pleased when his lordship told us we were to come here."

"You are part of his lordship's staff in London?" Kate asked, giving the beaming woman her full attention.

"Why, yes, my lady. Mr. Crayton and I were with his lordship's father, the late Earl of March. It was quite excited we were, coming to this foreign place, and all. His lordship said we needed a change of air, he did."

Kate pursed her lips. A journey from London to Switzerland must occupy the better part of a week. The Craytons would have had to leave England before Julien came to Paris. To verify her suspicions, she asked, "When did his lordship send you here, Mrs. Crayton?"

"We've been here nearly a week now, my lady," Mrs. Crayton confided, unaware of a sudden tenseness in her young mistress. "You see, my lady, his lordship told us he was going to be married in Paris and he wanted us to come immediately to have all in readiness for your ladyship. But, of course, your ladyship knows all of this already!" She smiled kindly at Kate. "Mr. Crayton is forever telling me that my tongue runs on wheels, begging your ladyship's pardon."

"Yes, yes, of course I knew, Mrs. Crayton," Kate hastened to say. Though the woman's tongue ran on wheels, they were quite informative ones, she thought. Damn Julien anyway! How very certain he had been of himself and of her.

Mrs. Crayton read the tightening of her ladyship's lips and the sudden frown on her forehead as signs of fatigue. "Do forgive me, my lady, for rambling on so. You just sit down and rest by the fire and I'll have Mr. Crayton fetch up a nice hot bath."

When Mrs. Crayton had removed her garrulous self from

the room, Kate yanked off the expensive bonnet and flung it on a chair. The blue velvet cloak that Julien had bought for her, she tossed in a heap on top of the bonnet. She sank down into the soft cushions of the setee that faced the fireplace and idly looked about her for an object that would make a likely projectile to fling at Julien, were he to present himself. She looked fondly at a small gilded mirror that hung over the mantel but thought pessimistically that he would handily duck it were it to be hurled at his head. Kate found that the mental image evoked by such a confrontation was so comical that she could not long maintain her seething anger. She even found herself thinking somewhat philosophically that it would have been most unlike Julien to forget so important an item as accommodations for their wedding trip. She wondered, indeed, if he ever forgot any detail, including the perfectly fitted satin undergarments that felt so delightfully luxurious against her skin.

Kate sighed and remarked to the crackling fire, "Well, my girl, there is no way of getting around the fact that you are married." She supposed that, once married, one remained married and made the best of it. She instantly took exception to her own thinking, roundly chiding herself that nothing had changed between them. She would not allow him to bend her to his will. As this resolve brought with it an unsettling sense of dissatisfaction, she closed her eyes and concentrated on thinking about absolutely nothing.

When Kate appeared in the cozy dining room closer to two hours later than one, she saw Julien standing in front of the long windows, his back to her, gazing out into the darkness. He turned as her rustling skirts announced her presence, and she was momentarily taken aback by the very serious expression on his face. But in an instant the expression was gone, and he lazily strolled to where she stood, took her hand in his, and kissed her fingers.

"How very beautiful you are tonight, my dear," he murmured.

"I fear, Julien, that you compliment the gown you chose rather than its wearer," she replied dryly.

"Do not forget, my dear wife, that I appraised the wearer long before I purchased the gown." He grinned at her impishly, and as Kate made no response, he asked, "Do you find your room adequate?"

"Yes, of a certainty. It is quite charming." She spoke with

more enthusiasm than she had intended, her pleasure with her room causing her to unbend a trifle.

"I trust also that you will find no fault with the sherry," he said, handing her a glass. "It is really quite excellent. The Conte Bellini's cellar rivals that of St. Clair."

"Which reminds me, Julien," Kate interrupted. "Mrs. Crayton informed me that they are not only in your household staff in London but they have been here for nearly a week! You told them you were getting married in Paris!"

A sleek brow shot up in seeming surprise. "But of course, Kate. Would you not wish to have all in readiness for you when we arrived here?"

"That is not the point, as you very well know," she retorted hotly. "You told them before you left England."

"Had I not, how else could they have been here in good time?" Julien drained the remainder of his sherry and regarded her with mild surprise, as if he could not comprehend why she would be upset at such a logical course of action.

Kate fidgeted with her glass a moment, realizing that to continue in her argument would only provide him with more ridiculous amusement at her expense. "Very well, Julien," she said, trying her best to quell him with a frown, "since you so conveniently refuse to acknowledge the justice of my point, I do not wish to haggle further with you. Oh, how nice, here is our dinner."

"Begging your lordship's pardon, but you said dinner was to be served when her ladyship arrived."

"Your entrance was exquisitely timed, Maria. Kate, my dear, would you care to be seated?"

"How very gracious of you, my Lord March," she replied formally as she seated herself gracefully at the table. "Do try the lamb, Julien, it looks quite delicious," she continued serenely.

"Yes, ma'am," Julien said meekly, and promptly fell to his dinner.

Some minutes later, Julien remarked casually, "Oh, Kate, I forgot to tell you. Harry wrote you a letter and asked that I give it to you."

"A letter from Harry?" she exclaimed, her lamb forgotten. "But how did you get a letter from Harry? No, no, please do not deign to give me a tedious explanation. How ever could I imagine that you would overlook my brother in all your machinations?"

"You begin to understand me, Kate." He grinned as he handed her the envelope. "I do apologize for not giving it to you sooner, but there were so many other . . . pressing matters that I forgot about it. Crayton found it when he was unpacking."

"Yes, yes," she said impatiently, taking the letter from him. It did not take her long to decipher the few lines of Harry's familiar sloping scrawl, and she raised a face pale with anger to Julien. She wadded up the sheet and clutched it in a tight fist.

"Good Lord, Kate, what ever did he write?"

"You put him up to this!" she spat, flinging the ball of paper at him. He caught the paper handily and smoothed it out in front of him. He had expected Harry to simply congratulate his sister, which of course he did, but in such a way that Julien could readily understand why it had raised Kate's hackles. Harry admonished her in no uncertain terms not to make a cake of herself; after all, she was a very lucky girl to be offered marriage by such a distinguished, amiable, and accomplished gentleman. Even this could be forgiven if in his zeal to commend himself to his brother-in-law Harry had not gone so far as to advise her to forget all her nonsensical notions, become an obedient wife, and conduct herself as a countess should. Undoubtedly Harry had meant to do him a favor. Lord, he hadn't meant to so impress the boy! The last few lines were difficult to read, and Julien, after making them out, decided that Kate had not read to the end of her letter. Perhaps it would alleviate her anger.

"Harry was a trifle . . . overexuberant in his advice, Kate. You should forgive him, for he was very excited over joining his regiment."

"Overexuberant!" she cried, and then pulled up short. "What do you mean . . . joining his regiment?"

"The last lines of his letter, Kate. He tells you that by the time you read his letter, he will be on his way to Spain."

"Spain," she repeated blankly.

"Of course, Kate. You knew that was his wish above all things. I made the arrangements before I left London. You need not worry for his safety, for there are only minor squabbles with the guerrillas since Napoleon's downfall."

Kate did not respond to him, but sat stiffly, her head averted. Misunderstanding, Julien said more harshly than he intended, "Good God, Kate, I do not comprehend you! Harry is a grown man. You are behaving as though he were still in short coats!"

"It . . . it is not that," she said unhappily. "It has just happened so quickly." She had the sudden feeling that the world she had known had crumbled about her. Harry had been everything to her after her mother had died. Of course she knew that someday he would leave her, but it had always been in a misty, vague future. But that he should leave without her even knowing it, without giving her time to reconcile herself to it!

It was on the tip of Julien's tongue to further assure her of Harry's safety when he saw her wan look of unhappiness replaced by tight-lipped anger. He realized that she was now dwelling on Harry's other words. He waited patiently for her outburst, but it did not come. Perplexed, he saw the angry look vanish, and to his consternation, she gazed at him steadily and said in a desperate voice, "So, my lord, I am to be your obedient wife and conduct myself as a . . . countess should."

Julien stretched out his hand and let his long fingers close over hers. "Advice that I soundly endorse, Kate," he said with a grin, hoping to make light of Harry's ill-chosen words.

But Kate was not to be drawn so easily from her gloomy state of mind. To Julien's discomfiture, a large tear gathered and rolled unheeded down her cheek. She did not sniff or blink, merely let the tear and those following it gather and fall, leaving a light streak to mark their path.

"Kate . . ." he began.

She calmly picked up her napkin, daubed the corners of her eyes, and wiped her cheeks. She said dully, "It seems that I did not know my brother. He is exactly like the rest of you . . . men. He cares naught but for his own pleasures and expects women to keep to their place. An obedient and, yes, undoubtedly, subservient wife . . . that is what he means. Of course, it is what you wish also, Julien."

Kate slipped out of her chair and without another word walked stiffly to the door. She did not turn, but let herself quietly from the room, picked up her skirts, and fled up the stairs to her room.

She looked blindly about her for a moment and then flung herself facedown on the bed. She was lost in her own private misery and was aroused only when the fire in the grate burned low and she began to shiver. Kate stood up shakily and smoothed with an automatic gesture the folds of her gown. It was hopelessly crumpled, but she did not care, for after all, it was Julien's.

She walked stiffly to the windows, found the cord, and jerked back the heavy curtains. The night was black save for a few errant stars that appeared through the heavy veil of darkness. She pulled the latch and leaned out, the cold night air pressing against her face. A picture of Harry in his yellow-striped waistcoat, proudly pluming himself in front of her, came into her mind. Harry, gone to Spain! Deep inside she knew that nothing could ever again be the same. For so long as Harry had remained near to her, a semblance of their years together, the happy moments of her childhood, was preserved. But now they had both crossed irrevocably into a different life, their past forever lost to them.

She suddenly felt very tired. She drew back into the room and slowly closed the window. Not without some difficulty she managed to unfasten the small buttons at the back of her gown. She let the gown slide to the floor and simply stepped out of it, leaving it where it lay. She slipped out of the silk chemise and shift and slid between the warm covers in her bed.

Long after the covers had been removed by the unobtrusive Mrs. Crayton, Julien sat alone in brooding silence. He held a glass of claret in his hand and stared into its depths vaguely. It was smooth, deeply red, and it warmed his stomach. Unfortunately, it had not yet spread its mellowing warmth to his mind. He felt a cold, impotent frustration. Kate seemed farther out of his reach than ever before, even though she was now his wife. Certainly he understood that Harry's admonishments galled her. But Harry's commission was another matter entirely. Why could not Kate accept the fact that Harry was ready for adventure and freedom? He rose from the table and walked slowly and thoughtfully to the fireplace. He leaned his elbows on the mantel and gazed into the dying flames. In that instant he cursed the woman who had so changed his life, the red-haired vixen who had woven her web so completely around him that he no longer desired any other woman. He strode quickly from the dining room and flung out of the villa into the dark night. Without really realizing what he was doing, he found himself walking to the side of the villa, to where Kate's room was located. Almost against his will he looked up at her windows. He sucked in his breath, for the curtains were open and Kate was standing in the middle of her room, clad only in her chemise. His heart quickened at the sight of her. He stood rooted to the spot and watched her after a long moment pull the straps of the chemise off her white shoulders. An ache in his groin became a fire as she let the chemise slip over her breasts and to her slender waist. He forced himself to turn away, cursing his own weakness, as the silken material fell below her waist and he glimpsed her white belly. Despite the coldness of the night, Julien felt sweat on his forehead. With a growl he broke away into a fast walk, forcing himself not to look back. He remained outside, until, finally shivering violently from the cold, he was forced back into the villa.

"His lordship is not here?" Kate asked Mrs. Crayton with a mixture of relief and surprise.

"No, my lady. 'Twas quite early his lordship left this morning to go into the village. He will be returning for dinner." Mrs. Crayton thought it strange that his lordship had not informed his countess of his plans. Indeed, she wondered at her ladyship's puffy eyes and remembered the crumpled gown she had picked up from the floor. She decided that they must have had a lovers' quarrel the previous evening.

"I . . . I see," Kate said, slipping into a wrapper. Perversely, she felt slighted that he had not told her, but then, she thought with a sigh, she had given him little opportunity.

Kate kept herself busy throughout the morning poking her head in and out of the elegant rooms in the villa. After a light luncheon she donned a shawl and strolled out into the grounds. It delighted her that there were no formal gardens, for she had never enjoyed her mother's pastime of pulling up weeds and putting in her favorite flowers. The vast wilderness of forest and mountains gave her a feeling of unrestrained freedom. From the edge of a cliff to the left of the villa she could make out the small village nestled in the valley below. She sat down near the edge and wrapped her skirt about her legs. Although she was used to being alone, particularly after Harry left for Eton, she found that now she did not enjoy her solitude.

She wandered back to the villa, selected a small volume of Lord Byron's poems from the shelf in the well-stocked library, and curled up in the window seat. But her attention was not long held by the poet's bold, haunting words, for she could not help remembering Julien's recital to her of Lady Caroline Lamb and her flaunted affair with the quixotic Byron. She had thought then of the excitement of belonging to such a world, of meeting people who cut such a romantic dash through London society. She sighed and leaned back on her elbows and allowed the thin vellum volume to drop to the floor. Somehow she still felt like the provincial Kate Brandon. She wondered when she would feel like a countess.

Later in the afternoon, bored with her inactivity, Kate sallied forth, and without any particular destination in mind, began to walk down the single winding road that led to the village. Being used to country life, she found the exertion invigorating and maintained a crisp pace. She saw not a soul and allowed herself to be drawn into the quiet serenity of the ageless forest. She bent down to stroke a soft fern that had wound itself around a tree trunk, when she was startled to her feet by a shrill cry. She wheeled around, and seeing nothing, hurried around a bend in the road. She pulled up short, not believing what she saw. A peasant stood in the middle of the road, flailing a mare with a mean, knobby stick. The horse whinnied and shied, but the man held her firmly, cursing and raining blows on her head and back.

Kate picked up her skirts and ran toward the man. He did not notice her presence until she grabbed at his arm and shouted at him, "Stop, you fool! How dare you strike that poor animal!"

The peasant jerked around, baring blackened teeth in an astonished grimace, at the sight of a well-dressed young lady, her face flushed with anger.

Kate realized that she had spoken in English, paused and gathered suitable denunciatory phrases in French. "What ever are you doing, you wretched creature? I demand that you stop beating this poor animal!"

"*You* demand my pretty young lady?" he snarled, derisively eyeing the slender white fingers that clutched at his arm.

"Just look at what you have done," Kate cried, disregarding his words. Flecks of foam dropped from the mare's mouth, and ugly red blood streaks crisscrossed on her head and neck. Kate moved to the horse to quiet her, but the peasant blocked her way and shook the stick in her face. "It is my horse," he cried hoarsely, revealing his blackened teeth, "and I'll give the beast the beating she deserves. Kicked me, she did."

"In all likelihood you deserved the kicking," Kate retorted, standing her ground. From long experience with facing Sir Oliver, ranting and waving his cane at her, she now felt no fear.

The peasant pulled up short at this attack from the foreign lady and narrowed his eyes at her speculatively. He licked his thick lips and looked meaningfully at the single strand of pearls about Kate's neck. "How strange it is that such a fine young lady is out walking by herself," he suggested. "Maybe I'll not beat the beast if you give me those fine pearls." He reached out a dirty hand, and Kate jumped back out of his reach.

"Don't be absurd, you cruel creature. You cannot frighten me! I shall have you whipped, which is less than you deserve, if you so much as lay a hand on me!"

"By whom?" he asked baldly, advancing upon her, the raised stick poised.

Without thought, Kate balled her hand into a fist as Harry had taught her and struck the man full in the face. He staggered back, more from surprise than pain. His rough features distorted with rage, and he cursed her loudly in words she did not understand.

Now frightened, she began to back away from him warily.

"I'll show you, you bitch!" The man rushed at her, swinging the stick in a wide arc.

He had no time to strike her, for in that instant the mare, now freed, reared on her hind legs and thrust her hooves at the peasant's back. He went sprawling and landed on his face mere inches from Kate's feet.

Kate saw her chance, and praying that the mare would not bring her thrashing hooves down upon her own back, grabbed her mane and swung onto her back. The mare snorted in surprise and reared back, her front hooves pawing the air. Kate hung on tight to her mane, disregarding a huge tear that rent her skirt. She saw only the man, who was rising slowly and painfully from the ground, his eyes cruel, narrow slits. Kate threw herself forward on the mare's neck and grasped the loose reins. She felt pain shoot through her leg as the peasant's stick came down on her. She bit back a cry, dug her heels into the mare's sides, and hung on with all her strength as the frightened horse shot forward in an erratic gallop. She did not look back and laid her face against the mare's neck. She realized vaguely that there was only the single mountain road and that they were heading in the direction of the village.

She heard the peasant yelling after her and she looked back in sudden panic, afraid that he had another horse. He was running after her, gesticulating wildly with his fists raised. She breathed only a momentary sigh of relief, for it soon struck her forcibly to wonder what the devil she was going to do. She had stolen a horse, albeit for the purest of motives, and was fleeing toward a foreign village, where, for all she knew, the people were as vicious and uncaring as that horrible peasant.

She felt a sudden surge of hope when she saw in the distance two horses coming up the road at a leisurely pace. It took her but a moment to recognize Julien, with Crayton following closely behind him. She urged the mare forward and waved wildly with one hand. As she neared, she pulled back on the reins. To her despair, the still-frightened mare gave a loud snort and plunged her head down, quickening her pace.

"Good God, Crayton, whoever the devil can that be? What foolhardiness on such a winding road!" Julien exclaimed, reining in his horse. The words died in his throat as he recognized Kate's auburn hair whipping about her face and saw her torn clothing. He dug in his heels, and soon they drew so close that he could see the flaring of the horse's nostrils. "Kate!" he cried as she streaked past him.

"I cannot stop her! Julien!" Kate shouted, flinging her hand back toward him.

Julien wheeled his horse about, and in what seemed an eternity to both of them, drew up beside her and grabbed the mare's reins. For a long moment he struggled with the terrified mare to bring her, finally, to a walk. He leaped from his horse and grasped the reins firmly and with infinite care calmed the animal.

"Oh, thank God, I did not think you would catch us," she panted. Kate slipped off the horse's back, found that her legs were as weak as water, and promptly sat down at the side of the road.

"My lord, whatever has happened?" Crayton exclaimed, dismounting and rushing toward them.

"I do not as yet know, James," Julien replied grimly, still quieting the trembling horse.

"The blood, my lord . . ."

"Yes, I see. Hopefully her ladyship is not harmed, but rather this wretched animal. Here, James, take her reins."

Julien dropped down to his knees in front of Kate, gripped her shoulders, and pulled her to her feet. "Kate . . . Kate, are you all right?"

She nodded mutely and brought up her hands to clutch at his shoulders, her fingers working convulsively. Though she knew now that she was quite safe, the enormity of what she had done rendered her speechless.

"Kate, tell me what has happened! What ever are you doing on a runaway horse?" he demanded, his fear for her giving a sharpness to his words.

His tone steadied her, and she drew back and gave him a rather weak smile. "I fear that I am now to face a magistrate, Julien. You see, I have stolen the horse."

As he looked at her stupefied, Kate gathered together her disordered thoughts and launched into her story. It required several interpolations from Julien to grasp the facts before she lamely came to a finish.

"You understand, do you not, Julien?" Kate pleaded, seeing a frown gather on his brow. "I could not let that horrid man continue to beat the mare. And he simply would not be reasonable about the matter!"

"This peasant, he tried to harm you, Kate?" Julien asked with ominous calm.

"Well, yes, but you see, I gave him great provocation by hitting him in the face," she replied seriously.

"Where is this man?" he demanded. He realized that for the first time in his life he was most willingly prepared to commit murder.

"The last time I saw him, he was standing in the road waving his fists at me. Back up there." She turned and pointed a grimy hand.

Julien turned abruptly to Crayton. "Take the mare, James, and let her ladyship mount your horse. Come, Kate, we are going to settle this matter right now!"

"But, Julien . . ."

He ignored her, took her firmly by the arm, and tossed her into the saddle. He ground his teeth at the sight of her bloodied, torn gown.

Kate found herself frightened, not now for herself, but rather for Julien. "Julien, please, I do not wish you to murder that man," she began.

He was looking like a thundercloud and she saw that her words fell on deaf ears.

"Can you manage the horse?" he asked impatiently.

"Of course I can," she replied, at once indignant.

"Very well. Cease your advice and pay heed to not falling off!"

Kate had not much choice in the matter, for Julien vaulted into the saddle and urged his horse into a gallop.

Julien was furious at the man who would dare try to harm Kate, and at Kate for being so foolish to walk out alone. That she had been quite brave and tried to save the mare, he stored away for future consideration. Fortunately, it was not long before his rational self asserted itself and he was forced to admit that Kate, after all, had quite unlawfully interfered and stolen the man's horse. His blood ran cold at the thought of what would have happened had she not had the quickness of wit to escape on the mare. Damnation! How could he wring the man's neck, when, if one were logical, he had had just provocation?

Kate was praying devoutly that the peasant would be gone. But when they rounded a bend in the road, she saw to her despair that he had not budged, and stood now, legs apart, the knobby stick held tightly in one hand.

Julien drew up some distance from the peasant and turned to Kate. "I want you to stay here," he commanded shortly.

"No, I want—"

"Dammit, do as I tell you! For God's sake, Kate, obey me just this once!"

"Very well," she muttered, her face drained of color. "But I would that you take care, Julien. I would not want us both to be hauled to the magistrate!"

Julien scowled at her before turning to Crayton. "Stay with her ladyship, James. And don't let her leave this spot!"

"Yes, my lord," Crayton replied unhappily.

Kate sat huddled in the saddle, wishing that a Swiss regiment would somehow magically appear. She watched tensely as Julien dismounted and strode toward the peasant. She hunched lower in the saddle and bit her lower lip as the man brandished the stick in Julien's face and yelled wildly in her direction. Kate blinked in astonishment, for the next moment, the man lay sprawled in the dirt and Julien stood over him, calmly rubbing his knuckles. When the man finally struggled to his feet, he appeared to have shrunken visibly in size, so it seemed to Kate. There followed a rapid conversation in French, dominated by Julien. Money changed hands, and to Kate's further surprise, the man bowed to Julien, dusted off his clothing, and walked quickly into the forest.

Kate clicked her horse forward and drew up beside her husband.

"Well, Kate, it seems that you now own a horse," he said, allowing his features to soften at the sight of her haggard face.

"But, Julien, he was such a vicious bully! How ever did you—?"

"You unman me, Kate," he interrupted her, grinning wryly. "When you meet Percy, he will tell you in the most condescending manner possible that I spend too much of my time sparring with Gentleman Jackson."

"The boxer?" she asked cautiously.

"Yes, my dear. Now, let us return to the villa. Both you and your horse are in need of attention."

For the first time Kate became aware of her disheveled condition "Yes, I . . . I am rather a sight," she said uncomfortably.

"But no worse off than your horse, Kate."

"She will be all right, will she not, Julien?" Kate looked at the pitiful specimen she had rescued.

"She will forget this experience more quickly than you will, I wager."

Julien's lightness of heart lasted only until they reached the villa. His anger fanned as he harked to Kate's foolhardiness, born undeniably from his fear for her, and he was out-of-reason cross when finally they drew to a stop. When he helped her to alight, he looked down at her and said wrathfully, "A fine day's work, madam! If you think that I will condone your altogether foolish behavior, you are sadly mistaken. That you would walk out in a strange country, alone, is in itself unforgivable!"

Kate knew she was in the wrong, but she did not understand Julien's consuming fury. "I think, my lord, that you are refining too much upon the . . . the incident," she ventured stoutly.

"Incident?" he growled. "Dammit, have you thought what would have happened if your horse had not so obligingly helped you? And what if I had not stopped your horse?"

"But you did, Julien," Kate said reasonably.

"You little idiot, that is not the point, as you well know!

Kate, I will strangle you myself if ever you again pull such a ridiculous stunt! Do you understand me?"

"It is impossible not to understand, you are ranting so loudly," she said, her temper rising.

"Oh, the devil!" he shouted in exasperation. "Go to your room and try to make yourself presentable. I will see you at dinner, in an hour." He gave her a none-too-gentle push to the door.

Kate walked without a word into the villa, trying in vain to hold together the gaping tear in her skirt.

"James, see to the mare," Julien called over his shoulder as he followed Kate through the front door. He heard Mrs. Crayton give a scream and thought, not without some pleasure, that Kate would receive a good trimming from yet another quarter.

Kate begged, cajoled, and threatened Mrs. Crayton not to inform his lordship when the woman discovered the swollen, discolored bruise on her thigh. She finally secured her reluctant agreement after assuring her mendaciously that it bothered her not at all.

For the first time, Kate entered the dining room not even one minute late. She was beginning to ache all over, as if the peasant had flailed her with his stick, and not the mare.

Julien had planned to lecture her at length during dinner, but at the sight of her exhausted face, such intentions vanished. Without thinking, he took her gently in his arms, and to his surprise, she raised her hands to his shoulders and pressed herself against him. After a few moments he murmured softly, his chin resting against her hair, "Please forgive me, Kate, for ripping up at you. It is just that if something had happened to you . . ."

Kate drew back and gave him a watery smile. "You were a worse bully than that horrible man, Julien."

"You are pert and headstrong, Kate, and most deserving of a trimming," he replied promptly.

She was disinclined to argue this point and said: "Cannot we now say that all's well that ends well?"

He was obliged to laugh. "What, Kate, more Shakespeare?"

"Julien, I am not a shrew and your veiled references are quite . . . odious!"

"Undoubtedly you are right," Julien acquiesced, not willing to give her reason to quit the circle of his arms. "You now have one task left, Kate, and that is to name your mare."

Kate grew thoughtful. "You know, it is too bad that she is a mare, for Gabriel would be my choice. You see, I was quite convinced that I had reached my judgment day," she explained candidly.

His arms tightened about her as he recalled his anxiety for her. "Then she shall be Gabriella, Kate."

She looked up at him fixedly for a moment, the expression on her face unreadable, and lightly slipped from his arms.

"What, another order, Julien?" she said over her shoulder with an attempt at lightness. A part of her wanted desperately to be pressed against his broad chest, to feel his strength and his gentleness.

"My only order, Kate, is that you do not get yourself strangled by any other man than myself."

"I shall endeavor, my lord, to do your bidding in this matter," she replied in docile tones, but her eyes twinkled impishly as he assisted her to sit at the table.

There was a companionable silence between them as Mrs. Crayton served their dinner, clucking worriedly each time she gazed at Kate. When she left the room, Kate looked up from her plate and remarked wryly, "The way she is acting, I feel as though I should curl up my toes and pass over to the hereafter."

"Oh, Julien," she continued before he could respond, "what ever were you doing in the village today? I thought perhaps that you were . . . not pleased here and wished to make arrangements to return to England," she said candidly.

He raised his brows in surprise. "Why ever should I not be pleased, Kate?"

She colored slightly. "Oh, I can really think of no reason—how stupid of me to say such a thing! Now, do tell me, Julien, what was your errand?"

"It was a matter of some importance, Kate, and I hope—indeed, I am quite certain—that the result will meet with your approval."

"*My* approval? Come, stop teasing me! What have you done?" Her lips were parted slightly, and her eyes shone with curiosity.

Rather than answer her immediately, Julien swiveled around in his chair, regarded the clock on the mantel, and appeared to give some weighty problem due consideration. He turned back to her, a smile on his face. "Perhaps we should wait until tomorrow, Kate. You have had a . . . try-ing day."

"Julien, it is too horrid of you!" she cried. "I assure you, I feel as fine as a new penny!"

"Very well. Go to your room—an instruction, not an or-der. You will find a surprise. I will expect you in the library in fifteen minutes."

Kate cocked her head in silent inquiry, but as he merely shook his head, she whisked herself out of the room. She had no idea what to expect, but when she found a pair of black silk breeches, a frilled white shirt, and a pair of elegant black boots set neatly on her bed, she was baffled. In but a trice she was gazing at her trim figure in the long mirror. She quickly drew on the boots, pulled her hair back, and secured it with a black ribbon.

She skipped out of her room and down the stairs, unable to contain her excitement. She pushed open the library door to see Julien standing in the middle of the room, dressed as she was, in breeches and shirt. In his hand he held two foils.

Kate pulled up short with a gasp of surprise. "Julien! You don't mean . . . foils? One is for me?"

His eyes lit up at her evident pleasure, but she did not no-tice, her gaze being fastened to the foils he held.

"I believe you expressed a desire to have fencing lessons, did you not, Kate?" He walked to her and placed a foil in her hand.

"Oh, yes!" she exclaimed. "Julien, you are too good!" She clasped the foil in sheer delight and bent it back and forth, testing its flexibility.

She looked up after a few moments of this pastime and said with wonder in her voice, "But, Julien . . . I lost our wager at piquet, do you not recall?"

"What has that to say to anything? It has been a great while since I have had a worthy opponent. I only hope, Kate, that I am not to be butchered, as was poor Harry."

"As long as there is a button on the tip, you have no need to worry!" He was rewarded with a dimpled smile.

Julien moved swiftly away from her to the center of the room and presented his side, his foil unwaveringly straight, in salute.

"*En garde,* madam!"

"*En garde!*" she repeated with great delight, and thrust her own foil forward.

Their foils clashed together in the silent room with a ring of steel. Julien was unsure of Kate's ability and at first rigidly controlled the speed and power of his thrusts. He discovered very quickly that she was an aggressive fencer as he parried lunge after lunge. She held herself perfectly straight, her form excellent. She appeared to have no fear whatsoever and executed the most daring of maneuvers. No wonder she rolled up poor Harry! Julien smiled as he tested for areas of weakness. Kate's foil was like her tongue—quick, sharp, and quite spontaneous. He slipped through her guard, drew up short, and pulled back. She merely laughed and in a quick flurry skipped forward and drove him back with rapid steps to the corner of the room. Their foils locked together for a moment before Julien, with a practiced flick of his wrist, sent her foil spinning from her grasp to the floor. She looked momentarily surprised, laughed at herself, and hurried to retrieve her foil. As she bent forward, the bruise on her thigh, to this point not at all bothersome, sent a flash of pain through her leg. She quickly averted her head and gritted her teeth, cursing the leg and the peasant who had struck her.

Julien saw the tiny furrow of pain on her forehead and instantly drew up and dropped his foil to his side. But he thought he must have been mistaken, for when Kate straightened, her face glistening and her foil held securely once more in her hand, she shot him a dazzling smile and cried gaily, "I do believe you are better than Harry! And now, Julien," she said, advancing on him, "I defy you to catch me so unawares again with your tricks!"

"Better than Harry? Such praise, Kate! As for my tricks, let us see if I catch you napping again."

As Kate lunged forward, shifting weight on the leg, another surge of pain distorted her face and she clamped her lips together tightly to prevent the cry that threatened to escape. She drew up and turned about. "It has been a long day, Julien. Though you have soundly thrashed me tonight, I shall seek redress tomorrow. You will see that I am not so easily vanquished!"

"That I caught you off your guard for a moment does not constitute a thrashing, Kate. Redress you shall certainly have." He added with undisguised pride in his voice, "I have indeed been granted a most worthy opponent."

"That is very kind of you, Julien," she began in a low voice, feeling at the moment strangely inadequate to express what she felt at his praise. She walked with great care to the desk to place her foil in the open case.

He strode to her with the express intent of placing his foil beside hers. To his chagrin, Kate misunderstood his motive and backed away so quickly that she stumbled into the desk chair. His jaw tightened. His open, confiding Kate was gone behind a mask of fear. He turned his back to her and began to carefully cover the foils with the velvet cloth. He said in a rigidly controlled voice, "It is getting quite late and you have had a rather strenuous day. I will see you in the morning."

There was no response, and Julien turned to see Kate clutching the back of the chair, her face chalk white.

"Go to bed, Kate," he said harshly. Why the devil didn't she move? Was she trying to taunt him?

"I would, Julien, but I . . . I cannot walk." Having made this admission, she lowered her face, perilously near to tears with embarrassment.

"What the devil!" He was at her side in an instant and drew her up against him. She cried out and he picked her up in his arms and deposited her gently on the sofa. Kate lay back against the cushions and took a deep breath. "I . . . I am sorry, Julien, in but a few moments I shall be fine. All that activity, you know—"

He interrupted her, his voice thunderous. "Kate, what is the matter? Why can you not walk?"

"It is nothing, I tell you. Please, Julien, just help me to my room," she pleaded, raising herself on her elbow.

"I tell you, Kate," he said, bending a stern eye on her, "if you do not this instant enlighten me about your inability to walk, I swear that I shall tear off your breeches and examine you myself!"

Kate capitulated, feeling altogether too wretched to argue further. "The peasant, he struck my leg with his stick when I jumped onto Gabriella. But I assure you, Julien," she continued hurriedly, " 'tis but a bruise. It only hurts because I bumped into the chair."

"Kate, dammit, I've a good mind to throttle you! That man struck you and you did not deign to tell me? And don't talk fustian to me about your leg hurting only when you bumped into the chair!" Julien struck his forehead with his hand in disbelief and exasperation. "Woman, you would try the patience of a saint. And you were foolish enough to fence with me with your leg hurt!"

Kate eased herself into a sitting position and gazed at her agitated husband. "Julien, I did not tell you because I knew you would make a great fuss. You are really quite as bad as Mrs. Crayton. As for my foolishness to fence with you, it is, after all, my leg, and I shall do as I wish."

She saw his eyes flash daggers and quickly added, "Julien, don't you dare go . . . murder that man! Although he is mean and vicious, he certainly got his just deserts today. I hit him too, do you not remember?"

"Commendable," he said acidly. "Kate . . . No, this argument is quite ridiculous!" Without further ado and ignoring her protests, he swept her up in his arms.

As he carried her up the stairs, she asked in a small voice, "You are just . . . taking me to my room, are you not?"

"No," he replied shortly, not looking at her face. "I am going to see just how foolish you have been by examining your *bruise* myself."

As she tensed perceptibly in his arms, he added in a most uncompromising voice, "And do not bother to argue the point, Kate, for my mind is quite made up."

He turned at the top of the stairs and called out, "Mrs. Crayton, we require your presence in her ladyship's room."

The peremptory tone of the earl's voice brought Mrs. Crayton scurrying from the kitchen her hands still covered with flour from the bread she was baking. She perceived her young mistress quite flushed in his lordship's arms, blinked rapidly, and bustled after them, wiping her hands on her apron.

Kate was only partially relieved that Julien had enlisted the aid of Mrs. Crayton. She was laid very gently on her bed and told roundly not to move.

Julien turned to Mrs. Crayton, who stood somewhat out of breath in the doorway. "Maria, I understand that her ladyship has a bruise on her leg. Don't look alarmed, for I am quite certain that she was most persuasive in convincing you not to tell me."

"Julien, I really think that you carry this much too far," Kate began in protest.

"As for you, Kate," he continued, disregarding, "Mrs. Crayton will undress you and preserve your modesty by leaving only the bruise visible. Call me when you have finished, Maria."

"Yes, my lord," Mrs. Crayton said quickly, relieved that she had escaped so lightly.

Julien entered the room not many minutes later and Kate turned her head away in embarrassment as he looked down at the goodly expanse of thigh that was exposed.

Julien swore softly under his breath. The bruise had swollen and turned a deep purplish black. Gently he probed around the area and slowly moved his fingers to the swollen bruise. Kate stiffened in pain but made no sound. He straightened and stood quietly in frowning thought. He said finally: "I do not think a doctor is necessary, Kate, but I fear that you must curb your activities for a while. Are you in pain now?"

"Oh, no, Julien, I assure you I am not!"

"Of course, I disbelieve you, my dear. Maria, fetch the laudanum. I think three drops in a glass of water will suffice."

"But I don't want to dose myself," she declared belligerently.

"Do be quiet, Kate." There was an edge of impatience to his voice, as if he were speaking to a recalcitrant child.

"Damnation, Kate! I could have pierced your heart at least five times in as many minutes! You must think constantly and observe me carefully. You are not fencing by yourself nor with a blind man! Never underestimate the skill of your opponent!"

Kate stood panting with exertion, her face glistening with sweat. "Aye, you are right." It did not occur to her to take umbrage.

"Lunge, withdraw! Lunge, withdraw!" She pushed herself until her arm trembled with fatigue.

It was invariably Julien who halted their lessons, not Kate. After one day of enforced inactivity, she had announced that she was fit as a fiddle and skipped several times in front of Julien to prove her leg no longer pained her.

"Very well," he had said, "but today, only riding, Kate."

During the next three days, their time had fallen into a comfortable pattern; they fenced in the mornings and explored the countryside surrounding the villa in the afternoons. Gabriella appeared to be favorably disposed toward Kate, her former life with the peasant forgotten.

But to Kate, their evenings together were a trial. Each time that Mrs. Crayton helped her to dress in one of her elegant gowns, she felt a sense of wariness descend over her. And yet, she felt it was Julien who was different. Dressed in his severely cut black evening clothes that seemed to emphasize the saturnine set of his elegant brows and the strong line of his jaw, he became a stranger to her, a threatening personage with frightening claims on her. If only their days could have ended after riding! She came to dread the hours passed in the soft candlelight, sensing in him a growing frustration, a barely restrained urgency. She would feel his gray eyes sweep over her, hungrily resting upon her mouth, then lower, on her breasts, devouring her with burning intensity. She cursed herself for showing her obvious discomfiture, but she could not help the disjointed and hasty excuse of tiredness that heralded her hasty departures to her room.

As she lay in bed each night waiting for sleep to come, she would try to close him from her mind. But she could not; he was there, stark and real within her mind, waiting. With him came a certain coldness and strange unexplained images that swept through her, leaving her confused and frightened. She would stare into the darkness and whisper a simple Scottish prayer her mother had taught her.

One day over luncheon, Julien informed her that he had business concerns to deal with that afternoon in the village and would be unable to accompany her on their daily riding expedition. Kate's face fell into lines of disappointment.

"Do forgive me, Kate, but it is likely that I will be late this evening. Do go riding. You know the countryside quite well, and I believe that Gabriella could outdistance the peasant if you happened to be so unfortunate as to cross paths with him again."

She replied with guarded lightness, "As you will. Shall you be here for dinner?"

"Were I not to be here, Kate, would you miss my presence?" He regarded her steadily, and although she answered him calmly enough, there were two bright patches of embarrassed color on her cheeks. "But of course I would. If you are not returned, I will simply content myself with a tray in my room."

"How could I ever doubt that you would miss me at night?" he asked sardonically, his question a rhetorical one.

She refused to meet his gaze, and even when he prepared to take his leave of her, she maintained a restrained silence. Before he mounted, he turned to her and gently touched his hand to her cheek. Startled, she drew back. She watched in embarrassed silence as his gray eyes hardened and he regarded her coldly. He turned quickly away from her and without another word passing between them, he mounted, wheeled his horse about, and was gone. He did not look back.

Kate was still pondering his words and his abrupt departure from her as she carefully guided Gabriella through the thick woods to the long, open meadow beyond. Freed from the embarrassed restraint she had felt at his nearness, she could not but feel now that his measured words, so calmly spoken, had been meant to taunt her. How aloof and cold his regard had been when he had left her! Even a week ago she would have rejoiced in what she would have felt to be a minor victory, but now she felt an unsettling confusion.

The wind tugged at her riding hat when she gave Gabriella her head across the long expanse of meadowland. She had always thought it strange that nature had carved this open land, so at variance with the dense forest that surrounded it. She gave Gabriella a flick of the reins and the horse tossed her head, easing into a steady gallop. Kate was a good deal surprised when suddenly her horse pulled up short and reared back on her hind legs. She grabbed at the pommel to steady herself and wheeled around in the saddle in panic, expecting to see the peasant rushing at her, flailing the air with that vicious stick. But it was not the peasant but rather a man on horseback, enveloped in a long greatcoat, riding purposefully toward her. She drew Gabriella up, thinking that he was perhaps lost and in need of directions. She felt merely curiosity until he drew near and she saw that his face was masked. In a croaking voice that did not sound like her own, Kate urged Gabriella forward, her mouth suddenly gone dry with fear. Her horse needed no further encouragement and shot forward. In but a moment the meadow blended back into forest, and after a moment's hesitation Kate knew that she could not escape through the thick underbrush. She jerked Gabriella about, driving her in a wide circle, skirting the edge of the trees as close as she dared. But the man was fast advancing on her, and she realized with a tingling fear up her spine that in but a moment he would cut her off. The horse's hooves pounded in her ears and even as her mind refused to believe that this could possibly be happening to her, she screamed in blind panic as a strong pair of arms pulled her up out of the saddle. She found herself held in an iron grip, so close to the man that she could hear his breathing.

The man pulled his horse to a halt and nimbly vaulted to the ground, still holding her pinioned against him. Instinctively she struggled wildly and pounded his chest, until he grasped her hands and fastened them against her sides. Kate kicked out at the man's shins. Her boot connected with bone and flesh and he gave a cry of surprise and pain. In the next instant she was on her back on the ground, the cloaked man out of reach of her flailing legs.

Her body froze when her captor leaned over her and said softly in guttural, accented English, his voice muffled by his mask, "I will not harm you. Hold still, *liebchen.*"

She forced her numbed mind to alertness, realizing that she must be calm, use her wits. The man had spoken to her; she must try to reason with him.

"What do you want with me?" she demanded, surprised at the cold authority of her voice.

He did not answer but fumbled for something in one of the pockets of his black greatcoat. She tried to squirm away but his other arm held her firmly. "Please," she pleaded, "what do you want of me? I have no money and I have done you no injury!" Dear God, where was Julien? The thought of him brought her new hope. Perhaps he did not know who she was.

"I have a husband, he is the Earl of March. He is an English nobleman and a very powerful man. You must realize that he will miss me. He will kill you if you do not let me go this instant! Do you not understand?" Kate's voice rose to an almost hysterical pitch, but still the man did not reply. She did not know if her words made any impression on him, for the mask and hat covered his head completely. It made him all the more terrifying, for he seemed to be faceless.

He withdrew a white handkerchief and with it a small vial of liquid.

"What are you going to do?" Kate's voice was hollow with fear. Before she knew what he was about, he leaned his body over her chest and wet the handkerchief with the liquid. He straightened, grasped her shoulders firmly, and brought the cloth over her face. A strong odor filled her nostrils and Kate began to struggle wildly. She thrashed her head back and forth, trying to escape the cloth. Without realizing it, she inhaled deeply and felt bitter fumes attack her senses. She began to feel lightheaded, her reason deserting her. The man eased his arm around her head and held her still. Kate heard herself cry out before she succumbed and slipped from consciousness.

10

Kate opened her eyes and blinked in rapid succession, trying to free her mind of the terrifying remnants of her nightmare. She shuddered and tried to rise, but her body would not obey her. She focused her eyes in an effort to clear the clinging lightheadedness and realized with a start that she was not in her own room. She had not dreamed the man, the drugged cloth pressed over her face. She made a determined effort to rise, only to find that her arms were pulled above her head and her wrists securely tied to the posts of the bed. She lifted her head from the pillow and tugged with all her strength at the bonds, but it was no use. She lay back panting and tried to calm herself. Why had the man brought her to this place? There had to be some mistake! She realized in that instant that she was not in her riding habit. She felt a soft, flimsy material covering her body. With terrifying clarity she pictured herself half-clothed, her arms drawn away from her body. He had tied her down; she was helpless. What did he want with her? her mind screamed. But somewhere, deep within her, she knew why she was tied down, knew what he wanted with her. Her mind seemed to snap with the knowledge, and sent her reeling to the edge of a yawning gulf of blackness. All she knew was lost to her, as the blackness engulfed her, sucking her down farther and farther into its depths. She saw herself small and cowering, then struggling frantically, caught and trapped by she knew not what. Intense, rending pain tore through her, and above the pain she heard cruel, taunting voices. Screaming, furious voices that somehow intensified the pain. She could not bring her hands to cover her ears to blot out the horror of the pain and the voices. She screamed and the images and the voices faded, drawing away from her, becoming as fragments of whispers, strewn as distant echoes to the farthest reaches of another place. She became aware of the anguished sound of her cries and felt beads of perspiration sting her eyes. Kate thought at that moment that perhaps she was mad, for she could not understand what had happened to her. The present righted itself and she saw that nothing had changed. She tried to regain her calm, forcing herself to gaze about the unfamiliar room, and found the presence of the solid pieces of furniture somehow reassuring.

The sound of a key turning in the lock brought her eyes, fearful, yet hopeful, to the door. The man, her captor, slowly entered the room, his long cloak swirling about his ankles as he turned and grated the key in the lock. He was still enveloped in hat and mask, even wearing gloves on his hands. Kate stared at him, her eyes dark green pools, widened and enormous with silent fear. He drew to a halt beside her, and before Kate could understand what he was about, he leaned over her and in a swift motion drew a length of black cloth from his pocket and folded it over her eyes. Kate was plunged into darkness. Like a trapped, frenzied animal, she thrashed her head from side to side as the man jerked her forward and tied the cloth in a secure knot behind her head.

In that moment Kate wondered if she had been brought to this place to die. Unbidden, Julien's calm, handsome face rose in her mind's eyes. She saw him turn from her in cold contempt.

She began to tremble violently, and the sickening, jeering voices pounded in her head, then receded as if they had never existed. Sudden anger kindled within her and burned away her trembling with its intensity. How dare this man bind and blindfold her! She jerked up her head and screamed at him, "You filthy pig—how dare you! My husband, the Earl of March, will kill you if you do not instantly release me! Do you understand me?" There was only a deadening silence, save for the rasping of her own breath.

The man's silence fanned her anger. "Damn you to hell!" she yelled at him. "You coward—are you afraid that I will see your ugliness? Let me see you!" She fell back against the pillow.

Still the man made no response, but she heard him move

away from her. As the precious minutes passed, she thought that he had understood and was going to leave her alone. To her horror, she felt the cover being pulled from her body and she saw herself clothed only in the flimsy material, exposed to this man's eyes. He sat on the bed beside her and she felt his breath on her face. His lips came down upon hers, gentle yet demanding. She clamped her mouth firmly shut and felt his lips move to her throat, and his hands lightly caress her shoulders.

The warmth of the room touched her skin as he slowly eased the material away from her shoulders and down over her breasts. She felt him untying the ribbons, pulling her body free of the gown. He slid the material to her waist, where it lay bunched about her.

The last remnants of what Kate knew, of what she understood, left her in that instant. There was a blankness in her mind and an undefined dread that mingled together, leaving her nearly senseless. Tiny points of light exploded in her mind, and she realized dimly that she had been holding her breath. She opened her mouth, and precious air flew past her constricted throat into her chest. She could feel her breasts heaving but she could not stop their deep upward and downward motion. His fingers were on her forehead, gently pushing back tendrils of hair. She tried to evade him, pulling away as far as her bonds would allow. But his fingers were tracing the line of her cheek, her lips, her throat. She wanted desperately to plead with him to stop, but she could find no words.

The man's hands were on her shoulders—firm, strong hands. Her body grew rigid as she felt his fingers move to her breasts. He was kneading her, caressing her nipples until they grew hard and taut between his long fingers. "I beg of you . . . please do not . . ." she whispered mindlessly.

His hands left her breast, and in the long silent moment that followed, Kate felt his eyes upon her face. She sensed a hesitance in him. If only she could see! Her eyes strained, but there was only blackness.

He came down over her body and enfolded her in his arms, burying his face against her neck, holding her so tightly that she could not breathe. She knew she had lost.

He lifted himself off her, and his hands traveled quickly, urgently, back to her breasts. She felt his mouth upon her, kissing and nibbling her throat and shoulders, until finally his lips and hands played together over her breasts. Kate cried out and tried to twist her body free of him. His hands moved to encircle her waist, and as she tried to arch and wrench away, he eased them beneath her to stroke her back.

Tears scalded her eyes and dampened the black cloth that blinded her. She heard her own voice, begging and pleading with him to stop, but her words broke from her mouth only as meaningless, incoherent sounds.

His hands left her back and tugged at the material about her waist. In a swift motion he slipped the flimsy cloth from beneath her hips, leaving her naked.

There was a sharp intake of breath from the man, and Kate knew that he was staring at her, examining her body. She had never been so aware of her body, of its purpose, and its meaning to men.

Kate knew she was rapidly growing exhausted. The futility of her struggles, her fear, was sapping her strength. She stilled, her body tensed. The damp cloth, salty from her tears, burned her eyes. She turned her head on the pillow and clamped her jaws together, waiting.

His weight came down on the bed and his naked shoulders pressed against her body. His lips touched her waist and roved downward to her belly, his tongue scalding against her skin. She pushed her hips down into the softness of the bed, but it seemed to excite him only the more. She felt shocks of fiery sensation where his lips touched her.

She could picture him, now balanced on his elbow, gazing down at her. His fingers played over the softness of her belly, and paused, ever so slightly, before closing over the curly auburn triangle of hair. His touch was feather-light, but she felt seared, irreparably marked by his touch. His fingers continued their exploration, pressing and probing the softness between her thighs.

Kate cried out in shock and humiliation, writhing frantically to rid herself of him. But slowly and rhythmically he stroked her, his other hand roving upward to fondle her heaving breasts.

Impossible to struggle free of him, for his hands seemed to touch and probe every part of her body, the gentle pressure of his fingers burning her flesh. Exhausted, Kate ceased her struggles. Deep rasping sobs broke from her throat. She felt defiled, her mind and body sick with fear. She tried to detach her mind, but she could not. She was aware of his every touch.

A gasp of shock broke her sobs when his fingers ceased their rhythmic caressing and she felt his mouth upon her. She jerked her hips from side to side, but he only slid his hands under her and lifted her upward. His tongue flicked over her lightly, tentatively, gently tugging, possessing her.

Kate could not move, her hips and thighs firmly grasped in his hands. She was locked against his mouth, as if he were a part of her. She lay stiff and unyielding, her body and mind outraged, when suddenly an intense sensation, an almost painful searing, exploded in her loins. Her mind plummeted and merged with the feeling, consuming her with its strength. The searing sensation faded, leaving her weak and uncertain of what had happened. She tensed every muscle and held her breath. But his mouth was burning her, white-hot and deep. Julien's image rose sharply in her mind. Dear God, she was betraying him! She could no longer deny her desire, her longing at the hands of another man, a stranger whom she could not even see. All the words her father had screamed at her were true. She was a slut, a whore, no better than Julien's lustful mistresses. How could she go back to him now?

She felt the sensation building again, fanning throughout her body. Her mind screamed for him to stop, but only low, feverish moans emerged from her mouth. Frenzied waves of the exquisite inflaming pleasure swept through her body. Somehow, in the distant recesses of her mind, she felt that if he were to stop, she would die. She lost her will to fight him and strained her hips upward toward his mouth, urging him, becoming one with him. Her moans and soft cries filled the stillness of the room. The feeling coursed through her, like great waves breaking, receding and building again. She trembled uncontrollably as shock after shock of ecstatic pleasure shot down her legs and up into her belly.

Slowly the waves of pleasure lessened, and a soft glow of warmth spread through her body, leaving her weak and shaking. The man's lips left her, and she felt an undeniable yearning, a sense of incompletion.

Julien shifted his position, and lay his full length beside her, his hands now moving over her belly and breasts with calm possessiveness. As he gazed at her, his desire grew. Her hair was spread about her face in tangled masses over the pillow, the stark black of the cloth deepening the pallor of her cheeks. He breathed deeply, schooling himself, ignoring the burning in his loins. His hands stroked her thighs, downward as far as he could reach, and then up, over and over, in long, sensual strokes. He let his hands move up between her thighs, caressing and savoring the white softness.

She was moaning, gentle cries of longing, of desire. Now he was certain that she was ready for him. He straightened over her and gently parted her. She gave a cry of surprise as he slowly entered her. Blood pounded in his temples, yet he knew he must control his thrusts, for she was a virgin and he did not want to hurt her any more than was necessary. He pushed deeper into her, feeling for her maidenhead.

She suddenly screamed, her voice hoarse with terror. She struggled frantically, wildly, to free herself of him. He drew back quickly in surprise, for he did not think he had hurt her. But his own desire was now an insistent throbbing. Though he felt her fear, he refused to withdraw from her. Slowly he allowed himself to ease deeper inside her. In the next instant he realized with undeniable certainty that she had no maidenhead. She was not a virgin! He jerked back, dumbfounded. No, he thought frantically, he must be mistaken! But her fear, her wild struggles, seemed to betray her. She had deceived him! Savage, uncontrolled fury swept over him. She had given herself to another man—or was it to other men? his mind screamed. God, how very gentle and careful he was, seducing his innocent, virgin wife!

Cruelly, violently he thrust deep within her, oblivious of her cries of pain. He tore through the small, tight passage, ripping her in his frenzy. He gripped her hips in his hands, his fingers digging mercilessly into her flesh, and forced her body to meet his thrusts. He pounded into her, pushing until he could go no deeper. Her screams rent the silence of the room, but he paid no heed, too consumed in his own fury. He wanted only to hurt her, to punish her.

He cried out as his own desire flooded over him, holding him in its grip for a brief moment. He drove into her with all his strength, spewing his seed deep within her body. Finally spent, he let himself fall on top of her, his head next to her cheek.

As if from a great distance, Julien heard Kate crying hopelessly. His fury slowly receded, and with it the cruel, animal savagery. Slowly he eased himself off her and stood staring down at her, his mind hollow with blank despair. His

wife. His innocent young virgin wife. God, what a mockery!
Strumpet . . . whore! he cried at her in silent anguish. She
was no longer crying, and he thought her unconscious, so
quietly did she lie, until she tried to bring her legs together in
a weak, futile gesture. A low moan escaped her lips. He
gazed bleakly at her exquisite body, wanting to laugh at his
own folly, his overweening pride. Bitter laughter mixed with
despair in his throat and he turned abruptly away from her.
Now he knew why she had not wanted him to touch her. It
was not fear as a frightened virgin, or a misbegotten desire to
thwart him as her husband, but rather her dread that he
would discover that he was not the first man to have her. His
hands clenched into fists. He wanted to shake the truth out of
her. Who had been the man to possess her? God, not that
bumptious ass Bleddoes! Kate herself had laughed at his tena-
cious courtship of her. But who? Who?

Julien found that he was shaking. Never before in his life
had he so completely lost possession of himself. He turned
back, almost unwillingly, to look at his wife, suddenly sickened with himself. He had savagely raped her, cruelly torn
her body. He had planned so carefully to teach Kate
pleasure, to force her to realize that she was a woman with a
woman's passions. With infinite skill he had thought to reveal
himself to her.

His jaw tightened in renewed anger at her. There had been
no need to teach her passion! God, she had forced him to go
to such lengths because of her lies, her deceit.

For a long moment he cursed her silently, trying to counter
the nagging disgust he felt at his own actions with her unforgivable perfidy. Suddenly he became aware of the time. He
thought it now impossible to reveal himself to her. He must
get her back to the villa. Yes, he had to do that first, then
think.

Julien removed the vial and cloth from the pocket of his
coat, doused the cloth thoroughly, and walked to the bed. As
he bent over her, she thrashed her head wildly to avoid the
cloth. He grasped her firmly and brought the soaked material
over her nostrils. In but a moment she was quiet. He held the
cloth against her face for several minutes to be certain that
she would not awaken too quickly.

He lifted the cloth and let it drop to the floor. Quickly he
untied the blindfold and pulled it away. He stopped short, realizing that it was wet with her tears. His proud Kate. Her

long thick lashes were wet spikes against her cheeks, and her pale skin was blotched with the streaking tears. There was a small drop of blood on her lower lip, bitten in her pain.

Julien forced himself to look away. With shaking fingers he untied the silken bonds from about her wrists, wincing at the dark, mean red welts. His eyes traveled to between her thighs. Mingled with his seed were dark traces of blood. He could feel again how he had torn her. He quickly bathed her and placed the cover over her body. He shrugged himself into his clothes and drew out his watch. A sense of unreality seized him. He had had Kate with him but three hours! It seemed unbelievable that his life could so change in such a short period of time.

He quickly drew Kate into her clothes, not bothering to confine her masses of tangled hair with pins. It did not matter now that Kate looked disheveled.

He lifted his unconscious wife in his arms and walked quickly from the room and out of the small thatched cottage he had secured for this one day. Julien lifted Kate over his shoulder, untied their horses, and mounted, taking the reins of her horse in his free hand. He eased her down into the circle of his arm, wheeled his horse about, and rode away from the cottage.

11

"Oh, thank God you have found her ladyship, my lord! What ever has happened? James searched the grounds and all of the meadow where her ladyship rides."

"She is all right, Maria. She must have fallen from her horse. I found her on my return from the village," Julien said as he strode past Mrs. Crayton into the villa.

"James, quickly, you must fetch a doctor immediately!"

"No!" Julien said sharply. "It is not necessary, Maria. I have examined her ladyship and there are no broken bones. She merely struck her head, and there is nothing a doctor could do that we cannot." Seeing that the Craytons were unconvinced, he added with a curl of his lip, "Would you that the village doctor—a foreigner—attend her ladyship?"

Mrs. Crayton appeared to be struck by the logic of this pronouncement. "What would you have me do, my lord?"

"Fetch hot water and laudanum," he said with cool authority. He turned abruptly and carried his unconscious wife to her room. Kate moaned like a small child as he laid her on the bed and began to pull off her riding jacket. He set his jaw and did not look at her face, but he found that his hands were none too steady in carrying out their task. She seemed so very fragile and vulnerable. He quickened his pace, not wishing her to awaken until he had tucked her into bed. He reflected inconsequentially that women wore too many layers of clothing. He ripped off her satin shift in his impatience, and as he looked down at her naked body, he felt no desire, only an intense despair. Another man had possessed her, had caressed her soft white skin. With a deep moan of animal pain he wrenched himself away and strode to the armoire. He found a nightgown, the one she had worn on their wedding night. He crumpled the soft material in his hands, remembering all too clearly his gallant consideration of her seeming virginal fear. With jerky movements he slipped the gown over Kate's head and smoothed it over her body. He turned at an urgent tap on the door.

"My lord," Mrs. Crayton cried, hurrying forward, "here is the water and laudanum."

"Thank you, Maria," Julien answered, forcing calm into his voice. "You may turn down the bed."

Kate moaned again as Julien eased her between the covers, this time turning her head slightly. Mrs. Crayton took a quick step forward, but Julien blocked her path. "As you see, Maria, her ladyship will be fine in but a moment. I will attend her. Do not worry, I shall call you if your assistance is required."

Mrs. Crayton cast a final glance at her young mistress, turned slowly, and walked from the room. She could not help but feel that his lordship was reacting too calmly to his young wife's accident.

Julien pulled a chair next to the bed and sat down wearily. It seemed that nearly a lifetime had passed in this one afternoon. He gazed at his wife's pale beautiful face and felt a numb coldness sweep through him. How he wanted her to suffer, to feel the deep, scarring humiliation he now felt. His rape of her was not sufficient revenge, for that pain she would soon forget. God, what a ludicrous bargain he had made!

Kate slowly opened her eyes and blinked rapidly to sharpen her blurred vision. She saw her husband sitting next to her, his face buried in his hands. She frowned in confusion for one brief instant before her memory righted itself. She cried out as the details of what had happened to her jetted through her mind.

Julien schooled his voice into false concern. "Kate . . . are you all right?"

She turned wild eyes toward him. Her lips moved and she said in a strangled whisper, "How am I here . . . oh, Julien, is it really you?"

Julien leaned over her and said firmly, "You had a riding accident, Kate. I found you unconscious beside Gabriella on my return from the village. You will be quite all right, I assure you."

"Riding accident?" she repeated vaguely, his words making no sense to her.

"Yes, Kate. A riding accident," he said flatly.

Kate did not notice the hardness of his voice and quickly turned her face away from him. Dear God, he did not know! She thought dully that her captor, having taken his pleasure with her, had drugged her again and left her to be found.

"Julien," she cried, struggling up on her pillow. "I must tell you . . . I did not . . ." The words died on her lips. Her story would sound utterly absurd and unbelievable. She knew that even if he were to accept her words, he would know that she was no longer a virgin, that another man had taken her. She choked back a sob and fell against the pillow.

"Kate . . ." Julien said unguardedly.

She whimpered and closed her eyes tightly. His voice was so very gentle. If only she had not scorned him, fought him, but now it was too late. What had happened to her was real and she would never forget or forgive herself.

She felt her head being raised from the pillow and a glass touch her lips. For an instant she relived the cloth being held to her face, the bitter fumes plummeting her to unconsciousness. She struggled frantically, jerking her head back and forth.

"Kate, it is but laudanum. It will make you sleep."

She quieted at the sound of Julien's calm voice. Sleep, yes, she welcomed the opportunity of forgetting, if for but a while. She opened her mouth eagerly and swallowed the soothing liquid.

"Oh, God," she whispered, "please let me never awake. . . ."

Julien recoiled at her words as if struck. With trembling fingers he set down the empty glass. He wanted her to suffer, to know regret and shame; but that she could whisper with such hopeless despair of death tore at his very being. The burden of guilt that he had fought against consumed him relentlessly, and try as he would, he could not dismiss the enormity of what he had done.

He watched her fall into a deep sleep and settled back in a chair to keep silent vigil. It was shortly before dawn, as he was building up the dying fire, that he whirled around at the sound of a low, piercing scream. He was at Kate's side in a moment. She was writhing, her body tangled in the covers, in the throes of a nightmare. Julien grabbed her shoulders and shook her, but the effects of the laudanum seemed to hold her from consciousness, and she cried out again and again. In desperation he slapped her face until a tremendous shudder passed the length of her body and she opened her eyes and stared up at him, her pupils dilated with fear.

She threw her arms around his shoulders and hurled herself against his chest. She trembled violently, and low sobs racked her body. Julien froze for a moment in shocked confusion. Without conscious thought he closed his arms about her and held her tightly against his chest. He scooped her up, pulling her covers with him, and carried her to a chair beside the fireplace. He could feel the strength of her terror, so tightly did she cling to him. He whispered low, comforting words, words that scarce made sense. Slowly the racking sobs lessened and she loosed her grip, as if exhausted from the effort. She lay against him quietly, her head lolling against his chest.

"Kate," he murmured softly, smoothing damp tendrils of hair from about her face. "Kate," he repeated, until she opened her eyes and met his gaze. He struggled with himself to speak to her of the nightmare, knowing full well what it must be, and realizing that to do so would encourage her to pour forth her story. He held back, suddenly aware that if she were to speak, he would be unable to hold the truth from her. Kate broke their long silence. In a voice vague from the effects of the laudanum, she whispered, "God, I cannot bear it . . . I know that I am going mad. . . ."

"Mad?" he repeated blankly, his mind arrested at her strange words. "What, Kate, cannot you bear?"

"The blackness, the voices," she whispered, again clinging to him as if for protection.

He frowned, for he had not the least idea what she meant. He tightened his arms about her in silent comfort and waited for her to calm. She spoke again, her voice cracking, the words jumbled. "The blackness—it has never been so strong, so real. It covers something horrible, something evil, but yet I cannot see what it is . . . it was so long ago. There is such pain . . . and the voices, cruel, jeering voices."

Julien tensed, his mind almost refusing to work. Long ago—not today. "Kate," he urged, "what was so long ago? You must tell me . . . what happened? What is this blackness, the pain, the voices? What did you dream?"

"I . . . I cannot be sure," she stammered. Then she stiffened suddenly in his arms. A low moan broke the silence and she fastened her gaze toward the fireplace, focusing upon something he did not see. In a high, hysterical voice, a child's voice, she cried, "Mother . . . why did those men hurt me? My clothes . . . Mother, the blood, why am I bleeding? No, Father, no! Do not hurt me! What have I done? Father, what have I done?"

Her voice suspended in a cry of pain. She winced and cowered, jerking her arms above her head as if to protect herself from blows raining down upon her.

Julien grabbed Kate's arms and shook her until the cries ceased and the dulled, glazed film dropped from her eyes. She looked up into his set face, and in a voice of great weariness she whispered, "Julien . . . I am so glad that you are here." She nestled her face against his chest and murmured drowsily, "Please do not leave me—I could not bear it if you left me." But a moment later he heard her even breathing and knew that she slept.

Early-autumn sunlight poured into the room before Julien raised his eyes from Kate's face. His arms ached but he did not move, not wishing to disturb her. She was in a deep sleep, a healing sleep. He was aware that he felt extraordinarily humble, his bitter anger and wounded pride stripped from

him. He understood her fear of him now, why she had not
wanted to marry him, even though she herself did not understand her reasons. He remembered the day when they had
ridden to the small copse, and the look of blank terror on her
face. A place of evil, she had said. She had not been able to
fathom her reaction, and he had not considered it important,
so intent had he been on his gallant offer of marriage. How
could he have been so blind? He felt the hair prickle on the
back of his neck at the thought of Kate as a small child being
attacked. Good God, what kind of man would rape a child?
His hands clenched and unclenched in black anger as he pictured in his mind a small helpless girl at the mercy of those
vile brutes. All too clearly he saw Kate's father, cursing at
her, blaming her, even beating her.

Kate whimpered softly and he tightened his arms about her
protectively. It occurred to him, as he gazed down at her
peaceful face, that his life had been singularly uncomplicated
to this time. He tried to weigh the enormity of the problems
he now faced. Although he could not explain why, he felt
certain that Kate would not as yet remember her nightmare,
even though his rape of her had penetrated the cloak of forgetfulness that had protected her all these years. He could
well understand how a child's instincts for survival had
forced her to lock away what had happened to her. But now
it could be only a matter of time until she remembered, and,
he thought bleakly, such devastating knowledge could easily
be too much for her to bear.

Julien rose slowly, careful not to disturb Kate, and gently
laid her in her bed. He found that his own physical exhaustion soon overtook him, and with a deep sigh he stretched out
in the chair and soon fell asleep.

Kate awoke, her mind alert and clear from the long hours
of sleep. She sat up in her bed and looked about her. She was
startled to see Julien sprawled in a chair beside her, his clothing disheveled and his head resting against his hand. She
frowned in confusion, remembering vaguely being held by
him. He had comforted her, had soothed away an awful fear.
She shook her head to focus the jumbled images, but they
melted away from her. She slipped out of bed and felt a
sharp pain between her thighs. She flushed with shame, recalling with vivid clarity all that had happened to her. Her eyes
flew to her sleeping husband. He had told her that she had
had a riding accident. Her mind clung tenaciously to this

fact. No one, save her and that man, knew what had passed between them, and she grimly resolved that Julien must never know. She walked to where he slept and shook his sleeve to wake him. Somehow it did not seem important that she was dressed only in her nightgown.

Julien awoke with a start and bounded from the chair. With great tenderness he grasped Kate's shoulders and pulled her against him. How very strange, she thought wonderingly, that she found his closeness and strength comforting. They stood thus for some time, until Julien drew back and with a gentle hand smoothed back her tangled hair from about her face.

"You are all right, Kate?" he asked tentatively, unsure of exactly what he should say to her.

She lowered her eyes, and a look of anguish passed over her features.

"Kate . . ." he began.

She looked up at him, her face now impassive, and interrupted him quickly. "I am quite fine now, Julien. I . . . I was not gravely hurt in the riding accident. Gabriella must have been frightened again. It is over . . . now."

Julien was relieved at her decision not to tell him the truth. If she were to tell him of her rape, he would not be able to keep silent, and what he told her would destroy her newfound trust in him. Somehow he must find a way to banish the terrible fears from her childhood before telling her.

He smiled at her and said lightly, "I fear, my dear, that if the Craytons were to witness the Countess and Earl of March in such a state of disarray, our consequence would be woefully cast down." He ran a hand through his own messed hair. "I propose that we both endeavor to repair our respective appearances."

Kate mustered a tentative smile in return. She raised her hand to her tangled hair and said ruefully, "Oh, dear, it will take Mrs. Crayton at least thirty minutes to brush out the knots."

He admired her greatly in that moment. Without thought, he pulled her against him again, gently brushed his lips to hers, and released her. She did not recoil from him, but rather stood silently gazing at him with a confused look on her face.

"Would you have breakfast with me, Kate? In an hour?"

"Yes, my lord."

Kate stood for some moments after he had left her room, unmoving. She thought of his kindness and of his gentle, undemanding kiss before leaving her. It touched her deeply.

Julien found that his fondest hope—that Kate would learn to trust him, and willingly wish to be in his company—was granted. In the days that followed, she became like a shadow, not allowing him out of her sight. On several occasions Julien found himself ruefully explaining to Kate that he had to leave her for but an instant to relieve his physical needs. Her face would flame with color, but she remained where he left her, doggedly awaiting his return.

It did not occur to Kate that Julien would think her behaviour odd, for her constant fear prevented her from understanding how much she had changed toward her husband. Somehow it had not even seemed strange to her when, the night following her riding accident, Julien gently informed her that he would no longer pressure her to consummate their marriage, that he wanted her to have as much time as she wished. From that evening on, Kate no longer wished to escape Julien's company as the hour grew later. Her bedroom was no longer a solace against him, but an empty, lonely place where her guilt and fear mingled with terrifying clarity, keeping her from sleep.

A week had passed when, near dawn one night, Kate awoke to the sound of her own cries. Vague, menacing shadows crowded about her; hands tried to grab at her, and taunting, jeering voices dinned in her ears. In panic she threw off the tangled covers and ran terror-stricken to Julien's room.

Julien heard her screams and had just thrown on his dressing gown when Kate burst into his room, looking like a white apparition, her hair streaming about her face and down her back. He caught her up in his arms and held her fast against him, feeling her heart hammer against his chest. "There is nothing to fear, Kate," he said softly.

"It was so awful, Julien, yet I cannot remember. Why cannot I remember?" she cried, clinging to his arms all the harder. "It must be the same nightmare as before. I am sure of it . . . I just cannot grasp it. . . ."

"You must trust me, Kate. Everything will be all right, I give you my promise."

She looked up at him, a small frown furrowing her brow, as she weighed his words. "Please let me stay with you,

Julien, I cannot bear to be alone." Her eyes were enormous with fear, and her voice pleaded.

"Of course you will stay with me, Kate. I will not leave you. You are safe with me. Do you understand, Kate?"

She nodded slowly. He swept her up in his arms and placed her in his bed. He lay down beside her, pulled the covers over them, and gathered her to him. Julien felt a long sigh pass through her body, and in but a moment she was asleep, her head on his chest.

Sleep did not come so easily to Julien, and he lay staring ahead of him even as gray shafts of dawn filtered into the room. His promise to Kate to keep her safe rang hollow in his mind. How could he protect her from her own fears, fears that emerged to terrify her at night, fears that she did not comprehend? During the day, she was living the guilt that he had forced upon her, and the misery in her eyes made him writhe with self-reproach. Try as he would, he could think of no way to separate her rape as a child from his own brutal rape of her. To speak to her of one could not but result in her knowing of the other. He had no doubt that if he told her now that he had been the man who raped her, he would lose her.

Julien closed his eyes and enjoyed the warmth and softness of Kate's body. He stroked her silky hair, feeling the soft waves sprng in his hand, as if alive.

When he awoke some hours later, Kate was gone. He was not the least surprised by this fact, for he could easily picture her embarrassment upon waking in his bed. Nor was he overly surprised to find her pacing outside his bedroom door, waiting for him to emerge, dressed in her breeches for their daily fencing lesson. Neither of them mentioned her wild flight to his room.

There were changes Julien saw in Kate that day. She hurled herself into physical activity, extending their fencing lesson until finally Julien dropped his foil, seeing her face white with fatigue. In their riding in the afternoon, she pushed Gabriella to a frenetic pace, until again Julien was forced to pull her up so that her horse would not drop under her with exhaustion.

She tried to maintain a flow of light, inconsequential chatter that evening, as if to prove to herself that all was well with her. But she could not cloak the haunted look that veiled her eyes whenever she slowed her frantic pace. Late that evening, after she had lost an imaginary two hundred pounds to him at piquet, he led her unwillingly to her room.

"But really, Julien," she protested, "I assure you that I am not at all tired. I . . . I really do not think that I can sleep."

He himself was exhausted, but he did not point out this fact. He looked down at her and smiled gently. "If you find you cannot sleep, Kate, come to my room and we shall talk until you are drowsy."

She turned her face away quickly, and he could feel her weighing her trust for him against her fear of being alone.

"Whatever you wish, Kate. Why don't you think about it?" He gently propelled her into her room, not wishing to push her for a response.

Julien had just eased his tired limbs into his bed when there was a light tap on his door and Kate slipped diffidently into his room. She stopped and stood in awkward silence, her fingers plucking nervously at her nightgown.

"Come, Kate," he said gently, patting the place beside him. "It is too chilly to have a comfortable talk . . . come, I do not wish you to take a cold."

She walked slowly, hesitating every few steps, and with a visible effort climbed into bed beside him. She was trembling violently, and Julien made no attempt to take her into his arms, only pulled the covers over them and lay on his back beside her. After a long moment of strained silence Kate said hesitatingly, "Julien, I do not wish you to think . . . that is, you must think it odd . . ."

He could feel her embarrassment, and so cut off her pitiful explanation. "Kate, I think only that I am very tired, for you have quite worn me to a bone today. Come, my dear, let us go to sleep."

He tentatively stretched out his arms and touched her shoulders. She tensed but a moment before she allowed him to pull her against his chest.

During the next weeks, Kate felt as if she were slowly suffocating from her guilt and shame. Julien's unflagging kindness during the days and his gentle understanding each night made her all the more miserable. She could allow no excuses for herself. That her unknown captor had forcibly drugged her and ruthlessly bound her gave her no justification, no forgiveness for herself, because she had experienced deep, stirring pleasure at his hands. Though afterward he had brutally raped her, she still thought herself guilty of betraying her husband. Her guilt ate at her relentlessly, and only her fear of losing Julien forced her to keep her secret to herself. Her only comfort was sleeping in her husband's arms each night. The terrifying nightmare had come to her two more times, but her low moans had instantly awakened Julien, and he had shaken her to consciousness before the fearful images grew strong within her mind. She tried each time to understand the meaning of the fearful dream, but something deep within her jostled the images, as if to prevent her from grasping their significance.

Kate developed the habit of gazing at herself in the mirror whenever she passed one in the villa. She was certain that some change must have appeared on her face, some knowing sign, perhaps in her eyes, that would reveal her lost innocence. She felt she must see the signs before Julien did. But each time, she saw only a pale, set face, her lost innocence evidently buried behind the depths of her eyes.

She thought occasionally of Harry, perfunctorily loving him, but his meaning to her was slowly changing. She was no longer his hoydenish Kate, spontaneously involving him in all her thoughts. She did not know whose Kate she was.

The Swiss weather remained comfortably cool during those weeks and then changed abruptly. The temperature plummeted and a light snow blanketed the ground.

Julien did not blink an eye when Kate donned her riding habit to accompany him to the village to secure carriages for their journey back to Geneva. Upon their arrival in the village, she dogged his steps, oblivious of the curious stares cast her way by the local folk, and stayed at his side as he conducted his business at the tiny inn. Her only comment when they left was that the owner had a bulbous nose and years of grime under his fingernails. Julien laughed. "Dirty or not, Kate, he much admired you, and I am convinced that I got a much better price because you were with me."

"Perhaps, Julien, I should have conducted your business. It is possible that I would have achieved even a cheaper price," she retorted, a smile momentarily lighting her face.

Three days later, their luggage securely strapped to the boot of their chaise, Kate and Julien took their leave of the villa, leaving the Craytons to follow at a more sedate pace in the second carriage.

How very different was their return to Geneva. As before,

they stayed at the Coeur de Lyon, but this time, by tact agreement, Kate shared Julien's room. Happily, it occurred to Julien to have a screen brought to their room to ensure Kate's privacy when dressing. He willingly played her lady's maid, buttoning and unbuttoning her gowns and helping her to brush out the tangles in her hair. He said not a word when she whisked behind the screen to complete her toilet.

"Do you recall, Julien," Kate said unexpectedly that evening over dinner, "when we were last here and you forced me to take that wretched walk with you to the lake? And I nearly contracted a chill because of your high-handed manners?"

He replied solemnly, "I find it very . . . interesting how memory becomes so quickly distorted. Why, as I recall, it was you, Kate, who was being stubborn and willful, by refusing to wear that most warm cloak I had bought for you."

"But it was *your* cloak, Julien. Somehow I felt that if I wore it, I would be . . . selling myself, that I would no longer be me."

Julien paused, an arrested look on his face. "I had not thought of it as you have expressed it, Kate. But it was a fascinating disagreement, do you not agree?"

A smile tugged at the corners of her mouth. "Yes, I suppose it was, particularly since you gained your ends in any case. Your wager in piquet was, I admit, a master stroke."

"You have shown some improvement," he conceded. "It has been some three weeks now that I do not quite disdain you as an opponent."

"Odious man! You will see, I am much the smarter and will serve you your just deserts!"

"I admit it as a possibility, if, in the dim future, I manage to lose my wits."

Kate was silent. She could simply not imagine the future, dim or otherwise. She counted her future in only immediate days. She became aware of Julien's eyes upon her and quickly commented on the tastiness of the roast veal.

They journeyed slowly through France, enjoying the warmer weather, halting to explore the Roman ruins in the south, and making their way far to the west of Paris. When they reached Calais, Kate was surprised to find Julien's yacht, the *Fair Maid*, moored in the harbor.

"I had forgotten your yacht, my Lord March," she said, looking quite demure.

"I trust I will not have to sling you over my shoulder and carry you aboard, Kate." Julien waved to a small portly man, uniformed in dark blue, striding toward them.

"I think it will not be necessary now," she replied, looking up with interest as the uniformed man bowed low to Julien.

"A pleasure to see you, my lord. The men were becoming a trifle restless," boomed Captain Marcham. He broke into a leathery smile and bowed to Kate.

"Her ladyship, the Countess of March, Captain Marcham," Julien said.

"An honor it is, my lady," the captain assured Kate, thinking privately that he was indeed fortunate that he and his men were not left longer to kick up their heels in Calais. Lord, were he the earl, he would have extended the wedding trip another six months!

The *Fair Maid* was finely appointed, with small elegantly furnished rooms and a deck that shone to a high polish. During the nine-hour crossing, Kate spent the majority of her time contentedly bundled in fur rugs on the deck. As she sipped a cup of tea, proffered to her by a shy young seaman, she remembered with wry amusement her flight to France on the small dingy packet.

"We'll dock at Plymouth within the hour, my lord," Captain Marcham informed them after what seemed an incredibly short time to Kate.

"Excellent time, Marcham. I hope you now have a better opinion of my yacht, Kate," he teased, turning to tuck the rug more closely about her legs.

"Aye, Julien, that I do. It is just that we have come so quickly back and I am . . ." Her voice trailed off and she stared out over the whitecapped water, her mind in some confusion.

"And you what, my dear?" he asked.

Kate gave a tiny shake of her head. "It is nothing. I am being quite foolish."

When they stepped ashore at Plymouth, it was teeming with travelers, harried seamen, and many indigenous specimens lolling about on the dock. Somehow the touch of English soil beneath her feet and the hearty cries of the English tongue sounding on every side of her made her feel terribly alone. Though Julien stood not six feet from her, giving instructions to Captain Marcham and to the flunkeys who were removing their luggage, Kate had the unaccountable feeling that the man whose life she had shared for the past two months was now drawing away from her, returning to a way of life that was alien to her. Two months ago she would not have cared, but now she felt that what she wanted most was to return to the yacht and let Captain Marcham sail wherever he wished.

"Come, Countess," Julien said, taking her arm, "a hearty English meal awaits us at the Wild Boar."

Kate mumbled her assent, cast one last fond gaze at the *Fair Maid,* and moved into silent step beside her husband.

12

"Good Lord, George, you don't mean my mother is here now?"

"Yes, my lord. Her ladyship informed me that she had the 'feeling' that you would be returning shortly. She has been waiting in the drawing room not a half-hour, my lord."

"I did not know she had such powers," Julien remarked with some exasperation to Kate. "Kate?"

"Oh, yes, indeed—how strange." Kate had a headache and she felt a trifle queasy after their long journey from Plymouth to London.

Julien looked down at her pale face. "George, call Eliza. Her ladyship is fatigued."

Kate did not take exception to her husband's order, thankful that she would not have to meet the dowager countess until she had time to gather her disordered thoughts and rid herself of the pounding headache.

"Mother will, of course, wish to meet you, Kate. But if you do not feel just the thing, I shall take you to visit her another day. Eliza, escort her ladyship to her room." Julien patted Kate's hand, turned and strode down the long marbled hall, and disappeared through a set of double doors.

"I will see to your luggage, my lady," George assured her,

snapping his fingers in the direction of a footman, whose presence Kate had not even noticed.

"Thank you, George," Kate murmured. "I would like to go to my room, Eliza." It did not occur to her at that moment to question Eliza's presence as her maid.

Kate removed only her cloak and bonnet before stretching out on her bed. She felt less wretched after Eliza had placed a cloth soaked in lavender water over her eyes. Her stomach settled, and some few minutes later she rose up on her elbows and said, "Eliza, I am beginning to feel much more alive than otherwise. Please fetch me a gown, for I would meet the dowager countess. Something modest, to suit a mother-in-law's taste, I think."

Eliza chose well, and not a half-hour later Kate walked down the curved staircase, dressed in a demure, high-necked muslin gown of pale green, her hair brushed into a knot of clustered curls atop her head. She felt no particular trepidation at meeting her mother-in-law, for she really knew very little about her, save that the several times Julien had mentioned his mother, he had spoken with a sort of affectionate impatience.

The doors to the drawing room were slightly ajar, and Kate paused a moment to smooth her gown before entering. She stopped, dismayed, upon hearing a woman speak in a reproachful, complaining voice.

"Of course, I scotched any scandal, Julien, after you left in such unnatural haste to Paris! But how could you chase that girl in the most shocking way imaginable? I told you there was bad blood in the Brandon family, and now you have saddled me with this wicked girl!"

Kate stood rigidly outside the door, waiting to hear Julien's response.

"Really, Mama, you have had two months to accustom yourself to the idea," he replied briskly.

"But even Sarah, my dear boy—"

"You forget, Mama, that Sarah is married. Surely you prefer a wicked Brandon to my running off with a married lady!" Julien's voice was sharp. Kate was not privy to the gleam of sarcastic amusement on his face.

She dismissed her immediate cowardly instinct to retreat to her room, raised her head, and rather like a condemned martyr, strode proudly to her judgment.

She drew up short as she entered, her eyes fastened on the

dowager Countess of March. A small dark-haired woman
swathed in several fine paisley shawls sat on a sofa with her
head pressed back against the cushions, her eyes tightly closed
as if she were undergoing the most dire of upsets. One thin
hand clutched a vinaigrette to her narrow bosom. Julien sat
opposite her, his hands clasped between his knees, his look
one of bewildered impatience.

Kate cleared her throat and forced her feet to move forward.

"Kate, my dear!" Julien hurried to her side and gave her a
wry smile and a wink before turning to his mother, who now
sat bolt upright, her dark eyes open and assessing.

Kate made a pretty curtsy and said demurely, "I am
indeed honored to make your acquaintance, ma'am. Julien
has of course told me much about you."

"Well, at least, child, you in no way resemble that im-
pudent father of yours," the dowager stated flatly.

"I am said to resemble my mother," Kate replied smoothly,
disposing her skirts neatly as she sat down beside her
mother-in-law.

The dowager was silent for a moment as she searched her
memory for a picture of the Lady Sabrina. She vaguely
remembered bright red hair set atop a rather pale, silent face.
"Yes, I suppose you do," she allowed finally.

"Would you ladies care for a glass of sherry?" Julien interposed.

"I do suppose it would be a soothing agent to my nerves,"
the dowager said with a sigh. As Julien poured the sherry, the
dowager turned back to Kate.

"You seem rather on good terms with my son now, young
lady. Perhaps you would be so kind as to tell me why you refused my son two months ago and ran away in the most ill-
bred manner possible—and by yourself—to Paris?" She sucked
in her cheeks and waved her vinaigrette in Kate's face.

Julien was annoyed. "Really, Mother, you bring up the
past, which is no longer of any importance. Any misunder-
standings Katharine and I have had are over and done
with—and certainly none of your affair in any case!"

The dowager gasped, and pressed her hands to her palpitat-
ing bosom. To Kate, Julien's measured words seemed only
the mildest of reproaches, but it was not so, she perceived, to
her mother-in-law. She quickly possessed one of the
dowager's limp hands into her own and patted it soothingly.

"Of course you have a right to know, ma'am. You must forgive Julien, for he is quite . . . fatigued from our long journey. You see," she continued earnestly, not looking toward her husband, "my father was quite Gothic in his attitude, demanding that I wed your son before . . . before I knew my own mind. Indeed you are right, ma'am, it was most foolish for me to travel unaccompanied to Paris. I can but attribute my thoughtless action to my . . . confusion of sensibilities. I do hope that you will now endeavor to forgive my exceptionable behavior."

The dowager found herself in something of a quandary. She saw from beneath her lashes that Katharine's prettily spoken speech had found favor with her son, and there was a kindness of expression, a warmth in his eyes that she had never before observed. Having, however, catalogued a rather impressive list of complaints to demonstrate her own ill-use, she decided to take her daughter-in-law to task on another matter.

"Your Aunt Mary informed me that Lady Katharine was a lady of quality, and now, I suppose that I must concur. "But"—the dowager paused briefly for effect—"she also told me that you, Katharine, appear to be no breeder. Of course, I do not in general like to speak of such indelicate subjects, but I think it is a matter of great importance that an heir be provided quickly for the St. Clair line."

Color flooded Kate's face. She could think of no smoothly sincere words to say, and were the lady not Julien's mother, she would have thought her woefully ill-bred to mention such a topic. She was too embarrassed to look at Julien to see the effect of his mother's words.

Julien was at the end of his patience, his anger fanned by the misery in Kate's eyes. He stood over his mother and bent a stern eye upon her. "Really, Mother, you go too far! It is obvious that you mean only to make mischief, and I will not have you badger Katharine with your tactless and altogether unnecessary comments. If you cannot bethink yourself of any conciliatory words, then I would suggest that you take your leave."

"Julien!" the dowager shrieked, more startled than distressed at the implacable hardness of her son's voice.

"Now, Julien . . . surely . . ." Kate began, throwing herself into the breach. Above all things, she did not wish Julien to have a falling-out with his hitherto fond parent. She removed the vinaigrette from the dowager's unresisting hand and waved it under her nose.

"Come, ma'am, let us try to forget this unpleasantness. Julien, will you not apologize—please?" Kate turned pleading eyes to her husband.

To Julien's surprise, his fast-fading parent turned half-tearful eyes to Kate and uttered in a tremulous voice, "Dear, dear child, how well you understand the frailty of my constitution. Gentlemen do not, nay, cannot share the sensitivity of our feelings!"

The dowager cast a baleful glance at her now-baffled son. Julien looked from his mother to his wife, threw up his hands, gave a grunt that carried no particular meaning to either lady, and strode to the long curtained French windows.

"You must forgive him, Katharine," the dowager said sadly, leaning toward Kate and patting her arm. "I am certain that you will coax him out of his sulks. Alas, a mother's influence wanes so quickly."

Kate received this expression of confidence without a blink. She hesitated to think of Julien's mother as a remarkably foolish woman, but the thought could not but intrude.

"I shall certainly try to bring him to his former good humor," Kate assured her.

The dowager looked rather soulfully at her son's back, and with a sigh of one sorely used, she began, with the assistance of Kate, to gather her shawls into a semblance of order about her thin shoulders. She even allowed Kate to assist her to her feet.

"Julien!" Kate said sharply. "Your mother is preparing to take her leave."

Julien turned about, a harried expression on his face. He walked to his mother and planted a light kiss on her thin cheek.

"My dear son . . ." The dowager sighed. "At least your father is not here to see—"

"Mother!" Julien threatened. "Father's misunderstanding with Sir Oliver has absolutely nothing whatsoever to do with Katharine. I would that you contrive to forget it."

Katharine added persuasively, "Dear ma'am, I would assure you that my father was always alone in his views regarding your esteemed family. My brother, Harry, and I have long been in disagreement with Sir Oliver in this matter. Indeed," Kate finished mendaciously, "after making your acquaintance, ma'am, I am more convinced than ever that he was quite . . . ill-judged in his actions."

"Dear Katharine, how noble, so refined in your observations!" The dowager's dark eyes grew bright, and the thin line of her lips turned up at the corners, albeit with some effort. She turned her face to Katherine and allowed her daughter-in-law to plant a dutiful kiss upon her cheek.

"I will escort you to your carriage, Mother," Julien said, taking her arm. He did not wish to risk a reversal of good humor in his now-more-rational parent.

When he returned to the drawing room, he was obliged to smile, for Kate bore a rueful, impish grin.

"You are a baggage, Kate," he remarked, taking her hands in his. "You speak of my turning Sir Oliver so sweet, and here you rolled up my mother, foot and guns! Well-done, my dear."

"I learn my lessons well, Julien." Her smile faded as she recalled her mother-in-law's comment about the Lady Sarah. "Julien?"

"Yes, clever Kate," he prompted as she paused.

"I . . . I could not help but overhear your mother speak of Lady Sarah . . ." Her voice trailed off, and she turned her head away, now embarrassed to bring up the subject.

"A beautiful, charming woman," he said outrageously.

She whipped her face up, her eyes darkening with sudden anger. "You wretched man," she began, only to pull up short as her own shame seared into her mind. She drew a deep breath and planted a tight smile on her face. "I look forward to meeting this paragon," she said lightly, avoiding her husband's eyes. Sometimes she felt that he saw too much, that he could probe her thoughts.

Julien sensed Kate's change of mood and dismissed further provocative comments. "Well, Kate, what do you think of my humble establishment?"

Kate took a more easy breath and gazed about the drawing room before observing, "Most elegant, my lord. Of course, I have still to see the majority of the rooms before I make my final judgment."

It did not take Kate long to applaud Julien's excellent taste in his furnishing of the town house and to compliment the quiet efficiency of his staff. She was particularly drawn to the stolid butler, George, whose gentle dignity she found comforting. It was he who eased her transition as mistress of the house, unobtrusively giving her advice on the management of the servants and the protocol of receiving visitors. In this matter, Kate was profoundly grateful, for in the next week the knocker was never still during the mornings. It appeared that all of London society wished to inspect the new Countess of March. Because of her own inescapable preoccupations, Kate was a great deal less nervous in the presence of her exalted guests, and many left the St. Clair town house to spread the gossip that even though the countess was, unfortunately, from the country and a mere baronet's daughter, she did seem to know her way rather well.

Of all the ton who paid visit to the St. Clair town house, it was Percy who found instant favor with Kate. After eyeing her for some minutes with his quizzing glass, he turned to Julien and remarked blithely that he was a lucky dog and quite unworthy of his good fortune. Kate felt a tightening in her throat at what she thought to be undeserved praise, when, but a moment later, Percy turned to her and asked what François was preparing for dinner. She blinked several times at this unconventional inquiry, noted that Julien was grinning roguishly at her, and responded truthfully, "Do forgive me, Sir Percy, I really have no idea. If, however, you will be patient, I shall ring for George."

"Not at all the thing, you know, Lady Kate, not at all the thing!" Percy said with severity, waving his quizzing glass at her for emphasis. "I shall be over first thing tomorrow morning and we shall plan the week's menus."

Indeed, Percy arrived punctually the following morning, and he and Kate spent a comfortable hour devising menus that would test François's culinary abilities. "After all," Percy announced, "you pay the damned fellow one hundred pounds a year—don't want to have him lazing about."

Kate could find no fault with this logic, and discovered after Percy took his leave that she had quite forgotten herself while in his company. She sought him out, and more often than not, it was Percy who accompanied her to Bond Street to do her shopping and to the park to ride at the fashionable hour of five in the afternoon. It was during one of these excursions that Kate chanced to see a very lovely lady dressed in the height of fashion raise her parasol in greeting. She was seated in an open carriage beside a gentleman who seemed to be remonstrating with her. Her piquant oval face was framed with blond ringlets and her eyes were a startling blue. Kate raised her hand in a hesitant reply and observed a rather mocking smile pass over the lady's lips. She wondered whether she should turn Astarte and make the lady's acquaintance.

"Kate," Percy hissed, drawing his horse close to hers.

"What ever is the matter, Percy?" she inquired. "The lady waved to me. Would it not be rude to ignore her?"

"No," was his clipped response. He click-clicked his horse into a canter, and Kate was obliged to do the same. After some moments, Kate drew up beside him and laid her hand on his sleeve.

"Percy, for heaven's sake, who was that lady?"

Percy stared doggedly between his horse's ears.

"Now, you're being quite cowhanded! Observe, Percy, you are jobbing your poor horse's mouth."

"Cowhanded!" Percy screwed his head around, incensed at the attack on his equestrian ability.

Kate chuckled. "Do forgive me, but I had to get your attention. You are behaving quite foolishly, you know." She paused for a moment. "It was Lady Sarah Ponsonby, was it not, Percy?"

As Percy regarded her in silence, she added in a flat voice, "She is quite lovely, is she not?"

"I suppose so," he replied coolly. "If one happens to like the china-doll variety."

"Do not, I pray, Percy, try to cozen me! We both know that the china-doll variety is quite to Julien's taste. Oh, don't look at me so strangely and don't try to deny the truth, Percy. Perhaps I should not know about her . . . liaison with Julien, but I do, and there's an end to it!"

Percy bit his lower lip in vexation. He said heavily, "Do not refine too much upon it, Kate. Julien dismissed her the moment he returned to London—long before your marriage."

Kate replied with forced lightness, "It would appear that the lady perhaps disagrees with you, Percy."

Though Kate quickly changed the topic and chattered with seeming unconcern for the remainder of their ride, Percy was not deceived, for there was a troubled look in her eyes and a nervousness in her manner that belied the airiness of her conversation. After depositing Kate in Grosvenor Square, Percy repaired to White's, as was his habit. Although not one to let other people's concerns trouble him overlong, Percy found quite to his surprise that he felt it his duty to seek out Julien and inform him of what had occurred. He ran him to ground in the reading room, conversing with the portly, good-humored Marquis of Halport.

"It's as I always predicted, March," Percy heard Lord Halport grumble with a shake of his nearly hairless head, "the regent makes a damned cake of himself more and more as each day passes. Though the Princess Caroline is really quite vulgar, and always putting up the backs of those around her with her gross want of manner, Prinny should have the good sense not to publicly scorn her. Bad judgment! I daresay his utter lack of pretense will be his undoing. I say, Blairstock," Lord Halport continued without pause, willingly admitting Percy into his conversation, "you must agree with March and me that want of mutual affection in the married state, particularly among those of high station, must not condone the public flaunting of the most sacred of mortal vows. I have always spoken my mind on this topic with Lady Halport, and *she*, I hasten to assure you, most adamantly agrees with me!"

"Just so," Percy readily assented. He kept silent as Lord Halport, needing no further encouragement to proffer his views, raised his voice stentoriously. Julien caught his eye in a wink of tolerant amusement. It was common knowledge that the mousy, timid Lady Halport mouthed her spouse's views with nauseating promptitude, having learned through enforced periods of solitude on the marquis' estate in the North that any contrary thoughts and opinions brought about swift wrath upon her head.

Another five minutes passed before Percy was able to detach Julien from the garrulous marquis. "Don't mean to be disagreeable, Halport," Percy managed to insert during a brief pause, "but I must remove March here. Need his advice on this nag up for sale at Tattersall's," he added mendaciously.

"Good Lord! Not Otherton's slope-shouldered bay, I trust, Percy," Julien declared wickedly.

"Now, see here, March—" Percy cried, instantly affronted.

"Devilish fine horse, if you ask me," Lord Halport interposed.

"I daresay, Halport," Julien said smoothly, "just exactly the type of showy creature to put between the shafts of your curricle. Perhaps Lady Halport would appreciate such a generous gift."

"My wife knows nothing of horseflesh, nothing at all," Lord Halport scoffed. "Give her a donkey and she wouldn't know the difference!" Lord Halport turned to Percy and asked politely, "If you wouldn't mind, Blairstock, think I'll take a look at Otherton's bay. As March says, he's a showy creature. I always like to maintain a full stable, you know."

"Not at all, dear sir. Don't mind a bit," Percy said with composure.

"Servant, March. My regards to your lovely countess. Blairstock!" Julien and Percy returned Lord Halport's creaky bow, and when the marquis was out of earshot, Percy said indignantly to Julien, "You, Julien, of all people, know that I would never consider that broken-down bay of Otherton's! Just couldn't think of another excuse to get rid of the fellow. And as to *him* claiming Lady Halport wouldn't know the difference between a donkey and a horse—why, the poor lady's been living with an ass these past ten years!"

Julien grinned broadly. "Well said, Percy. Now that we have as good as sold Otherton's bay for him, why do you not join me in a glass of sherry?" Julien waved his hand to a somberly clad footman.

"Now, Percy, what ever is the matter? You're looking positively blue-deviled."

Percy rearranged his elegantly clad bulk into a more comfortable position and eyed Julien in agitated silence. Seeing his friend so very calm and composed, he began to doubt the wisdom of poking his nose into the earl's affairs.

"Good God, Percy, it cannot be so bad as all that!" Julien sipped his sherry and smiled lazily into his friend's agitated countenance. "Your tailor been dunning you?"

"Dash it, March," Percy exclaimed, goaded into reply. "Kate has seen Sarah!"

"She was bound to, sooner or later," Julien pointed out, unruffled. "I can see no cause for alarm. Pray, do not excite yourself."

"Easy for you to say, Julien, but you did not see the look on Sarah's face or the way she waved to Kate. Like a cat with her claws curled! I swear she's up to mischief. You know as well as I do that she grows quite bored with Sir Edward. Wouldn't be at all surprised if she set her cap for you again."

"You forget, Percy, that I spoke to her before Kate came to London. Just a woman's jealousy, no more."

"Well, Kate seems to think that you much admire Lady Sarah. Told me so, in fact. Tried to act like she didn't care, but you know Kate, she can't hide her feelings."

Julien silently damned Sarah but was obliged to admit

upon brief reflection that he was not displeased that Kate was distressed. Could it be that she was jealous?—a sure sign to him that she had truly come to care for him. He met Percy's gaze and said quietly, "Do not concern yourself further. I shall take care of the matter. And, Percy, I thank you for your kindness to Katharine. She is aware, I believe, what a very good friend she has in you."

Percy coughed, suddenly embarrassed by this tribute. "I say, Julien, deuced nice of you to say that, but you know ... well, Kate is such a *trump!*"

"That she is, that she is," Julien said, more to himself than to Percy. "Oh, by the by, Percy, what is François preparing for dinner this evening?"

Percy pursed his lips in thought before replying cordially, "Thursday ... ah, yes, veal in a delicate herb sauce, a brace of pheasants—"

"Enough," Julien said, grinning wryly. "I trust that you will grace us with your presence."

Percy beamed. "Dashed nice of you to offer, March. Don't mind if I do."

After Julien and Percy had parted, Julien could not help but wonder if he was not living in a fool's paradise, pretending that there were really no problems at all, when in fact they were growing wildly in number. He knew that there had been no recurrence of Kate's nightmare, for though she slept in her own room, he quietly opened the adjoining door each night before retiring. For the present, he could think of nothing better to do (to his mind, Sarah presented only a mild inconvenience), and decided there was no reason to take Kate to St. Clair before Christmas, as he had planned.

13

Lady Sarah Ponsonby let her vellum-bound copy of Lord Byron's *The Corsair* slide off her lap onto the pale blue carpet, reached out for a sweetmeat on the table beside her, thought of her figure, and drew her hand back. She was bored, not only with her doting elderly husband, but also with her lover, Sir Edward. Though his adoration for her had not diminished over the past several months, she found him unimaginative in lovemaking and trite in his gallant offerings of flattery. She could not help but make comparisons between Sir Edward and Julien, and found in all particulars that her portly lover was a decided second to the Earl of March.

She felt a sudden knot of anger at the thought of the pale-faced girl Julien had wed. She was far too tall, in Sarah's estimation, and she found it altogether disagreeable that some considered the young countess to be quite beautiful. Well, beautiful or not, she thought, brightening, the baronet's daughter was not enjoying her good fortune, for all was not well between the earl and countess. How fortunate it was that one of her lackeys was enamored of a talkative serving maid in the earl's household, for he provided her with a steady source of prime information. From her own experience, she knew Julien to be a passionate man, and she had first dismissed the careless bit of gossip that he did not visit his wife's bedroom. But then she had wondered why their wedding trip had been of singularly short duration. Now, after more than two weeks in London and many more bits of information let slip by her lackey, she was convinced that something was definitely amiss with their relationship. Her vanity tempted her to believe that Julien realized that he had made a shocking misalliance and was simply biding his time to again seek her out. It was an exciting thought, and she refused to dismiss it. After all, Katharine was but a girl—the thought rankled a bit—but she, Sarah, was an experienced woman, and a beautiful one, as she had been told countless times.

Her smooth brow furrowed in concentrated thought as she cudgeled her brain for the most expedient way possible to bring Julien to his senses. It did not take her long to hit upon Lady Haverstoke's ridotto, which was but two days away. What better opportunity to show Julien that he had made a mistake in his choice of brides. She would dress as Cleopatra, perhaps even paint her toenails, and wear the golden sandals. Dampening her petticoat to make the flowing white gown cling to her body was a bit uncomfortable, but it would serve to make her only the more alluring. With more energy than she was wont to show, Sarah rose from her couch and rang

imperiously for her maid. She found that she was even looking forward to riding with Sir Edward.

"You are silent, Julien. Does my costume not please you?"
Kate asked.

"It is not that it does not please me, Kate. It is simply not
quite what I expected you to wear," he answered in an even
voice. Secretly, he was appalled. He had supposed that Kate
would perhaps choose a shepherdess costume for the Haverstoke ridotto, or some such gown that would not call attention to herself. Instead, unbeknownst to him, she had attired
herself as a courtesan of the last century. She had powdered
her hair and piled it high atop her head. Her gown was of
crimson velvet, with full skirts worn over panniers, and cut
very low over her white bosom, a narrow row of lace suggest-
ing more than revealing the curve of her breasts. Perhaps
what shocked him most were her reddened lips and the small
black patch placed artfully beside her mouth. She wore heavy
ruby earrings and necklace, and even to the least exacting
taste, too many bracelets adorned her arms. He thought she
looked the whore, albeit a very expensive one.

"Perhaps, Kate, you have become enamored of Madame
de Pompadour's portrait?" he asked, trying to check his anger
at her appearance.

It was Kate's turn to be silent, and she turned the bracelets
on one wrist before replying slowly, "Yes, I had the gown she
wore in the portrait copied by Madame Bissotte. Of course,
she was Louis XV's mistress, but still . . ."

"She was a trollop," Julien said more harshly than he intended. "I do not wish my wife to emulate such an example."

His anger died as quickly as it had come, for her face
paled beneath the rouge and she turned quickly away from
him. He realized with a shock that in some strange fashion,
Kate was acting out the role of a whore because it was how
she felt about herself. He wondered fleetingly if she herself
was aware of what she was doing. He walked quickly to
where she stood and gently placed his hands on her shoulders.

"Do forgive me, Kate. It is just that I have no great liking
for the Pompadour. Indeed, my dear, you look striking . . .
the flamboyance of your costume serves only to enhance your
beauty." Though through his eyes, his words bespoke a blatant untruth, he was certain that the ton would see nothing

amiss with Kate's appearance and would even applaud her daring originality. "Come," he said, as she remained silent, "it grows late, Kate, and the Haverstoke mansion is several miles from London."

Kate turned to face him, a look of confusion in her eyes. She asked in a tight voice: "You do not go in costume, my lord?"

"My concessions are a domino and a mask. Had I but known that you so admired the dress of the last century, I would have dressed as Louis XV."

"Oh, no, you could not have! Madame de Pompadour was only his mistress! It would not be . . . that is to say . . ." Kate halted in consternation and gave her head a tiny shake.

With a flash of insight he realized that Kate did not see him as her lover, so in her eyes she could not see him as Louis XV. Aloud he said gently, "I hardly think it matters, my dear. Ah, here is George."

"Your carriage is in readiness, my lord," George announced, unaware that he had rescued his lordship and ladyship from a rather trying scene.

"Oh, yes, indeed! I have but to fetch my domino," Kate exclaimed. She turned on her heel and brushed past George.

Julien gazed after her before turning to his butler. "Thank you, George. Please inform Davie that we will be down presently." Julien picked up his black satin domino from the back of a chair and nonchalantly flung it over his shoulders. He fingered the soft black velvet mask before he slipped it into the pocket of his waistcoat. He thought grimly that he was indeed living in a fool's paradise, and it was crumbling bit by bit around him. When he walked past his butler into the entranceway, his face remained outwardly impassive.

Kate met him presently, an even more striking picture enveloped in her long crimson velvet domino. She had fastened on her red velvet mask, and not one auburn strand was visible through the white powder in her hair. If he had not known she was his wife, Julien would not have recognized her.

Their ride to the Haverstoke mansion occupied the better part of an hour, and after many minutes of strained silence, Julien endeavored to ease the tension between them by describing the various members of the ton she would meet. He maintained a steady discourse, which was punctuated only at rare moments by questions from Kate. She became animated only at the mention of Percy's name.

"I believe Percy plans to appear as a medieval lord of the manor, complete to battleaxe, so he told me," Julien said.

"I do but pray that he will not drop it on his foot."

"Rather on his foot than on yours when you dance with him." Julien grinned into the dim light.

"And will Hugh be present?" Kate asked, relieved that she could contribute to their conversation without causing awkwardness.

"Certainly. Like me, Hugh will relax his taste only to the point of domino and mask."

Kate did not comment, for the swaying of the carriage was making her stomach churn uncomfortably. She leaned her head back against the white satin squabs and closed her eyes.

The Haverstoke mansion was a two-storied pale red brick structure dating from the Restoration, set back from the main road by a rather rutted graveled drive. Lights blazing from every window and countless carriages lining the drive gave ample evidence of the success of the ridotto. As Bladen opened the carriage door for his master to alight, his eyes veered to the lighted servants' hall, where he was certain he and Davie would enjoy frothy mugs of ale.

Lady Haverstoke had rigged out her entire staff in the formal livery of the last century, a startling yellow and white, and had insisted, much to their consternation, that each wear a wig of sugarloaf shape. Thus it was that her hawk-nosed butler was busy grumbling to himself and twitching at his wig when the Earl and Countess of March were ushered into the main hall. Elkins, his second in command, looked like an exotic yellow bird, a canary, the butler decided with a curl of his thin lips, for a canary sounded both exotic and yellow. And the way he was fluttering ingratiatingly among the guests in his strutting manner was simply not to be borne! The butler grimly resolved to put the little creeper in his place the moment the guests departed. He was obliged to cloak his violent intentions as the earl and countess approached. The butler's bow to the earl was of the perfect depth, though his knees trembled in complaint as he straightened more slowly than he had descended.

"If your lordship and ladyship will please to accompany me," he announced grandly. The earl nodded briefly, and the butler smiled smugly as he conducted them up the winding stairway to the large ballroom on the second floor. Elkins, with his thin, high-pitched voice, would never be able to perform this duty with impeccable grandeur.

He managed to gaze surreptitiously at the new Countess of March and was disappointed that he could not make out her features through her mask and her powdered hair, as white as his sugarloaf wig.

"The Earl and Countess of March!" the butler announced in the most booming voice he could manage. He hoped that not too many more guests would arrive, for the assembled company was so boisterously loud that he was growing quite hoarse in trying to be heard over the laughing chatter and that wild German music—the waltz, it was called, Elkins had condescendingly informed him.

Kate had only a few moments to scan the startling colorful sea of guests for a familiar face before a large woman with a more than ample bosom, swathed in yards of purple satin, swooped down upon them. Her hair was tightly crimped, and a myriad of tiny sausage curls fluttered about her heavy face. Kate blinked at the two enormous purple ostrich feathers implanted atop her head that swayed precariously as she walked.

"Ah, my dear March! And your new countess! So delighted you could come. Quite unusual you look, my dear—Marie Antoinette, I daresay. And you, my Lord March, so disobliging of you not to come in costume! But no matter." She beamed at them, revealing large, protruding teeth.

"You look quite dashing, Constance," Julien remarked as the lady halted her monologue for a moment. "Yes, this is Katharine, my wife."

Lady Haverstoke favored Kate with a tap on the arm with her ivory *brisé* fan. "The hair creates quite an effect, my dear. So *very* white! But look—you are in good company. Only regard." Lady Haverstoke pointed her ubiquitous fan in the general direction of a small knot of elderly women, each attired more outrageously than the other. "Lady Waverleigh and that monstrous pink wig! That lady in the lavender silk, Elsbeth Rothford, how very youthful she would like to appear! And, of course, there is Lady Ponsonby, surrounded by her gallants, her court, as I call it." She looked expectantly to see some signs of agitation in Katharine, but seeing none, hid her disappointment and added for effect, "Scandalous, in my opinion! Cleopatra, she informs me—in that clinging wisp of material. And her toenails—painted gold!" Still observing no noteworthy response from either the earl or countess, she contented herself with the fact that the evening was far from advanced.

"Well, my dears," she said brightly, the feathers dipping dangerously low, "I really must see to old Lady Ranleigh. Such a bore! Of course you know your way, Lord March. *Such* a pleasure . . . Katharine!"

"My *dear* Lady Ranleigh!" Katharine heard her say as Lady Haverstoke moved with amazing speed away from them, soon lost to view among a throng of guests.

"Lord Haverstoke must be a man of great forbearance—or deaf," Kate said, shaking her head wonderingly.

"Lord Haverstoke had 'the good sense to depart this world some years ago," Julien replied wryly. He wished he could see behind Kate's mask to see what effect Lady Haverstoke's calculated words had on her.

"Come, Kate," he continued, taking her arm, "I believe that I have located our lord of the manor—battleax and all!"

"Oh, and there is Hugh, Julien. He looks terribly somber, does he not? All that black satin."

"Do I look equally as somber, Kate?"

"How ridiculous! Of course not! You look . . . rather dignified," she offered handsomely, "perhaps like a statesman."

"High tribute, certainly. If ever I take an active role in the house of Lords, my first act will be to comdemn auburn hair."

"Then you will find your bills for white powder will grow monstrously."

"Julien, at least have the decency to tie on your mask. You look like some sort of hell-fire parson bent on destroying the world!" Percy thrust forward his hand and shook Julien's heartily.

"Kate tells me I appear more like a statesman," Julien said, unable to refrain from smiling as he surveyed Percy's noble proportions encased in a jerkin of light yellow wool. His battleax dangled from a large leather belt about his waist.

"How grand you look, Percy . . . so very prepossessing!" Kate laughed gaily as Percy endeavored somewhat unsuccessfuly to favor her with a gallant bow. "Good evening to you, Sir Hugh."

"Lady Katharine. If my memory does not fault me, you have copied Pompadour's gown. I must commend your originality and the skill of your modiste. An unusual lady she was, to say the least."

Kate sensed more than observed a stiffening in Julien at Hugh's appraisal. She said quickly, "The portrait took my fancy, Hugh. But you know, the black patch is most bothersome. It itches excessively."

"Well, I would most willingly exchange your patch for this deuced cumbersome ax!" Percy said, shooting a look at Hugh. "Never should have let him talk me into wearing it."

"*Me* talk *you* . . ." Hugh expostulated.

"March," Percy continued, ignoring Hugh's astonishment, "don't mind if I dance with Lady Kate, do you?"

"If Kate does not fear for her toes, I suppose I can make no argument."

"Not at all," Kate said stoutly, placing her gloved hand on Percy's arm. Percy bore her off, and soon they took their places beside other equally colorful couples on the dance floor.

"Well, Hugh, which do you prefer—parsons or statesmen?"

"Considering the regent's problems with retaining statesmen of worth, I believe we should choose the latter and offer our services."

"And would you recommend our good Percy to command the army?"

Hugh tied on his mask. " 'Twould give me great pleasure to see our dandy mount a horse in that getup."

Julien's deep laugh dissolved into a grunt of impatience as he chanced to look up and see Sarah beckoning to him in a most imperious manner. Hugh's eyes followed Julien's and his nostrils quivered in perturbation. He frowned as he appraised her in her Cleopatra's costume, trying to remember if it was an asp or a viper that brought about the queen's demise. He became even more indignant when Lady Sarah blithely detached herself from her knot of admirers and calmly approached them.

"Do not be so obvious, Hugh, in your condemnation. Percy informs me that Sarah grows tired of Sir Edward, and if she chooses to seek out old quarry, it must be dealt with."

The two men's eyes met through the slits in their masks, and though Hugh was uncertain of Julien's intent, he was obliged perforce to maintain his silence.

"I pray you will excuse me, Hugh," Julien said briefly, and walked toward Lady Sarah.

"My dear Julien! Such a bore that you did not come as Caesar or perhaps Mark Antony. What a very attractive couple we would have made together." Sarah raised wide, wistful eyes to Julien's face and sighed with soulful innocence.

"You have need of no one to further enhance your image, Sarah. Does your barge await you outside?" Though Julien had been scandalized by Kate's costume, he was rather amused by Sarah's outrageous daring, and was unable to prevent his gaze from traveling the length of her flimsy, clinging gown. "And the gold toenails—quite the crowning touch."

"Yes, are they not?" she said, pleased at his masculine response. She laid her bare hand on his arm and said softly, "Will you not dance with Cleopatra, my Lord March? I vow she has awaited your coming all this evening."

"If you wish, Sarah. It is just as well," he remarked, more to himself than to her. He slipped his arm about her slender waist and whirled her into the throng of dancers.

Lady Constance Haverstoke watched with glittering eyes as the Earl of March led Lady Ponsonby to the dance floor. She turned to her companion, Lady Victoria Manningly, and remarked complacently, "What is the saying about moths flying forever to a flame?"

"March should take care, I daresay," Lady Victoria said with pursed lips, "else he will find himself quite at odds with his new bride. That is she, is it not, over there?" She pointed to Kate's graceful swaying form, rendered less so by Percy's ungainly costume. "She is a very proud girl, I have heard it said—but of course not unbecomingly so," Lady Victoria added hastily, remembering suddenly that for some strange reason Mrs. Drummond Burrell had taken an unaccountable liking to the girl.

Lady Victoria judged from Lady Haverstoke's brazen attempt to draw attention to the earl and Lady Ponsonby that she was not privy to this bit of information. It would serve her right, Victoria thought, if the earl's bride were to cause a commotion. Certainly that cat Sarah Ponsonby would not show to advantage in the eyes of society. She wondered if perhaps she should drop a hint in Constance's ear. She was surprised suddenly from his meanderings by the touch of Lady Haverstoke's hand on her wrist. "Do but look, Victoria," she hissed in her ear, "March and Lady Sarah are leaving the floor!"

Both ladies watched in silence as the earl led Sarah to the

large curtained windows at the end of the ballroom, parted them, and slipped outside behind them.

"Perhaps it is not moths to a flame after all," Lady Haverstoke mused with the superior grin of one who has accomplished her goal, "more like bees to the honey pot!"

"Lord March is unwise," was all that Lady Victoria Manningly said.

"My dear Julien, how very thoughtful of you," Sarah breathed, her hand caressing his arm. "It was growing so terribly close. How I longed for a breath of evening air."

"Did you indeed, Sarah?" he asked, very much aware for one unwanted moment of her hand stroking his sleeve and the pervading odor of her musk scent. He said coolly, "I understand, my dear Sarah, that Sir Edward has lowered in your estimation. Really, my dear, you are too fickle."

"I have missed you, Julien," she said simply, leaving her lips parted in the most provocative way. She felt the strength of him through the black satin of his evening coat and raised her hand to touch his face. "Oh, Julien, how ever could you have tied yourself to that whey-faced girl?"

"Whey-faced, Sarah?" Julien stiffened at the unflattering description of his wife. "Surely you have not regarded her closely."

She tossed her golden curls. "Very well, perhaps, she is . . . passable-looking. But, Julien, she is but a girl!"

"Indeed, my reputation would suffer were it otherwise, Sarah."

"Come, you know very well what I mean. Why, it is common knowledge that—" She ground to a halt as Julien's hand gripped her wrist.

"Just what, I pray, is common knowledge?"

Sarah drew back at the coldness of his voice. "Well, it is not precisely *common* knowledge," she temporized. She knew she was unwise to continue, but her dislike of Katharine propelled her into hurried speech. "I know, Julien, do you hear, I know that you do not . . . sleep with your bride, that you do not even visit her room." He made no response, and Sarah was emboldened to continue. "It is a mistake, my dear Julien, to have wed an inexperienced chit. Is she frightened of your passion? That is why, is it not, that you returned so quickly from your wedding trip?"

In the dim moonlight she could not see Julien's pallor, nor

the hardening of his mouth. She thought him to be struggling with himself, and she pressed her body against him, and slipped her white arms up about his shoulders. "Oh, Julien, can she give you this?" She stood on her tiptoes and touched her lips to his, her hands entwining in his curling hair and pulling him down to her.

Percy wiped his forehead with a fine lawn handkerchief that was oddly at variance with his woolen jerkin, and heaved a sigh. "Lord, Kate, 'twill take me an hour to regain my breath! Too deuced fast, that damned German music. Enough to send a fellow toppling early into his grave!"

"You were magnificent, Percy," Kate assured him, all the while searching for Julien and Hugh. "Drat, how vexatious this patch is," she complained, and lightly rubbed her cheek around the offending black satin.

"There you are, my dear."

Kate and Percy turned at the commanding voice of Lady Haverstoke.

"How terribly feudal you are, Lord Blairstock!" She looked around her complacently. "A sad crush, is it not?"

"Yes, indeed, ma'am," Kate agreed without a moment's hesitation. It was an expected compliment, for the success of the gathering was assured by the number of couples in attendance.

Lady Haverstoke lowered her voice and said in a conspiratorial whisper, "How charming Lord March looked, dancing with Lady Sarah. Several of the ladies were disappointed when they left the floor."

"They left the floor, ma'am?" Kate asked, feeling sudden nausea rise in her throat.

"For a breath of fresh air, no doubt," Lady Haverstoke said in a way that was a trifle too offhand.

"Well, it is deuced hot in here, Lady Constance, deuced hot," Percy announced. Now, what the devil was the smug old tabby up to? he wondered silently. It came as a bit of a shock to him that Julien would commit such a folly.

"Come, Kate, let us try some of that excellent champagne." Percy took Kate firmly by the arm, nodded briefly to Lady Haverstoke, and propelled her toward the punch bowl. "Don't listen to her, Kate," he admonished, "just trying to stir up some mischief, that's all."

"Is she, Percy?" Kate asked, stopping and gazing up at his perspiring face.

"Good Lord, Kate, don't be a nodcock! Julien is your husband, not some old roué to sport around with every pretty face."

"You are right, Percy. It is overly warm," she said, disregarding him. "If you will excuse me . . ." She felt the words choke in her throat as she sped away from him before he could form a protest.

"Damnation!" Percy exclaimed aloud, accidentally bumping his battleax against a lady's elbow. "Apologies, ma'am," he muttered.

When Kate broke away from Percy, she thought perhaps to seek out some quiet room where she could regain her calm in peace. But somehow she found that her legs were quite at odds with her mind, and moved resolutely the length of the ballroom toward the long windows. She was beginning to feel quite ill, her stomach churning uncomfortably and a steady pounding growing in her head. She silently cursed her own physical weakness and stopped to press her fingers against her forehead. Her lacings were too tight, that was it. Eliza had tugged and tugged until Kate had gasped for breath. She smoothed the tight velvet about her waist, drew a deep breath, and wondered as she pulled aside the heavy curtains what was happening to her, what was so overwhelmingly compelling her to search out her husband. She found that she was quietly pleading to some divine power to find Julien alone. As she slipped through the narrow opening, she felt as though someone's fist had struck her hard in the stomach, for she saw Julien and Lady Sarah, standing very close, the lady's hand possessively holding her husband's arm. She heard Lady Sarah say with devastating clarity, "Is she frightened of your passion? That is why, is it not, that you returned so quickly from your wedding trip?"

"Oh, dear God, Julien, she cried silently to herself, please, please . . ." Kate could not see her husband's face, but his continued silence dinned in her ears.

"Oh, Julien, can she give you this?" she heard Lady Sarah say in a voice husky with desire.

Kate pressed her face against the windowpane to blot out the picture of Lady Sarah locked tightly against Julien's chest, her lips upon his. She was filled with sudden fury, and without thought she stepped forward, her hands balled into fists. Her long gown caught itself on the hinge of the window and pulled her up short. She bent down and gave the skirt a vicious tug and found that her anger was dissolving into a dim haze of misery. She looked down at her dress—a whore's gown, was it not? God, what right had *she* to rain down curses on Lady Sarah's head? Kate pressed her hand against her mouth and turned about quickly. She knew she was about to be violently ill. She hurried back into the ballroom and made her way to a more distant row of windows. She slipped out quietly and ran along the flagstone balcony, until, unable to help herself, she leaned miserably over the railing and lost her dinner.

Kate sat huddled against the railing until she was brought to her senses by voices quite near her. She was seized with panic, thinking that it was perhaps Julien. He must not find her like this! Remnants of pride patched themselves together. Kate rose slowly to her feet, pressing her lace handkerchief to her mouth and gritting her teeth against a new wave of nausea. With automatic motions she smoothed her gown and forced her face into an impassive mask as she sought out an antechamber to bathe her face and mouth. She felt strangely empty, as if nothing now seemed to matter to her. She was grateful for the numbness, the feeling of detachment, for when Julien later approached her, as she chatted with the utmost unconcern with a young matron dressed in the accepted shepherdess costume, she was able to greet him with the semblance of a complacent smile.

"Lady Ridelow," Julien acknowledged with a slight bow before turning to his wife. "My dear, Percy is in quite a taking, claiming that you most disobligingly abandoned him at the punch bowl. Come, you must make reparations before we take our leave. A pleasure to see you again, Lady Ridelow," he said politely as he assisted Kate to rise.

As Julien guided her through the now-thinning company, he said softly, "Actually, Percy was in quite a taking over my behaviour, not yours."

"Your behaviour, my lord?" She looked up at him, striving for calm.

"Yes, Kate, and undoubtedly I owe you an explanation. By taking Lady Sarah to the balcony, I evidently gave the gossips a delectable topic of conversation. You, I am persuaded, must know my reason for doing so."

"Indeed, my lord, it is not for me to question your actions," she answered shortly, her eyes focused straight ahead of her.

"Come, Kate," he said sharply, frowning down at her profile, "you have taken me to task on practically every one of my actions since the day I met you. That I perhaps chose an awkward place and time to set Lady Sarah straight is very much your affair."

Kate felt a deep bitterness invade the comforting numbness that surrounded her. Yes, she thought sadly, I saw just how well you handled the lady.

"I see I am to judge by your continued silence that you either understand my motives or that you are jealous. Which is it, Kate?" He grasped her arm and pulled her up to face him.

"As you say, my lord," she replied finally, her voice wintry and far away, "I understand your motives perfectly. I assure you, there is no need to explain further."

He regarded her steadily, and said at last, "As you like, Kate. We have not yet danced. Would you perhaps—?"

"No! That is," she added hastily, "I am quite fatigued. If you would not mind, my lord, I would as soon leave."

"Very well," he said shortly.

Gray flecks of dawn were penetrating the darkness of the room when Julien awoke at the sound of a piercing scream. He bounded from his bed, threw his dressing gown about him, and rushed through the adjoining door into Kate's room. She screamed again, tangling herself among the heavy bedcovers.

He leaned over her and grabbed her shoulders, shaking her none too gently. "Kate! Wake up!"

A long shudder passed the length of her body, and she forced her eyes open. Julien was balancing over her, his face pale in the dim light. She cried out in protest as he shook her again.

"It was the nightmare again," she gasped. She struggled up and pulled her hands from beneath the covers to push damp masses of hair from her forehead. She threw out her arms to clasp him to her, but as she did so, the sensuous face of Lady Sarah rose in her eyes, and she fell back against the pillows and turned her face away.

Julien drew back, baffled. Always before, she had wanted him to comfort her, to hold her. Slowly he straightened and automatically began to smooth out the tangled covers. He saw that she was trembling uncontrollably. "Kate . . ." he said softly. She made no response, and he eased himself down beside her. Above all things, he did not wish to frighten her, and thus he contented himself with gazing at her averted face, satisfied for the moment at least that he was close to her. Gradually the trembling lessened and her breathing became more regular.

She turned her luminous green eyes back to his face. "I . . . I thank you, my lord, for waking me." Her voice was dry and crackling in the silent room, like fragile autumn leaves falling from branches.

"Do you wish me to stay with you, Kate?" He reached out his hand and lightly touched her damp cheeks.

She whipped her head away as if his touch seared her. "No!" she cried. "No, my lord, I assure you that I am quite all right now," she said more calmly. "I pray that you forgive me for waking you in such an unseemly—"

"Enough, Kate." His voice seemed angry to her, and she closed her eyes tightly, turning back within herself. But there was only a vast, lonely emptiness there. She heard him rise from her bed and felt his eyes upon her as he stood beside her.

"Good night, Kate. You have but to call if you have need of me."

She did not trust herself to speak, and so lay in stiff silence until she heard his retreating footsteps. She opened her eyes, and unbidden tears welled up and rolled silently down her face. She tried to piece together the nightmare, but as always, it escaped her, drifting back into unknown depths of her mind, waiting there; she felt it would never be gone from her. She took an edge of the covers and wiped the tears from her face.

Sleep did not again come to her, and she pushed back the bedcovers. She eased her feet into her slippers. She padded to the windows and curled up in the window seat, her face pressed against the blue brocade curtains.

It was some hours later that Eliza found her, huddled and shivering, asleep in the embrasure.

"Damn it, Julien! A bloody fool, that's what you are, and if you weren't my friend . . . and a better shot," Percy added judiciously, "I'd call you out right now!"

It was a rare occasion indeed that Hugh would not call

Percy to task over such an outrageous speech. This time, he looked steadily at Julien and nodded his agreement.

The three men stood outside White's, their overcoats buttoned high to their collars to keep out the blistering winter wind.

"You must have known that Constance Haverstoke would take the first opportunity to fill Kate's ears with Sarah. And *you*, of all things, *you* had to parade her in front of everyone onto the dance floor!" As a gust of wind threatened to whip Percy's beaver hat from his carefully pomaded locks, he momentarily ceased his strictures.

"It is quite true, Julien," Hugh continued in Percy's stead, bending his dark gaze on his friend. "She is so . . . young, Julien, and you should have realized how she would feel."

"Kate assured me that she quite understood my motives," Julien said stiffly.

"Besides being young, she is quite proud," Hugh said with some impatience.

Julien threw up his gloved hands. "All right, that's enough from both of you!" He raised haughty brows and added sarcastically, "You are acting as if Kate were your sister. I was on the point of telling you both, before Blairstock here ranted at me like a madman, that I intend to leave London with Kate on Friday. We go to St. Clair. Does that satisfy your chivalrous meddling?" He felt justifiably irritated that anyone, even Hugh and Percy, should dare suggest that an Earl of March did not conduct his private life as befitted his station.

"And Sarah?" Percy asked darkly, undaunted.

"Neither of you have further need to trouble yourselves about that lady."

"Ah, so you came to an understanding with her when you took her outside to the balcony," Percy pursued.

Julien jerked his head around. "It appears that my actions are quite common knowledge," he remarked acidly.

"Lord, Julien. You may be a fool, but Kate isn't. As I told you last night, Lady Constance gave her an earful!"

Julien's anger died as he pictured Kate in the dim morning light, silent and withdrawn from him. He raised weary eyes to his friend and said quietly, "The matter is settled. Do not, I pray, call me out, Percy," he added with a glimmer of a smile. "Now, I suggest, if you gentlemen are quite through cutting up my character, that we repair to White's and have a glass of sherry."

It was strange, Hugh thought, as they were divested of their greatcoats in the cloakroom of White's, how very serious life had become since Julien had got himself wedded. And to see Percy in such a pucker over any matter that did not involve his personal pleasures made him wonder uneasily if he did not know more of the situation than he had disclosed earlier that morning, when he had unceremoniously burst in, most effectively dampening Hugh's appetite for his breakfast. He gazed beneath hooded lids at Julien and noted the tense lines about his mouth and eyes. No, he decided, finally, Julien was too closemouthed, and like Kate, too proud to unburden himself to anyone.

They drank their sherry in silence, each feeling acutely strained in the others' company. Hugh thought the sherry tasteless.

"It's like you could cut the air with a blade," George said behind his immaculate white-gloved hand to Mackles, a young footman who had just received a blistering set-down from a usually polite, calm master.

"It ain't so much his lordship," Mackles said after ruminating over George's comment for several moments. "It's her ladyship. Like a ghost she's been, so pale and quiet-like, if you know what I mean." He glanced sideways toward the breakfast room, thankful that the door was firmly closed.

George knew very well what the footman meant, but he was suddenly aware that such a conversation, were it even with a superior servant, was unseemly. "Well, just never you mind about all that, my boy," he said formally, bending a stern eye on the hapless Mackles. "You just help Eliza with her ladyship's trunks. His lordship and ladyship should be finishing their breakfast shortly and will wish to leave."

On the other side of the breakfast-parlor door, Julien was sitting across from Kate. "Do at least try some of your eggs, my dear. 'Twill be a long journey."

"Aye, my lord," she answered, her head down. She did not feel at all well this morning, and the thought of the eggs made her stomach turn. But as she did not wish him to know, she tentatively raised a morsel to her lips and forced herself to swallow.

"Your gown is very smart. Madame Giselle?"

Kate nodded, thinking privately that the dove-gray dress emphasized her pallor and the dark shadows under her eyes most unbecomingly. She had pulled the gown from her wardrobe to the sound of Eliza's disapproving clucking.

"How long do you intend to remain at St. Clair?" Kate assayed, seeing Julien frown at her nearly full breakfast plate.

"If it pleases you, at least until the new year. You do have a say in the matter, you know."

She quelled a disbelieving rejoinder and merely nodded. She could remember no occasion when any opinion of hers affected his decisions. Indeed, she had learned but two days before that they would be leaving for St. Clair.

Not many minutes later, the Earl and Countess of March said hasty good-byes to the assembled servants in the marble entranceway.

"Have a safe journey, my lord, my lady," George said in his superior butler's voice as he opened the front doors.

"I will keep you informed as to the date of our return, George," Julien said over his shoulder.

Kate looked with something akin to dread at the open carriage door. "Maintain a smart pace, Davie," she heard Julien say to their coachman, "I wish to halt at Bamford for luncheon."

"Yes, my lord," Davie answered with a salute. He shot a smug smile at the gimlet-eyed Bladen, who was not to accompany the earl on this trip.

Julien assisted Kate into the carriage and handed her two fur rugs to wrap about her legs. He swung himself in and settled himself comfortably, then tapped the roof with his cane. He briefly looked out the carriage window to ensure that the other carriage containing Eliza and Timmens was also in motion.

Satisfied, he sat back and stretched his long legs diagonally across from him. "Are you warm enough, Kate?"

"Yes, my Lord March," she answered, not turning her head to face him.

"So formal, Kate?" he asked lightly. "Would you that I call you 'my lady'?"

Kate watched Grosvenor Square disappear behind them before saying with a forced smile, "If it suits your fancy. With all those servants at your command, it seems more natural for you to be a Lord March, and not a simple Julien."

"They are also your servants, Kate," he said, steadily regarding her.

Two slight patches of color appeared on her pale cheeks. "As you will . . . Julien."

Not a very auspicious beginning, Julien thought glumly, watching Kate from the corner of his eyes.

As the carriage rumbled through Hounslow Heath, Julien attempted some unexceptionable conversation. "It looks quite barren, does it not?" He directed her attention to the forlorn leafless trees set against a gray, fog-laden landscape. "Our most famous highwaymen have frequented this place, and still do, for that matter. I myself was stopped here some years ago."

Kate showed some signs of interest. "You were robbed?" she asked incredulously.

"Well . . . not precisely. I had to send the Bow Street runners for two of them, and the other fellow managed to escape with a bullet in his arm."

Julien chuckled. "You should have seen Davie. Foolishly brave he was, waving about his blunderbuss and screaming curses at the villains."

"You . . . you were not hurt?"

"Oh, no. Merely late for Lady Otterly's drum." He did not add that the lady who was accompanying him flew into the most damnable hysterics.

"It must have been quite exciting," Kate said naively. "I have never met a highwayman."

"I must admit to some relief, my dear. A most unsavory lot, and not at all dashing or romantic, as the stories puff them up to be."

"I am not a silly girl, my lord," she said, taking exception. "I was merely wondering what it would be like to . . . shoot someone."

"I trust you will never have the occasion to find out," he said dryly.

She shivered.

"Are you cold, Kate?" He leaned forward and tucked the rugs more securely about her.

She drew back at the hint of his nearness. "No, no, I was merely thinking of Harry . . . and hoping that he is unharmed," she said, nervously tugging at her handkerchief.

The carriage lurched over an uneven stretch of road and Kate gritted her teeth against a wave of nausea. Even as she closed her eyes tightly and prayed that she would not be ill, she was forced to say in a strangled voice, "Julien, please stop the carriage. I am going to be sick."

Julien took one look at her strained, pale face and drove the head of his cane hard against the roof of the carriage. The carriage pulled to a halt, and Julien threw open the door and jumped to the ground.

"Come, Kate," he said crisply. "Give me your hand."

She stumbled toward him, her handerchief pressed hard against her mouth. He took a firm grip on her arms and swung her to the road beside him. She leaned heavily against him, the world spinning unpleasantly about her. Julien let her slip to her knees at the side of the road and held her shoulders firmly as she retched violently. He silently cursed himself for forcing her to eat what little breakfast she had had. The retching eventually subsided into dry-heaving spasms that shook her whole body. Julien ruthlessly pulled off her fashionable bonnet so that she could rest her head on his thigh, and drew his greatcoat around her to protect her from the blustering wind.

"My lord," Davie said diffidently, "perhaps her ladyship would feel a mite better with some of my . . . medicinal brandy."

"Thank you, Davie. The very thing." Julien took the flask from his coachman, wet his handerchief, and gently wiped Kate's lips. "Come, Kate. This will make you feel much better." His calmness steadied her, and though she was now consumed with embarrassment, she slowly raised her head and allowed Julien to place the flask to her mouth. She took a long draft and felt the fiery liquid burn its way down her throat. Her stomach churned anew at the unwelcome intrusion, but to her profound relief, quieted after but a moment.

Kate felt too weak to struggle as Julien gently lifted her into his arms. Nor did she protest when, once inside the carriage, he held her firmly on his lap, her head resting against his chest.

"My lord, is her ladyship well enough to continue now?" Davie poked a concerned face through the carriage door.

Julien took quick mental stock. "How far are we from Barresford?"

"But a mile or so, my lord."

"Good. There is an inn there . . . the White Rose. I think her ladyship should rest there before we think of continuing.

Drive slowly, Davie," he added, tightening his hold about Kate's shoulders.

Kate burrowed her face against Julien's chest. Between bouts of the wretched dizziness, she felt there could be no greater shame than being vilely ill in front of someone else.

"Why did not you tell me you were sick, Kate?" Julien asked after some moments.

"It is but a touch of the influenza, I think," she answered, her voice muffled.

He felt inordinately guilty that he had not guessed that her unnatural silence and pallor reflected more than her unhappiness. He frowned above her head, wondering why the devil Eliza had not informed him.

"If you had but told me, we could have delayed our trip to St. Clair."

"No!" she cried with unwonted energy. "That is . . . I did not wish to stay . . ." Her voice trailed off and he felt her tense in his arms.

"It is all right, Kate," he soothed, letting his chin rest on her hair. "If you are not feeling better this afternoon, I will send Davie back to London for a physician."

"Please do not, Julien. I shall be fine—you will see. I would not wish to cause you any more . . . inconvenience."

"It is not an inconvenience to wish my wife to be in good health," he said with some asperity.

She sighed and was silent.

The White Rose was a staunch red brick inn nestled amid elm trees across from the village green. The landlady, unused to Quality visiting her humble establishment, quickly wiped her large hands on her apron and bustled forward, waving imperiously at two of her sons as she did so.

"Quick about it, Will! Open the door." A large, ambling boy of about seventeen years hurried forward and pulled vigorously at the carriage door.

Not without some difficulty, Julien alighted with Kate in his arms. "Davie, stable the horses and keep your eyes sharp for the other carriage."

"Right this way, my lord." Mrs. Micklesfield hurried to stand beside the open doorway for Julien to enter. He had to lower his head, for the smoke-blackened beams were perilously low.

"I require a bedchamber for her ladyship," Julien said,

looking about him at the dim but cozily warm taproom. He hoped there would be no bugs in the mattress.

"Yes, indeed, my lord, if you will please to follow me." For a large woman, Mrs. Micklesfield moved with amazing rapidity up the worn wooden staircase. She opened the door at the top of the stairs to a small but sparkling-clean bedchamber containing only a large old-fashioned four-poster bed and an ancient armoire.

Kate did not particularly wish to relinquish her warm, hidden position against Julien's shoulder. Her eyes met her husband's as he gently laid her on the bed. She was a good deal surprised to see a frown of worry furrow his brow, for, in truth, she had rather expected some sign of impatience at having his trip so disrupted. He leaned over her and plumped the pillow beneath her head. "Now, my dear, Mrs. . . . ?"

"Mrs. Micklesfield, my lord," she hastily supplied.

"Yes, Mrs. Micklesfield will undress you and tuck you up. I will return and look in on you in a little while."

"As you will, Julien. But you will see, I shall be fine in but a few minutes," said Kate, trying to rally her forces.

"Stubborn Kate," he said softly. He squeezed her hand, straightened, and walked from the room.

"Now, my lady," Mrs. Micklesfield said, moving resolutely forward, " 'Tis high time we made you comfortable." With deft movements she unfastened the myriad of small buttons on Kate's gown and slipped it over her head. Her petticoat and stockings followed her gown, and soon she lay snug beneath a soft down quilt.

"Thank you, Mrs. Micklesfield. That is indeed much better."

"I should think so, my lady," she declared as she carefully hung Kate's gown in the small armoire. "Now, you just rest and I will fetch you some food and a warm broth. 'Tis just the thing to make you feel fit as a trivet."

Kate felt dubious about the food, but she was too weary to quibble. She closed her eyes and concentrated on righting her disgruntled stomach.

Julien stepped out of the taproom a few minutes later to see Mrs. Micklesfield preparing to mount the stairs with a tray of covered dishes in her arms.

"Ah, my lord! Quite knocked up, her ladyship is, but I've just the thing to make her feel better." She beamed at him in what Julien thought to be an uncommonly motherly fashion.

"But food, Mrs. Micklesfield?" he asked, feeling every bit as dubious as Kate had.

"But of course, my lord. A lady in her condition must keep up her strength. All that racketing about in a carriage unnerved her—it is to be expected," she added with some severity.

"A lady in her *what?*" he asked sharply, disregarding the rest of her words.

"If I may be so bold as to wish your lordship my congratulations," Mrs. Micklesfield said, softening her leathery features. "But as her ladyship is breeding, you really must not rush her hagglety-pagglety about the countryside, if you will allow me to say so, my lord."

It took a moment for her words to penetrate Julien's befuddled mind. Kate pregnant! He felt as if he had just stepped into some bizarre play in which he was the main character and Mrs. Micklesfield his audience, and he had no idea of the lines he should speak.

As all the tortuous implications of this bizarre situation flashed before his eyes, he found that he was leaning heavily against the door, his eyes fixed dazedly on Mrs. Micklesfield. There can be no greater irony, he thought—my wife pregnant by a wild German lord, who is I. Yet in the same moment he felt a certain sense of masculine pride. He remembered his blithely spoken words to his Aunt Mary Tolford. He had promised her an heir within a year. It was his audience of one who forced him back to the complexities of reality.

"Shall I take the tray up to her ladyship, my lord?"

"No, Mrs. Micklesfield, I shall take it up." It occurred to him that Kate might not know she was pregnant. "Mrs. Micklesfield," he began, choosing his words carefully, "you did not mention her ladyship's condition to her, did you?"

"Why, no, my lord, I assumed . . ."

"Excellent. I pray that you will not. You see," he added mendaciously, "her ladyship is not quite used to the idea as of yet. I would not wish her further upset."

Mrs. Micklesfield nodded slowly. As the earl mounted the stairs, she shook her head, puzzled. Breeding was breeding, after all. Natural it was, she thought, remembering how her own five children had slipped so easily into the world. The Quality are peculiar, she concluded, and turned toward her kitchen, where a freshly plucked chicken awaited her ministrations.

Julien paused a moment outside Kate's door. He felt convinced that she did not yet know she was pregnant. After all, she had spoken so earnestly about her influenza. But, good God, how could she not know? Did not women understand these things? Surely, when she missed her monthly cycle . . . No, he thought, it was entirely possible, nay practically certain, that she did not know, caught up as she was in her own unhappiness and her dreaded nightmares. He made rapid calculations in his head back to that day, to that small cottage in Switzerland. It could not be much longer before she must realize that she was with child. Several days, a week perhaps. It did not allow him much time. He schooled his features into those of simple concern and tapped lightly on the door. He entered to see Kate struggling to pull the covers over her bare shoulders. He found that he was regarding her closely, perhaps expecting to see some change in her. But if anything, from the brief glimpse he was allowed of her arms and shoulders, she seemed more slender than before.

"Well, wife," he said crisply, moving forward to her bedside, "Mrs. Micklesfield has kindly prepared some food for you. It will make you feel quite the thing, so she informed me."

He set the tray beside her and picked up a smaller coverlet. "Here, Kate, would you like to wrap this about you? I would not want you to catch a chill."

As she modestly wrapped the coverlet about her shoulders and pulled herself to a sitting position, she turned to Julien and said with some surprise, "It is very strange, you know, but I find that I am really quite famished. I have never had the influenza before, but it is *odd*, the way it affects one."

"Indeed, I have found that to be true," he answered with great seriousness. He felt an urge to gather her in his arms and tell her that she was pregnant with his child, but he thrust his hands into the pockets of his breeches instead. He must first get her to St. Clair; then, as much as he abhorred the notion, he must see Sir Oliver. He was convinced that he himself had first to know all that had happened to her; then perhaps he could help her to understand and forget.

Kate consumed every morsel of food on the tray and lay back with a sigh of contentment.

"Poor François would be positively unnerved if he witnessed the quantities of food you just consumed," Julien observed.

"He is forever burying the most delicious foods in those outlandish sauces of his. He could take a few hints from Mrs. Micklesfield, I think." How very normal we are acting toward each other, Kate thought, when he is away from that *woman*.

Julien walked to the windows and gazed out onto the gray afternoon. A light drizzle had begun, and raindrops were running down the glass in zigzag rivulets.

"Julien," Kate said presently, "you would not wish me to quack myself like . . . your mother?"

"Quack yourself, Kate? I hardly think that resting after you have been vilely ill qualifies as quacking." He turned away from the window and approached her bedside.

"What I meant was . . . well, I feel quite marvelous now, and if you would not mind, I would that we continued to St. Clair."

She did indeed look the picture of blooming health. "Very well, my dear, if you are certain . . ."

"Oh, yes, my lord, quite certain. But fetch Mrs. Micklesfield and I can be dressed in a trice."

It was not beyond a half-hour later that Julien assisted Kate into the carriage and climbed in after her. Despite the drizzling rain, she waved her hand out the carriage window and smiled brightly at Mrs. Micklesfield and her grinning son.

It was Kate who urged that they push to Hucklesthorpe before they halted for the night.

Though Julien would have preferred to leave early the next morning, he judged from his brief experience that Kate needed time after breakfast to settle her stomach. She did not seem to notice that he ordered a light meal for her, nor did she take exception at their delay in leaving. They were both rewarded by Julien's careful planning, for Kate did not suffer a moment's illness throughout that day.

It was well after nightfall when their carriage finally turned from the main road down the long elm drive to St. Clair. Mannering was not expecting them, but Julien knew there would be cozy fires in their rooms and a warm dinner ready for their delectation within an hour of their arrival.

"My lord . . . my lady!" Mannering at first edged the great doors open and then flung them wide.

"It is so good to see you again, Mannering." Kate stepped quickly forward and shook the butler's hand warmly.

"Ah, Lady Katharine . . . to see you here, as mistress of St. Clair, such an honor, such an honor! Allow me to offer my congratulations, my lord," he continued, turning to Julien. "Dear me, how very late it is. If your lordship and ladyship will allow me to escort you to the drawing room, I shall inform Mrs. Cradshaw."

"My lord," Kate interjected, turning to her husband, "if it pleases you, I would prefer to have dinner in the drawing room. The dining room is so terribly . . . glum!"

"Certainly, Kate. Whatever Cook has available, Mannering. will be fine."

"Yes, my lord." Mannering bowed and conducted his master and new mistress to the drawing room.

"I do hope dinner will not be long in coming," Kate said as she stripped off her lemon kid gloves and tossed them on top of her bonnet.

"On that score you need not worry." Julien smiled. He knew that the mild-spoken Mannering, when confronted with an emergency, bullied, cajoled, and otherwise threatened mayhem on all his staff who did not immediately perform in the most exacting and speedy manner possible.

After a footman had unobtrusively laid a fire, Julien seated himself opposite Kate next to the fireplace and stretched out his legs toward the crackling logs. As always, he felt a sense of deep contentment at being in his ancestral home.

"It feels so very . . . strange to be seated in this room, as if I belonged here," Kate said, more to herself than to Julien. She ran her hand tentatively along the red brocade of the armchair.

Julien shook out the ruffles over his wrists, pondering, it seemed, the great ruby signet ring on his right hand. "It would seem to me, Kate," he said at last in a voice of forced lightness, "that you are far more at home here at St. Clair than at your father's house."

"Perhaps. I certainly *look* more elegant than that poor wretchedly dressed girl at Brandon Hall did." She paused a moment, a frown puckering her brow. "Julien, you do not think it necessary that I visit Sir Oliver, do you? You have guessed, I am certain, that a genuine welcome is simply not in his nature."

Julien thought of his impending visit to Sir Oliver. Whatever the outcome, he himself did not imagine that it could be in any way cordial. It was likely that Sir Oliver would be the one to sever all relations. He shifted his position in his chair and crossed one gleaming Hessian over the other. "I naturally understand your reluctance," he said finally. "Let us see what the next few days bring, shall we? And as to that poor wretchedly dressed girl, as you so unkindly call her, I thought she showed a great deal of spirit. I cannot but remember your breeches with a certain fondness. The combination of your breeches, leather hat, and pistol were altogether irresistible."

A slight smile played over Kate's lips, and Julien could very nearly picture the laughing dimples. "Well, at least in that instance, Julien, you must admit that you looked rather foolish . . . and so top-lofty!"

"You were a sore trial to my consequence. Would you accept a challenge to duel with me? Breeches and all?"

"Only if I find my leather hat," she replied swiftly. "But surely, sire, you will perforce again fear for your consequence. To be beaten by a mere female!"

"That, my dear," he said imperturbably, "remains to be seen."

Kate stood up and shook out her skirts. "I do wish Mannering would bring our dinner. My stomach is knocking against my ribs."

"Ah, Mannering, here you are. Lady Katharine was just this moment expressing a desire for your company."

"Your dinner, my lord," Mannering announced as he entered, followed by a footman staggering under the weight of several covered trays.

As Kate settled herself beside a small table to enjoy baked chicken and warm bread, she heard Mannering clear his throat and inform his lordship that the second carriage had succumbed to an unfortunate mishap. "The axle sheered clean through, so Mr. Timmens informed me, my lord."

"Good Lord, Mannering. I presume that her ladyship's maid is now stranded?"

"Yes, my lord. In Tortlebend, Mr. Timmens tells me. 'Twill be several days before the carriage is mended."

Julien turned to Kate, who was in the process of wiping her fingers. "I hope you do not mind Mrs. Cradshaw looking after you, Kate. It would appear that Eliza is enjoying a forced holiday."

"Not at all." Kate could not but admit a certain relief. Sometimes, she thought, it seemed that Eliza saw too much.

"As to the work you ordered, my lord," Mannering continued to Julien, "it was completed just last week. An excellent job the carpenters did, if you don't mind my saying so. One would never guess that the rooms did not originally adjoin each other."

"What work was Mannering talking about, Julien?" Kate asked after the butler had bowed himself out of the room.

"I merely ordered that our bedrooms be connected by an adjoining door, that is all, Kate," Julien replied nonchalantly. He chose to ignore the two bright patches of color on Kate's cheeks and made an elaborate pretense of eating his chicken.

14

"The Earl of March is here, my lord, and awaits your presence in the drawing room."

Sir Oliver ceased tugging at his boot for the moment and looked up at Filber. "He is, is he?" The perpetual lines that drew down the corners of his mouth lifted, and to Filber's surprise, he gave a grunt of amusement. He wet his hands with his spittle and ceremoniously slicked down his frizzled gray hair.

Filber quickly averted his eyes and gazed down at the toes of his black shoes. He hoped that his abhorrence of Sir Oliver's distasteful habit would go unnoticed by his master.

Sir Oliver rose, picked up a cravat from the dresser top, and carelessly knotted it about his neck. He peered at the result in the mirror, seemed satisfied with what he saw, and turned toward the door. "Let us go, Filber. After all, we would not wish to keep my august son-in-law kicking up his heels." He gave a cackle of mirth and thwacked the stoop-shouldered butler jovially on the back.

There was an air of suppressed excitement about Sir Oliver that made Filber uneasy. It was barely nine o'clock in the morning, a time when his master was at his most dour and disagreeable. It was strange too, he thought, that Lady Katharine had not accompanied her husband.

"Is it not gracious of his lordship to pay us a visit, Filber? And such a gray, unpleasant day it is, too." Filber quickened his pace in front of his master down the staircase. Now that he thought about it, the earl, though polite as always, had acted differently, rather too serious, perhaps even abstracted.

Filber reached the drawing room and flung open the double doors. "Sir Oliver, my lord."

"My *dear* sir! How very pleasant to see you!"

A common-enough greeting, Filber mused, as Sir Oliver brushed past him into the room and firmly closed the doors behind him.

Julien turned from the window and faced his father-in-law. He nodded only slightly in response to Sir Oliver's greeting and did not move forward to take his outstretched hand.

Sir Oliver was not at all discomfited by his son-in-law's coldness.

"You are a long time in coming, my lord. If the truth were to be told, 'twas much sooner I expected to see you. Will your lordship be seated?" he offered with a flourish of his hand.

Julien's jaw hardened. "No, I think not. But perhaps, sir, it would be to your advantage to be seated."

"Don't mind if I do." Sir Oliver flipped up the tails of his coat and eased himself down into a thread-worn chair. "Deuced cold day, eh, what?" he asked.

"I am not here to discuss the merits of the weather," Julien replied harshly.

"And how is my dear, *dear* daughter? No use shilly-shallying around, my lord. That is why you are here, is it not?"

"Katharine enjoys good health. And as you say, it is because of her that I am here."

Sir Oliver dropped his eyes from his son-in-law's set face and smiled, pretending to study his knuckles with rapt interest. "Now, my dear boy, there was nothing in your most thorough marriage contract about the . . . return of damaged goods." He looked up and met Julien's gaze, a malicious gleam drawing his eyes more closely together. He chuckled. "Well-stated, is it not, my Lord Earl?"

Julien drew a deep breath and for the moment kept his anger in check. He said steadily, "Katharine's purity and innocence are not, I assure you, in question." A look of deadly contempt passed over his face. "I would add that I now marvel at this, considering that she sprang from your seed. Has it occurred to you that you are speaking of your own daughter? If your Methodist preachings allow you a soul, sir, I would suggest that you look within yourself, for if you have a soul, it is withered and rotted. Your body reeks of its putrefaction."

"How dare you . . . you arrogant, foppish . . ." Sir Oliver jumped panting to his feet, his face suffused and mottled red with fury.

"Sit down!" Julien thundered, advancing purposefully. Sir Oliver sagged back into his chair.

Julien planted himself in front of Sir Oliver, gripped the arms of his chair, and leaned close to his face. "Now, you will listen to me. It is obvious that you knew I would come, that you have indeed looked forward with a twisted delight to spewing your venom in my face! Did you honestly expect that I would return Katharine to you, spurned and disgraced?"

Julien straightened quickly, repelled by the closeness of this man. Sir Oliver's face was still blotched with his anger, but now his eyes were wary and he licked his lips nervously.

"Then why are you here?" he muttered.

"Ah, now we are to make progress," Julien said softly. He moved away and leaned his shoulders against the mantel. "You know, I presume, that Katharine has no conscious memory of her rape and your subsequent treatment of her. But did you know that it haunts her like an elusive specter, emerging with terrifying confusion in her dreams at night? She is close to unlocking the truth, yet it eludes her still, and she lives in a suffocating dread. And that is why I am here— to learn all of the truth so she can finally be cleansed from this ugliness."

Sir Oliver's pent-up hatred of his daughter took full rein. "You *defend* her," he spat, "you believe her a pure, defenseless child. She has made a fool of you, my Lord Earl! Well, I will tell you, she is a slut and she was a whore even then. Those wild green eyes, and that hair—red as all the sins of Satan—hanging loose down her back! And my doting wife, blind to the evilness of her own daughter, let her flaunt her wiles to the countryside. . . . Oh, yes, I remember well that day, the lying little strumpet screaming that those men had hurt her! She deceived my wife with her tears, but I saw through her pretense. I beat her . . . yes, thrashed her to an inch of her life, to scourge the evilness from her, to exorcise her vile spirit! And then the little harlot feigned illness. Lifeless she lay in her bed, with her damned fool mother, half-crazed, crooning over her——" Sir Oliver felt his voice choked off by a painful tightening in his chest. The blood pounded in his temples, and for several agonizing seconds he could not breathe. As quickly as the pain had come, it receded, and he gulped in the precious air, feeling his chest expand again with life. He tried to remember what he had been saying, and the image of Katharine as a child rose before him, her large, silent eyes staring at him, deep pools of fear. He heard himself give a crack of laughter.

"She forgot, you know," he said slowly. "But I reminded her and, yes, I beat her . . . to keep the wickedness out of her." Sir Oliver's eyes blazed again in sudden passion. "Do not you understand? I saved her soul from eternal damnation!"

He paused and looked up to see the earl still standing motionless by the fireplace, a curious, unreadable expression on his face. "She fooled you too, my *dear* Lord Earl, did she not?" Julien did not answer, and Sir Oliver sat forward in his chair, a look of grim satisfaction marking his mouth. "Allow me to wish you much . . . pleasure with your virgin wife, my lord. But beware that she does not cuckold you before your precious heir is born!"

Julien looked dispassionately at the leering old man before him. He felt moved by a deep tenderness for Kate, stirred by a helpless sense of pity and regret at her having spent so many years with this man. If only it was not too late for her now.

"It happened at the copse, in the wooded area close to Brandon Hall?" Julien was surprised at the calm of his voice.

"Eh?" Sir Oliver looked with confusion at his son-in-law.

"The copse—the place where Katharine was raped," Julien repeated patiently.

"One of her favorite haunts, the copse." Sir Oliver's voice rose suddenly. "It was her own private kingdom, she would say. But I know why she went there—to traffic with the devil, to learn the evilness of her body!"

"Enough!" Julien interrupted, suddenly sickened. He wanted now nothing more than to leave this oppressive, airless room. "I have nothing more to ask you. You have provided me with all the information I need." Julien straightened and walked quickly to the door. He added softly as he turned the knob, "Of course you will understand that Katharine will not be paying you a visit."

He saw Sir Oliver gazing blankly down at his hands as he pulled the doors closed firmly behind him.

"Your coat and hat, my lord."

"Thank you, Filber." Julien shrugged himself into his greatcoat and moved rapidly to the front doors.

"Is Lady Katharine well, my lord?" Filber asked, his voice softening. "She will be much better soon, Filber, I assure you." Julien could not prevent his eyes from straying momentarily to the closed drawing-room doors.

"If you pardon my saying so, my lord, all of us here wish Lady Katharine the very best. If you would be so kind, my lord, as to give her our . . . regards."

"That I will, Filber, that I will." Julien strode down the front steps and without a backward glance mounted his horse.

It was late in the afternoon when the sound of Julien's voice reached Kate through the half-open door of her bed-chamber. She heard his sure stride on the staircase and stood rubbing her sweaty palms on her skirt, in an agony of indecision. Oh, dear God, she thought wildly, I cannot yet see him!

Kate's instincts for survival propelled her into motion. "Milly!" she cried, rushing toward the startled maid. "Quickly, go to the door and tell his lordship that I am not well . . . that I am asleep!"

With feverish rapidity Kate tugged off her dressing gown and scrambled into her bed. "Milly, hurry!" she hissed, her dread of seeing Julien sharpening her annoyance at the maid's slowness.

"Yes, my lady," Milly said in a flurry, moving as quickly to the door as her plump figure would allow. She shot a furtive glance over her shoulder at her young mistress, now burrowed beneath mounds of covers, her eyes tightly closed. Milly gulped and stepped into the hallway, her nervous fingers closing the door behind her. Like most of the newer members of the St. Clair household, she held the earl in reverent awe, and as he approached nearer and nearer to her, she began to feel almost incoherent, her tongue lying thick in her mouth.

"Good afternoon, Milly," Julien said politely to the bobbing girl in front of him. He motioned an elegant gloved hand to the closed door. "Is her ladyship in her room?"

"Yes, my lord," Milly managed to say in a strangled whisper. As the earl made to move past her, she rushed into desperate speech. "Her ladyship is not well, my lord . . . that is, she was not well, but now she is sleeping. She did not wish to be disturbed, my lord." She bore up rather well, she thought later, under the earl's close scrutiny, but was aware at that moment only that her stays were much too tight. She shifted her weight to her other booted foot and looked at him hopefully.

"Very well," Julien said slowly.

Milly breathed a sigh of relief, but to her consternation, the earl moved to the door and quietly opened it. She wondered frantically whether she would be able to secure another such excellent position as this.

Julien peered into Kate's room, now bathed in the somber gray late-afternoon light. A lone candle cast its withered light above the mantel, blending in curious patterns with the smooth orange glow of the fire. He could still picture his mother sitting on her favored spindle chair, remorselessly plying her needle into a swatch of material that never seemed to become anything. Only Kate's collection of hairbrushes scattered above the dresser top gave proof that another now occupied the bedchamber. He stood silently, hoping to see some movement from the bed, but the blue velvet goosedown quilt remained firmly in place. He could make out only the general outlines of her slender figure, the rich hair fanning out about her face on the silk pillow giving her Kate's identity. He stepped forward, stopped, and again retreated. No, it would be better not to awaken her, he decided, pulling the door closed behind him. The maid, Milly, still stood where he had left her, like a small plump pug, parading as a watch dog at his mistress's door. He raised an inquiring brow. "Yes, Milly?"

Milly gulped. "Oh, nothing, my lord. That is, if you wish me to stay with her ladyship . . ."

"No, I think not. Let her sleep. She will undoubtedly ring if she has need of your assistance." Julien nodded dismissal, turned, and walked to his own room, his greatcoat swirling about his ankles.

Milly bobbed a curtsy to the earl's back, cast an uncertain glance at the closed door, turned, and fled down the hall to the servants' quarters. There was a thankful prayer on her lips.

Although Julien forced the sniffing Timmens to go slowly in assisting him to change into evening clothes, no word came from Kate that she would join him for dinner. Hunger finally drove him to the library, where Mrs. Cradshaw brought him a covered tray.

"Has her ladyship kept to her room all day, Emma?" he asked, uncovering a succulent lamb stew.

"Yes, she has, my lord," replied Mrs. Cradshaw comfortably, peering over Julien's shoulder to make sure the kitchen maid had put a salt shaker on the tray.

Julien swiveled about and looked at her sharply, but was greeted by only a bobbing of her head, for the girl hadn't forgotten about the salt. "Will that be all, my lord?" she inquired, a smile on her broad face that crinkled up the wrinkles about her eyes.

A damned disturbing smile, Julien thought, searching her eyes for some clue, with no idea of what he expected to find there. The dark brown depths remained unmoving, as she complacently regarded him. Rather sourly he waved her from the room and turned his attention to his dinner. The tasty stew did nothing to alleviate his mood, which was one of disgruntled melancholy. Good Lord, to be faced with his lunatic father-in-law, a smug housekeeper, and an absent wife all in one short day was enough to dampen anyone's spirits. Still hopeful for a message from Kate, he endeavored to while away the long minutes by penning a letter to his fond parent. As no neutral phrases leaped from his quill, he gave up the attempt. With a sigh he rose and stretched, and cast an unenthusiastic eye toward the rows of leather volumes meticulously lined up on endless shelves. He finally selected a volume of Voltaire's *Candide*. He made his way upstairs, pausing a moment outside Kate's door. No light shone beneath the door and there was no discernible movement from within. He raised a hand to the door, thought better of it, and continued slowly to his own room.

The hands on the mantel clock moved inordinately slowly, and it seemed an eternity before they softly chimed twelve strokes. Julien looked down wryly at the few pages that his fingers had relentlessly turned and could not recall what he had read. He sniffed out a gutted candle and lit a new one. At least he did not have to concern himself overly with

Kate's health, since he knew the cause of her illness. But Sir Oliver—if only he could rid himself of the distorted, leering features, the twisted, damning words. He gave up the attempt to sleep and resolutely turned his wandering attention back to Voltaire.

He did not know what caused him to look up, perhaps the veriest whisper of movement or a change in the soft shadows cast by the candlelight on the walls. His book dropped to the covers unnoticed.

Kate stood motionless at the foot of his bed, clad in a white satin gown that shimmered in the flickering light. Her hair was unbound and cascaded about her face and her shoulders, falling in shiny deep waves to her waist. Her eyes rested calmly and steadily upon his face, the pupils so enlarged in the near-darkness that they glowed with an intense blackness.

"Kate?" he asked uncertainly, sitting upright in his bed.

Her dark eyes widened under his questioning scrutiny, but she remained silent, her pale lips parted only slightly. She began to move stiffly toward him, her gown clinging to her in gentle folds, her eyes, great luminescent pools, never leaving his face.

"Have you had the . . . nightmare?" he asked quickly. Julien pulled back the covers, realized that he was naked, and covered himself again.

She stood quite close to him now, and his eyes were drawn to her full breasts gently outlined by the flimsy material. He felt desire for her flame from deep within him and did not trust himself to speak.

"Julien . . . may I stay with you tonight?" Her voice was soft, a tantalizing whisper from deep in her throat.

God, I must be dreaming, Julien thought, blinking away what surely must be an apparition. He felt a gentle hand on his bare shoulder. "May I, Julien?"

Her touch sent waves of molten feeling coursing through his body. He drew a deep breath, and with a sense of wonderment gently took her hand in his. "Kate . . . I do not understand . . ." he began. Her fingers fastened about his hand, and he forgot that he did not understand anything.

Her lips curved into a smile, a gentle, tentative smile, yet one full of promise. She slipped her hand from his and took a step back. Her slender white hands moved to the white ribbons about her throat, and slowly she began to pull them loose, one after the other. The gown parted in the wake of her fingers and revealed to him the full curve of her breasts. Her hands dropped to her sides, and she stood motionless for what seemed an eternity to Julien. She lowered her eyes from his face and in one long fluid moment shrugged the gown from her shoulders. The soft satin floated down about her waist and rested momentarily on her hips before falling light as a feather about her feet. Almost defiantly she tossed back her head, her long hair swirling about her face, and gazed at him questioningly. "You have not answered my request, Julien," she said in a husky whisper.

Somewhere in the back of his mind Julien dimly realized that he was being seduced, not an altogether new experience, but one that could not but be ironic, given that the lady was his wife.

"Come, Kate," he said with simple tenderness. He tossed the now-meaningless novel into the dark corner of the room and moved toward the center of his bed. "I trust, my love, that the pleasure will be both of ours." He held back the covers, and without pause Kate slipped in beside him.

Julien balanced himself on an elbow above her, not yet touching her. He needed to savor the fragile moment, one that he had awaited for so long. Kate, of her own desire, coming to him.

"How very exquisite you are," he murmured, allowing his hand to smooth waving tendrils of hair away from her face.

"I would give you . . . pleasure, my lord," she said in a low voice, her lips parting slightly.

A discordant note sounded sharp in his mind, but dissolved away as Kate lifted slender arms and wrapped them about his neck, pulling his face down to hers. He met her lips hungrily, pent-up desire overcoming for the moment the tenderness and wonder he felt at her coming to him. He tasted the sweetness of her mouth and grew more demanding, probing possessively for her tongue. He felt her stiffen and cursed himself for his clumsiness; he stilled his raging desire and released her. He saw a flicker of fear in her eyes before she quickly lowered her lashes.

"Kate," he began softly, "if you would rather not . . ."

He sensed a hesitance in her. He gently touched his fingers to her cheek, and she raised her eyes to him again. With a fierceness that took him off his guard, she arched her back upward, letting the covers fall from her breasts, and pressed herself against his chest. She held to him tightly, her hands sweeping down his back. "Oh, yes, Julien . . . please. It is what I want."

Her voice was breathless, somehow unnatural, but now he was aware only of Kate and his undeniable need for her. Impatiently he threw back the covers and gathered her to him. He swept his hands down through her fragrant hair to her slender hips and pressed her hard against him. She buried her face against his shoulder, and he felt an exquisite rippling of pleasure as she dug her fingers into his back.

"Oh, Kate, my dearest Kate," he whispered, his voice low and husky with passion, "if only you knew how long I've waited for this moment." He buried his face in her hair, savoring the rich softness.

He felt her fingers, feather-light, touch his hair. "Do you not . . . want me, Julien?" There was an insistence, an impatience in her movements as her fingers moved to his face, and in her voice, almost an urgency.

A smile came to his lips, and he cupped her chin in his hand so that he could gaze into her full face. "I think the answer to your question should be fairly obvious, my love." He grinned at her and moved gently on top of her.

She flushed and tried again to look away from him, but he held her chin firmly and planted a light kiss on her lips. "So impatient, little one? I would give you pleasure first. How could you think me so ungallant?" He gazed into the depths of her dark eyes with intense tenderness.

"Oh, no!" she cried. "That is . . . please, Julien, I would that you take . . ." Her voice trailed off in an agony of embarrassment.

"Hush, Kate," he said softly, closing his mouth over hers. He remembered her gentle cries and moans of pleasure, the warm softness of her, and drew away from her, letting his hands move down her shoulders to stroke her white full breasts. Almost unconsciously his eyes roved over her body to see some signs of her pregnancy. Perhaps her breasts were more rounded, but he could not be certain. Her waist was still slender, but there was, he saw, a slight fullness to her belly. She lay perfectly quiet in the crook of his arm as his hand moved at will over her body. She stiffened against him only when he closed his lips over a soft pink nipple. He felt exquisite delight as the nipple grew taut at the touch of his probing tongue. He willed himself to go slowly with her, as he had done so long ago.

The quickness of her response surprised him, a long quiver that rippled the length of her body under the exquisite kneading and stroking of his hands.

"Julien . . . no, please," she pleaded.

"Would you truly rather that I stopped, Kate?" He paused and looked up at her face. She bit her lip and looked away. "Would you, Kate?" he repeated, his voice commanding an answer.

"No," she said faintly, the small word, so great in its significance, wrenched from between her parted lips.

The silence of the room was broken at first by her low, throaty sighs of pleasure. As she arched against him, her hands moving insistently over his shoulders and through his curling hair, her moans became cries of consuming pleasure. She thrashed her head wildly about, her nails raking his shoulders. He gave her that instant, intensifying her pleasure to the fullest, before moving quickly astride her. His fingers parted her and he felt himself engulfed in the small, soft warmth of her body.

"Julien, Julien . . ." She repeated his name over and over, arching her hips to draw him deeper into her. He thrust his full length into her, and despite his intentions, found that he could not control his pent-up desire. He covered her lips with his and felt long-awaited release, moaning his own pleasure into her mouth.

"Am I crushing your ribs, Kate?" Julien asked presently, drawing himself above her on his elbows. He felt almost absurdly happy, a sense of warmth and caring for her that rivaled their moment of sensual release. He was held in the curiousness of the feeling, for he had never before experienced with any other woman such tenderness and deep satisfaction following lovemaking.

Kate's lips parted, but before she could respond to him, he closed his mouth over hers.

"It would appear, my love, that I am quite unable to allow you conversation. Your lips are much too inviting." He kissed the tip of her nose and smiled into her eyes. He touched a finger to the corner of her mouth. "You may smile, however, for I wish to see my favorite part of your person . . . your dimples," he prompted.

Slowly she curved her lips into a deep smile and the

dimples appeared as if by magic. He kissed each dimple solemnly.

"Perhaps . . . my ribs, Julien," she whispered, trying to shift her weight slightly under his body.

Julien had thought his desire sated, but at her movement, he felt himself grow hard within her once more. "I have a solution, my love, that both of us, I hope, will approve." He slipped his hands beneath her back and in a swift motion pulled her over on top of him. Cascades of auburn hair buried his face. He smoothed her hair back and was tenderly amused to see a flush of embarrassment on her face.

He grinned. "Why, my dear wife, I have given you the upper hand . . . so to speak. It does not please you?"

She tried to slip away from him, but he gripped her shoulders. "By all the laws of nature, if I were to let you go now, I would have myself hanged from the nearest elm branch. Sit up, Kate, for I would look at you."

She seemed to struggle with herself for a moment before she slowly pulled her legs up to straddle him. As he settled her atop him, he felt himself move deep within her.

"Do I hurt you, Kate?" he asked, lifting up her hips slightly with his hands as she tried to shift her position.

Masses of hair swirled about her face as she shook her head.

"Oh, Julien, I must tell you . . ." Her voice broke off, strangled, and she stared at him numbly, naked misery in her eyes.

He could not allow her to speak, not yet. He could picture the horror in her eyes at what she would think his betrayal of her, his animal lust, his savage cruelty.

He pushed her hard down against him, and she moaned— whether in pain or pleasure, he could not be certain. He wound his hands in her thick masses of hair and pulled her face to his and captured her lips. There were no more words between them. He possessed her body, as completely as if she were a part of him. With infinite patience he forced her to pleasure, willing her for the moment, at least, to forget.

15

When Julien awoke the next morning, he languidly reached out for Kate and found that he was alone. For a brief instant he wondered if he had dreamed of her coming to him. He smiled a deep satisfied smile, stretched his full length, and brought his arms up behind his head. He was not overly concerned that Kate had left him before he awoke. It was quite likely that she felt deeply embarrassed after having initiated their lovemaking. He calmed his resurgent desire at the thought of her naked in his arms, rose from his bed, and rang for Timmens.

He took a long drink of hot black coffee and stared out of the morning-room windows onto the gray winter day. If only it would not rain, today of all days. There was much to be done. There was a light tap on the door, and Mrs. Cradshaw eased through the doorway.

"A good morning to you, my lord," she said brightly, and deposited several covered dishes on the sideboard.

"Such quantities of food would certainly make Lord Blairstock's eyes light up, Emma," he remarked as he buttered a slice of hot bread.

She chuckled. "I daresay it would, my lord. Do you know that Cook has never enjoyed herself more? Despite the presence of the Frenchman, of course." She hovered near the table, as if she were unwilling to leave the room. Julien granted her the privilege of an old retainer and did not dismiss her, sensing that she wished to speak to him of other matters.

"Her ladyship will be down presently," he said with confidence. Although Kate had not stayed in his bed, she was no coward, and he did not believe it in her character to purposely avoid his company.

" 'Tis natural, if you'll pardon the liberty, my lord, that she be a trifle late in the mornings."

Julien momentarily forgot the slice of crisp bacon on his fork and gazed at Mrs. Cradshaw fixedly.

"But another two or three weeks and her ladyship will be enjoying an early breakfast again with you, my lord," she said placidly, beaming at him in a motherly, knowing way.

He forced a smile. She has been fussing about me since yesterday, he thought, and that sentimental look—she knew last evening! "I suppose you have been giving her ladyship all sorts of good advice and time-honored remedies."

"Oh, yes, indeed, my lord," she said in a flurry. "I am so happy that she has told you! Made me promise, her ladyship did, not to say a word to you—wanted to tell you herself. Such wonderful news it is, my lord! Fancy, opening up the nursery again."

Julien cursed to himself silently as the truth burst upon him. Here was Kate's motive for willingly offering herself to him last night. He could imagine the hours she had passed arriving at such a desperate and daring solution. He could not allow Kate to discover that he knew. "Mrs. Cradshaw, her ladyship does not need your assistance. Indeed, I expect her momentarily. I would much prefer that you meet with Nurse and inspect the nursery." He spoke firmly, and she at once responded to the authority in his voice.

She brightened. "Right away, my lord," she said, curtsying.

Julien nodded his dismissal, and when the door closed behind Mrs. Cradshaw, he rose slowly and walked to the windows. Poor Kate! How could she have been so naive as to believe she could deceive him into believing the child was his? Did she not even realize that a man could tell whether or not a woman was a virgin?

He turned abruptly as the door to the morning room opened and Kate tentatively ventured in. With a palpable effort he said calmly, "Good morning, Kate. Do come and have your breakfast. Cook must have threatened the chickens, for there are mountains of eggs. And as for the pigs, I dread to contemplate their fate. The bacon is crisp, as you like it."

He realized he was rambling on with inconsequential conversation, but he wished to give her no clues as to his own thoughts, and to lessen her nervous embarrassment at seeing him.

Her eyes did not quite meet his, and she mumbled an unintelligible greeting as she slipped into a chair.

He continued in a heartening voice: "When you have finished, I would that we ride this morning. I do not think it will rain, and the fresh air will be invigorating."

He saw agreement register on her face before she spoke. Riding, she would not be obliged to converse with him. "Yes, I would like that, Julien," she said, forcing a momentary smile.

"I will leave you, then, my dear, and see to having the horses saddled. Would half an hour be sufficient for you to finish your breakfast and change?"

"Oh, yes, 'twill be fine." She was unable to quell the look of relief that swept her features as he left the room.

Dressed warmly, a thick, lined velvet cloak buttoned to her throat, Kate ventured past Mannering out onto the front steps, where Julien held Astarte and his own powerfully built stallion. "Stay, Thunderer," he commanded, and released the stallion's reins to toss Kate into the saddle.

"They are restless and ready for a gallop, Kate," he said over his shoulder as he mounted. "Take care that Astarte does not get away from you." Although he did not believe that riding at a sedate pace could harm her in her condition, he had felt a moment's hesitation about their outing on horseback.

"I suggest that you see to your own horse," she returned with some spirit as Thunderer sidled and pranced about. "Astarte is far too much a lady to give me a moment's worry."

"Yes, ma'am," he said mildly, and reined in his horse beside her to canter side by side down the graveled drive.

Julien found to his relief that Kate seemed to pay no particular attention to the direction they took. It was not until their horses broke through the woods into the small meadow that bordered the copse that Kate suddenly reined in Astarte and said sharply, "Julien! Whatever are we doing here?"

He pulled up beside her, and before she knew what he was about, he grabbed Astarte's reins from her gloved hands. "It is time to bury old ghosts, Kate."

She stared at him in confusion. "I . . . I don't know what you mean."

"The copse, Kate. We must go there." He whipped the reins over Astarte's head and urged Thunderer forward.

"Julien! No! I do not wish . . . I cannot . . . Please, let us leave this place!" There was a rising note of panic in her voice, and she tugged furiously at the reins, trying to pull them from his closed fist. Julien quickened their pace, and she had to grab the pommel to retain her balance.

"Julien, no!" she cried, her voice breaking pathetically.

Julien drew in at the edge of the copse, jumped from Thunderer's back, and walked quickly to Kate's side. She tried to draw away from him, but he grabbed her arms and pulled her down to the ground, holding her for a moment hard against his chest. He shook her lightly, and she turned a pale, drawn face up to his. "Kate, listen to me," he commanded. "You can no longer live in dread of this place. Have you not guessed that your nightmare had its beginning here? Look about you, Kate. There is nothing for you to fear here, not now. Do you remember the small girl who played in this copse? It was her fairy kingdom, her private world, a place of security—until that day when the men came upon her. Look, Kate! Do you not remember?" He gently pushed her away from him, into the depths of the copse. Her hands twisted at the folds of her cloak and she stared ahead of her, unseeing.

"Was it summer, Kate, that day?" he pursued, moving to her side.

She did not answer him, and he saw that she was looking fixedly at an old tree trunk that was very nearly covered with thick ivy. She raised a gloved finger. "That was my throne," she said softly. "How overgrown it has become." She moved lightly toward the tree stump and gazed down at it, frowning.

Julien stood motionless and watched her in silence. She fluttered her hands about her, and she seemed to move more lightly, her step shortened.

"Ah, but the mushrooms still flourish. So lush they are! The palace guards picked them for the queen. They should be flogged, the floor of the throne room is such a mess. All those brambles and that wretched encroaching ivy! And the queen's musicians, playing soft music through the green swaying leaves . . ." She sank down to her knees, her cloak billowing about her, and slowly began pulling away the tangled masses of ivy. She began to hum in a faraway voice, a child's lilting song, as she brushed away the dead leaves from the top of the tree stump.

"The men came, Kate?"

She became suddenly quiet and crouched over, turning on her heels to gaze through him. "Oh, do but be quiet, all of you. Do you not hear the sounds, the strange noises? Heavy, wooden boots—strangers coming here. Quickly, cease your playing, your music will attract their notice!" She put a finger to her mouth and looked furtively about her. "Hide, all of you! Oh, I am still to be seen." A hard, proud look froze her eyes into bright slits, and her mouth was a straight, tight line. "I am the queen," she declared haughtily. "Look, they approach." A spasm of uncertainty, then open fear, crumpled her features. She swayed back and forth on her heels and gazed, openmouthed, mutely ahead of her.

"Kate, do you remember what happened? The men burst in upon you. They approached you." Julien moved silently to her and went down on his knees beside her swaying form. She shook her head slowly back and forth, as if willing herself not to remember. She closed her eyes tightly and averted her head, willing herself not to see.

"What did the men do, Kate? Did they . . . hurt you?"

Her eyes flew open and she thrust her hands out in front of her to ward off something he could not see. "No! No!" she cried out shrilly, shaking her head violently from side to side. She tried to scramble away from him, but Julien clasped her shoulders and held her firmly. "What do you want here? This is Brandon land. You must go! Do you hear me?" The fear in her voice, the pathetic defiance, made gooseflesh rise on his arms. Through her eyes, he could picture the men, rough peasants, coming upon the beautiful child, their callused hands clutching at her long hair, ripping at her clothing, savagely exposing her.

Kate stiffened suddenly, pain suffusing her pale face, and cried out—a shrill, terrified cry that rent the silent woodland. She crumpled forward, and he caught her against his chest. Julien was beyond words, helpless and impotent in a fury that grated into his very soul. No retribution, no reckoning; and now it was too late, years too late.

With shaking hands he pressed her against him, trying somehow to make her feel his understanding, his compassion. Over and over he whispered her name.

Julien was long aware of the damp chill air creeping

through his greatcoat before Kate stirred in his arms, pushed her hands against his chest, and raised her white tearstained face to his.

"It is all over now, my love. There is nothing more for you to fear. Do you understand, Kate?"

The naked pain in her eyes wrenched at him, propelling him into further speech. "You must face it, Kate. It's been over now, over for years upon years. The child's pain can no longer be your pain. You must banish it from you. The ghosts are dead, Kate. Do you understand me?"

"Ghosts . . . bury the ghosts," she said dully. "That is what you said when you forced me here, is it not?"

"Yes, Kate, that is what I said." He gently brushed the tears away with his gloved fingers.

She gave her head a tiny shake, her eyes narrowed in confusion. "But . . . but I do not understand, Julien. How did you know, for I did not. How?"

"The nightmare, Kate. You remembered and spoke in your sleep. To be certain, I spoke with your father."

To his surprise, Kate flung away from him and rose shakily to her feet. She shrieked at him in a strangled voice, "Why did you not tell me? Why did you force me through all this?" She flung her hands widely around her. "Why, Julien, why?"

"Kate . . . I could not. If I had told you, simply recounted what I knew, I could not be sure you would remember, or understand. There was so much that—"

"Well, now you have your confession, my lord!" she flung at him. "Did Sir Oliver give you every sordid detail? Did he tell you all about his slut of a daughter?"

He rose to his feet, staring at her incredulously. "Kate, you misunderstand! What I have done was for you, to help you."

She sneered at him, her hands balled into fists on her hips. "For *me*? Dear God, how you lie to yourself, Julien, as you have always done! There were no nightmares until you forced me to wed you. There were no ghosts until you resurrected them! Did I play my part well, my lord?"

"Kate, damm it! You are blinding yourself to the truth. If you will but listen for a moment—"

"No, Julien," she said scornfully, "I have your full measure now, my lord! Do you intend a second visit to my father to tell him he was correct about his harlot of a daughter? Do not hope that he will take me back. Or do you still believe my innocence? Do but recall how very passionate and abandoned I was in your bed last night. Come, Julien, was your precious Sarah ever more eager for your embraces that was I?"

"Enough, Kate!" he thundered at her. "By God, you will stop this nonsense!" He moved quickly forward to grab her, to shake some sense into her, but she evaded his outstretched arms and rushed to Astarte. She tugged the reins from the withered branch and threw herself onto her horse's back.

"Kate, stop! Damnation, don't be a fool!" Julien shouted, running toward her. He lunged forward to grab the bridle, but Kate jerked up on the reins and Astarte snorted in surprise and plunged backward. Kate wheeled the startled horse about and dug in her heels.

Cold desperate fear gripped him. God, Kate, the child, remember the child!

Astarte was galloping erratically, crashing through the undergrowth of the woods, naked winter branches ripping at both horse and rider. Her riding hat was torn from her head, drifting gently earthward, buoyed by the vivid blue ostrich feather, until it lay stark and helpless on the mossy floor of the woods, ground but an instant later into the bright shreds by Thunderer's pounding hooves.

The woods ended and both horses cannoned onto a narrow lane, beset with deep treacherous ruts, gaping wide, an arm's length, many of them. Astarte veered off the road, as if sensing herself the dangers of those yawning holes, into a barren field.

Agonizing minutes passed, as Thunderer strained to close the distance.

A long, low stone wall, for many years a meaningless boundary between properties, cut across the field to either side, its cold gray edges stark against the clouded sky. Surely now Kate would stop, she must stop.

"Kate, no, do not! Astarte does not jump without command!" His ragged voice filled the empty space. He made a last desperate attempt to reach her, but she evaded his outstretched arm.

"Astarte, over!" The futile command hung about him muting his hearing. He watched in helpless despair as Astarte reached the stone wall, gave a frightened snort, and veered sharply, grazing the jagged stone edges. Kate cried out as she lost her hold and was thrown, strangely huddled and small, across the wall to the ground beyond.

Julien whipped Thunderer forward, and the horse sailed gracefully over the stone wall. Julien leaped off his back and ran to where Kate lay motionless, on her back, the velvet cloak fanned out about her, a soft blanket of deep blue against the hard, rocky earth.

He fell to his knees beside her and gathered her into his arms. He loosened her cloak and felt for the small pulse that was beating steadily in the hollow of her throat.

Her lashes fluttered and she opened large eyes, filled with dumb fear. "Julien . . . the child."

He acted without conscious thought and quickly slipped his hand up underneath her riding habit to the soft shift that covered her belly. He had no practical notion of what he should do, but instinctively he gently pressed his hand against her belly. She was soft and smooth to the touch. "Do you feel any pain, Kate?" he asked, as he continued to gently probe with his fingers.

"No . . . no, there is no pain." She sucked in her breath and gazed at him in consternation. In a voice devoid of emotion she said flatly, "You knew of . . . the child."

"Yes," he acknowledged realizing that he must not now keep anything from her. "You remember when you were ill, the morning we left for St. Clair. The landlady at the inn where you rested told me."

"Then you know as well that the child . . . is not yours." Julien had to lean very close to her face to hear the whispered words. The hopelessness in her voice wrenched at his heart.

"You are wrong, Kate. The child is mine," he said calmly.

"Do not make mock of me, Julien," she cried bitterly. "Dear God, is there nothing you do not know?"

He gently shook her shoulders. "You must listen to me now, Kate. I know that is must seem incredible to you, but it is true. I was the wild German lord who drugged you, who abducted you. It was I who raped you. I had thought to teach you pleasure, to make you admit to yourself that you cared for me, indeed, that you wanted me as your husband in every way."

"Oh, Julien, no! Please, stop, it cannot be true!" But as she spoke, memory stirred deep within her. Memory of that man's hands on her body, his lips scalding, possessing her, and Julien's touch the night before, creating in her the same frenzy, the same passion. "I . . . I was so frightened last night; I thought myself the cheapest of women to react so . . ." She pressed her fist against her lips.

"No, love, do not think that of yourself, for I knew, as I knew why you came to me last night. How I have hated myself for the deception, for forcing you to live with this misery!"

She seemed not to hear his words, and searched his face with dazed anguished eyes. "But why did you . . . hurt me?" she wimpered pitifully.

Julien drew a deep breath, and for an instant, could not meet her gaze. "When I entered you, I realized that you were not a virgin. I thought your fear of me was a sham, that you had given yourself to someone else before me. I cursed you in that moment and sought only to give you pain. I wanted to hurt you as I thought you had hurt me.

"It was only later, that night, when I realized the truth. The nightmare, Kate. My rape of you made you remember, but only in that tortured dream. You spoke in fragmented images of the men—of the cruelty of your father. You remembered nothing of it the next morning." Julien saw in her eyes the gulf of misunderstanding that separated them, and he hurried to answer her unspoken question. "I could not tell you, Kate. You trusted me so completely that I feared the consequences of speaking the truth. That is why I brought you back to London. I thought, foolishly perhaps, that you would forget."

"You could not tell me," she repeated dully, the woman struggling with the child's pain. She fumbled to grasp the child's horror, to bring her through the intolerable years, to somehow make her part of herself. As she opened her lips to speak, a long, sharp pain tore through her belly, and her words, jumbled and fragmented, tore from her throat in a jagged, meaningless cry. She was held in senseless surprise as the pain dissolved, freeing her mind for a brief instant, then seared again through her, its force doubling her forward.

"Dear God . . . the child! Kate, quickly, I must get you back!"

She looked at him blankly, her eyes dulled with shock and pain. Julien pulled her cloak closely about her and lifted her into his arms. The stabbing pain engulfed her once again, and she clutched at his arms, her cry muffled in his greatcoat.

She became aware of her hair whipping about her face, the loud din of horse's hooves pounding in her ears. The pain was becoming a part of her, rending her, and only dimly did she realize that she was crying aloud. If only she could ease the pain. She tried to bring her knees up to her chest, but could not move against the strong arms that held her.

Julien tightened his fierce hold on her, her cries of pain rendering his face set and grim. "It is not much farther. You will be all right, by God, I swear it."

The words had no meaning to her. All understanding plummeted into a void of pain, dissolving shreds of reason. Incredible forces were tearing her asunder. She screamed her pain, thrashing wildly against the arms that held her. Voices, loud voices, coming as if from far away, shouted, babbled, incoherent sounds. Suddenly a great lassitude numbed the agonizing pain, scattering it apart from her, making her once again at one with her body. She wondered, almost inconsequentially, if she was dying. How strange that death would be like this, a creeping, paralyzing darkness that closed so gently over her mind. She whimpered softly to herself, a sense of undefined regret, a brief shadowy flicker, blending into the darkness.

Kate's head lolled from his shoulder as Julien carefully dismounted from Thunderer. He cradled her in one arm, freeing the other to feel for her pulse. He blinked in dazed shock at his hand; it was covered with blood, Kate's blood.

A sharp command burst from his mouth. His groom was running ahead of him, throwing open the front doors, quickly stepping out of the way, his mouth agape.

The set-down that automatically rose to Mannering's lips at the undignified impertinence of the groom was swallowed in consternation.

"My lord!" He nearly toppled backward, so quickly did he step aside as Julien swept past him.

"Mannering, fetch Mrs. Cradshaw immediately," Julien shouted over his shoulder as he bounded up the stairs. "The groom is off for the doctor. Send him up the moment he arrives!"

"Yes, my lord, right away, my lord!" For a moment Mannering stood staring after the earl, unable to remember where to find Mrs. Cradshaw. In frustration, and for the first time in his well-ordered life, Mannering threw back his head and bellowed, "Emma! Emma!"

Julien passed the maid, Milly, on the upper landing. "Her ladyship has suffered a miscarriage. Bring hot water and clean linen—quickly, girl!"

Milly gulped her garbled response, turned, and scurried down the stairs to the kitchen. "It's her ladyship! She's lost the baby!" she shrieked as she passed Mrs. Cradshaw on the stairs.

Julien carried Kate to his bedchamber and laid her gently in the middle of the large Tudor bed. She was so deathly pale! He pulled off her cloak and cursed his shaking fingers as the small buttons refused to open. He ripped off her habit, his fear lending frenetic speed to his movements. There was so much blood, clots of dark purple, covering her legs, weighing down her shift and skirt. He threw the soaked clothing to the floor and stripped off her stockings and riding boots.

He heard a sharp intake of breath behind him. "Emma, bring me towels. She is still bleeding!" He did not turn from Kate, and only the rustle of Mrs. Cradshaw's black skirt told him of her movement.

He could recall nothing, not a shred of information about miscarriage, a subject never spoken of in a gentleman's presence. The bleeding was now a purple pool stark against the pale green of the bedspread. He had to stop the bleeding! Julien rushed to his armoire and grabbed several fine lawn shirts. With all his strength he pressed the shirts against her to stem the flow of blood.

"My lord, the towels," Mrs. Cradshaw cried, her own face white and pinched with anxiety.

"No, Emma, I do not think it wise to lessen the pressure. Bring blankets, we must keep her warm."

His arms were buried by the covers, and though they began to ache, he pressed his hands all the harder against her.

Mrs. Cradshaw stood away from the bed, her gaze drawn to the bloody, torn clothing on the floor. "Did she lose the child, my lord?" she asked faintly.

"Yes," Julien replied briefly, not looking up.

"I will . . . remove the clothing, my lord." She leaned over, wrapped the soaked material in the towels, and rose, somewhat shakily. "Would you prefer that I remained, my lord?"

"No, Emma, it is not necessary. Take the clothing and burn it." The sharp command was cold, impersonal, but there was haggard misery in his gray eyes.

She moved slowly to the door. "Dr. Quaille should be here shortly," she said by way of reassurance, more to herself than to the earl.

Tentatively Julien eased one hand from between Kate's thighs and rested it briefly on her abdomen. It was an absurd gesture, for he had no idea of what he was probing for. He moved his hand to her breast and flattened his palm to feel her heartbeat. Though rapid, the beat seemed regular and steady.

He had begun to despair of his actions, when the door was suddenly thrown open and the portly, red-faced Dr. Quaille bustled forward, his stark black cloth suit proclaiming his profession.

"My lord! I came as quickly as I could." He panted from his exertion at running up the stairs.

"The countess has had a miscarriage," Julien said grimly. "I was uncertain what to do for the bleeding. It would not stop." He slowly pulled back the blankets. "As you see, I have pressed the cloth against her, hoping to stop the bleeding."

"Excellent, my lord, excellent," Dr. Quaille assured him as he drew some rather formidable-looking instruments from his worn leather bag.

"Now, my lord, if you would allow me to examine her ladyship," he said crisply.

Seeing the earl's obvious reluctance to move, he added gently, "You have done just as you should, my lord. I myself could not have contrived better, under the circumstances."

Julien slowly removed his hand. His shirts were soaked through with blood. He winced and said in a voice of despair, "It seems I have failed, for she still bleeds profusely."

"It is to be expected, my lord," the doctor soothed, seating himself on the bed. "Would you care to wait outside, my lord?" he asked, feeling it quite improper that a gentleman should witness what he was about to do.

"No," Julien said sharply.

The doctor lowered his brows, but as he could not gainsay an earl, he had no choice but to proceed. He removed the shirts from between the countess's legs. There was little new blood now. "As you see, my lord, your stratagem worked. The bleeding has nearly stopped."

Julien watched tight-lipped as the doctor plied some of the

more unpleasant-looking instruments of his trade. Thank God Kate was not yet awake.

There was a sharp insistent rap on the door, and Julien moved swiftly to answer. Mrs. Cradshaw, Milly, and two footmen laden with tubs of hot water and mountains of clean linen stood in the corridor, their faces white and stricken—the mirror image, Julien thought, of his own.

"Ah, excellent," the doctor proclaimed, looking up as Julien set the tubs on the floor beside the bed. To Julien's relief, he tossed the instruments aside and rose. "You need worry no more, my lord, for the countess will soon be on the mend again. In large measure due to your quick thinking, my lord," he added handsomely.

"And the bleeding?" Julien frowned down at the scarlet-spotted cloths.

"It is quite natural for the bleeding to continue, in fact, for several more days. And, I would add, my lord, that my examination indicates no internal problems. What I mean is," he amended, seeing the questioning look on the earl's face, "the countess is young and quite healthy. You will be honored with many sons and daughters, of that I am certain."

"My thanks, sir," Julien said simply.

"Now, my lord, I suggest that Mrs. Cradshaw put the countess in her nightclothes and then we shall awaken her."

16

After Mrs. Cradshaw left the room with Dr. Quaille in tow, Cook having prepared a light luncheon for his delectation, Julien dragged one of the tubs of hot water into his dressing room, stripped off his bloodied clothing, bathed, and quickly dressed. He walked back into his room and looked up at the clock on the mantel, surprised that it was but early afternoon. There was no movement from the bed. Kate still slept, a healing sleep, he had assured Dr. Quaille. Reluctantly the doctor had replaced the vinaigrette in his black bag.

Julien tugged his cravat into a more or less acceptable shape, drew up a chair, and sat himself beside Kate. For perhaps the fourth time the morning's events made a tangled procession through his mind, violent human emotions jostling against each other, so intensely destructive that he began to despair of a resolution that would bring about forgiveness.

Kate sighed and buried her face in the pillow, as if loath to leave her dreamless sleep. Strangely, it was the total absence of pain that forced her to awareness. "How very odd," she whispered to herself, "I am not dead. At least, I do not think I am."

"That, Countess, I would never have allowed." Julien smiled, clasping her hand in his. "How do you feel, Kate? Is there any pain?"

Her mind planted itself firmly into her body. She heard Julien's voice; his hand was holding hers. "No, there is no pain." The question seemed foolish to her, but she had answered, out of habit. There was a great soreness, as if someone had mercilessly battered at her, but of course, she could not speak of it. Her hand moved as if by purposeful design to her abdomen. It was smooth—empty. "The . . . child?" She faltered.

"I am sorry, Kate. There was naught I could do." Julien paused a moment, carefully weighing his next words. "The doctor assures me that the accident has not harmed you in any way, that—if you wish—there can be as many children as you desire."

Odd, she thought, staring silently away from him, he speaks of children and yet I knew of the child for but one day; poor wee thing, never really existing. She felt, somehow, strangely suspended in a vague present, where painful memories—ghosts, Julien had said—and now the loss of the insignificant small being that was inside of her, did not quite touch her. The future, the tomorrows that must irrevocably weave themselves into the present, were mercifully clouded. She looked at her husband and turned her eyes quickly away. The past was mirrored in his eyes, wrenching pain, deception, and suffering. She did not wish to remember, to feel. She struggled to pull herself up on the pillow.

"Kate, for God's sake," Julien began to remonstrate with her, unable to cloak the anxiety in his voice.

She gasped, fear suddenly filling her eyes. There was a warm stickiness spreading between her thighs.

"Kate, what is the matter?" he commanded, rising from his chair and leaning over her.

"I . . . I think I am bleeding," she whispered.

"Lie still," he said grimly, and before she knew what he was about, whisked back the covers. Small patches of purple stood out starkly against the white of her nightgown. He quickly slipped one hand under her hips and with the other stripped up her gown. His trembling fingers stilled, for the pads of cloth had simply slipped away in her effort to pull herself up.

"Oh, do not, please do not," she begged, consumed with embarrassment.

"Hush, Kate," he said sharply, disregarding. "The bleeding is natural, and nothing for you to fear. Your sudden movement dislodged the cloths, that is all."

She tried to draw her legs together as he straightened above her.

"Do hold still," he said with some impatience. "I must bathe the blood from your legs."

"I would prefer that you did not," she gasped.

He interrupted her brusquely: "Kate, after this morning's events, it is quite absurd that you should be embarrassed. Surely you would not prefer a stranger."

She made a choking sound and lay tensely miserable as he gently bathed her. He seemed a stranger to her. All she knew were strangers; she felt alien even to herself.

"Surely that was not so bad, was it?" He spoke rhetorically, expecting no answer. As he tucked the covers about her shoulders, he let his fingers gently brush across her flushed cheeks. "Now, my dear, if you would be so reasonable as not to execute any further violent movements, I shall fetch you some lunch and let our good Dr. Quaille in to see you."

He was another stranger, yet she had known him from her childhood. Why could she not be left alone? She wanted no more orders, no more gently veiled commands for *her* care. She raised bleak eyes. She wanted somehow to lash out at him, but she said only, "You . . . you take much for granted, Julien."

"No, Kate," he replied quietly, "I take nothing for granted. I wish only to see you well again."

Damn him! She did not want his kindness or his solicitude. She watched wordlessly as he strode from the room.

Julien soon reappeared, bearing Dr. Quaille in tow. "Ah, my dear Lady Katharine, there is color in your cheeks already! As I assured his lordship, you will be much your old self in but a modicum of time. One of the many advantages of youth!" He clasped her hand and was not surprised to find her pulse rate still rapid.

"I must say," he continued heartily, "you are the most fortunate of women in your choice of husbands." Seeing her look of bewilderment, he hastened to add, "But for his lordship's quick thinking and intelligent actions, you might have suffered severe complications."

"Dr. Quaille is overgenerous in his accolades, Kate," Julien said lightly.

"His lordship's natural modesty, my lady! But in any case, I do not wish to see you overtired." He patted her hand in a fatherly way and straightened. "I have given his lordship instructions for your care. No running up and down the stairs." He chuckled. "I shall come and see you tomorrow. I daresay you will be much more the thing then."

Dr. Quaille executed two swift bows, and Kate heard him exclaim to Julien as he passed through the bedroom door, "A most delicious repast, my lord. The ham slices, so wafer-thin, a delight, my lord, a delight!"

"Is it true, Julien—what the doctor said?" Kate asked stiffly when he returned to her bedside.

"I acted as I thought best, Kate, that is all."

How calm he is, how very self-assured, she thought. "As you have always acted for the best in my regard, my lord," she said aloud, her voice a blend of sarcasm and bitterness. "Perhaps in this instance, it would have been preferable had you not succeeded so well." There, it was said. Oblivion, she thought, yes, I would have preferred oblivion to the pain of my gratitude to you.

"Do not ever speak thus again, Kate! Whatever follies I have committed in the past, whatever pain I have caused you . . ." He broke off a moment at her distraught face. "Perhaps you will not believe me, Kate, but, yes, I have always acted toward you as I thought best, for both of us, for our life together."

"So glibly you dismiss brutal rape, my lord, and vile deception!" She could not stem the destructive words, they overflowed as from a cup full to brimming.

He straightened, his lips a thin line, and said tersely, "You are in no condition to talk of such matters now. You are becoming overwrought and will make yourself ill. When you have regained your health and are capable of speaking more calmly—"

"Damn you, Julien! I am not overwrought, and even though you may not like it, I am in full possession of my faculties! You have remained silent for so long now, my lord. Is it that you have forgotten the rational motives for your so despicable behavior? Must I give you more time to weave reason into your paltry arguments?" She fell back panting against the pillow, appalled at the rising note of hysteria in her voice. "Oh, God, why did you not let me die!" Unwanted, scalding tears coursed down her cheeks.

"Here is her ladyship's lunch, my lord," Mrs. Cradshaw announced as she came into the room. "Oh, dear, I did not know . . ." She stood frozen in a precarious stance and stared in dismay.

It was with an effort that Julien tore his eyes away from Kate. "Give me the tray, Emma. Her ladyship will be all right presently." He added under his breath, "Fetch me the laudanum, it will calm her."

He turned and stood above her. "Here is your lunch, Kate."

"I am not hungry," she said tightly.

"In that case, you can take your medicine and rest."

"I would rest quite well, were it not for your presence."

"You will have your wish as soon as you drink your medicine."

When Mrs. Cradshaw reappeared with the laudanum, Julien dismissed her and carefully measured out the drops into a glass of water.

Kate took the glass from Julien's outstretched hand and quickly downed the contents. There would be forgetfulness in sleep.

"Now, as you wish, madam, I shall relieve you of my presence," Julien said flatly. He turned and walked from the room.

He returned again, some thirty minutes later, saw that Kate slept, and sat down beside her. He had lost her at last. The admission cost him dearly. There were no more plans, no new strategies to make her understand. At least with the secrets, the necessary deceptions, he had been able to nourish hope.

"Deuced strange to think that my sister lives here!" Harry exclaimed, stamping freshly fallen snow from his top boots. He whipped off his many-caped greatcoat, stood proudly a moment in his scarlet regimentals, and clicked his heels together in grand military fashion.

"A fine figure you present, Master Harry," Mannering said fondly, removing the greatcoat from Harry's outstretched hand.

"I daresay it is rather dashing," Harry concurred, looking to his brother-in-law for confirmation.

Julien rose nobly to the occasion. "Have you left a score of broken hearts in your wake, Harry?"

"I fancy not above a half-dozen." Harry grinned. He stripped off his heavy leather gloves and gazed about him. "Always thought this place was like a tomb. But trust Kate to like it, always did, you know. She used to stand, mouth agape, mind you, staring at those ridiculous suits of armor. Claimed she would have been a fine figure of a knight; jousting and that sort of thing."

Harry pulled up short in his monologue. "Speaking of Kate, where the devil is she? Surely she ain't out fishing in the snow. Ah, I have it! I'd wager she's on one of your favorite stallions, careening all over the countryside."

Julien put a firm hand on Harry's sleeve. "No, Harry, Kate is here. Before you see her, though, I must speak with you privately."

"Eh, what's this? Is she brewing some new mischief?"

"Come, Harry, let us go into the library."

Harry shot his brother-in-law a puzzled look and said with an insouciance that Mannering readily forgave: "Do see that my hack gets stabled, will you, Mannering?"

"Certainly, Master Harry," Mannering murmured, at his most dignified.

Harry followed in Julien's wake into the library and moved quickly to the blazing fire to warm his hands.

"Will you join me in a glass of sherry, Harry?"

"Don't mind if I do. Hellish weather, but to be expected, I suppose, it being winter and all."

"No doubt," Julien said, handing Harry his glass. "When must you rejoin your regiment?" he inquired politely.

"Not until after Christmas." Harry deposited himself with practiced grace onto a rather fragile setee that groaned in protest under his weight. "Wanted to see what Kate is about—and then there is my father, of course," he added with a marked lack of enthusiasm.

"If you prefer to stay with us," Julien offered with a smile, "I am certain that Kate would welcome your company."

Harry sensed suddenly a tenseness in his brother-in-law's voice. Never one to tread warily, he demanded, "What of Kate? She is not ill, is she? Never been sick a day in her life!" But there was a rising alarm in his voice.

"No, Harry, not precisely," Julien said slowly. "She has suffered a miscarriage but three days ago. She is much better now, but is still confined to her room."

"Good Lord!" Harry jumped to his feet, forgetting for the moment the dignity he owed to his rank. "I had no idea that she was . . . that is to say—"

"She was not far along in her pregnancy," Julien interjected calmly. "But as I am certain you will understand, it was quite a shock." He gazed at Harry spectulatively beneath half-closed lids. Unexpected though his visit was, it could not have been better timed. Perhaps Harry would succeed where he had failed.

"Damned shame," Harry muttered, somewhat shaken. He brightened almost immediately. "I've just the thing to cheer her up. I brought her a present, you know. A trifle really, but I fancied she would like a real Spanish mantilla. All the ladies wear 'em over there, you see."

"She will be delighted, Harry. Now, if you like," Julien said, setting down his glass, "you can visit with Kate. I will not intrude on your reunion."

Kate lay languidly on a sofa near the fireplace, a finely knit cover spread over her legs and a paisley shawl draped about her shoulders. An embroidery frame with but a few overly large, uneven stitches covering its muslin surface lay precariously near to the edge of the sofa. She heard a light tap on the door and quickly lowered her head, as if suddenly preoccupied with her stitching.

"Well, I say, Kate, that's a fine way to greet your only brother!" Harry admonished cheerily as he stepped into the room.

"Harry!" Kate struggled into a sitting position, her initial shock at seeing him giving way immediately to a tearful smile. "Oh, my dear, it is so good to see you again! Oh, how very fine you look!" She alternately clasped him tightly against her and pushed him back, as if to verify that it was indeed he.

"Ho, Kate," Harry protested after several of her fierce embraces, "don't want to wrinkle my coat, old girl!" He patted her pale cheek, endeavoring to keep the worry from showing on his face. Lord, but she looked down pin, and dreadfully thin.

To Kate, who knew her brother perhaps better than she knew herself, Harry's thoughts were mirrored in his wide blue eyes. She forced a smile and said lightly, "Do sit down, my love. As you see, I am a trifle pulled—but it will pass, Harry, and there is naught for you to worry about. Come, my dear, pull that chair closer, and tell me about your regiment."

Harry could find no fault at all with her suggestion, as it appeared she had no wish to speak of herself. He'd give her thoughts another direction, that's what he would do. "Deuced hot in Spain and Portugal," he declared, stretching himself easily in the chair opposite her.

"Was there much fighting, Harry?"

"Oh, no, just scattered packs of ruffian bandits. We routed the scurvy lot, let me tell you. No match at all for our men!" Harry sat forward in his chair, warming to his story. "We had a couple of native guides, though of course we really didn't need them, just had them along to point us through the scrubby paths. Damned rocky terrain, you know, ground dry as a bone. But our men were hearty goers, rounded up the villains, no matter how cunning they were."

Kate sighed. "Oh, Harry, how I wish I could have been with you! I wouldn't have minded the heat, and the excitement . . ."

Harry said severely, "Now, that is not something for a countess to wish, old girl. Cursed rough work, you know." He paused and gazed around the elegantly furnished chamber. "Lord, I never thought to see you so . . . regally placed."

"It does seem strange. I daresay, though, that Kate Brandon never wanted or sought such . . . honors."

"Ridiculous, sister," Harry protested, disregarding the sadness in her voice. "Do you not recall that we could find no solution for you and . . . Sir Oliver . . . when I left for Oxford? Then the Earl of March—dashed fine fellow, by the

way—swoops down and rescues you, just like in those romantic novels!"

She lowered her eyes and drew her lips tightly shut.

Harry eyed her with a frown. "I can see that you have
indeed fallen into the doldrums, Kate. Trust me to cheer you
up," he said bracingly.

"Harry, you will stay here at St. Clair, will you not?" she
thought to ask, her voice pathetically eager.

"Think I very well might. The earl already asked me, you
know. Sir Oliver won't quite like it, but I shall pay him a
visit . . . or two."

"You must call him Julien, Harry. He would not care for
such formality from his brother-in-law." At the mention of
her husband's name, she lowered her head and asked with
forced lightness, "You have seen him, then?"

"Very proper that I should, Kate. As a matter of fact, he
met me downstairs and told me of your accident." Abashed
at his unwitting slip, he cursed himself for alluding to her
misfortune and made haste to recover. "I am sorry, my dear.
Bound to have more children, you know." He felt suddenly
that he had stepped into uncharted land and was quite out of
his ken. He could not unsay the words he had already spoken, so he merely looked at her hopefully.

"Of course, Harry," she said dully.

As he could think of nothing to say for the moment, Harry
picked up a periodical from the table at his elbow and casually flicked though the pages.

Kate sought to divert his attention, chiding herself for
making him feel awkward and uncomfortable. " 'Twill be
Christmas in but two weeks, my dear. If you do not think
your dignity will suffer, we can decorate the hall. There are
holly and berries in abundance in the home wood."

Harry readily applauded the suggestion, though secretly he
thought it would be a dead bore. He suddenly remembered
the mantilla carefully wrapped in tissue paper in his portmanteau. Kate loved presents; surely it would be just the thing to
cheer her up.

He rose and said mysteriously, "Don't want you to move,
Kate. I have a surprise for you."

He was rewarded, for Kate's eyes lit up, quite in the care-
free manner of his hoydenish little sister.

"A present, Harry? Oh, how very kind of you, my dear!"

"Let me fetch it, and while I am about it, I'll see if the earl

. . . Julien," he amended quickly, "will now join us. Said he didn't want to interrupt our reunion."

Kate said nothing to gainsay this suggestion, and Harry betook himself from the room, his step jaunty. Dear Harry, she thought, so innocently does he step into the boiling kettle. She planted a smile on her lips, for Harry's sake.

By the time Christmas Day arrived, St. Clair had undergone a magnificent transformation. Under Harry's nominal direction, the servants had festooned countless bunches of bright green holly, dotted with deep red berries, all along the walls and beams in the hall, even going so far as to fasten clumps—most disrespectfully, Mannering thought—atop the stern armored knights. Colorful paper strings of red and green garland were hung in deep scallops over the doors, and much to Kate's delight, Julien and Harry had hauled in a mammoth pine tree and given it a place of honor in the library. From a long-forgotten chest Mrs. Cradshaw had unearthed a collection of small hand-painted glass bulbs and hung them from the outstretched branches.

On Christmas morning, after Julien and Kate ceremoniously dispensed gifts among the staff, they repaired to the library to join Harry. Julien presented Kate with an elegant pair of diamond drop earrings and a narrow gold bracelet dotted with small exquisitely cut diamonds that matched those of the earrings. She accepted them with a smile, conscious that Harry was watching at her elbow.

"Just the thing to go with your mantilla, Kate," Harry declared enthusiastically.

"How very right you are," she said fondly. "I thank you, Julien," she continued with pained correctness, "they are quite lovely. I am sorry that I did not have the opportunity to—"

"My birthday is in January, Kate. I shall expect two presents from you on that date."

Harry gazed at them, baffled. He had felt acutely uncomfortable more than once during the past two weeks at being in their company. Several nights as he had made his way quietly to the kitchen, he had noticed a light shining from beneath the library door. He had trodden softly to the door, cracked it open, and seen his brother-in-law sprawled in a large chair gazing fixedly into the dying fire. He had recalled Kate's aversion to marriage with the earl, quite inexplicable to him, and her flight alone to France. But, be damned! She had married him, and for a while, at least, carried his child. Certainly no aversion there!

Late one night, as Harry gazed proudly at his scarlet uniform, pressed by Timmens' careful hands, he was drawn by the sound of loud voices coming from far down the hallway. Blessed with a lively curiosity, Harry stealthily opened his door and peered down the darkened corridor. He realized with a start that the loud voices were coming from Kate's room. It came as something of a shock to him, for during the length of his stay Harry had never before heard Julien and Kate raise their voices to each other, much less argue, and in such an unrestrained fashion.

He retreated back to his room and closed the door, reflecting as he did so that perhaps marriage was not such a divine state as it was touted to be.

Above all things, Harry disliked problems, particularly those he did not understand. It occurred to him that staying with Sir Oliver might not be so bad after all. Certainly, at Brandon Hall, he knew exactly what to expect from his dour parent.

But Harry was totally unprepared the next morning, when he trotted down the stairs, to see his brother-in-law in the hall, his head bent in conversation with Mannering, his luggage stacked near the front doors.

"Ah, Harry, there you are," Julien said pleasantly, turning to face his flustered brother-in-law. "I have decided to return to London; there are pressing matters that require my attention. Kate has decided to remain here awhile longer . . . before joining me," he continued serenely, ignoring the look of patent disbelief on Harry's face. "I drive my curricle. Would you care to join me?"

Harry would have liked very much to remonstrate with the earl, to defend his sister with scathing demands as to the earl's reasons for such a peremptory departure. But under Julien's cool inquiring gaze, he was made to feel that such an action would be grossly impertinent. He fidgeted with a gold button on his scarlet coat and said finally with stiff formality, "As you wish, my lord. I will accept your offer."

He looks for the world like a ruffled banty rooster, Julien thought as he turned his attention back to Mannering. He wondered if Harry would drop his reserve and take him to task on their journey. He really had no idea, at the moment, how he would respond to such inquiries.

They ate their breakfast in strained silence. Julien carefully laid down his fork, drew out his watch, and consulted it. He transferred his gaze to Harry, at once amused and rather touched by his obvious agitation. He cleared his throat to gain Harry's attention and said gently, "I applaud your sentiments, Harry, but you must understand that it is Kate's wish. I am certain that you have noted an atmosphere of tension between us."

"Yes," Harry muttered, instantly retiring again behind a barrier of silence.

"As a gentleman, you must know that I cannot divulge the reasons. To do so would be a great injustice to your sister."

"Is it because of her miscarriage?" Harry asked abruptly.

"Perhaps . . . in part." Julien turned the subject. "I have already said my good-byes to your sister. I will await you in the curricle."

Harry was not a great deal mollified, but he felt that to persist would make him appear boorishly forward. He rose slowly and laid his napkin down beside his half-empty plate. He was a trifle disconcerted by the hard glint in his brother-in-law's eyes.

He turned nervously and walked to the door. "Yes," he said over his shoulder, "I shall say good-bye to Kate." He wondered as he slowly mounted the stairs if he appeared poor-spirited to the earl. He knitted his brows a little over this, but by the time he lightly tapped on Kate's door, he had managed to rally his forces. It was in a heartening voice that he called, "It is I, Kate. May I come in?"

"Of course, my dear," she called. As he walked into the room, she rose, shook out her skirts, and stretched out her hands to him. Harry pulled her rather gruffly into his arms and said in a low voice, "If you prefer that I stay with you, Kate . . ."

"Do not be a ninny, Harry," she said briskly, drawing back. "You know very well that you would pine away within the week for want of your laughing, gay companions."

"But the earl . . . Julien, Kate. He has offered me a place in his curricle to London. It does not seem the thing to leave you alone." He ground to a halt, seeing in her eyes the same hard look he had so shortly before witnessed on his brother-in-law's face.

"Oh, Kate," he said unguardedly, "I do not wish to see you unhappy. God, to see you this way after all those years with Sir Oliver! Is there nothing I can—"

She cut him off without preamble. "This is not a Cheltenham tragedy, Harry. I fear you have much distorted the matter. The earl merely journeys to London . . . on business matters. That is all."

"Your husband's name is Julien, Kate, not *the earl*. Do you take me for a gull?" he demanded caustically. He would have said more, but he checked himself at the sight of her drawn face.

"Do forgive me, Harry," she said after a short pause. She looked up at him, the merest hint of a smile on her pale lips. "How ignoble it would be to think of you as a *gull*. I would fear that you would *plant me a facer*."

He grinned at her knowledge of boxing cant.

"Now, my dear, I know that you must be off. Pray do not concern yourself further about my stupid affairs."

He eyed her dubiously for a moment, but rather to her surprise, said nothing.

"Take care, Harry, and don't cut up too many larks!" She dropped a light kiss on his cheek, hugged him briefly, and drew back.

"You will write to me if there is anything—"

"Yes, yes, of course," she assured him hurriedly, not wishing that he probe further. She felt quite composed and did not want to chance any faltering on her part.

Some moments later, from her vantage point at the window, Kate watched the footman strap the luggage onto the boot of the curricle. Julien and Harry, scarves knotted securely about their throats against the light flakes of falling snow, climbed into their seats. The groom handed Julien the reins, and Kate fancied she could hear the crunch of hardened snow beneath the wheels of the curricle. She maintained her vigil at the window long after new snow filled in the wheel tracks on the drive.

Although the household staff were astounded at the earl's abrupt departure without the countess, no word reached Kate's ears, and to the casual observer there was no sign of disruption in the daily activities of St. Clair. Privately, of course, there were speculative comments, even by the second footman, a circumstance that Mannering heartily deplored but was unable to curtail. That the countess roamed through the various rooms, silent and aloof, was obvious to everyone, even those of the meanest perceptions. Never sure how long the countess would wish to remain in any one room, footmen scurried to lay fires against the chill, only to discover not many minutes after their efforts that the room was empty again.

Luncheon and dinner trays were returned to Cook with scarce a morsel taken from the plates. A firm believer in the benefits of pork restorative jelly, Cook artfully hid spoonfuls of the thick gray jelly beneath a cutlet or among sauced vegetables. "The only one who is benefiting from my jelly is that miserable tabby," she mourned to Mrs. Cradshaw, as she dished yet another uneaten plate of food into the cat's bowl.

Kate had no idea that she was inadvertently adding to the culinary pleasure of the kitchen cat, so closely was she locked into herself.

One afternoon, after wandering into the estate room, she returned to her room and huddled into a chair close to the fireplace, pulling a cover up to her chin. She had tried so hard not to think, not to remember, that she felt as if her mind was weaving itself into circular patterns. Finally, unable to withstand the onslaught of the bitter, confused thoughts, she allowed her mind to dwell upon the painful memories, each of them in turn. As once she had sought frantically to forget, she now forced herself to recall every detail, vividly recreating the past five months.

She rose sometime later, reluctantly, to light candles against the early-winter darkness. As she carried a branch to a table near her chair, the glowing lights blended for an instant with the orange embers in the fireplace, creating a lifelike shadow that loomed up on the wall in front of her. She could almost feel Julien's presence near to her. It was almost as if she could reach out and touch him; she had but to listen to hear him speak to her. The large shadow flickered and flattened into an insignificant blur.

Kate sank into her chair and buried her face in her hands. With appalling clarity she remembered their last night together, when she had taunted him until, finally, his calm, impassive facade crumbled. With a fury that matched her own, he had shouted at her.

"You speak so scathingly of *my* unbridled passions! But listen to yourself, madam, you rant like an uncontrolled, hysterical termagent! You cannot say that you were mistaken in my character, for indeed you have never exerted the slightest effort to determine the sort of man I am. You have stupidly and childishly ignored the wants of anyone but yourself, preferring to rely on ignorant assumptions of your own making!"

"How dare you—"

"How dare I what, Kate? Speak the truth? Make you realize that this mockery of a marriage is not only of my making? How many times you have hurled at my head that you dance to my every tune! I will tell you, madam, that the piper no longer plays!"

She rushed at him with clenched fists. "Of all the filthy lies!"

"Don't do it, Kate," he said in a voice of deadly calm. "Nothing would give me greater pleasure at this moment than to thrash some sense into you!"

"Ah, *your* pleasure, my lord!" She drew up, panting. "I have been naught but an instrument for your pleasure! Your token countess, whom your gentleman's code forbade you to seduce. You were forced to marry me to gain your lecherous object!"

"Forced to marry you!" he looked at her thunderstruck. "Is that what you believe? You witless little fool! Hear me, Kate, I can have any woman I desire. My choice of you for my wife, as the Countess of March, had very little to do with the gratification of my sexual appetites. Only your irrational refusal of me caused me to act in the way that I did."

"How very fortunate for you, my lord, that women find you so irresistible, else you would be forced to expend considerable energies staging your elaborate rape scenes!"

"I seem to recall, madam, that it was you who staged our last so memorable seduction scene. And if my lamentable memory serves me correctly, your own passion rivaled mine."

"Oh, stop it! Stop it!" Kate cried, clapping her hands over her ears.

"No, I will not stop and I have not said all that I wish," he said savagely, forcibly pulling her hands to her sides. "Dammit, Kate, listen to me! The young girl who was brutally raped no longer exists. You have seen her again, felt her misery. But now you must let her go. You are a woman, with a woman's needs and desires. You will destroy yourself if you do not banish that child's fears."

She wrenched herself free of him, her eyes grown dark and

enormous. She gulped convulsively, and hated tears sprang to her eyes.

"Kate," he whispered, and extended his hand to her. When she backed away from him, mutely shaking her head, he dropped his hands to his side, and his face hardened.

"Would that I never see you again, Julien," she cried with deadly contempt.

"If that is what you wish, Kate," he said grimly, his eyes boring ino hers.

"It is what I wish above all things."

"Then I bid you good-bye," he said tonelessly. Without another word he turned and left her room.

Kate raised her head from her hands, realizing inconsequentially that they were wet with tears. She rose slowly and placed more wood upon the dying fire.

The snowstorm ceased during the night, leaving a thick white blanket in its wake. Soft flakes fell about Kate as the steady pounding of Astarte's hooves shook the low, snow-laden branches.

She did not slow Astarte's pace until they had traversed the small meadow that bordered the copse. She waited for the gnawing fear to come as she slipped off her horse's back and carefully tethered her. Watchful of her footing, Kate walked into the small hollow and looked about her. Several inches of fresh snow were piled high on the familiar tree stump. The small patch of mushrooms was buried. She bent down and swept the snow from the tree stump. It seemed so much smaller than she remembered, her two hands almost spanning its surface. She felt nothing except a slight chill from the crisp winter air.

She sat down and pulled her riding habit and cloak close about her. She waited silently, still expectantly, but she could not recapture her child's excitement, nor her child's terror. There was nothing here for her, not the soft, sighing music woven from her child's thoughts, not the sound of men's heavy wooden boots coming upon her. The copse was simply a place, a small hollow of land.

She rose finally and walked back to Astarte. She did not look back as she retraced her steps.

17

"My lady! What . . . *what* a surprise! We had no idea that you—"

"Good evening, George," Kate said brightly, sailing past the astounded butler, beckoning as she did so to two lackeys. They staggered into the entrance hall under the weight of several trunks, portmanteaus, and bandboxes.

"I find myself shockingly short of funds, George," she said with a disarming smile. "Would you be so kind as to settle with the coachman, and, oh, yes, that very stern-looking fellow who, I am informed, was an excellent outrider."

"Yes, my lady, certainly," George managed to reply, his voice a trifle higher than usual. He motioned to a hitherto silent footman, who moved forward somewhat clumsily, unaccountably bumping one of her ladyship's bandboxes. George shot him a look that promised a scathing retribution, and after giving the hapless fellow instructions, turned back to the countess. He removed from her outstretched hands her ermine-lined cloak, gloves, and a dashing bonnet.

"It has been a long time, George. I trust all goes well with you."

"Yes, indeed, my lady," he replied in a more normal voice, his resumption of dignity belied by a nervous tic that formed in the corner of his eyes.

"Is his lordship here, George?"

Kate followed the butler's despairing gaze up the long circular staircase. "Yes, my lady. That is, his lordship . . ." He faltered.

"Yes, George?" Kate prompted, her head tilted in sympathetic amusement at the stammering of the usually elegantly coherent butler.

"His lordship is not alone, my lady!" he said baldly.

271

"Well, no matter," Kate said kindly with more aplomb than she felt. "I am certain that his friends will not mind."

"It is not exactly his *friends*," George amended in desperation.

"Oh? How very curious, to be sure! I was not aware that his lordship admitted his enemies into his house." Kate bent a disconcerting stare at the butler, who realized with inescapable inevitability that the countess was not to be put off. He said miserably, "The Lady Sarah is with him, my lady. She arrived not fifteen minutes ago, demanding to see his lordship."

There was a decided militant sparkle in Kate's eyes, but she said with a shrug of her shoulders, "Is *that* all, George? I daresay the *lady* is just this moment on the point of leaving!"

George had always thought the young countess to be a quiet, rather biddable lady. Tears, perhaps, he could have readily understood, but certainly not this calm, somewhat amused hauteur.

"Shall I inform his lordship of your arrival, my lady?" he asked hopefully, in a last effort to avoid what he believed would be an unavoidable scene.

"Not at all, George," Kate said with great composure. "Indeed, I shall surprise his lordship. I assume he is in the drawing room," she added rhetorically, having already decided the matter from the direction of George's anguished looks.

As George stood with his mouth unbecomingly open, unable to fit two more words together, Kate turned and walked jauntily to the stairs. She heard George say in a decidedly pettish voice, "Get about your business, my lads! Don't stand there gawking!"

Kate clutched her skirts and walked purposefully up the stairs. George's evident agitation at Lady Sarah's tête-à-tête with the earl had, strangely enough, given her confidence. Trepidation is for fools, faint-hearts, and butlers, she decided, not for countesses.

The door to the second-floor parlor stood partially ajar, and Lady Sarah's caressing voice reached Kate's ears before she actually saw the lady.

"Oh, Julien, let her stay in the country. She will be much more in place there. I always thought her awkwardly uncomfortable in society."

"How *very* kind of you, Lady Sarah, to have my welfare

so much at heart," Kate said sweetly as she swept into the room. Though she suffered a momentary setback at seeing the lady's arms about her husband's shoulders, she thrust her chin up defiantly and eyed her from head to toe with a cold contemptuous look.

Lady Sarah uttered a surprised exclamation and quickly dropped her arms to her sides.

"Good evening, my lord. I trust I find you well." Kate gave her husband a dazzling smile.

Julien gazed at her, an arrested gleam in his eyes. "Tolerably well, Kate, tolerably well," he replied.

"Now, my *dear* Lady Sarah," Kate said affably, bending her eyes on the flushed lady, "although it is a comforting thought to think of one's husband in such . . . *capable* hands, I think it time to have a changing of the guard, so to speak. I daresay your own husband would much appreciate such solicitous regard."

Although Sarah had never before been confronted by such a calm, contemptuous lady, she was made of sterner stuff than Kate imagined. The earl had been quiet since her arrival, attending to her every word with obvious interest, so it seemed, and had not appeared to be at all disinclined to accept her passionate embrace. Indeed, Sarah was emboldened to believe that the earl had been on the verge of succumbing to her ardor, had it not been for the untimely arrival of his country mouse of a wife.

"I do not believe, *dear* Lady Katharine," Sarah said with a triumphant glint in her wide blue eyes, "that you judge the situation quite correctly. You speak so quaintly of solicitous regard—why, my dear, it is common knowledge that you do not accord the earl even a modicum of regard, shrinking from even your most intimate duties as a wife."

Kate stiffened almost imperceptibly as the lady continued smoothly, "I am quite certain that the earl has grown quite impatient at your coldness, which I understand cannot but result from forming attachments outside one's class. Do you not think it wise, dear Lady Katharine, to return to your quiet country life, where, I am assured, you will get along so very comfortably?"

Kate wondered briefly how bunches of the lady's blond hair would look wrapped around her fisted hand.

"Although I cannot but be genuinely touched by your so obvious concern," Kate replied, pleased at the deceptive coolness of her voice, "I find you and your observations, dear Lady Sarah, a dead bore, though I must admit to being struck by your overly lively imagination. Now, if you please, I find your presence quite fatiguing, and must ask that you leave."

"Julien!" Sarah cried with an unbecoming shriek. "Will you let her talk to me in such—"

"You intrude upon my comfort, Lady Sarah," Kate snapped, not daring to look at her husband. "Leave my house this instant, else I shall forcibly eject you!"

"*Your* house!" Sarah tittered contemptuously. "I think that the earl must have other opinions on that subject!"

"Well, half of the house is mine," Kate amended scrupulously. "And indeed, the parlor is in the very center."

"Julien, would you cease this senseless charade and send her packing?" Sarah grabbed his arm and gave it a light shake.

There was a sudden silence, and Kate found that she could not meet her husband's eyes. She had absolutely no idea of what he was thinking, for he had acted the interested but detached onlooker since she had entered the room. She wondered with a sinking heart if the unmeasured words she had flung at him their last night together had finally driven him away from her, and if, indeed, he now viewed her as Lady Sarah had so unattractively painted her.

She forced herself to look up and saw that he was regarding her with an oddly keen expression that she could not fathom. She wondered dispassionately if he would allow her a dignified exit from the situation.

"Sarah," Julien said finally, "I do believe that her ladyship is in the right. The parlor is indeed in the very center of the house. Regrettable as it may appear, I am unable to gainsay her most persuasive logic."

Kate blinked in rapid succession, thankful that no words were required from her.

Two bright spots of color flew to Lady Sarah's cheeks, and she exclaimed incredulously, "Surely you don't mean, Julien—"

"Yes, Sarah. Shall I ring for George?"

"By God, you are . . . besotted!" Her voice shook with mortification.

Julien did not immediately respond, but rather turned his

gaze upon Kate, who was looking, to his amusement, quite bewildered.

He said softly, "Perhaps you are right, Sarah. I am quite ... besotted."

"I hope you will not live to regret this action, my lord!" She picked up her skirts and walked with haughty dignity from the room, casting Kate a glance of scathing dislike.

"Close the door, Kate," Julien said after the lady had whisked herself from the room.

Without a word Kate turned and pulled the door closed.

"Now, come here." She drew up in spite of herself at the hint of a command.

"Please," he added with a very disturbing smile that sent a tingling sensation up her back and at the same time produced a tongue-tied shyness.

"Perhaps you would like ... me to ring for tea, Julien?" she asked somewhat faintly.

"No, my love. What I would most prefer is to have my shrew of a wife in my arms."

"Oh!" She blushed hotly, cursing the absurd knots that tangled about her tongue. Her feet, however, seemed to have escaped similar affliction, and she moved toward him without hesitation.

She thought rather giddily that it was not so bad after all to have the breath squeezed from one in so ruthless a fashion. Somewhat shyly she lifted her face and saw that her husband's eyes were twinkling attractively. As he cupped her chin in his and pressed his mouth against hers, she felt an altogether delicious sensation, and when he released her, her eyes clouded with disappointment.

He grinned down at her in a rather boyish fashion. "But consider my love, how very shocked the servants would be to discover the earl and countess making love in the drawing room!"

"I assure you, Julien, that the thought of ... making love in the drawing room did not occur to me!" she protested. "I ... I was but humoring you," she added lamely.

"Most proper," he said promptly. "I trust you will continue to do so from this time on."

"Well, I fear that I have no choice in the matter," she said impishly, "else I shall spend my remaining years throwing hopeful ladies from the drawing room!" Kate gave a gurgle of laughter, recalling her arrival. "Poor George, I have never before seen him rendered so hopelessly inarticulate. He must have believed that murder would be done in this house."

"Perhaps a few beatings, but I assure you, wife, no murder," he said with a distinct gleam of amusement in his gray eyes. "And if you please me, I shall not beat you too hard, but only once in a while, and, of course, in my half of the house."

"Does that mean, my lord," she asked, "that I may take you to task whenever you encroach in that high-handed way of yours in *my* half of the house?"

Julien sighed heavily. "Being that I have wedded a shrew, I can see I have no choice but to agree."

A flush rose to her cheeks, and she quickly averted her face. "I would not have you believe that I am always so," she said in a small voice. "It is just that I was so terribly uncertain and . . . confused. I fear that I did not treat you with a great deal of . . . consideration."

"Which time do you refer to, Kate?" he asked, smiling. She gave her head a tiny shake. He drew her arm through his and led her to the sofa. "Come, my love, let us sit down."

She acquiesced, but did not allow herself to be drawn into the circle of his arms. She fixed her eyes instead on an elegant Dresden figure above the mantelpiece.

"You were speaking of all the many times you have unjustly abused me," he prompted, and squeezed her hand in a speaking way that robbed his words of flippancy.

"There was but one time, as you very well know, my lord," she said hotly. "Our . . . our last night together at St. Clair. I know that I did not treat you as I ought, and . . . and, oh, Julien, I am so very sorry." she blurted out.

"I was no less guilty of like offense, Kate," he said gently. "You know," he said after a brief pause, "I cannot recall having wished more to throttle you, save the time you most foolishly stole that peasant's horse."

"That was a *very* different matter entirely, Julien, as you well know!" she protested. "How abominable you are to remind me."

"Now that I have quite diverted your thoughts, my dear, you can surely not object to . . . *humoring* me again." He pulled her straightaway into his arms and kissed each smiling dimple before seeking her soft lips. He released her only when she pulled away, gasping for breath. He laughed softly. "I can see, Kate, that I must give you proper instructions.

Really, my dear, it is most dampening to quit such pleasurable pursuits all for the want of suitable breathing!"

She returned his smile saucily. "Surely, my lord, you would not wish your *wife* to be so consummately skilled as your mistresses."

"Since you are so strangely adamant in refusing me their charming company, dear one, I think it only fair that you oblige me in this matter." He shook his head in mock reproof. "Poor Sarah, have you not one shred of conscience over your violent assault on that hapless lady?"

"I would that you be serious, Julien! Hapless lady, indeed! If you do not recall, my lord, that evening of Lady Haverstoke's ridotto, I most assuredly do. How dared you take her out to the balcony and . . . make love to her!"

"Kate, I cannot believe that *you* were eavesdropping on that most affecting scene."

"How can you make so light of it?" she cried, her bosom heaving and her eyes flashing her agitation.

Although he did not allow her out of the circle of his arms, he was silent for a moment, frowning thoughtfully. "Then assuredly you can have no cause to doubt me, Kate, if you were witness."

"But I saw her kissing you, Julien! I heard her speak so . . . so unkindly of me and of our . . . marriage." She gulped angrily.

To her surprise, he threw back his head and laughed merrily. "I gather, little shrew, that you did not wait to see how I handled the situation."

"No," she admitted in a tight voice. "I got vilely sick, you see, and had to remove myself very quickly." She added with spirit, "Evidently, my lord, your splendid tactics did not carry the battle. After all, the lady seemed most sure of herself this evening!"

"Alas, I have this fatal charm," he mourned, shaking his head. "I am so relieved that I now have such a fiercely faithful wife to protect me from such temptations."

"Wretch!" she exclaimed. "You must be careful, else I shall write a most affecting, encouraging letter to *dear* Squire Bleddoes!"

"Ah, Kate, do you dare to threaten me?"

"I do not make threats, Julien, merely statements of fact," she replied demurely.

"Little cat!" he said appreciatively. "Much you cared about my high-flown rantings."

"You are mistaken." She drew an audible breath, slight color suffusing her cheeks. "After you . . . forced me to wed you, I lived in dread of your assurances to . . . to make me your wife in every way. I was so very afraid of you, and perhaps of myself." She faltered for a moment, then said slowly, "I could not seem to help myself. I've thought back so many times since you returned to London, and I realized that even during our stay in Switzerland, I was beginning to . . . care for you."

Julien looked at her searchingly, knowing how much her words had cost her. He responded seriously. "You must believe me, Kate, that I saw no evidence of your caring for me. Indeed, until that last afternoon when I left you at the villa, I looked at you closely, hoping to see the slightest sign of change. I believed you implacable in your conviction to thwart me. I thought you arrogant and proud, and thus I caused you what I thought until this evening was irreparable pain and disillusion."

Kate fastened her gaze upon the intricate folds of Julien's snowy cravat and carefully meditated upon his words, before reflecting gravely: "That is what I wished you to believe, Julien. You see, I did not understand my fear. When the nightmares began, I despaired of ever escaping from them. They were all the more terrifying because of the confused images, the half-truths. I understood only when you took me to the copse."

"I know, my love. Forgive me, I didn't know of any other way."

"But it was I who was terribly in the wrong," she protested. "My uncontrolled anger, the shock of remembering . . . I lost our child . . ." Her voice broke.

"Kate, look at me!" he commanded sternly. She raised her eyes to his face unwillingly, for she was perilously close to tears. "Your miscarriage was an accident, Kate. If there is to be blame attached, it must rest upon my shoulders. Do you understand me?"

"Oh, no! Julien, it was I who—"

"Do be quiet, Katharine." He clasped her arms in his hands and gave her a shake. "I cannot allow you to continue in this spate of guilt. We must, both of us, bury all the ghosts, else we shall spend our days in silent recriminations.

Of course, I am sorry for the child, but my first concern was and always shall be with you." He touched his fingers to her mouth to silence further protests and added in a lighter voice, "If you wish a future Earl of March and many beautiful daughters, you may be certain that I shall most willingly oblige you."

She was silent a moment as many memories jostled about in her mind. She said thoughtfully, "Do you recall, Julien, you spoke of burying ghosts once before—at the copse? I went back there, you see, but a few days ago. It was the strangest thing . . . the place was so very common—there was nothing evil or frightening about it. That is what you meant, is it not?"

"Yes, Kate, that is exactly what I meant," he replied, his eyes lighting with relief.

She regarded him with the merest hint of a smile. "I wonder if I would now find that wild German lord equally as commonplace? It does follow, does it not, that he must be a quite ordinary fellow, devoid of rational thought, of course, and not at all above the second-rate?"

"Oh, no," Julien replied smoothly. "I cannot allow it to be so. Surely, Kate, he was not an *ordinary* fellow? Do you not feel that one should make allowances for the oddities of foreign gentlemen?"

"Odious man! You are the most complete hand, Julien. But surely, my lord, you should not quibble when a lady chooses to bury a hatchet, rather than a ghost?"

Julien shifted uncomfortably. "Come, Kate, no more talk of that fellow. I daresay that he would most welcome being assigned to oblivion."

"Ah, such a faint-heart you are! Defending him so stoutly and then consigning him willy-nilly to oblivion. And I thought that you men regarded such swift changes of opinion as the prerogatives of the weaker sex."

"Indeed, it is so," he said, smiling wolfishly. "It is just that I do not wish you to feel the foibles of your sex more than is necessary. Surely, even you cannot deem such nobility of character *ordinary* or devoid of sensibility?"

"How very paltry it would be of me, to be sure," she agreed with a dimpled smile.

"Precisely so. Now, my dear, if you are quite finished cutting up my character—"

She protested: "But your character is so marvelously deplorable in so many as-yet-unmentioned ways! For instance, what about your shameful fleecing of me at piquet?"

"Far off the mark you are there, Kate," he said gravely. "My fleecing of you had nothing to do with a deplorable character, but rather with your slowness of wit. I see now two very promising areas for instruction."

"Slowness of wit indeed! I find, my lord, that your wits are shockingly disordered!" She paused and cocked her head inquiringly to one side. "Two areas needful of your instruction? Pray, tell me, what is the first?"

"Breathing," he replied, and pulled her against him.

When he released her a few moments later, Kate gazed up at him and said with a soulful sigh, "Alas, my lord, in some things I am so very slow to learn. Perhaps, in this instance, you will not think my backwardness a sore trial to your patience?"

"What a lovely mouth you have, my love," he said huskily, tracing the curve of her lips with his fingertips.

"You are digressing in the most nonsensical manner, my lord," she chided, "and have not answered my question."

"Question, Kate?" he asked.

"I . . . I think that subtleties of language are entirely lost on you, Julien." Her fingers nervously tugged at a bright button on his coat, and it was some moments before she raised her face and whispered, "Will you think me quite brassy, my lord, if I remind you of your promise to most willingly oblige me?"

"Anything, dear love. Which promise?" he asked, all the while twining his fingers around the soft auburn ringlets clustered about her flushed face.

"The future Earl of March," she murmured, blushing more furiously.

George chanced to look up and saw the Earl and Countess of March emerge from the parlor and stroll arm in arm down the carpeted corridor, the earl's fair head bent close to the countess's cheek. A slow smile spread over his face as he watched them disappear from his view. He decided that he should inform François that the succulent sirloin of beef, so lovingly basted with herbs and wine, would undoubtedly not be called for this evening by the Earl of March.